W.A.S.P.

SISTERS OF THE SKY

ISBN: 978-0-9975689-0-5
Library of Congress Control Number: 2016941927

The Women's Airforce Service Pilots –or W.A.S.P.—was a real organization during World War II. Although based in part on actual events and actual historical figures, this book is a work of fiction. Other names, characters, places and incidents are products of the authors' imaginations or are used fictitiously. Any resemblance of such non-historical persons or events to actual ones is entirely coincidental.

This book contains an excerpt from the forthcoming book *Sisters of the O.S.S.* by Teri McLaren & Bobby Garcia. This excerpt has been set for this edition only and may not reflect the final content of the forthcoming edition.

Teri McLaren dedicates this book to her father, H.C. Patterson, 1926-2005, who spent WWII in service to his country as a Naval officer.

Bobby Garcia dedicates this book to his sister Mary Garcia Owen, and his nieces Eileen Garcia, Elizabeth "Lizzie" Garcia, and Grace Garcia— all strong, beautiful women.

ACKNOWLEDGMENTS

Thank you, my alpha reader friends—Matt Wilson, Cheryl Randolph, Donna Broyles, Stacie Durbin, Betty Shiffman, David Hornback, David Hutcherson, Megan Scott, and Terri Johns—for your unwavering support, good humor, and conscientious efforts in helping to make this a better book. Thank you, Bobby, for all the laughter we shared in discovering our characters, their world, and their stories. Sláinte, my friend.

—Teri McLaren

Thanks to my family, friends and alpha readers—Johnny Garcia, Devin McGregor Ketko, Tara Knabenshue, and Stephen Blackehart—for your encouragement and your inspiration. And thank you, Teri, for showing me the way. Chairs, my friend.

—Bobby Garcia

Both authors wish to thank the brave, determined women of the WASP for their service.

NOVELS AND SHORT STORIES

by TERI McLAREN

Song of Time
Shadows of Time
The Cursed Land

"Nature of the Beast"
"Dragonfear"
"Vallenwood"

as TERI WILLIAMS

Before The Mask
The Dark Queen

"Mark of the Flame, Mark of the Word"
"The Final Touch"

SCREENPLAYS by BOBBY GARCIA

The Truest Valor
Lunatic Psycho Chick
Stoner Girls
The Dead Princess
Fotobook Killer

TERI McLAREN
&
BOBBY GARCIA

W.A.S.P.
SISTERS OF THE SKY

PROLOGUE

January 1943, Casablanca Conference, Morocco –

QUICKLY GLANCING AT his wristwatch, Franklin Roosevelt fidgeted in his wheelchair as a valet knelt to lace the shoes he had just placed on the President's polio-stricken feet. In only a few minutes, British Prime Minister Winston Churchill would blow through the door, trailing cigar smoke and wielding razor sharp wit, and Roosevelt wanted to be ready to receive him. One had to be on one's game when Winnie was in the room, and the valet was taking so long that Roosevelt feared Churchill would catch him at this vulnerable, unprepared moment. That simply would not do. Personal weakness never inspired international confidence. Especially in wartime.

"Push me toward the balcony, please, Herbert," said Roosevelt, as the valet finished and steered the chair into the bright Moroccan sun. The President and Churchill had conferred for several days publicly already, but Winston had requested some time to speak privately with Roosevelt, away from the reporters' flashbulbs and the hovering entourage that normally followed the two leaders everywhere they went. *What's on your mind, Winnie,* thought Roosevelt, as the palms swayed overhead and the cool January breeze blew in from the Atlantic. The smells of cooking fires, the sea, and sweet jasmine incense permeated the air.

He didn't have long to wait before finding out. The knock came and the valet answered it. "Enjoying the fresh air and sunlight, I see, Mr. President," Churchill's gravelly, unmistakable voice came from behind the chair before the man himself appeared.

"Yes. Still too damned cold for my taste," Roosevelt said, grinning over at his friend. Churchill's big face split into a lopsided smile as he pulled a chair opposite Roosevelt's at the patio table and settled his bulk onto the groaning metal frame.

"Franklin, I'd like to get to it straightaway, if you don't mind." Roosevelt nodded and Churchill began. "While you seem solidly decided on the subject, I simply must be heard on this matter of Europe—I think your plans for a cross-channel invasion are premature. It is my deep and abiding belief that the Allied effort in Europe would be best served by an invasion of Sicily, where German forces, once pulled south, would encounter great difficulty in later moving into France to repel your channel landing at Normandy. The Chief of the Imperial General Staff quite agrees with me."

"Ah, General Brooke, is it?" Roosevelt asked, his bespectacled eyes drifting over the rounded, Moorish buildings of the city. "He would be the same man who counsels you against committing more military resources to the Pacific. He thinks rather highly of that axiom written by a famous countryman of yours—'Let every eye negotiate for itself, and trust no agent,' does he not?" Churchill pursed his lips and stared at the white and blue tiles beneath his feet for a moment before responding.

Then he looked Roosevelt in the eye and said, "Mr. President, delaying the invasion of France now would have the added benefit of your army facing a severely depleted and demoralized German army later. That is, *if* the Germans continue to smash themselves upon the rocks of the Eastern Front, so to speak, in the meantime," Churchill said, drumming his blunt fingers on the mosaic tabletop.

"So the United States should bear the burden of routing the Japanese from New Guinea and Burma, territories of the British Empire, while you dictate the strategies for Fortress Europe. Hmm. Winston, we are old friends, but make no mistake—it is I who am saving your country with the Normandy invasion, and I will do it in my own time and place," Roosevelt said.

Churchill sighed, seeing the argument was stalled. "I could do with a spot of lunch, if you don't mind, and a drink," he said, lighting a fat cigar. Roosevelt nodded to the valet, who went to the bar, poured a lowball, and brought it over to Churchill, who drained the glass before he refocused on Roosevelt. The valet quietly made a room service call as Churchill continued. "I have very current intelligence which might persuade you otherwise," he said, studying his cigar ash. "We've recently learned that several months ago, the Nazis successfully tested a new fighter aircraft, which they are calling the *Sturmvogel*. And unlike our own nascent jet programs, this craft is completely turbojet powered, and is rumored to achieve nearly transonic speeds. I don't think I need to tell you what havoc several squadrons of these aircraft would wreak on your cross-channel invasion force."

"There are many ways of moving forward, but only one way of sitting still, Winston. I have the utmost confidence in America's—and Britain's—ability to achieve air superiority," Roosevelt said. "Since we are now sharing technology with you, advances are being made much more quickly. Besides, if we move on Normandy now, the Germans won't have these turbojets in the air yet."

"Oh, but they could!" Churchill exclaimed, the ash on his cigar sparking away as he slammed his beefy hand on the table. "And with those jet fighters, the Nazis will rule the skies! Your bombers would be no more than target practice for them! Your troop transports and gliders would be shot down by the dozens! And what of your invasion forces on the beach? There is no air defense in existence that could prevent the Germans from strafing and attacking your troops *at will*. Your men would never get a boot on the beach! Are you receiving my message, my dear Franklin?" Churchill said, his face flushed red with desperation.

"That depends, Prime Minister," Roosevelt said quietly, "First, I'd like to have access to this new intelligence, and then decide for myself if it should alter the plans."

A knock on the door signaled lunch had arrived. The room service attendant wheeled the large trolley over to the heads of state and stood waiting beside it.

Churchill glanced over at the attendant and smiled. "I had anticipated your response, Franklin, so here is the man who can tell you what you want to know."

Roosevelt followed Churchill's gesture and then frowned in confusion. "Winston, that is a waiter, unless you are seeing someone I am not," he said, clearly irritated.

"I do indeed see someone you do not. Mr. President, meet Gabriel, MI-6's finest." Gabriel folded a tea towel over his arm, gave a quick waiterly nod, and smiled at Roosevelt, who was having a hard time comprehending that his lunch attendant was actually a member of Britain's elite group of spies. Gabriel was a man so average and unremarkable in every way that he was almost invisible.

Roosevelt raised an eyebrow as Gabriel said, "Pleased to meet you, sir. And sorry for the theatrics, but my work demands that I navigate as discretely as I can. That means I am often hiding in plain sight. May I proceed?"

Roosevelt was laughing now. "Yes, please do!"

Gabriel began, resting one hand on the cover of a ceramic tagine. "Sir, the Germans might have the edge in technology, but they need and lack strategic materials to mass produce it. In particular, superalloys of high melting point, capable of withstanding the temperatures generated by turbojets." He lifted the lid on the covered serving dish and Roosevelt saw that instead of lunch, there was a lump of gray metal sitting in it. Gabriel picked it up and handed it to him as he explained, "This is chromite, sir, and from this raw ore, we get chromium. Ugly, isn't it, to have a name that means 'color'? Yet, it's what makes rubies red and various oil paints green and blue and yellow. It also has an industrial application. Chromium is what the Germans need to keep their components from melting at turbojet temperatures."

"What are you saying?" Roosevelt asked, turning to Churchill.

"We're saying the stuff is thin on the ground, or rather *in* the ground, so the United States and Britain must seize control of the worldwide supplies and choke the German jet program out of existence, Franklin," Churchill muttered. "We must divert those materials to *our* jet programs, and beat the Nazis at their own game," Churchill continued, "and only then can we successfully plan a Normandy invasion."

Roosevelt sat thinking for a moment. "I see. Where does it come from?" he asked, hefting the chromite sample.

Gabriel answered. "As raw ore, mostly from South Africa, but that's a long passage through U-boat patrolled waters, and many of the transport vessels have either been sunk or don't want to risk the trip anymore. Finland is currently Germany's supplier, but the Allies have pressured them to stop. You have a bit of it in your western states, so you could partly manage your own program, but it's not enough for us Brits to share, and with no deposits of our own, we'll need it as badly as the Germans. However, one of my contacts found a most interesting geological survey from one of your southern states—Georgia. There is evidence of a new vein of chromite in the piedmont area around a little town called Lowland Mill. In fact, the farms there, and one in particular, which belongs to Randall Shannon and his daughter Sprite, are sitting on enough chromite to keep us both going for some time, if you can acquire the land and mine it quickly."

Roosevelt steepled his fingers and then looked gravely over to Churchill. "I see what you mean, Winston. I will, of course, want to look over the dossier, but if the information checks out, I am willing to table the Normandy invasion for awhile. No matter what, though, I think we should stop this stuff going to Germany."

As he handed Roosevelt a stained leather case, Gabriel added, "Sir, I know you will appreciate that one of our other agents, Michael, is missing in action and another, Uriel, gave his life for you to have this information."

Roosevelt nodded grimly. "Yes, of course. I certainly do. Upon confirmation of your report, I'll have one of my generals, Henry Arnold, find one of his team to deal with the Lowland Mill site to get it in the works immediately. Meanwhile, Winston, I think we had better ramp up our own jet programs. It looks to me like we need an operation that not only diverts this chromium, but also puts us ahead of the Germans in terms of design and production." He looked over at Gabriel. "Gabriel, you said your fallen and missing comrades' names were Uriel and Michael—your monikers put me in mind of the Biblical archangels of the same names."

"Well done, sir," said Gabriel, "It is precisely why we chose them. Agent Uriel was head of covert intelligence gathering, and named for the archangel of wisdom. He was partnered with our weapons strategist Michael, named for the captain of the heavenly host. I sometimes travel with our physician Raphael, named for the healing archangel, and I am the head courier and the herald of British intelligence, as Gabriel the archangel is written to have been a messenger."

Churchill harrumphed from the table. "Now that we've figured this bit of bother out, could we please have that lunch?" Gabriel bowed respectfully and pulled another covered dish from beneath the trolley's draped cloth, set the hot tagine down in front of the Allied commanders, and lifted the lid with a flourish worthy of a Cordon Bleu trained maitre d'. Roosevelt and Churchill tucked into their chicken stew and khobz, the local bread, but when Roosevelt looked around to invite Gabriel to join them, the man had vanished into the air like the spirit being whose name he shared.

Churchill chuckled at Roosevelt's puzzlement. "He's the best, Franklin. The whole team are—were."

Roosevelt nodded, considering the cost of the news Gabriel had brought. He sat in silence for a moment and then said, "I think we ought to call this joint operation 'Archangel.' What do you say, Winston?"

PART I

CHAPTER 1

May, 1943, Dublin, Ireland – neutral state in WWII –

MAJOR WALLACE SEAMUS Doyle, US Army Air Forces, staff officer to General Henry Arnold, stepped out of the black taxi onto the busy Dublin street corner near Trinity College, where his fiery Irish girlfriend Coreen was to meet him. His serious brown eyes wandered over the long, tall buildings, and he was surprised at how few students he saw walking to classes. But then, with the war on, even though Ireland had chosen to remain neutral, more of its young people might have taken war related paths instead of the academic ones meandering through Trinity.

The air was cool, even for May, and steely skies threatened rain, but Doyle walked to a stone bench near the Companile and sat down to wait for Coreen. Today, he would ask her to marry him, and she would say yes. What did a little rain matter? His life would soon be so much better! His father, the longtime US Ambassador to Ireland, would hate that his sole surviving son would marry a Protestant—politically, it would be a dreadful hindrance for the old man in this religiously volatile, Catholic country. It might even ruin his illustrious career. That made Doyle smile a bit wider. Wallace had never been good enough for George Doyle; had never been the hero his brother Parker had been. But Parker was dead now, killed at Pearl, and Wallace had been drafted into the US Army, much to his disdain. America claimed him as native son, but Wallace did not claim America as motherland. He had been born in Ireland and had grown up there. It was absurd for him to be serving a country had had never known. He had wanted to stay neutral, like Ireland. But the war would be over soon and he and Coreen could return to Dublin and begin their life together, and George Doyle would just have to retire if his daughter-in-law was unacceptable to the Irish Prime Minister, the Taoiseach.

After a half hour, though, Doyle began to wonder what had become of Coreen. It wasn't like her to not show up. He had told her he would be back in Ireland for only a few days, meeting the Brits in Antrim tomorrow afternoon to be briefed about their end of General Arnold's ultra-secret project, an operation called Archangel. Today through tomorrow was his only free time, and it was quickly passing.

He gave her another twenty minutes and then began to amble down the sidewalk, his feet crunching and scattering last fall's wet hazelnuts shed from the overhanging hedges. He went back and forth several times, and each time the bench came within view, he was sure Coreen would be sitting there, ready to let him have it for being late himself.

But no. Coreen was nowhere to be found, and it now was an hour past their agreed time. Doyle felt his heartbeat quicken and the muscles in the back of his neck tighten. Where was she? He sat down on the damp bench, thinking she might be caught in conversation with a professor or her class had run late. He didn't want to miss her.

But another half hour and ten thousand terrible scenarios later, a soft drizzle began, so he got up and started walking to the restaurant where he had made their dinner reservation. He would find Coreen there, he thought, and she would hug him and tell him how boring her class had been.

When he arrived at The Seaside, all he could think to do was get out of the rain. He glanced at his watch; yes, she would no doubt be waiting for him there, having sought shelter herself. Doyle strode into the foyer, and was greeted by the maitre d', who pointed him toward the coat check. Searching all the tables for Coreen, Doyle began to shuck his big raincoat, and the girl behind the counter peeked out from the racks of coats she was brushing and came forward to take the garment.

When he handed the coat to her, she let it fall on the counter, and that brought his eyes around.

"Oh, sorry," he began, thinking she might have dropped it because of his sloppy hand off.

But the girl, a tall, thin, Nordic blonde with striking blue eyes and a red-painted mouth, smiled at him from behind her Rita Hayworth hair-style and said, "You'll be wanting this, Seamus."

Seamus was his middle name. Nobody called him that except Coreen.

The woman handed him an envelope which smelled faintly of Coreen's Coty Emeraude perfume. Baffled, he turned his back and read the contents while the clerk took another customer's coat.

Dearest Seamus,

I am writing to let you know first of all, I am all right and unharmed. And I am sorry for what this is putting you through, especially since you didn't find me waiting for you as planned. What must you have thought?! These people, and I don't know who they are, have taken me somewhere near the coast, because I can smell the ocean, but other than that, I could not tell you where.
They have let me write so that you will know by my hand that I am alive and well. They have told me that you must cooper- ate with them, or things will not go well for me, so I urge you to do as they ask. That is all for now, my darling. Please hurry. Please, Seamus.

With all my love,
Coreen

When the customer had gone to his table, Doyle looked sharply at the blonde woman, who stood placidly holding a garment bag. "What have you done with her?!" He quietly snarled, reaching across the counter toward the woman, who deftly dodged him and held out the garment bag.

"Now, Seamus, you've seen the letter and you know it's hers. Put these on, make no more of it, and come with me. I can't speak further about it here," she said, voice low and commanding blue eyes leveled at him.

Doyle took the bag, finding it to be heavier than he expected, and the woman ushered him into a closet behind the counter. Doyle opened the bag and saw a coat, a fisherman's sweater, trousers, a linen shirt, a belt, socks, and a cap. All of the clothes reeked a bit of fish, and the sweater bore a few permanent dark stains. The overcoat was good quality, though—Donegal tweed. It would shed the rain well enough. He took a deep breath and began to take off his uniform, folding it precisely into a squared pile, shoes on bottom, hat on top, and pulled on the other clothing. There was no mirror, but he didn't need one to know he now looked as common and unremarkable as any boatman on the beach. *Invisible again*, he thought, *Story of my life.*

He still had Coreen's letter, and held it to his nose, inhaling the scent. *What have they done with you, my pet*, he thought, the smell of her perfume reminding him of the last time he had seen her, with her golden blonde hair blowing in the sea breeze and her mischievous smile teasing him to chase her down the beach. "I'm coming for you, Coreen. Just hold on. I'm coming," he muttered aloud. He looked down at his sock feet, and saw there was a pair of old boots next to them. He exchanged them for his own freshly shined shoes, and found the fit and the look of them to be less than happy. Having refrained for as long as possible, Doyle put on the ratty newsboy cap, noticing its interior band had been well worn and stretched a bit, and was stained with another man's sweat. Sadly, it fit. He stepped from the closet and the woman took his uniform. She hung it in the same garment bag, which she then placed on a hook in the closet. "You'll get it all back," she said, and then off-handedly added, "Well, probably."

X

Within a few minutes' walk, they came to a car park, where the woman opened the back of a produce lorry and motioned him to get inside.

He climbed aboard and settled on a crate of cabbages, their green pungency turning his already unsettled stomach. He hated cabbage and everything in its botanical family. Then the double doors of the white lorry swung shut and left Doyle sitting in the dark. With stinking cabbages. He ground his teeth in anger and waited for his eyes to adjust to the darkness. There was nothing to see—just the scraped metal interior and the crate he sat on. In a moment, he heard the driver's door shut, then the motor started and they were backing away from the car park, shell and sand crunching under the lorry floor. *North,* he thought, *we were parked facing north. Then a left turn, west. Then another left—south. They were heading south.*

Doyle listened intently as he bounced along on the cabbage crate. He heard city sounds for a while and then, for a very, very long time, only the silence of country roads, and finally, the slither of grass beneath the tires and along the lorry's sides. The ground was rough now, and he had to hold onto the crate to keep from spilling forward. Then the lorry stopped, the doors swung open again, and the thick, salty smell of bladder wrack and seawater hit him full in the face. A stiff breeze blew and the tide was low somewhere… yes, the gulls were wheeling overhead and calling to each other. He was on the southern coast, and the pink in the sky told him it was the hour before sunrise. He had ridden for the entire night. That could put them almost anywhere along the coast of County Cork or Waterford.

The woman stood holding the doors, and motioned for him to dismount. He climbed from the lorry, stretching out after the cramped ride, wondering if he could run if he had to.

"Stay planted," the woman said. She held a small Walther pistol on him, opened the crate he had been sitting on, and fished around in the cabbages. Beneath them was an assortment of weapons. Doyle, to his great dismay, had forgotten the drill they had taught him in his short training period after he was plucked from his civilian job with a manufacturing and mining company and appointed into the army. Always look for a way to escape or turn the tables. Use whatever is around you.

Check everything. *So all this time*, he thought, *I have been sitting on a crate of guns....*

The woman smiled ruefully at him, seeming to read his thoughts. "Not much of a military man at heart, are you?" she said. "Ah, well, that's why we wanted you, so don't be thinking badly of yourself. And the ammunition was up front with me, anyway. Let's go," she said, pointing with her gun.

Doyle trudged on until they came to a dolmen, one of the hundreds of Neolithic stone structures scattered across the country. It rose six feet above the uneven ground, and a huge capstone, weighing perhaps thirty tons, sat pinnacled on the tiny points of two other upright stones. The woman stopped behind him there and looked south, as though searching for something. Doyle thought about trying to make a grab for the woman's gun, but then, to what end at this point? If she had taken Coreen, he'd never find out where. There was nothing to do but follow along until he could find her.

Their view, illuminated by a mist shrouded sunrise, encompassed a green ridge above the shoreline, and a flock of brown and black sheep, damp and stringy from the fog, stared back at them with disinterested amber eyes. A few tall gorse bushes bloomed bright yellow in the pasture, and then, her eyes alighting on one of them, the woman began to sing a song that Doyle knew from his school days in Switzerland. It was a German folk song, *Im Märzen der Bauer,* and while she used no words, he followed her tune in his mind with them.

She finished her verse and waited. A heartbeat later, the gorse bush, apparently a tenor, broke into the same tune. The woman chuckled as a man who appeared to be a shepherd stepped out from behind his thorny yellow cover, waved his staff, and strode toward her. When he got close enough, Doyle saw that he wore clothes similar to his own. The man pointed with his eyes, cocked his head to the right, and the girl took up her position in front of the dolmen. Then the "shepherd" dropped his staff, ducked under the enormous dolmen and then beckoned to Doyle, saying, "Step into my office, sir. We'll have us a little chat." Doyle complied.

Beneath the capstone of the structure, the chill from the wind diminished along with its constant whine. "Here, Dr. Doyle," he said, motioning to the ground. The man's quiet words seemed to echo slightly in the chamber, giving them a sense of otherworldliness. Doyle sat where he was told, on a long, flat, lichen covered rock, and waited. The man stood.

"My name's Gallagher, Dr. Doyle," the man said, his accent clearly from the Gaeltacht, the Gaelic speaking part of Ireland. "I am the deputy commander of the IRA County Cork Brigade." He cracked a broken toothed smile as he put his hands on his hips, letting his coat open slightly to reveal a Webley revolver tucked into his waistband.

Doyle stared up at Gallagher, swallowed drily and said, "You have the advantage, sir. How exactly do you know me?" The confined space of the dolmen, with that thirty-ton rock balanced so impossibly above their heads, made Doyle feel cornered and vulnerable.

"That'll be unimportant. What is important, though, is that we have your lovely Miss O'Dell, and you'll be doing what we want for the sake of her life," replied Gallagher, cocking his head at Doyle, who had paled at the mention of Coreen's name.

"There will be inquiries if anything happens to either of us," Doyle said, but there was little conviction in his voice. "My father—"

"Hmm, yes, your father. I think we both know how far the American Ambassador wouldn't go to help you. And cold comfort official searches would be to you, down under this slab here," Gallagher snorted, tapping the rock with his toe as he offered Doyle a cigarette. Doyle accepted it, and Gallagher smiled down at him, moss green eyes taking note of his captive's shaking hands. "But let's not be followin' those fox trails down a hole just yet. We want to take you to someone who very much wants to meet with you. Come along on the little journey, and then we'll return you and your fair colleen to Dublin, and all's right with the world again."

Gallagher stepped out from the dolmen and Doyle got up and followed, saying, "Wait—now? Right now?"

"No, the day after you're dead," snarled Gallagher. "Of course right now. And if you'll look just to your left just there, boyo, you'll see your darlin' girl. Proof to remind you of why you are cooperatin' with us."

And there was Coreen, standing right beside the lorry, the blonde's gun pointed at her head. The woman nodded to her, and she made a mad run for Doyle.

Coreen, her face streaked with tears and her wild golden hair flying in the wind, slammed into his chest, crying, "Seamus! I thought I would never see you again!"

"Where…how? Coreen, are you all right? Did they hurt you?" Doyle pushed his face into her neck and lifted her in a bear hug. She was tiny in his arms and light as air.

"Ah, ya big gormless idjit! They've held me in a basement and I've had no food for two days, so am I all right?!" she said, laughing and crying at the same time. Doyle held her away from him and searched her face. Two days….

"That's enough. Now you've seen her and know her to be alive, so Greta will be takin' her back for safe keeping," said Gallagher, taking Coreen by the arm.

"NO!" Doyle shouted, and she held his hand tightly.

"Just give us one moment, please," she pleaded. All Irishmen being romantics, Gallagher rolled his eyes and released Coreen's arm.

"I haven't found the right ring yet, because it has to be as rare and special as you are, and I wanted to ask you properly," Doyle said. "But when this is all over, will you marry me?" Then he kissed her hard, and Gallagher instantly hustled her off into the lorry, putting her in the back with the cabbages. "You are my beloved, my very heart, Coreen! I'll do whatever I must to get you back!" Doyle said.

"You shan't! I know what they really want now! Don't give it to them, Seamus!" she screamed over the wind, "*Coinnigh ort go deo!* There's far more at stake here than my life!"

Then the doors to the lorry slammed shut and he heard no more. Doyle stood in the stinging wind, Coreen's words ringing in his heart, and stared across the pasture at the disappearing lorry until Gallagher caught him by the arm and marched him at gunpoint toward the strand.

✗

Doyle felt his stomach lurch as the Grumman Widgeon amphibious plane banked hard to the left. Down below them was, by his reckoning anyway, the southernmost part of the Irish Sea, gray-green and misty. *Where on earth are we going?* he wondered.

The seaplane touched down in the water an hour and a half later, the swoosh of its V-hull loud in Doyle's ears. A motor launch separated itself from the shadow of a larger craft, a cargo vessel with "Irish Rowan" painted on its bow, and came toward them as they waited, rising and falling with the great ocean swells. Gallagher cracked the door of the seaplane and caught a line that a man in the bow of the launch tossed up to him. He pulled it taut, allowing the launch and the seaplane to more or less move together as one. "Jump, Dr. Doyle, and make sure of your landing. You wouldn't last long in this cold water," Gallagher warned. Doyle put his head out the door of the plane and looked down. It was only a few feet below, but both of the craft were constantly moving with the rough water. It made him dizzy to look, so he closed his eyes, hoped for the best, and jumped, landing partly on the gunwales of the launch and falling the rest of the way into the boat. Gallagher followed, making a more practiced landing, and then they were off to the *Rowan*. The seaplane waited until they reached the cargo ship, then roared into life again and lifted off, trailing streams of water behind.

In a few seconds, Doyle felt the launch scrape against the starboard side of the *Rowan*, and heard winch hooks unwinding above his head. A boarding ladder was tossed down, nearly hitting him, and Gallagher said, "Up you go, boyo," as he pushed Doyle forward, and then quickly followed. At the top of the deck, a party of six men greeted them.

"Cotched a new kind of fish, there, have ye, Devlin?" said a man that Doyle thought must be the captain. He wore a knit cap like the rest of the crew, but his demeanor was one of command.

"Oh, aye, Cap, I have," said Gallagher, laughing. "But we'll save him for later, and eat whatever your crew has left us now, if you please. I'm near like to starvin'!"

The captain gave one of the men at his side a nod, and Doyle was taken to the ship's mess, where a group of second watchmen were dining on beans and cod. Doyle sat down between two of them, taking the only other place at the table, but Gallagher waited outside for a moment and then came in with a large waterproofed parcel. He tore it open as he took the place of a man who moved over, and examined the contents. Sliding them over to Doyle, he said, "These are yours. Learn 'em up, in case we're stopped and they ask you questions."

Doyle stared down at the papers and was shocked to see his own photograph pasted to a carnet, with the name "Seamus Conaill" typed on the document. Conaill was his mother's maiden name…. The photograph was old, one he recognized as taken during his graduation year at Trinity College Dublin. Whoever these men were, they knew far too much about him.

"What's this for?" Doyle asked.

"Guernsey," said Gallagher. "How's your Irish?"

"Guernsey?! That's German-occupied territory," Doyle spit out, his mind beginning to race. If he set foot on Guernsey, a British Crown possession captured by the Germans at the start of the war, he could be executed as a spy if anyone discovered him to be an American army officer. He narrowed his eyes at Gallagher, silently asking for more information.

Gallagher smiled wickedly, and shoved a huge bite of cod into his mouth. Gallagher knew exactly what kind of peril Guernsey meant for Doyle. "You'll be taken to my friends, but you'll need to sound like me and not an American army officer, y' see? Can't have any onlookers 'tween here and there finding you out. Ya never know who has an ear out. So I'll ask you again. How's she cuttin'?"

It had been awhile since he's spoken the language he'd learned at the knee of a Gaelic nanny and used with friends in school. His father, unable to understand it himself, had forbidden it to be spoken in his presence, but Doyle had never forgotten the musical, lilting tongue of the land of his birth, a land that was more home to him than America ever would be. Of course his Irish was good. He was a native, and Gallagher would already know that. He fixed the man with a cold stare.

"*Is fearr Gaeilgi briste, na Bearla cliste*—broken Irish is better than clever English," he said, matching Gallagher's own accent.

"That'll do, boyo," Gallagher smiled, and broke into good-natured laughter.

An hour later, Gallagher led Doyle down the gangway to the docks of St. Peter Port on the Bailiwick of Guernsey. The twenty-four square mile island was situated in the English Channel, perilously close to Occupied France, and Britain had offered no resistance when the Germans took it to use as a launching base.

A contingent of Waffen SS soldiers waited for them, and Doyle felt his chest constrict with a different kind of fear than he had ever felt before. His life seemed to collapse and reform before his eyes. He was no longer the American army major on assignment overseas. He was a captive in enemy territory, really there, really among the Nazis. They were no longer mythic images in a news report or statistics on General Arnold's desk. They were now only a few feet in front of him, in the living, breathing flesh. And they were everything dreadful he had imagined and more.

A young *Oberleutnant*, his hair buzzed down to the skin on the sides of his head under a *Schirmmutze* officer's cap cocked to the right, stepped forward and appraised Doyle.

"Wait. Who is this one? I have not seen him before," the Oberleutnant said to Gallagher in carefully correct English. Gallagher shrugged. The Oberleutnant's nose crinkled up and his slate-gray eyes lingered on Doyle's forged carnet. Doyle felt his knees nearly buckle when the officer summoned two rifle-bearing, steel-helmeted SS soldiers, their faces stony as the cobbles beneath Doyle's feet.

"Your name?" the Oberleutnant queried. He raised those flat, soulless eyes to Doyle's and Doyle felt his hands go cold and his throat tighten.

Hoping his muscle reactions would not constrain his voice, he said, "Seamus Connaill." The words sounded rusty, and his mouth was dry.

The Oberleutnant smiled blandly and nodded to one of the SS soldiers, who raised his Mauser K98 stiffly and drove its steel buttplate into Doyle's solar plexus. Doyle's knees did buckle this time, and he fell onto the hard cobbles in abject agony.

"Take him to the command bunker and sort him out," ordered the Oberleutnant, and the two SS soldiers slung their rifles and grabbed Doyle by the arms to drag him away. Remembering how rifle butts in the gut felt, some of the striped-pajama-clad Jewish laborers averted their eyes. Doyle gagged and spat, bringing up pink spittle, then blacked out when the soldiers pressed harder on his upper arms.

※

With no clue as to how long he had been out, he regained consciousness in a windowless, water-stained concrete room. Only an overhead bulb, naked and glaring in his eyes, lit the dismal, cold space. He squinted into the dark beyond the bulb's aura and saw that he was in some sort of fortified bunker.

When he tried to bring a hand to his eyes, he discovered his arms were shackled to a chair. A long wooden table, its several stains reminding him of old blood, stretched before him. His breath came in gasps, and his gut hurt so badly he thought he might have internal bleeding—no, he was sure of it. Then he heard the creak of a steel hatch opening behind his back, and the crisp clicks of what had to be a pair of spit-shined cavalry boots walking slowly across the concrete floor. The Oberleutnant again? It must be. But then Doyle's sense of smell jerked his head around to follow the odor of fresh bread. Was he hallucinating?

No. An SS officer had entered and was carrying a tray bearing a sandwich, a cup of coffee, and a thick file, all of which the man placed on the table in front of Doyle. The officer stayed in the darkness just beyond the small bulb's circle of light, and said, "Cigarette?" in German, as he removed two Gauloises from a pack. He offered one to Doyle, who of course could not take it, and then the man laughed apologetically and placed it on the table as he lit his own.

"I'm so sorry about the blow to the stomach," he continued in German, "Our man is eager and a bit cruel. He was supposed to bring you to me without damage." Doyle tried to make out the face of the man as he came forward a bit. The pain kept him from thinking of much else, but there was a sense of familiarity in the officer's voice. In silhouette, the man had the same closely polled, neatly slicked back haircut that all the Waffen SS seemed to favor. Doyle could see the Ritter Cross hanging from the center of his stiff collar. The four-diamond rank of an *Obersturmbahn-furher* decorated one side of that collar and the SS runes marked the other. "Now that I see you," the man chuckled, "I think bringing you food was maybe a bad idea. Sorry. Just consider that hit payback for our last rugby match at school, the one when you rammed me with your head in the very same part of my body. I was in bed for days!" The officer stepped fully into the light.

Doyle's focus sharpened in on the smiling face and at the last words, a dawning recognition swept over him. "God in heaven!" he said, also in German. "Mattias?" A wave of something almost like relief washed over Doyle, for he realized that the officer was indeed a much older Mattias von Esslinger, his chum and roommate from Lyceum Helvetica St. Gallen, the prestigious Swiss boarding school that Doyle had attended all through his teenage years. "Mattias... I can't be here! Can you help me? What are you doing in that absurd uniform?" The words tumbled out of Doyle's mouth almost on top of each other.

Without answering, von Esslinger moved around to Doyle's side of the table, unlocked the shackles, picked up the French cigarette and reoffered it to him. Doyle accepted this time, let von Esslinger light it for him, and then dragged deeply on it. Exhaling, he felt the nicotine steady his bloodless hands. Mattias leaned in to him.

"My friend, you are in dire straits," he smiled, noticing his own pun. "And I can only allow you to help yourself. The Oberleutnant wanted to force you with more pain, but I told him that would not work with you. The Commandant agreed."

"Gallagher, the woman—they abducted me," said Doyle. "What do you have to do with this? They have my girlfriend."

"Yes, they do. They work for my Commandant," said Mattias, laughing. "You met my darling Greta? What a woman!"

Doyle thought he was hallucinating again, and *he* was certainly not laughing along with Mattias. "Your Commandant did this? You brought me here?" His relief promptly drained away and the muscles in his lower back clenched into spasms. Mattias really was a Nazi.

"*Ja*. There was no other way. We had to be sure you would not be followed," said Mattias, resting on the corner of the table nearest Doyle. In a warm, soothing voice, Mattias continued, "Wallace, I know that you have spent your life seeking the approval of those who are too blind and uncaring to appreciate your talents. Your father, the ambassador—so distant he is, given completely to his own career. Your mother never loved you and always preferred your brother Parker, even more so since his heroic death at Pearl Harbor. Are these not the things you lamented night after dismal, lonely night at St. Gallen? And what of America, the country that drafted you into military service against your will, to fight for a nation you barely know and care little for?" Mattias smiled sympathetically at his old friend. "Dire straits, indeed."

Doyle heard him. Heard every word's truth. He pressed on, saying, "But why I am here, Mattias?"

"Ah, yes, it's time to tell you," said Mattias, opening the file and removing a bound report. He read the title page aloud: 'Analysis of Super-alloy Coatings in Critical High-Temperature Applications,' published 1936 by Wallace S. Doyle, PhD, Massachusetts Institute of Technology. "That is why," said Mattias, holding the document reverently. "You are brilliant. You have only just begun to tap your potential. You see, Wallace, my superiors appreciate your considerable talents and accomplishments. We also know you have been hand picked to oversee the American branch of Archangel."

"Archangel!" said Doyle, wondering how the Germans could know of his involvement with the secret operation. Doyle had been ordered to report to Santa Sabina airbase in California after the Antrim meetings, along with General Arnold and some young engineer pilot by the name of Halcyon James. He had found out about Archangel only two days before, and he hadn't even met James. All Doyle had heard was a rumor that the operation was about new jet technology.

"Though we are winning the war, of course, we are having a bit of trouble with some of our engine designs, Wallace, as I am sure you have already heard," said Mattias. Doyle had heard. German engines could operate for only a few hours before their components melted and had to be replaced.

"What about Coreen?" said Doyle, quietly cutting to the heart of his concern.

"Miss O'Dell is safe. In fact, once you have agreed to help us, we will put her on the *Irish Rowan*, the same cargo ship that brought you here. It'll take her to the Azores, where you had always meant for her to go— yes, we know everything. It was your original plan upon marrying her, was it not?" Mattias said. "She will be very comfortable. It all depends on your answer, however. Will you help us?"

What could he say? Doyle knew he wouldn't survive the trip home if he said no. You don't tell Nazis "no" and live to talk about it. Maybe his momentary "yes" would at least assure that his darling Coreen would be safe.

"She'll be truly safe?" Doyle asked weakly.

"Don't you trust me on my word?" Mattias gently replied, putting a comforting hand on Doyle's shoulder. Doyle didn't trust anything that came out of Mattias' mouth anymore, but he nodded his head woodenly. What else could he do? Doyle kept wondering what had happened to his old friend and if he had ever really known him. Mattias continued, "After we win the war, you will have a home with us, Wally. Where you can explore your talents to their fullest. State-of-the-art research facilities pursuing the latest technologies: advanced composites, new production methods. But yes, as soon as you prove you are loyal to us, we will put her on the *Rowan*. Until then, she will be cared for by Greta." Doyle listened and then a frown crossed his face when he realized there was another variable in Mattias's proposition.

"What if I can't become part of it, Mattias, because I am removed from the program? Or what if they catch me?" said Doyle, carefully.

"Ah, well, Wallace, we will see that your work is unhindered. We have people everywhere. And I think you are rather more clever than to be caught. Especially since Coreen's life depends on your success," said Mattias.

Success. Success as a traitor. It was true that Doyle had never been much of an American patriot in his heart. His only real allegiance was to his birthplace and early home, Ireland, so maybe this would be easier than it seemed. He could give Mattias what he wanted in order to save himself and Coreen and then just disappear from both the Nazis and the US Army before either of them knew it. The only option was to continuing playing along until he could get Coreen to safety.

"What do I have to do to prove myself and get her on that ship?" said Doyle.

Mattias studied Doyle's pained expression and smiled. "There are two things. First, when you return to America, find a way to acquire a good bit of chromium for us. We must have it, you know, and we cannot get this element any other way. And second, right now, confirm your acceptance of our terms," Mattias said, as he offered Doyle a typed index card. "I feel so bad this had to be done painfully. So, here is an anonymous numbered account, at the cantonal Bank of Zurich, with, shall we say, a 'token' initial deposit." Mattias held it out to him. Doyle made no move to accept it. "From me to you—my own personal funds. Please, for the inconvenience of coming to Guernsey, for our friendship," Mattias said, smiling, "and for your agreement to help us. Today you call the bank and accept the deposit, and then when you have a plan implemented for the chromium, we will put your girl on her ship." Doyle continued to stare at the card. Mattias nodded and laid the information card on the table. "That balance can grow on a regular and ongoing basis. Payable in Swiss francs of course… or in gold, if you prefer. Just call the bank and say 'yes' when the banker asks if you accept the deposit."

Doyle sipped his cooling coffee and systematically memorized the number on the card, but all he could think about was Coreen.

"Bring me a telephone," he said.

CHAPTER 2

Lowland Mill, Georgia, July 1943

TOO MANY PEOPLE had gathered in seventeen year-old Sprite Shannon's house, and all she could think about was getting outside, where she could breathe freely again. Earlier, a brilliantly hot summer sun had come out after another morning rain, making the noon funeral service uncomfortably steamy. The Reverend had been brief, but the sparse trees around the little family graveyard provided too little shade for so many people. The freshly turned red clay of her father's grave had melted into a soft, waterlogged mound, and the pallbearers had had a hard time shoveling it back over the casket in the thick, oppressive air.

It was an almighty hot Georgia summer day out there, but it was worse inside the house, because the parlor smelled of old potato salad, sweet pickle relish, and Pine Sol instead of fresh-cut grass and fertile soil. For the past three days, people had come by and given Sprite peach pies, biscuits, and soda cracker casseroles made of last year's canned beans and things that had no business passing for meat, even during the war. July was not a bad time to share food in Georgia, with the fruit trees full of peaches and plums, and the gardens coming in, but even if it had been, these people—folks her Daddy worked with and for, her friends from town who knew her from school and church—seemed like these people would have brought her their last potato and been glad to do it, and never once would have let on about it. It made Sprite's heart swell when she thought about that. Maybe things would be all right for her. Maybe she didn't need to feel so scared and alone.

Anyway, all of Lowland Mill's good farm people were pressed into her tiny parlor and kitchen, standing elbow to sunburned elbow, murmuring softly, respectfully. Now and then, Sprite heard a few stray words while she sat on the sofa with her best friend Letty.

"...and nobody knows why them other guys was even there behind the mill and got burnt up, too...."

"I hear tell Randall had engine trouble and it was sheer dumb, bad luck he couldn't set down the plane down before he hit the windmill, but you know, he was flyin' in the dark—that part don't make no sense to me, does it you? Randall never did nothin' that crazy before, even if he did drink...."

"...said her father's cousin was comin'. I think that's him standin' over there with the fancy woman by him, yeah, the bleached blonde with the Betty Grable hair-do. He kinda looks like Randall, don't he?"

Sprite sighed wearily and glanced over at her second cousin. He did look like her Daddy. Maybe a little too much to bear right now. Jeff was six or seven years older than Randall and, long before Sprite was born, had moved to Pennsylvania to do some kind of work in a steel mill up there. He had met and married Josephine Dupree, the bleached blonde Grable girl, but they hadn't had any kids. They had arrived here yesterday, surprising Sprite and bearing a faded family reunion photo with Jeff and her father in it. It was clear that they were expecting to stay awhile, since Josephine had brought three bags for herself alone.

"Um, Letty, darling, could you go get me some water, please, and I would be ever so grateful if you would put a little more ice in it this time. I am about to melt in this room," Jo laughed, making a funny face and fluttering her fingers. Her voice was high, and a little raspy, like a rusty hinge.

"It's because she smokes like a freight train," said Letty, reading Sprite's mind. "I'll go get her water, but 'No, Miss Priss, there ain't no more ice down here in the hot hollers, 'cause you done used it all up!'"

Letty whispered to Sprite, miming Josephine's hand movements perfectly. It made Sprite smile, and when Letty came back, Sprite thought it was a good time to bring up the question that had troubled her all afternoon.

"Why you think they came all the way down here, Letty?" she said, under her breath, looking at the cousins. "They've been real good to me since they got here, takin' care of all the arrangements for Daddy, even payin' the minister. But I never met 'em before in my life. Why would they care a thing about me?"

Letty looked discreetly at the couple and then away quickly, opened her mouth to begin, and then stopped, as if she didn't want to say something out of turn. She began again. "I don't know. But I'm glad you have some family now to be with you, even if they are Yankees. I gotta be back home tonight and you'll be here alone with 'em."

"What's wrong with that?" Sprite said.

"You know what my momma says about relatives in the house. They are your blood, but they ain't your friends! Keep honest people honest. Better hide the good silverware!" Letty held up the bent-pronged tin fork she had just licked clean of apple pie, and they both laughed weakly. Sprite pulled out a hand fan and sighed, knowing it would be a few more hours before she could breathe freely again.

By late afternoon, the crowd had thinned down to two or three women who were scraping dishes and washing mason jars. Sprite said goodbye to Letty, then walked back into the parlor, where she found Jeff and Josephine alone.

"How are you feeling, honeybelle? You have had such a long, terrible day, and you look like you're ready to drop over. Why don't you go on to bed now and Jo and I will tidy up down here," said Jeff. Jo nodded her agreement, brassy curls on her forehead bobbing.

Sprite searched their eyes, and finding only concern, she said, "Cousin Jeff, I sure do appreciate all you and Jo are doing for me. I know Daddy would have, too."

"Oh, think nothing of it, darling," said Jo, fanning herself with a folded newspaper. "That's what family is for. We'll stay with you as long as you need us."

Sprite smiled a little crookedly and said, "All right. I'll leave the windows open for you, but when it gets dark, we can't have any lights on, you know—the war and all."

"We know, honeybelle," said Jeff. "I'll take care of that. It's the same up North."

Sprite turned and left them, but she didn't go to her room. Remembering a duty she had not yet done, she eased up the stairs to her father's bedroom, where Jeff and Jo were staying, and went to his desk. Opening the wooden drawer slowly, quietly, she removed a sealed envelope with "Sprite" written on it and crept back down the stairs and outside, into the early evening light. It was much cooler out there now, and Sprite could smell another storm coming. She looked for the thunderhead, but the sunset, pinks and golds and purples, stretched all the way across a clear sky. However, the birds were swarming in great hordes over the nearest neighbor's pecan trees, lighting and rising, time and again, as if they couldn't find the right tree for shelter from the oncoming heavy weather.

She remembered what her father had told her when he was teaching her to fly last year. "See those birds, Baby? And notice that smell in the air?" he'd said over the radio. "You can't tell it yet, but the birds can. A storm's coming in and they're taking shelter. When you see that sign and you smell the rain, it's time for you to take your own bird home. Now set 'er down right smart, like I taught you. We got maybe ten more minutes before she hits."

Sprite had looked all around the blue sky and had seen nothing but white, fluffy clouds. But she obeyed her father, and the two of them, each flying their own Stearman crop dusters, banked for home. Sure enough, a little while later, as they'd huddled in the hangar, a huge black thunderhead had sprung up and begun to release torrential rain and hail the size of green peaches.

Daddy always knew, she thought. One day she had asked him about it. He'd told her it was just experience with the weather, but he also had a bit of the gift of the Sight, or the "knowing," as Randall called it. For him, it was a little warning voice or a knowledge he hadn't consciously learned. But her Irish mother Sherilene had also had the gift, and in her, it had been much stronger.

Sprite also had those "knowings," like the time she'd had to land a plane before she'd ever flown one. Her father had blacked out while they were in the air, and all Sprite could do was hold on and feel how the plane responded to the controls in her cockpit. Somehow she had managed to set them down in a soft cornfield, though the landing was ragged and rough. It was as if her hands had done it before, though afterward, she couldn't remember how.

Sprite took her good shoes off and squished up the lane toward the hangar through yesterday's rain puddles. When she got there, she slipped into the door, shut it behind her, and locked it from inside. She breathed a long sigh of relief at being alone and in the hangar, with its familiar smells of machine oil, polish, and bug dust, and its high, airy ceiling. Opening the sealed envelope in the dimming light, she read its contents again and again, tears soon falling upon the words, reviving the old dry blue ink and blurring letters here and there on one of the two copies.

> *Dear Sprite,*
> *I am writing this to make it legal that everything I own, and*
> *everything I have been entrusted with for you, will pass to*
> *you, my only child, Enid Shannon, when you turn twenty-one*
> *years old.*
> *Signed on the 19th of May, 1941, Calder County, Georgia*
> */Randall M. Shannon/*
> *Witnessed by:*
> */Mrs. Annie Johnson/*
> *Notary Public.*

The big round wheel of the notary's seal had embossed the page next to the woman's signature. Sprite wiped her eyes, blotted the pages with a clean polishing rag, and folded the papers back into the envelope.

Her father had shown her this envelope before, explaining what it was and where he kept it in case of, well, something like what had just happened. It had been after dinner on her fifteenth birthday, shortly after he'd had to sell part of her inheritance from her mother's side, about a hundred acres of prime cotton land, to make the payments on the planes they used in the crop dusting business. He presented it with a gift, which was her mother Sherilene's wedding ring on a gold chain, and told her, "This ring was your Ma's. So it's from her. But the envelope is to you from me, Baby. See your name right here on it? The paper inside says when you turn twenty-one, everything goes to you. You gonna let me stay here with you then?" he had kidded her. She had, her face serious, allowed he could remain on her property. They both had a big laugh, and Randall had walked her up to the hangar and let her take her first solo flight. It had been a wonderful day... just a couple of years back, but now it seemed so long ago.

"Enid. My name is Enid," she whispered, the memory of her first knowledge of that name flooding over her. One day, when she'd pestered him all morning, her father had sighed and figured she was old enough to know, so he told her about her birth... she had come into the world kicking and screaming after the thirty-one hour delivery that had killed her mother. Thinking the baby would surely be a boy, Randall had even painted a new sign for the hangar that read, "Shannon & Sons." He and Sherilene hadn't even picked out a girl's name. When her mother, most of the blood run out of her, had laid her hand on his and taken her last breath, Randall had removed her wedding ring, a rose and green gold Claddagh, put it in his pocket, and walked out of the room. He went straight to the hangar, leaving the newborn in the arms of the midwife, and promptly embarked on a two day, full-bore bender. When the preacher had come to bury Sherilene in the family plot out back of the house, the good Reverend had found Randall soaked to the bone in corn liquor, slacked up against a stack of bags full of "Enid Springs" calcium arsenate that he used to dust crops. The preacher had coughed politely, saying he could do the christening right after the funeral if Randall wanted, and then asked him what the baby's name was.

Randall had looked up at him through two days of grief and an empty quart bottle of his best whiskey, dropped his eyes to the stack of bags, and said the first thing that came into focus. "Enid...."

The minister had said, "Uh, Randall, did you say 'Enid'?" Randall had closed his eyes, becoming dizzier with every thought.

"Yup," he'd mumbled. "That'll do. Her name is Enid."

A few days later, when he had sobered up, he had looked at the baby's handwritten baptismal certificate and winced, vowing never to call her by that name. Then, a new name had come to him that very night, when he dreamed Sherilene had whispered it in his ear.

"Sprite should be her name, Randy. She'll be a wind sprite one day, just like in my grandfather's stories from Ireland. She'll have wings like the fairy folk." And the next morning, Sprite was her only name from then on as far as Randall had been concerned. Sprite had often thought about the story of her naming through the years, but had never felt anything more than sad for the mother she had never known.

She folded the papers, put them back into the envelope and then into her long skirt pocket. It had gotten very dark in the hangar, and the first few heavy drops of rain began to pepper down on the tin roof… the big storm had arrived.

✕

It had rained so hard that Sprite had decided to stay in the hangar and sleep on the cot Randall kept there. The next morning, before full light, she walked back down the soupy lane, red puddles still dancing with a few sprinkles of rain, and passed through the back door without making a sound. Her night had passed fitfully, with waves of grief washing over her again and again, until at last, her throat had opened and released a wail as primal as a wolf's cry into the nightlong thunderstorm. She had awakened with one hand tightly clenched over the Claddagh ring she wore on her other hand.

Now, the little ring felt like fire on her skin, reminding her of how her father had died, how her mother had named her, and that she was all alone now.

I'll put it on again later, when I can wear it without crying, she thought, removing and stringing it back onto its gold chain. Sprite had no jewelry box, so she put the chain in her little white Bible as a bookmark at the 23rd Psalm, the one the preacher had read over her father's grave. She tucked the ring between the spine and cover at the top of the Bible, and left the chain trailing at the bottom, satisfied that the heirloom was secure.

A few minutes and a hot sponge bath later, she appeared at the break-fast table, where Jo had laid her place, and ate an entire plate of pancakes with peach preserves and a little butter on them, and a half piece of their rationed bacon.

"Well, goodness, girl," said Jeff, laughing, "you ate like somebody was going to take it away from you!" Jo gave him a funny look, but she sat down and smiled at Sprite, closing her Tangee orange mouth over smoke-yellowed teeth.

"What will you be doing today, darling?" she asked, spreading pre-serves on a biscuit. Sprite looked into her empty plate, and then toward the hangar as she thought.

"I think I'd better see to Daddy's customers. The last three days of rain's washed all the poison off the crops, and they'll be needin' a dust now."

Josephine almost dropped her biscuit. "What!? What do you mean?" Jeff was listening intently for Sprite's answer.

"Well, I mean I'm goin' to put the dust in the hoppers and fly the plane real low over the crops, and dump the dust on the crops, you know…" she patiently explained, wondering if these two were a couple of dim bulbs. But, of course they wouldn't know anything about what her father's business really meant in terms of its work. She instantly felt a little less than gracious in her judgment of them.

"You? Fly that plane out there?" said Jeff, stunned.

"Yes, me—I got my licenses last year and I been workin' with Daddy ever since," Sprite replied.

Jo rolled her eyes and laughed, this time showing her ugly teeth. "Well, I never! You can really fly? I can hardly believe that! Jeff, she says she can really fly!"

"Yeah, yeah, I heard her," Jeff nodded. "Well, OK, then! Crank her up and we'll watch from the ground." Sprite smiled, surprised that she was enjoying the attention, though it was a slightly embarrassing feeling for her. Flying was just her job, not something all that glamorous, but if it made 'em happy, well, at least she could repay their kindness by entertain-ing them. The dust runs could wait until the afternoon.

A half hour later, she was in the air. She did a few simple maneuvers for the cousins, and they cheered and clapped and waved every time she flew over their heads. Sprite hadn't felt that good since, well, seemed like a long, long time ago, even if it had been just last week.

Still waving and watching from the hangar door, Jeff and Jo were talking to each other through their big, painfully stretched smiles. "I couldn't tell you earlier, Jo, because you might have blabbed it," said Jeff, trying to talk through clenched teeth.

"Well tell me now, and stop pretending you're some kind of spy. She can't hear you way up there. Just talk normally," Jo said, in full voice.

"OK, OK, but keep your voice down. Who knows what she can or can't hear up there. As I was saying, you should know about all this now, because you'll have to be there while I do the deal. Won't be hard—girl's already accepted us, and now all we have to do is hang tight until this Captain Smith comes and pays us. We'll get her settled into a factory job and she'll never know anything about the money. Then we'll be on our way."

"You *sure* this is gonna work?" Jo said.

"That guy Smith, first time he called, when I was at work, he said this little piece of paradise is the only parcel of land left that the government needs. He's buying for the army. Smith's boss is overseeing some kind of Army Corps of Engineers mining project in the works, but these hayseeds don't know anything much about it yet. Smith said Randall never took the government dollars."

"I don't see what's so special about this dirt hole," Jo said.

"Well, lo and behold, this piece is the lynchpin of the whole deal, because of the minerals and that artesian spring out back. But that was Randall—bullheaded and dumb. Never did know how to make an easy buck!"

Jo waved and blew a kiss to Sprite and she did a loop-the-loop. "What spring out where?" said Jo, forcing herself to continue to look up at the plane.

"Over there, behind the hangar. That big pond. It's not like other ponds if you look at it. No, don't look at it now! We can't seem interested or she'll wonder why. That's where this Poplar Creek that runs all around the county starts. Right there in that pond, and then the spill makes the creek. And the government needs that water. Who knows for what, but that's why Smith hunted us up and got us down here when he read the paper and saw Randall's last name was same as ours. I guess they were trying to find next of kin. I'd never have come down here just for Randall—we didn't get on much. But hey, want the best news?" His eyes never left the sky.

"You know I always do," said Jo, her neck beginning to ache.

"Smith is coming here tomorrow to pay us for this land, so don't unpack, Jo; our ship is coming in, and we need to catch it quick!"

A few fancy moves later, noticing she needed gas, Sprite landed the plane and came rolling up to her cousins, who were applauding her. She hopped out, let Jeff give her a big hug, and then took care of the fueling. While she was waiting for the tank to fill, old Mr. Wakely, who owned most of the cotton she and her father dusted, drove his big green truck up the lane and got out, waving to her. She'd seen him only yesterday at the funeral. He had been so nice to her.

"Hey, Sprite. Ah, again, I sure am sorry about your father. I just came to tell you that all us farmers, well, we know you'll be closing the business now, and we'll be going over to that bunch out of the Mississippi Delta for our dusting. They got a new branch here. I just thought it was the courteous thing to do, and would save you a difficult call."

Sprite looked at him, bewildered. "Mr. Wakely, I'm the one been dustin' for you, and most of them as well, these past two years. That's been me up in that plane as much as it was my Daddy. I do a good job and I plan to continue right along. Only way I know I can make a livin'."

Wakely's sun-reddened face smiled kindly out from under his cap. "Aww, Sprite, honey, don't make this hard on me. I know you can fly real good and all, but I can't be trusting my business to a little girl, now can I?"

Sprite couldn't answer. 'A *little girl?*' Wakely's words now, others' words later. She just sighed and dropped her head. They'd give her their last potato, but not their business....

"And, honey, you know the five farms down from me are gonna tell you the same. We done discussed it, and I'm real sorry, but you see our predicament, don't you?" he added, confirming her last thought.

Sprite saw it all right. Men wanted to do business only with other men. "Thank you kindly, Mr. Wakely, for bringing me word of your change of service providers. I will be goin' back to work now, if you please," she said curtly, avoiding his rheumy gaze.

Jeff and Jo looked at each other with practiced sad eyes and compassionate frowns. "Sprite, honeybelle, it'll be alright. We're here with you now and we'll work through all this together. I think I might even have a way to help you out, but I don't have the details straight yet, so that's all I can say. But we're going to help you somehow," said Jeff.

Wakely, seeing that he had been deftly pushed out of the conversation, got back in his truck without saying goodbye, and left them to it.

"Thank you Jeff," said Sprite. "I think I'm goin' over to Letty's for a while." And with that, she capped the tank with a snap, and strode off down the road.

※

"Aww, Sprite, they're just a bunch of ignernt ol' men! Who do they think is doin' all the men's jobs up in the munitions factories and on the rivet lines, even pumpin' their gas? It's us, that's who! It's the women they left here when they went off to fight. Somebody's gotta do it and we do it just fine," Letty huffed, petting her calico cat, Turtle. "What's the differnce with you dustin' their crops instead of your Daddy? Dust is dust, ain't it? And you don't even drink! Oh, sorry, honey. I didn't mean to say it like that, I just meant you don't drink, like a lot of people do, like—"

"Letty, it's alright. I know what my Daddy was like. But just so's you know, the onliest time I ever saw him drink and then get in the plane was the night last week he went after those men from the bank that broke into the hangar and shot at him and tried to hurt me, I swear," said Sprite.

That had been the night of the crash. Randall, furious and desperate after his attempts to pay off the predatory loan, only to meet with the bank's ham-fisted attempts at collection, had chased the men down the road in his plane and buzzed them until he was out of fuel. When the men's car had pulled behind the old windmill, Randall had put his plane, out of gas and gliding its last few feet before an inevitable crash, neatly into one of the turning sails, causing an enormous explosion that had taken the men's lives as well as his own.

"Well, I think you orta fly us both down to the State Peach Festival outside Atlanta this weekend," said Letty, trying to bring her friend's thoughts back to the present. "Hey, I hear they got a lot good lookin' boys down that way!" Letty bounced up and down gleefully on the blue-flowered sofa next to Sprite.

"That's a real good idea, Letty," said Sprite, slowly brightening. "But your momma wouldn't let you go with me, you know that. Not after Jesse… it'll be a long time before she's gonna let you anywhere out of her sight." Letty wilted, acknowledging the point. Jesse, her brother and Sprite's first and still secret love, had been killed last fall in battle on Guadalcanal.

"But you know what?" Sprite continued.

"What?" said Letty, already knowing what, but playing her part.

"I am gonna go over there with the plane and put me up a sign and charge me some money for little up and down 'see Atlanta from the air' jaunts," said Sprite, her green eyes twinkling. "I'm gonna do that for sure. I've never seen Atlanta, high or low either one, my own self."

CHAPTER 3

"NOW BE REAL careful, honeybelle," said Jeff, his serious brown eyes locked onto Sprite's as she settled into the cockpit of her Stearman. "We'll look for you back late tomorrow, or we're 'draggin' the river,' as my momma used to say." Sprite quirked the side of her mouth a bit, pondering his momma's repeated phrase. Something about the way Jeff said it made her uneasy. When she'd told the cousins about the Peach Festival, they seemed almost too happy she was going. They didn't even want to follow in the truck and Jeff hadn't asked her for her route, or quizzed her on what she would be doing or even where she would stay, for that matter. Not like her father would have done.

"You got your sandwiches and thermos? And your clean clothes?" asked Jo, fluttering around, cigarette jumping nervously in her hand.

"I will be back on time and I have everything," Sprite patted the stubby red and green plaid bottle. "And I've done my flight check," she said, feeling her heart begin to race at the thought of going out on her own, and to the biggest city in the state. Well, not the city itself, maybe, only the fairgrounds outside the city, but still, it was a long way from Lowland Mill.

In a couple of minutes, she was in the air, rising far above the rooftop, the red dirt lane, the waving cousins, and all that was home.

)(

An hour and a half later, the lush rolling piedmont of Georgia had flattened out a little bit, the river had disappeared into pine forest, and she began to watch for the landing field her father had described so many times before. He'd told her he had been to this festival with her mother when they were first married, when he was still doing barnstorming as a hobby.

Throughout the flight, Sprite had seen twisted, red dirt roads become straight country lanes that turned into paved two-lane highways that crisscrossed ever more frequently until they gathered themselves into a big tangled mess at the heart of Atlanta. There was a low-lying cloud of white smoke rising from five or six distant factory stacks, and it seemed much hotter the closer she got to the city. The smells of sulfur and lime and burning coal drifted up to greet her, and she began to descend a little, veering upwind of them. Then she saw bright red, white, and blue banners flapping in the light breeze all around a big circle just outside of town, with a flat, grassy landing field right beside it. Four other planes with military markings already sat staked in their places, and it looked like hundreds of people were milling around the white canvas topped booths and open air tables inside the circle. She tipped her wings, circled twice, and a man in all white clothing ran out to the end of the airfield and waved a big semaphore flag back and forth, signaling her in for landing.

The Stearman rolled to a perfectly controlled stop in an empty spot in the row of planes, and Sprite cut the engine and unbuckled her harness. The man in white had made it back from the end of the field, and now he was huffing up to her, face as red as his hair.

"Well, hey there, little lady! Have we found Amelia Earhart at last?" A shining river of sweat trickled down out of the big man's close cut gray hair. "My name is Homer Montgomery and I'm the program director, so welcome to our little Peach Festival! We didn't expect any other air traffic aside from the recruiters, but I am absolutely sure they won't mind sharing the field, seein' how you must be with the WASP." Homer Montgomery slapped his big hand on his white seersucker pants and gave Sprite a showman's smile.

"What's a WASP?" Sprite asked, knowing he couldn't have meant the insect.

"They're the Women's Army Special Pilots or some such. There's a lady pilot here from their group. I thought you must be with her…” Homer said, disappointed in his guess.

“Well actually, I… I was hopin’ to do a little business, Mr. Montgomery,” said Sprite as she climbed down from the Stearman. Suddenly, she felt alone and very small. Atlanta was all a bright fairy tale from the air, but down on the ground, its tall buildings loomed huge and menacing and seemed much closer than they really were. “I want to give plane rides to your festival folks and I guess maybe you are the man to tell me where to set up.”

Homer looked the Stearman over, seeing the “Shannon & Sons” logo painted down the side of it. “What does Shannon and Sons do, um—didn’t get your name, darlin’.”

“They call me Sprite. Sprite Shannon. This is my plane. Daddy and I have—” Sprite corrected herself, “I have a crop dusting business over in Lowland Mill.”

“Lowland Mill! Was that the little town up to the east where that man lost control and ended up with his airplane stuck on that windmill and killed a family of five on the ground last Wednesday night? We heard all about that here in Atlanta,” Homer said, his mind working to recall all the details of the news report.

“Yes, sir, that would be the place, but it was three men, not a family of five,” said Sprite, hoping he would not press her for more information about it. People seemed to be making all kinds of stories up about her Daddy’s wreck, and the farther away from the crash site the stories got told, the farther away from the truth they wandered. She set her chocks and stood up, brushing her hands on her coveralls.

“Well,” said Homer, a bit chaffed at being corrected on his gossip, “Sprite, please follow me and we can get you fixed up. Usually, our vendors make arrangements a year in advance for this festival, but we can make an exception here with you, I think,” said Homer, thinking about what his percentage take might be on such a novelty as plane rides. “Yes, such a novelty! Say, there used to be a guy from somewhere around your town that came here to do barnstorming tricks a long time ago, when we had barns here. Had the prettiest wife—Sher… Sheryl? Sherrie? Something like that. And he was the best I’ve ever seen at what he did. I guess he's in the war now, dropping bombs on Gerry," said Homer, leading Sprite to the Chamber of Commerce tent, "Might be dead now for all we know." Sprite grimaced at that, but said nothing.

In a few minutes, Sprite was sitting on a little white "First Baptist Church of Atlanta" folding chair, the Stearman a few yards away, holding Homer's quickly painted cardboard sign that read, "See Atlanta from the air. Plane rides, $3." Within a very few minutes, a couple of high school boys walked over to her.

"Hey, girl, where's Shannon? Or the Sons? I think my friend and I would like to engage his services and take a ride. We'll be joining the air corps in a few months if the war can last, and we'd like to see what it's like up there!" The one with the buzz cut red hair and the big freckled face pointed at the plane. The other one let his friend do all the talking, but he eyed the plane with interest. Before Sprite could answer that she would be their pilot today, a small crowd had appeared behind the boys—men, women and their young kids, and more teenage boys. Many more teen-age boys.

Sprite took a deep breath, thinking that she could maybe get only a few of them in the air today, and said, "Well, everyone, my name is Sprite. Sprite Shannon. And this is my airplane, and I will gladly take you up one at a time today for as long as it's light out. I think these boys here in front were first, though!" She gave the crowd a big smile.

The freckled face boy's head cocked to the side, and he looked at her like he thought she was playing a joke on them. "Girl, let's get to it, OK? The war ain't gonna wait on us. Go find your Daddy or your brothers and get us up in the air," he said, a little bit of irritation in his voice now.

Sprite shook her head. "My Daddy... my Daddy is somewhere else and I don't have any brothers. I'm the pilot, and I flew this plane here from Lowland Mill not one hour ago," she finished, watching the crowd evaporate as quickly as it had formed. The red-headed boy spit a big gob of tobacco juice at her, just missing her feet. Then the two boys just snorted and walked off, punching each other in the arms and laughing, repeating her last sentence and mimicking her voice.

And so it went for the rest of the day. Someone would approach, ask for a ride, and then back off when she told them she would be flying them. By late afternoon, she was exhausted and forlorn and needed to find a bathroom. On her way back to her seat, she passed the recruiters' tables. Army, Navy, Marines—behind all of them sat handsome young men in their tailored, pressed uniforms, talking avidly to each boy or man in the front of their line. Sprite wove her way through the string of soon-to-be recruits, and then came to a little table, lower than the rest, at the end of the group. There was a single chair just like the one she had been given folded and leaned against the table, and on that, a stack of flyers fluttered in the breeze, a big rock on top holding them down. Sprite walked up to the table and took a flyer. It read, "W.A.S.P. - Is the new Womens' Air-force Service Pilots program for you? Apply now!" Sprite glanced over to the next table, where a handsome Marine shook the hand of his latest recruit. His buddy beside him had ducked to retrieve one of their paper forms from the ground. "Sir," she said, tentatively, "Do you know any-thing about this?" She held up the flyer.

The first young man said, "No, Miss, I don't. But the lady who was at that table has just left for the day. Her name is Ethel Sheehy, and you might still catch her. She just walked away not two minutes ago, and she was headed for the airfield. Right Hal?"

His friend—Hal—swung up from his paper save, and stood up to point the way for her. "Airfield is right over there, Miss," he said, remov-ing his white officer's cap and giving her an easy, genuine smile.

Sprite stared at him until she realized her rudeness and then pulled her eyes away from the most attractive man she had ever seen. Like his buddy, he wore the dress blues of an officer. He was as tall as Jesse had been, built solidly, with lean muscles, broad shoulders and a straight back. His eyes were a clear cornflower blue that caught the late afternoon sun and lit up his friendly face, and when he spoke, his words were colored with the faint-est of Northern accents. There was something about the way he didn't come down hard on his "r" sounds, just left them hanging gently in the air—Sprite couldn't place it. His pale blond hair, worn a little longer on top than some of the other servicemen's, lay straight and neatly combed. "Oh, thank you. Um, my name is Sprite Shannon," she said, red-faced.

The handsome Marine nodded and replied, "Captain Halcyon James. Pleased to meet you, Miss Shannon."

"Likewise. Sorry to bother you, thanks," she said nervously. She had already turned to go when the young Marine called after her.

"The other way, Miss Shannon..." he said, laughing, replacing his cap back on his head, but there was no meanness in his voice, no condescending tone. Just good humor.

She laughed too, whirled to the correct direction, and ran toward her little white chair, but she knew she was too late when she heard the engine of an Interstate L6 Cadet crank and saw it turn out of the line of aircraft where her own plane was parked. In another moment, the olive-green Cadet took the air in a graceful leap and Mrs. Sheehy was gone.

※

Sprite sat by the Stearman, on the ground now because Homer had come for his chair, saying, "Aww, sorry nobody gave you any business, Sweetie-pie." And he maybe he was, even if he didn't quite sound like it. "You can try again tomorrow if you like. Just come find me. Facilities are, well, you probably know where by now."

Sprite nodded, then said, "Mr. Montgomery? Where...do I sleep tonight?" The sun had set and the festival was closing for the night.

Homer looked at her, his eyes widening a bit. "Well, Sweetie-pie, everyone local here either goes home or has their own camp, like always. Just behind their booths, so they can watch over their wares at night. You don't have any place to stay?"

Sprite laughed uncomfortably, and replied, "Oh, sure, Mr. Montgomery. I have my plane here if that's the way it's done. I'll be fine."

Homer nodded absently and ambled into the empty circle, past the closed booths, chair in hand.

Tired and depressed, Sprite fumbled in the cockpit for her thermos and food, and settled onto a patch of soft grass beneath the Stearman, sandwiches by her side. Their waxed paper covers had melted into the creases of their own folds, retaining the shape of the bread, but she flattened the pinked-edge paper carefully and refolded it, saving it for another use or two. The bread was a little stale now, and tasted faintly of wax, but the peanut butter and jam was good, and the food and water made her feel a little better. She rolled onto her flight jacket, used the bundle of her clean clothes for a pillow, and tried to sleep.

Smoke from the other vendors' fires wafted on the warm July breeze, bringing with it the smell of roasting corn and some kind of fish. In a short while, the distant voices of those campers dropped out of the night, and except for the low hum of Atlanta, punctuated sometimes with a short siren flare-up or a train whistle, the evening was what city folk would call quiet. But Sprite's life had been spent in the natural rhythm and music of the country, with its birdcalls, cicada song, and sough of the wind through tall pines, so the city's different kind of noise was just enough to keep her hovering at the edge of sleep.

The evening darkened gradually, and a wide, star-filled sky appeared. All of Atlanta was blacked out, so there was no artificial glow competing with the brilliance of the stars. Sprite, wide-eyed despite her bone-weary fatigue, lay awake, looking up at the sparkling constellations, naming them off by position, ending with Sirius the faithful Dog Star by the side of Orion, the Hunter, his belt of three stars almost appearing to be red and orange at the edges of her sight.

Sprite recalled that when she had been maybe seven or eight, her father had been fascinated with Orion, and Sprite would often find him sitting outside on moonless nights, even when it was cold, looking up at the constellation. Randall would beckon her over to him, settle her on his lap, and point out the hunter's shape, saying the names of the stars. "That's Rigel, on his left knee. That's Bellatrix on his left shoulder, and Betelgeuse on his right one." That name always made her smile, because it sounded a bit like "beetle juice," when he said it, and it had been years before she actually saw the correct spelling of it in her science book at school.

"Doesn't sound a thing like it's spelled!" she had said to Randall, indignantly.

Her father had said, "Yep. Some words, like some people, sound different than you might read 'em."

When she had turned a year or two older, he'd taught her about finding her way in the dark, when there was no sun to tell her which way was east. He explained that whatever time of year it was, only certain stars were visible, and that the sky always changed season to season, and the stars never stayed in the same place during the night, except for one. He had pointed to the North Star, the big bright one that seemed anchored at the top of the sky. "You can always find your way home if you can remember to look up," Randall had told her. "Find Polaris, the North Star, and then you know whichaways the other directions lie, and you will never be truly lost."

"Well, I feel pretty doggone lost right now, Daddy," she whimpered aloud, the loss, rejections, and failures of the last two days overwhelming her. "You left me here by myself to make do, and don't tell me it was just because you couldn't find another way to deal with those rough thugs the bank sent. Did you do it apurpose, that night? Did you know you were gonna do it when you took off after those guys and left me standing in the road? I think you knew it, deep down. You never got over Momma dyin', and it always seemed like you wanted to be with her more than you wanted to be with me. Don't lie to me, Daddy, I know that's why you drank all the time these last few years and why you had to a' chosen to give yourself up to that crash. Even if you thought it was the only way to keep those bruisers from hurting me, I want you to know your dyin' hurts me, too. Why did you quit your life? You told me it's never right to quit! And you never woulda hit that mill if you hadn't aimed at it! You always flew exactly where you looked and that night, you were looking at Momma, over in Heaven. You were the best pilot ever, and you can't tell me that crash was an accident. You chose it! You chose her over me! And I miss you… so, so much, Daddy." And then the hot, angry tears were coursing down her face and ridiculously into her ears, making her turn her head from the sky, from the beautiful light of the constellations, from the North Star itself, and she fell into the deep, black void of sleep at last.

She never heard the soft steps of the Marine recruiters as they passed by on the way to their plane, never saw Captain James stop to look down at her for a long moment and then smile at how beautiful he thought she was. Only the rumble of an engine at the end of the field roused her briefly from desperate, sweet unconsciousness, and not making sense of the sound, she went back to sleep again. Dreams of fire and smoke and windmills assailed her, and then they faded into another vision where she saw herself looking into a night sky as vast as time, unable to focus as dangerous lights danced around her and the loud thrum of engines hurt her ears. Something bright filled the sky, and the most awful sadness washed over her. Then, the dream's strong wind and rain lashed her face and she was falling and sliding into the sea until she saw the anxious face of the Marine called Hal, and felt his strong arms around her. She finally fell into deep peace as his face faded from the dream.

She awoke the next morning to pink dawn light, a low hanging mist, and the smell of fresh horse manure. Three roosters crowed again and again as though they were competing for best in show.

It took a minute for Sprite to remember where she was. On the ground, under her plane, at the Peach Festival, all alone. She grimaced and sat up, massaged the crick in her neck, then rubbed her face with a sleeve. Her hair hung in strings, having escaped her ponytail sometime in the night, and her clothes felt sticky and damp. *Ah, the mist*, she thought, looking up at the Stearman's big belly. Fat drops of water had collected there in a long line down the center and hung for an impossibly long time before finally dripping onto her, and her clothes had become almost totally soaked on one side.

"Well, great," she pronounced dispiritedly, the cobwebs of last night's bad dreams still clinging to her mind. *Time for me to just pack up and go home. At least the cousins are there. And Jeff promised to help me. Thank God I'm done with school and can maybe get a job for the war effort someplace if they won't let me fly the crops. Jeff and Jo could stay at the farm if they wanted while I was away... keep things up until the war is over.... Gee whiz, I'm hungry. I wish I had saved a half a sandwich, at least*, she thought, stomach rumbling. She had planned to buy today's food with her earnings. Those boys had been so evil to her. There had been no call for that. No call whatsoever.

She slung her clean clothes bag over her shoulder and made for the facilities, and on her way back, feeling much better for changing into dry clothes, she found a basket of peaches, huge and red ripe, fragrant and fuzzy, sitting by her plane. She looked around for the benefactor, and one of the women she had seen yesterday at a produce booth caught her eye, smiled, and waved at her from across the circle. Sprite waved back as she bit into the soft, sweet-sharp peach, juice dripping from her hand. Wartime brought out the worst and the best in everyone, she thought, mounting the plane.

CHAPTER 4

"I CALLED SMITH, and he's coming now, while she's gone. Take that apron off, and *will* you stop lighting those things for one tiny little second, Jo? This man might not like you smoking in front of him; some people don't, you know," he said, meaning himself.

Jo ignored him and torched up another Lucky. "Then he can talk fast and get out," she said, blowing a cloud of blue smoke into Jeff's face. Then she jumped at the sound of the knock on the door, turned herself around and smashed out the cigarette in the sink.

"Why, thank yew, my dear," said Jeff, his own cloud of sarcasm taking the place of her smoke in the air between them. Jo batted him away like a fly and picked at her curls. The Georgia humidity had started to stretch them too far down her forehead, making her look more like a bleached blonde poodle instead of Betty Grable.

"Come right in, sir," said Jeff, holding the door for the sallow skinned, long nosed man to pass. Jo plastered on her big red smile, hiked up her bosom, and bounced out from the kitchen to shake his hand.

"Please sit down, Mr... uh—," she said, offering him a chair in the parlor. He took it, crossing one leg over the other, and sniffed at the air, pulling a sour face. Jeff, moving very close alongside Jo, smiled sweetly at her as she absently tapped out another cigarette, then swiveled his shoe onto her slipper clad toes purposely, meaningfully, and applied corrective pressure. She muffled a yelp behind her hand and promptly put the Lucky back in the pack. They both plopped down onto the sofa on the other side of the coffee table and looked at the man expectantly.

"Captain. Captain Smith," said the man, finishing her sentence, not directing the comment toward either one of them in particular. "I believe the army is expecting your signature on these papers." He snapped open his case, took a manila envelope out and slid it over to Jeff. There was a government seal on the front of it.

Jeff put a finger out and touched the corner of the envelope, then dragged it toward him. Jo, wanting to smoke, squirmed on the sofa. Jeff opened the envelope and Jo swanned over it, trying to read. When they had both gone through the first page, Jeff skipped to the last one, where the dollar amount for the property should have been quoted, and his eyebrows took a hike up his forehead. He looked up at Captain Smith, silently searching for an explanation. Smith just gave them a bored sigh, and began to fill them in. "I'm sorry, but things have changed since we spoke. We have discovered that your cousin was attempting to pay the bank at the time he died, but he died intestate, and still owed them money. That puts a bank lien on the estate. If the bank has a lien, then the government can foreclose and pay nothing for the property. I just need you to sign for Mr. Shannon's minor daughter to acknowledge she has been served with this eviction notice and that the property has been seized. Sorry to have put you out."

"Ah, yes, Captain Smith, if you wouldn't mind to excuse my wife and me for a few minutes while we talk this over in the kitchen, I would appreciate it," said Jeff, his mind working.

"Of course," said Smith, looking at the wall. He hated this part. He hated every part, actually. Total waste of time. They always tried to bargain out of it. Major Doyle would be fuming out there in the car.

Smith's eyes wandered around the room. Major Doyle really wanted this place condemned, and by yesterday. Smith still couldn't figure out why a member of General Arnold's staff had been sent down with him to oversee the dinky little mining project. What did anything they could take out of this no account red clay have to do with the government? And why would a guy like Major Doyle—with a PhD in chemistry—get himself assigned to such a lowly job? Rumor had it the Major had actually requested it. Smith just couldn't figure it.

Once behind the kitchen door, Jo swatted Jeff on the arm, saying, "What does he mean, 'We pay you nothing?'"

Jeff pursed his lips and gave her a frown. "Because they always have to say that before they pony up their real offer."

"He isn't bargaining, Jeff! Why do you need to play your game with him?" said Jo, wringing her hands at him.

Jeff closed his eyes, feigning patience, and then said, "Alright. I'll try something, then. Where're those papers you found in the girl's pocket when you were doing the laundry?" It had been such a stroke of luck that Jeff had hardly believed it when Jo found the envelope. Their ship might still be coming in.

Jo stretched up gingerly on her bruised toes to pull the papers from the top of a cabinet. They were still in the envelope with Sprite's name written across the front of it in Randall's hand. "Here," she said, shoving it at Jeff. "Now let's get back in there before the girl gets home. I got a feeling she's coming back early."

"Captain Smith?" said Jeff as they came back into the room, "Here is proof of our guardianship rights on the place. We are Enid Shannon's only living kin, as you have said. Her father, my dear cousin, gave this into my keeping for her. Will this do for a will?"

"No," Smith said, not bothering to read the page. "It doesn't clear the loan with the bank, no matter what." He put a copy in his briefcase anyway and handed Jeff a fountain pen and the official notice of eviction and seizure. Jeff reluctantly signed, and then he and Jo sat stonily before Smith while he packed up.

Once the screen door closed, they turned and looked at each other in silent complicity, then jumped up and took off in separate directions, racing around the house. Jeff rooted through Randall's desk for cufflinks, his good wallet, and anything else that looked portable. Jo pawed through Sprite's things, but the girl's clothes were far too small. She scraped the movie money Sprite had saved off of the dresser into a good leather purse that had been Sherilene's, then rummaged a bit under the bed, finding only some old movie magazines and a Tootsie Roll wrapper. There was a shelf of pretty rocks, a few aviation books, some hair ribbons, and a small white Bible on the nightstand, but Jo didn't like rocks, didn't read much, didn't wear hair ribbons, and certainly didn't want anything to do with that Bible. Jo quickly scanned the room one last time, but it was clear that the girl really didn't have anything worth taking. Disappointed in her haul, she met Jeff in the kitchen, and they both began to empty the pantry of jams and other canned goods. Jeff swung the ice box open and found four boiled eggs. He stuffed them into his pocket. Jo grabbed a plastic flower arrangement one of the mourners had brought for the funeral and stuffed it into the purse.

Ten minutes after Captain Smith strode out the front door, Jeff was loading Randall's truck with their booty and suitcases while Jo stood by and lit her first cigarette since Smith had appeared. Ruefully, she held the second copy of Randall's notarized letter to Sprite in one hand, took the Lucky out of her mouth with the other, and touched the burning end of it to the document.

⋇

Five minutes from home, Sprite descended gradually in a clear sky and watched the roads below. She saw their supplier Jable T. Clort's white truck, the bed of it loaded with bags of pesticide he sold to the crop dusters. A little farther on, the mail carrier had stopped on the road by Mrs. Rogers' house. A quarter-mile from there, a truck going toward town raced up the road, kicking up dust, obscuring the color and make of the vehicle. "Where's the fire?" Sprite wondered aloud. When the truck had to slow to avoid hitting the mail car, the dust settled enough for Sprite to see it more clearly.

It was her Daddy's truck. Her truck now. And the woman on the passenger side had brassy blonde hair that hurt the eye when the sun struck it through the dusty windshield. Now she wondered if there really *was* an emergency—where were her cousins going at that speed? And why were their suitcases in the bed of the truck?

Sprite flew onward, and then dropped the plane as fast as she dared, landed, and brought it to a stop at the hangar, jumping out almost before the prop stopped spinning. She could see that there was a big black car up by the house, and a tall, dark haired man in an army uniform stood beside it. He walked up to her front porch, opened the door, and went inside like he owned the place. Trying to make some sense out of it, she remembered her father and Jable T. talking about the army wanting all the property around Lowland Mill for some kind of mining. Had they sent someone to her house? And what was he doing going straight in without a welcome? She would just find right out!

Sprite started to run to the house and then her intuition sounded a warning in her mind. *I can't be in the house alone with a strange man! Something is very, very wrong!* she thought, stopping to look for a place to hide and watch for a while. She had just settled in behind the sparse cover of a big crepe myrtle when she saw another man get out of the car and begin walking toward the hangar. She froze with fright for a moment. *He's coming up here! I can't let him see me....*

She jumped from the myrtle bush like a startled rabbit, but quickly saw she would be out in the open if she ran any other way than toward the back porch, through the "victory garden," as it was now called. The garden was long and narrow, stretching from the back of the hangar to the back porch. Her father had liked to walk through it on his way back from the hangar, so there was a narrow path of sorts through the rows. The bean stakes and the tall corn would hide her almost all the way to the back door, and maybe she could get close enough to see or hear what was going on in the house if the windows were open. She scrambled toward the garden, quietly as she could, just as the driver's footfalls became audible.

In and out of the close corn rows she wove, watching the tops of the plants, edging along sideways to keep them from rustling and waving and giving her away. The driver had no doubt meant to find who had flown the plane in and would be soon looking around for her in any and every direction. If she could make it to the house before he turned his head, she could crouch beneath the parlor window and still be hidden from view.

In another two breaths, she was there, heart pounding, flattened to the side of the house just under the parlor window, listening. She heard the tall man walking all through the ground floor of the house, his steps measured and precise, his stops at each room all the same length of time. When she was sure he was in the kitchen, she raised her head ever so slowly up to the windowsill and peered over. The man's back was turned to her, and he had something on a chain in his hand. He lifted it to the window at the kitchen sink. It swung before him, his head all but obscuring it, and Sprite had the sensation of him smiling, even though she could not see his face. In fact, he was standing right in front of the window's blinding morning light, so she couldn't see anything but his shape. Then he moved a little and that bright light caught the chain and it shone gold. He was spinning the small circular thing on it around and around, bright pink and green-white flashes of light dancing upon it. *Mama's Claddagh ring!* she thought. *Why did I ever take it off? He got it out of my Bible! How did he even find it? But no wonder he took it,* she thought. It was made of Welsh gold mixed with something called 'electrum' that made the gold greenish white on the hands and crown that held and topped the copper alloyed gold of the little pink heart. The ring even had its own language—worn on the right hand, heart toward fingertips, it meant "single; looking for love." On the same hand, heart pointed toward the wearer, it meant "in a relationship." On the left hand, heart pointed toward fingertips, meant "the wearer is engaged." On the left hand, heart toward the wearer, meant "wearer is married." The ring had come down from mother to daughter in Sprite's Irish family for a couple of centuries now. In the old country, it had been lost for a long time once and stolen a few times before, but had always come back to its rightful owner. One time, the thief himself had brought it home, begging for her grandmother to "remove her curse." Her father had not lived to tell her all of those stories, and neither had her mother, but the Claddagh ring was Sprite's only link now to their love for each other and for her. A cold rage came over her and her eyes bored into the man's back; still, she dared not show herself.

The tall man abruptly shoved the ring and chain in his pocket and turned around, sensing that he was being watched. She ducked quickly and rolled under the high crawl space of the house, frantically combed the bent grass back upright where she had been standing, and heard his footsteps begin again, this time, directly over her head. Sprite held her breath, willing herself to be invisible and silent. The floorboards, only a few inches from her nose, gave slightly with his weight and she saw the bow in them where he had stopped at the window, no doubt looking at the very spot where she had just been hiding.

"Ha," came a deep voice above her. The floorboards muffled it but she could still hear the words he was saying to himself. "Cat," he said, chuckling. Sprite looked out from the crawl space and saw Turtle, Letty's calico, stalking something at the edge of the garden. Turtle pounced on a mole she had scared up and Sprite heard the man above laugh again, apparently satisfied it was the cat that had been watching him.

I have to get out of here and find out what's going on, she thought. *If I can get to Daddy's pistol... I wish that guy would go into another room... is that a spider? Yes.* She nonchalantly flicked it away.

A minute or two later, the man walked to the front of the house. Sprite heard the screen door slam and the floorboards of the front porch squeak. She crawled from beneath the house and through the open window, then ran softly to her father's room and reached into the corner behind his big standing wardrobe. She triumphantly pulled out Randall's always-loaded revolver. Tiptoeing to the open door, she saw that the man was still standing on her front porch, his back to her, smoking a cigarette. She didn't bother with stealth any longer.

"Don't move, Mister—" she said, surprising herself with her own steadiness. "You're in my sights."

Without turning around, the man dropped his cigarette, ground it out with a highly polished shoe, and said, "Hello, there. You must be the daughter. I wondered where you had gone after you landed the plane. Impressive that you can fly it."

"Who are you, and what are you doing in my house?' Sprite said, her voice low and menacing. An anger-fueled strength had welled up in her from some unknown depth, and she was not going to let this man take what was hers.

"May I turn around?" the man said, a note of amusement in his voice. "I'm unarmed."

"Please do. But put your hands up and keep them up," she said, keeping a tight grip on the revolver. The man stiffened at the sound of the cocking hammer, and when he turned around, hands in the air, he was no longer in a laughing mood. Piercing dark eyes glared at her from under his hat and his lips stretched into a thin, hard line.

"I am Major Wallace Doyle. I am here to take possession of your forfeited land and homestead. Everything here now belongs to the government," he said coolly, keeping his eyes on hers.

"Says who?" said Sprite, her aim on his chest unwavering.

"Says the US Government, Miss Shannon. It is Miss Shannon?" he snapped.

"It is. And I don't believe you. My father paid for this farm over and over, and the bank kept tellin' him he owed. But he didn't. And now it's mine, and I haven't said I'm selling or leaving or anything else, so just get in your big black car and drive away, and never come back here," she finished.

"Oh, I don't think that will happen, Miss Shannon," said the Major. "I have the official signature of your adult guardian, your uncle, right here on this paper. He signed it all over to me, paid for or not."

Sprite's eyes widened at that, and she looked at him sidelong. "You are lying. Jeff wouldna done that. And if you are here for the government, why didn't I know about it before today? Something here ain't right, Major Doyle. I just know it."

The Major slowly and carefully produced some papers from his breast pocket, Jeff's name scrawled at the bottom of the last page. "Jeffrey Shannon did know about it before today. Your uncle and aunt are perhaps not the loving family you seem to think they are. If you don't believe me, just look around. They've taken everything but the paint on the walls. What kind of relatives steal from a little girl, especially just after her father has died? Now, if you will just lower your weapon, we can talk about maybe finding you a place in a factory job or maybe work in the new mine office, as reparation for your unexpected loss," he said, coaxing her.

"I don't want a factory job, Major Doyle. I want my own job. I want to fly my plane and stay right here," Sprite said. Doyle laughed again at that.

"Your own job? I don't think you have one anymore. At least, that's what your former clients agreed to when I suggested they move their business to the Delta dusting group."

Sprite could hardly believe it. But no wonder Wakely had come to tell her that the farmers had decided not to use her to dust any longer. "You did that? You took my living away so you could run me off of this place? Tell me, Major Doyle, why is my farm so important to you? Has to be some reason you are pouring money into making sure I'm gone. And what new mine are you talking about? There's no mining around here," Sprite said, her heart now pounding in her ears.

Doyle almost seemed to squirm a bit at the mention of the mine, but he recovered and said, "Well, while there is no current mining, there soon will be, and dear girl, I need your farm for the water and mineral rights. You've got a vein of chromite under your feet that will win the war, so just step up and be a patriot. I can't tell you any more than that. Now if you will please get that pistol out of my face, I will let you collect some of your things and leave quietly. I won't press charges."

Sprite was not finished with him. "What about that ring on the chain you took from my Bible? Is that the government's now too? If it is, then why is it in your pocket? I saw the way you looked at it in the kitchen window. You're keeping it for yourself, aren't you? So what kind of army officer steals from a girl, especially right after her father has died?"

Doyle shrugged and smiled ruefully, as if to say, "What are you going to do about it?"

Sprite heard the unspoken words as clearly as if they had been whispered in her ears. Then she remembered the stories about the ring and smiled knowingly. "Major Doyle, you will want to give me that ring back. It was my mama's and her mama's before her on down the line, and it's mine now. It made of Welsh gold and it comes from Ireland. You might even say it's a bit magical," she said, eyebrows raised.

Doyle did laugh at that. "Magical? Seriously, Miss Shannon?"

Sprite just nodded and said, "Yep. Always comes home. The stories say it's been lost or stolen before a few times, and you know, ill-gotten gains and all. So you can give it to me now and save yourself a lot of trouble, or you can take it and let it come back to me however and whenever that might happen. But don't say I didn't warn you."

Still laughing, Doyle frowned and shook his head. "Folk tales told by ignorant country people, my dear. I'll bet your momma 'had the

Sight,' right? Ha! She did," he added after Sprite's eyes had narrowed at the remark. "Listen, Miss Shannon, I was born in 'the old country' and I've heard them all. I hope you don't believe that kind of thing yourself," he said.

"Give it over, Major Doyle. And then be on your way," Sprite said, matter of factly. Her hands did not shake as she pointed the revolver at a spot at the very top of his right ear.

Doyle rolled his eyes, lowered his hands and lunged toward her. Sprite was quicker. She fired and the blast deafened him as a shot flew past, nicking his ear. He stopped in his tracks, stunned.

"I told you, Major Doyle. I warned you. And the next one is going through your chest. When the police come, you will have been shot dead because you were an intruder and you forced yourself on me and I killed you in self-defense. My ring, please," said Sprite, her voice sounding muffled to her own sound-shocked ears.

Doyle just stared at her in horror, raised a trembling hand toward his stinging ear, and said, "You... you shot me! You little bitch! An inch to the right and you could have killed me! You just shot an army officer in wartime, and that's a capital offense, tantamount to treason!" Doyle mastered his rage, glowered at her and said, "You will pay for this, Miss Shannon. I'll be back shortly, with the Sheriff, to arrest you. It will go far easier for you if you wait for me, but if you are gone by then, make no mistake, I'll find you and see you punished if it's the last thing I ever do!" Thick blood oozed from the tiny nick of Sprite's bullet. Doyle touched his finger to it and brought it back dripping and red. Shaking with pent up anger, pointing the bloody finger at her in mute promise, he turned and ran for his car.

Sprite stood stock still for a moment, her mind whirling. She hadn't thought she'd really have to shoot the man. But she had, and now his car's engine was revving and the tires sprayed gravel and Major Doyle was gone. And so was her momma's Claddagh ring.

Sprite stayed where she was for another several agonizing minutes, still holding the warm gun, her mind racing to figure out where she could go that Major Doyle would not find her.

She figured for too long. She had forgotten about the other man, the one who had walked up to the hangar. The sound of her plane's engine reached her ears, and she ran outside the house toward the lane. She stood powerless and stunned as her plane soared over her head. A few peaches dropped and exploded like miniature bombs, and then a piece of paper fluttered to the ground at her feet.

Without bothering with it, she turned and made for house again. When she reached the kitchen, she found dirty dishes in the sink and a government eviction notice along with a note on the dining table.

> *Dear Sprite,*
> *We are sorry. We wish you the best.*
> *Signed,*
> */Jeff and Jo/*
> *PS: They will be coming for everything this afternoon, and*
> *bringing in the dozers, so better get your things and go.*

Jo had added that, Sprite could see. It was her wispy handwriting. She dropped with a thunk into one of the chairs and let the note drift to the floor. After a few numbing moments when her brain refused to work at all, she got up suddenly and raced up to her room. Doyle had told the truth about her uncle and aunt. Her belongings had been thoroughly rifled, and anything of value had been taken. The same with her father's room. She collapsed on the floor by his desk, her knees so weak they wouldn't hold her up any longer. Then she saw that the floorboard where her father kept their savings seemed undisturbed. Heartened, she pried up the loose board, sighing in relief that Jeff and Jo—and Doyle—had not found the sock full of dollar bills. She lifted it out, stuffed it into her pocket, and ran back to her own room. She threw some clothes, her other pair of shoes, her log book, licenses, and the little white Bible into a pillowcase along with the sock. She ran downstairs to find some food, but the pantry had been emptied.

Of course it had.

Sprite sighed and looked around the kitchen one more time, knowing it would be her last. Accompanied only by the singing of the cicadas, she walked the quarter mile to the family graveyard and stood for a moment in front of the line of graves that held her entire family. Her grandparents' stones had sprouted lichens and moss, and the names on them had begun to blur. Her mother's stone was a little less weathered, but its granite had darkened a bit with age. Freshly turned red clay covered her father's grave as it stretched before a temporary brass marker. She had thrown some grass seed on top of the dirt, knowing it would settle in with the next rain and sprout, soon healing over the scar on the plot. Would that even matter now? What would become of them? What would become of her? She sat down on the grass and began to talk to Randall.

"Daddy—I miss you so much. I need you right now and you're not here. In fact, nobody's here," she said, frowning at the other gravestones. "I don't know what to do… and I've shot an army officer! In wartime! They can hang me for it. That Major Doyle said it was a capital offense, tantamount to treason!"

The wind whispered through the pines beside the little graveyard and pushed high, white, puffy clouds past the distant treetops. She began to cry. Great, defeated sobs wracked her body until she thought she could not stop. All she could think of was how alone she was and how much trouble she would be in when Major Doyle came back with his men. She had shot him in the heat of the moment to stop him from coming at her, but what defense was that? She was a girl, and he was an army officer. Who would anyone else believe? He was a thief, for sure, but he had also been unarmed. They would arrest her, at the very least, and never believe her part of the story. There was also something desperate behind that man's hard and vacant eyes that really terrified Sprite—she really had believed he meant her harm, no matter how polite he had tried to be. The thought of him pointing that bloody finger at her made her cry all the harder.

After a few moments, she stopped sobbing, her energy spent and her mind empty, and she listened to the silence. Like a miniature tornado, a great wind suddenly came up, dragging at her hair and straining the trees, tossing their branches fitfully. Then it was gone and quiet surrounded her like an embrace, and even the cicadas stopped their earsplitting summer serenade. A strange, hopeful peace settled into Sprite's heart, and she decided that maybe she did know what to do after all. "That's the best I'm gonna get, isn't it, Daddy? Well, you told me to take heed of the knowing, so I will. I love you Daddy. You, too, Mama. I reckon I'll never be back here, so goodbye… all of you."

Dry-eyed and determined, Sprite turned from the graves, the old ones and the fresh one, a new vision filling her heart. She walked across the field and then cautiously onto the lane, thinking to say goodbye to Letty and ask her for a ride to the bus station. Looking over her shoulder and listening for the sound of Major Doyle's tires on the gravel road, she picked up the flyer that had blown out of the cockpit of her plane. It said that Sweetwater, Texas, was where the Women's Airforce Service Pilots trainees were assembling to report for duty. She studied the paper for a long moment.

"Sweetwater it is, then," she said softly. "You'll never find me there, Major Doyle." As she turned to go, she looked back at the hangar wistfully.

The "Shannon & Sons" sign now lay face down in the red, sandy clay, victim of the whirling winds of change.

CHAPTER 5

A DAY LATER, in the bunker at Guernsey, Mattias and the Ober-leutnant played two-handed bridge while it poured rain outside. An SS soldier rapped on the doorway and stood at attention until Mattias wordlessly beckoned him inside. The soldier stiffly presented Mattias with a communiqué, which he read silently on the spot. When dismissed, the soldier raised a hand to Hitler and left the room. Once he was out of earshot, Mattias said, "*Ha! Gut, gut!* Wallace has secured access to the new vein of American chromite! They are breaking ground immediately and expect to be in production in a very few weeks. He'll be skimming ore from the shipments that Archangel has scheduled to send to the English. Phase one is complete, and phase two is underway!"

"Do you think he will really carry through with it, *Herr Obersturm-bahnfuhrer?* I still question whether he will try to tell his American Ambassador father about this. He wants the old man's approval so very badly, even at his age," said the young Oberleutnant as he drew on his cigarette. "I find him pitiful and weak. How is it that he was ever your friend, I wonder."

Mattias waved away the comment. "He will do it, Franz. I know Wallace Doyle. He is pitiful and weak because he is starved for love, and only the girl gives love to him," answered Mattias, flipping through Gallagher's intelligence on Doyle. "Even more than the ambassador's approval, Wallace wants his girl safe and he will do anything we tell him to in order to keep her that way. Why do men betray their country? Power, money, and revenge. Wallace wants the power to save his girl. He wants the money he thinks is still in the Swiss account. *Ja.* I removed it. And he wants revenge for a thousand fatherly slights—he would far rather unravel his father's political career than help it. We have offered him all of those things. Even so, send word to Gallagher to make sure that Wallace is watched even more closely. Meanwhile, I will appeal to his sense of fairness and trust— put the girl on the *Rowan* with one of Gallagher's men and send her to the Azores. The man's 'expertise' will assure Wallace's continued cooperation once his fiancée arrives."

CHAPTER 6

SPRITE STEPPED OFF the train and onto the platform of the Texas & Pacific Railroad Depot in Sweetwater, Texas, still carrying the pillowcase containing her clothes and few belongings. Looking around, she saw travel-weary businessmen in wrinkled suits flagging down porters to help them with their luggage, but then she noticed a girl, maybe a little older than herself, standing alone, her arms crossed over her chest, her foot tapping nervously. The girl's pink gingham dress looked crisp and new, despite having been worn for at least a day on the train— the last station stop had been Dallas. Under the wide brim of a matching hat, the girl's dark eyes darted here and there as if she were searching for someone. *Maybe she's here for the same reason I am*, Sprite thought, as she made her way slowly toward the girl.

"Hi... are you here to join the WASP?" Sprite asked her, coming up from behind. The girl spun around to face Sprite while holding one hand on top of her hat to keep it from flying off. A pleasant face broke into a shaky smile when her eyes landed on Sprite.

"Yes! I sure am! I'm Phoebe Summerfield!" she said as she automatically extended her white-gloved hand, and then withdrew it a little, as if, upon closer examination, she was not quite sure about making friends with the ragamuffin in front of her.

Sprite extended her own hand, saying, "Well, Phoebe, I'm Sprite Shannon, and I'm gonna be a WASP, too, as soon as I get out of these awful clothes and get a bath! I've been on that train since Atlanta!"

Phoebe took her hand and shook it briefly, seeming a bit more cordial after Sprite's explanation of her appearance.

A porter removed several bags from his cart and dropped them on the platform next to Phoebe. Sprite watched as Phoebe counted them, then reached into her purse and gave a quarter to the man, who smiled at her generosity. "Thank you kindly, ma'am," he said, tipping his red cap.

"Gosh, that's a lot of luggage," Sprite said, admiring the matching navy blue Samsonite suitcases. "Do you want some help carryin' these?"

"I could sure use a hand, but what about your stuff?" Phoebe asked, looking around for Sprite's luggage.

Sprite looked at her pillowcase and shrugged, suddenly even more embarrassed. "I travel light," she said, shifting the pillowcase behind her back. "So, where are we supposed to go?"

"A real nice lady on the train told me that all the WASP girls check into the Bluebonnet Hotel before they go to Avenger Field, so I guess the Bluebonnet is where we're headed. It should be close by," said Phoebe, looking beyond the platform toward town. "Oh, there it is! The lady said it was the tallest building in town. Let's go!"

Laden with Phoebe's two heaviest cases, Sprite followed Phoebe down Oak Street, and then Broadway, and then yet another long block to the hotel. Sprite had instantly broken into a pouring sweat in the midmorning August sun, but Phoebe seemed unaffected by it. *Sure is different from Georgia out here*, thought Sprite, looking out over the flat, parched landscape. They came to the Bluebonnet, and Sprite stepped into a thin line of shade while she waited for Phoebe to trundle more of her overstuffed suitcases up to the door.

"My Daddy's in the oil business," Phoebe said blithely, "but I've always dreamed of flying, just like Jackie Cochran does—Bendix races, trans-continental speed records, ocean crossings, you know. I guess all my heroines are female pioneers, like Alice Robertson. She was the second female member of Congress, and she went to University of Tulsa, just like me, only I studied languages, especially French. And Dr. Mary E. Walker? Well, she was a surgeon during the Civil War, and she was the first woman awarded the Congressional Medal of Honor, even though she was technically a civilian, and you've heard of Lt. Colonel Margaret Craighill? Did

I mention I just graduated from University of Tulsa? What about you? What did you study in college?" Phoebe chattered on, rearranging her suitcases so that they lined up by diminishing size and pointed exactly the same direction, but Sprite had stopped listening at about the "Alice" point in the girl's list of admired women.

I'm so glad that hotel was only a couple of blocks away from the station, Sprite thought. When Phoebe stopped to take a breath, Sprite realized there had been a question pointed at her and said "Oh, what? Me? Well, I haven't had the chance yet—"

"—And I just barely got the minimum thirty-five hours of flight time logged to get accepted for the WASP, but I guess they're gonna take care of that for us, won't they, by the time we're done? We'll be flying practically every day for six months I hear, doncha think? And confidence, you know, they'll give us that as well," Phoebe said.

Where did all those words come from? thought Sprite. The girl never seemed to run out of them. She processed the last bit of information and then asked, "So you got accepted already? How'd you do that?"

"Well, of course you have to get accepted, so you can be issued a report date. That's how you know when to come to Sweetwater." Phoebe tapped on the hotel door, summoning the porter, and then looked at Sprite. "Didn't you get orders with this report date?" Phoebe asked, puzzled. "Isn't that why you were on the train?"

"No, I just heard about the WASP from this flyer I got from the Atlanta Peach Festival, and then some things happened at home and I just got on the train, and here I am," Sprite said, her stomach lurching as she answered Phoebe's question.

"Well, that's just not how things are done, Sprite Shannon. That's not how they're done at all," Phoebe shook her head, instantly exasperated. "I do hope you'll be able to straighten things out. My class, 44-W-1, is due to report in three days. I came down early to make sure I had everything in order, but here you are just showin' up? Do you even have a pilot's license? You do know how to fly, don't you?" Phoebe asked, peering down her long, straight nose at Sprite as she continued to impatiently tap on the door.

That's the part I'm sure I have covered, Sprite thought, meeting her gaze and holding it. "I had my own plane, back in Georgia. I was part of the family business. I've been flying since I was fifteen, and I've got over five hundred hours in my logbook," Sprite said, raising one brow slightly. Phoebe's face went slack in wonder.

"Your own plane? Your own plane? Then you are just gonna have to get yourself straightened out, Sprite Shannon," Phoebe said as the hotel porter held the door for them. "So Sprite, until then, what do you think about sharing a room?" Phoebe continued as she counted what was left in her coin purse, "We could save some money."

Sprite smiled, cocked her head to the side a bit, wondering if she could stand the girl's incessant talking, but then nodded. The money in her sock was running low and she needed to save some back—no telling how long she would have to be here if she couldn't get in to the WASP right away. She quickly chased that thought from her mind.

In the hotel lobby, big ceiling fans turned slowly, pushing the warm air around, but at least the slight breeze dried the perspiration at Sprite's hairline. With Phoebe's wheeled luggage rack loaded, the two girls took a moment to look around.

The carpet that covered the vast expanse of floor had Texas bluebells woven into it, all dancing in zigzag lines toward the huge room's corner, where a group of a half-dozen college-aged girls congregated on blue couches and chairs. Their chatter rose and fell over introductory hugs, giggles, and squeals. Their wrists sparkled with bracelets and their clean hair shone in the window's strong light. They used polished gestures that made their hands look like restless butterflies, and their happy voices blended in waves of laughter.

Phoebe broke into a radiant smile, looking as though she had just found her long lost family. She stepped in front of Sprite, pushing her back and toward the desk, saying, "Sprite, you get us a room, and I'll try to find out what's going on. These girls must be joining the WASP too!"

"Well," Sprite said, bewildered, looking over toward the reception desk. She'd never stayed in a hotel before, but she'd seen people in the movies check into them, and she didn't want to look like the dumb country bumpkin in front of these fancy girls, not that they were looking at her. They seemed interested only in talking to each other. She made her way to the front desk, again hiding the lumpy pillowcase, and held up a small hand, mimicking the girls in the corner.

The desk clerk, an older gentleman with dusty, horn-rimmed glasses, smiled up from his paperwork and said, "Checking in?"

"Yes sir," Sprite said, unable to control the shake in her voice.

"Are you with the WASP?" he asked.

"Yes," Sprite said, smiling to herself when she saw the man's face brighten.

"Then you'll be wanting to stay for three nights. How many in your room?" he asked.

"Um, me and Phoebe," Sprite replied.

"Two of you. Very well then, three nights, double occupancy, three dollars per night, comes to nine dollars and forty-five cents with tax," the clerk said, and he turned around to the wall to retrieve two keys from a little brass hook on the room number board.

Sprite winced in shock at the price he had named. Her train ticket had been the largest personal purchase she'd ever made in her life, and that had drained her money down to about ten dollars. She dug into the old sock for the bills while saying a silent prayer that she would have enough. *Well, Phoebe's splitting it with me, so it's really only half that amount,* she reasoned, so she counted out the required sum in wrinkled bills and a handful of coins, and dumped it all on the counter.

The desk clerk spun the guest register book around and held out a pen for Sprite to sign in. She took the pen, and the clerk attended to straightening the bills and sorting through the coins, fastidiously placing his index finger on each coin and sliding it out of the pile until he reached the total of $9.45. Sprite scrawled her name, and then turned around just in time to see Phoebe and three other girls approaching.

"You will need to sign the register," Sprite said, trying to sound experienced in such matters, holding the pen out for Phoebe.

"Oh, Sprite honey, my plans have changed!" and she pointed to her left at a bored looking, weak-chinned girl with tiny, darting eyes and buckteeth. Sprite looked her up and down and couldn't help thinking about how her body didn't match her face. From the neck down, the girl could have been a pin-up model. "This is Liesel—she went to Bryn Mawr and her family is French—she and the girls are going to Abilene, since we have three days before we report, so I'm just gonna hop in with them," Phoebe said, nodding her head in tight little jerks and squinching up her nose. "I'll see you in a jiff, Sprite Shannon!" Phoebe had already started to walk away with the other girls, but added, "If you're still here when we get back."

Sprite looked at her in astonishment. "But I just paid for both of us for three nights, Phoebe!"

Phoebe turned her head and acted as though she had not heard Sprite, and the girl named Liesel started talking to the little group. As they left her standing alone in the lobby, Sprite heard Liesel say to them, "Abilene is a real town, with nice hotels and cocktail lounges, and the USO... and Camp Barkeley, where all the officer candidates are! *Très bien, n'est-ce pas?*" The group met this news with a small explosion of feminine excitement as they gathered a few more girls from the corner.

"Phoebe! What about the money for the room?" Sprite called after her loudly enough that every conversation in the big room stopped for an awkward moment.

"Oh, honey, take it easy. It's just a few dollars. I'll pay you back later. Geez, Louise!" Phoebe called back with a bitter, pinched look on her face. The giggling, lively group headed out the door and the strained moment passed. With a pleading look in her eye, Sprite turned to the desk clerk. The man had seen what had happened and was already searching his register.

"I can put you in a single. It's two dollars and twenty-five cents per night, plus tax, for a total of seven dollars and eight cents," he said as he began counting out the refund. Sprite felt her cheeks burn and her eyes water as she scooped the refunded coins into her hand and dumped them quickly into the sock.

X

Trudging up four flights in the echoing stairwell, Sprite began to feel really hungry. On the train, she hadn't eaten lunch, opting to save her money for breakfasts and dinners. Even so, it amazed her how much simple food cost when you didn't grow it yourself.

She opened the door to room 405 and looked around. There was a twin bed made up with a blue chenille spread, frayed tassels dragging the thin carpet that seemed to have stretched itself all the way from the lobby to her room. *Probably in every room*, Sprite thought. Texas sure loved its bluebells. She pushed her pillowcase and logbook under the mattress, toward the middle, and then sat on them to even out the lump they made in the thin bedding. She opened the single window and let the hot breeze in for a minute, then decided it was cooler with the window shut and the blackout drapes closed. "Where… is the bathroom?" she wondered. She put her head back out the hallway door and saw a sign at the far end that said, "Women's Restroom—Shower" and sighed. An indoor outhouse, that's what that was. In a fancy hotel and she still had to hike to use the toilet.

She smiled a little at that, and then decided to find food and maybe see some of the town. Turning to go, she almost left her logbook and licenses, but then thought better of it. She prudently retrieved them and placed them in the bib pocket of her overalls.

She figured she had enough in her sock to buy a jar of peanut butter and a loaf of bread, and she could put that in her room and have something to eat for the next three days. She could get water to drink from the sink in the restroom, although she'd have to find a cup or a glass. She suddenly missed her garden plot and orchards back in Lowland Mill, where she could pick food right off the stalk, vine, or tree. But this was a different world now, and she'd just have to learn to live in it. She made sure her room was locked up tight and then made her way downstairs.

Out on the big thoroughfare they called Broadway, about a block down the street, Sprite saw the marquee of the Texas Theater, where the new Gene Tierney movie *Heaven Can Wait* was playing. Gene Tierney was the most glamorous starlet in Hollywood, and Sprite's Daddy had once told her that her mama Sherilene kind of looked like Gene Tierney, with her dark hair and blue eyes. In a dark theater, Sprite could imagine that Gene was her mama for a little while, and that always made her happy.

"Well, then, if the peanut butter is not too expensive, I'll go. I could use a little happiness right now," she said, talking to herself out loud.

Sprite wandered the street, peeking in windows, and marveling that this town had a Montgomery Ward department store—she had seen Letty's catalog back in Lowland Mill—and the store took up the entire building! It was filled with clothes, and kitchen wares, and she saw some hardware, too, on the far wall. *When I get my hands on some money, I'm coming back here*, she thought. *I wonder how much they pay the WASP girls?* She walked on.

Then, as she passed before the large front window of the Applejack Diner, she halted mid-step, almost falling over her own feet. Inside, an attractive, dark haired woman sat in a booth eating her lunch. She was wearing a serge gray uniform with a white collared shirt and what looked like a matching gray garrison cap lay on the table. She had the unit patch of the Army Air Forces on her left shoulder, and the wings and propeller insignia of the Air Forces on her lapels, but most impressively, the woman wore the shiny silver wings of a pilot above the left breast pocket of her jacket. *Oh my gosh*, thought Sprite, *a real-live WASP*. Sprite pushed through the front door of the diner, and a little bell attached to the inside handle gave a jingle, which naturally caused the WASP woman to look up. Sprite gathered her nerve and ambled up to the woman's table.

"Ma'am, I'm sorry to bother you, but I saw your uniform and, well, are you a WASP?" she asked timidly. The woman leaned back and took a look at Sprite, clearly noticing Sprite's threadbare sneakers, her rumpled overalls, and her dirty hair. Sprite's face colored with embarrassment and she nearly turned around and left, but then the woman looked Sprite in the eye and gave her a gentle smile. The woman looked a little like Gene Tierney when she did that, thought Sprite.

"I'm an instructor pilot for the WASP, at Avenger Field. I'm Meredith Lowe—and what's your name?" the woman asked, extending her hand. Sprite accepted the handshake and pumped Meredith's arm enthusiastically.

"I'm Sprite Shannon, and I came all the way from Georgia on the train, and I was hoping you could tell me how to join the WASP," she said, the words tumbling out in a great flood of enthusiasm. Her stomach then growled loudly, adding a gurgling exclamation mark to the end of her sentence.

Meredith smiled again, and then looked down at the barely touched sandwich on her plate. "Pleased to meet you, Sprite Shannon. You know, I will never eat all of this, and we can't waste food, especially in wartime. Would you like half of my sandwich?" She gestured and Sprite sat down opposite her in the booth.

Meredith pushed the oval plate into the center of the table. Sprite sat down and eyed the sandwich. There was a big dill pickle slice weeping juice alongside the tall stack of bacon, lettuce, and tomato, and there was mayonnaise on the bread, too. It all smelled wonderful. Meredith raised her hand to signal the waitress over. "I think we could use a couple of Cokes, and I always finish lunch with a small chocolate milkshake. Would you have one with me, Sprite? My treat," she said, as the waitress scribbled down Meredith's order.

The waitress returned with two fountain Cokes and a clean plate for Sprite, on which Meredith placed the sandwich half. Desperate to eat, but a bit hesitant to take the food, Sprite hesitated. But then hunger overcame inhibition, so Sprite grabbed her half of the sandwich and tore into it, almost choking on the hard bits of bacon. Meredith handed her a napkin, and Sprite fumbled for the flexi-straw in her Coke and sucked down a huge gulp of the cold, fizzy drink. Then she remembered to eat more slowly and breathe between bites. It had been days since her last decent meal.

"The minimum requirements to join the WASP are a private pilot's license, and thirty-five hours of flight time. Do you think you qualify?" Meredith asked.

Sprite swallowed a smaller bite and reached into the bib pocket of her overalls, pulling out her licenses and logbook. "I got my licenses right here, private and commercial, and I got over five hundred hours flight time in my logbook, but I heard you have to get orders and a report date," she trailed off, her eyes finding Meredith's. "See, I had my own plane 'cause I flew crop dusting service with my Daddy and he just died and the army took the farm and my plane, and now, I'm just...."

"Just trying to find your way in the world," said Meredith, taking the items from Sprite. Sprite nodded and ate in silence while Meredith inspected her logbook. Sprite could see she was impressed with the hundreds of hours Sprite had logged over the past year and a half. A small spark of hope began to glow in Sprite's heart. Just then, the waitress returned with two milkshakes and set them on the table. Meredith bent her straw to her lips and took a sip.

"Well, Miss Shannon, the regular procedure would be for you to have a sit-down interview with Mrs. Sheehy, where you present these documents, and then if you're accepted, she'll issue you a letter with a report date. Problem is, Mrs. Sheehy is traveling, and isn't due back to Avenger Field for a few days," Meredith said. Sprite dropped her eyes. "But Sprite, I'll tell you what," Meredith continued, "I am heading to the airfield to get in a little 'stick' time this afternoon. How'd you like to do a little flying with me, and see Sweetwater from the air?"

Sprite took another bite of sandwich, sipped her Coke, sipped her milkshake, and then nodded her head excitedly. "Yes ma'am, I'd love to," she said. The spark of hope burst into a small flame.

"Let's see how you do in the cockpit," Meredith said, "and then maybe I'll see about putting in a good word for you with Mrs. Sheehy."

CHAPTER 7

LESS THAN AN hour later, Sprite having finished both hers and
Meredith's lunches, they sat on the runway of what Meredith said
was Avenger Field's auxiliary airfield, in a Stearman PT-13 biplane,
almost exactly like the one Sprite had flown for the last couple of years.
Sprite climbed into the front cockpit, usually reserved for students, and
Meredith sat in the rear one, just like Sprite's father did when he was
teaching her to fly. Sprite took a moment before finishing her flight check
and ran her fingers over the dials and controls, their faces and shapes happily familiar to her touch. After all that had happened to her in the last
couple of weeks, this place, the cockpit of the Stearman, was a reassuring
refuge. She was home now. She closed her eyes in a silent prayer of gratitude, sat back, and completed the check. Meredith waited patiently in the
back, then at Sprite's word, gunned the engine down the dusty runway
and they lifted off with the smoothness of Sprite's long practice.

Once Meredith had flown them well away from the airfield and the
scrubby desert was zipping past below, Sprite felt the plane out, extending
her awareness to every part of it, taking its pulse and noting its idiosyncra-
sies. At Meredith's first touch of the throttle, Sprite had noticed the same
immediate responsiveness of her own plane back home, and now she was
sure that this plane was its twin sister. Her father had modified both of
their Stearmans to carry the heavy crop dust, and that meant much more
power. Crop dusting required a real workhorse of a plane, but when that
same plane was empty of cargo, it was as quick and nimble as a dragonfly.

She was not surprised when Meredith's voice crackled over the intercom in Sprite's earphones saying, "Sprite, this isn't the standard Stearman. It has the R1340 Lycoming 600 horsepower upgrade, so it's probably going to be much more responsive on the throttle than you're used to."

"Yes ma'am," Sprite said gleefully, "It's exactly like the one I've flown for a couple of years now!"

"Got your harness on tight?" came Meredith's voice again over the intercom, and Sprite turned around and gave her a thumbs-up. "OK then, Ladybird, you have the stick. Show me what you've got," Meredith said.

At several thousand feet, Sprite took them out of level flight, gently pulled back on the stick, and pitched the nose up about ten degrees. Putting the elevators back in neutral position, Sprite banged the stick left and the big Stearman snap-rolled over like a hound dog asking for a belly scratch, two full revolutions, 720 degrees. She continued all the way over to right-side up again and squealed with delight, enjoying the way her voice blended with the sound of the engine. She did two more of those rolls and then with a little pitch up, they were back to level flight. Sprite prepared for the loop-the-loop, listening to the engine, feeling its throbbing rhythm in her bones, its deep, resonant voice speaking to her very soul. Sprite tapped the big radial engine's commanding power to push the plane skyward in a vertical rush, arcing back over the top of her loop, where she and Meredith hung for a second or two between heaven and earth, suspended in their harnesses, almost weightless. Then she hit the downhill run, picking up airspeed, zooming to the end of the loop with a triumphant roar. She leveled out parallel to the earth below. Sprite breathed deeply, happily, excited to be back in the air. Then she heard Meredith say over the 'com, "What next, Ladybird?"

"Hammerhead!" Sprite replied as she giggled and once again put the biplane into a steep climb and this time, did only a one-quarter loop, holding back power to avoid the inversion. She slowed to about twenty knots in the vertical and then gave it full left rudder with the pedals, full opposite aileron with the stick, causing the Stearman to cartwheel and begin plummeting groundward, spinning methodically at moderate speed. Sprite shivered, and while she always felt the naked vulnerability of the open cockpit on this move, this time she felt a little more than vulnerable.

In fact, she felt a little bit like she was about to black out. But, like always, Sprite chased the sensation away with a few deep breaths, tightening her stomach muscles to push blood toward her brain, and then she applied full opposite rudder and opposite stick, and several moments later, they were stable and level again. She proceeded directly into an Immelman turn and again started her climb for the next maneuver.

At the top of the climb, when she got to the half-loop, she rolled the plane over from inverted to erect, waiting and ready to execute Meredith's request. "What's your pleasure, Mrs. Lowe?" said Sprite, tapping her earphones.

"Anything. Just don't do—"

"The English bunt?" Sprite laughed, pushing the stick forward. The Stearman screamed downward like a runaway roller coaster. Massive g-force pulled at them in the cockpits, but their harnesses dug into their shoulders and kept them from tumbling through the sky. Sprite giggled and screamed as they completed their outside half-loop and came safely level, though upside down. A quick snap half-roll, and Sprite brought them right-side up. She banked right, heading back toward the direction of town.

Then Sprite caught a glimpse of some movement on the horizon. It was a westbound Texas & Pacific passenger train, chugging and steaming away toward a small Whipple-truss bridge that spanned a dry riverbed twenty feet below. Sprite descended, came around and lined up the biplane perpendicular to the bridge. She could see the passengers in the train pressing their faces against the window, watching the approaching Stearman.

"There's kind of a windup for the next maneuver, Mrs. Lowe. If the timin' is good, when I'm closer, I listen to the heartbeat of the engine; listen 'til my own heartbeat matches it. I block out everything else and I always keep my eyes on the airspace. I think about how I'm not tryin' to miss the supports—I'm tryin' to catch the air between them. That's what I aim for, 'cause you will always hit what you are looking at," Sprite said. Behind her, she felt Meredith jump a little in her own cockpit.

"Trying to miss the *supports*? Sprite, the supports of *what*?" Meredith said, fear rising in her voice as she looked at the bridge and made the connection.

Sprite pushed forward on the stick, and the Stearman dropped down into the wash. *If the river wasn't dry, our landing gear would be getting a nice rinse right now,* Sprite thought. As the plane closed the distance to the bridge, the train blew its steam whistle in a useless warning. The panicked passengers at the windows fogged the glass with their screams, and Meredith bellowed something unintelligible over the intercom, but Sprite flew the roaring Stearman straight under the bridge, under the speeding train, between the supports, and out again on the other side, climbing up once again into the cloudless desert sky.

"That's for you, Daddy!" Sprite said softly as she pushed the stick left and allowed herself a slow victory roll. When they were upright again, Sprite tapped her headphones. She could hear Meredith gasping for air, and for a split second she thought the woman might be having an asthma attack. Thinking she'd better slow it down, Sprite reached a safe altitude and then turned around in her seat to visually check Meredith in the rear cockpit. Meredith huffed and puffed, chest heaving. Her leather helmet had shifted down over her eyebrows, and her goggles now sat twisted below her nose. Her face looked totally drained of blood, but she was conscious. She raised a shaking arm and slowly gave Sprite an unfocused, wobbly thumbs-up.

"So Mrs. Lowe," Sprite said, relieved that Meredith seemed all right, "Do you think you can get me that face-to-face meet-up with Mrs. Sheehy?"

"No need. You just finished your interview," Meredith gasped.

CHAPTER 8

THE NEXT DAY at Avenger Field, deep inside the Administration Building, Meredith knocked on the office door of Mrs. Ethel Sheehy, the official Field Recruiter for the WASP. Without waiting for an invitation, Meredith strode in and planted herself in front of Sheehy's cluttered desk. Meredith stood "at ease," with her feet shoulder-width apart and her hands behind her, at the small of her back, waiting for Mrs. Sheehy to look up from her paperwork. Meredith knew she was intruding, but she also knew she had something important to say and it couldn't wait. Mrs. Sheehy, in her late forties, was an experienced pilot herself, always on the move or in the air, and finding her sitting at her desk was rare. She looked up at Meredith over the top of her half-pane reading glasses, not bothering to hide her annoyance at the interruption.

Without waiting to be asked, Meredith said, "Mrs. Sheehy, I've seen a great many girls come through these gates and trained quite a few of them myself. We've had plenty of the debutante sorority girl variety that Jackie Cochran seems to favor, but a privileged background doesn't always make the best pilot."

Mrs. Sheehy removed her reading glasses and leaned back in her chair. "You mean young women with privileged backgrounds like your own." Meredith winced a little, because it was true. Meredith Lowe, neé Meredith Thayer, thirty-two years old, was a Cornell graduate and a certified member of the New York social elite. From an old-money family at Oyster Bay, Long Island, she had married into another old-money family, the

Lowes of Wall Street banking fame. Until the war, she had led a life of luxury and ease. Her wealth had allowed her to become one of the early aviatrix adventurers—a member of Amelia Earhart's "Ninety-Nines," and before the war she had been an annual Bendix race competitor.

"Yes, Mrs. Sheehy," replied Meredith, "I mean girls like me. But to my point, yesterday, I flew with a girl from a different background—she is from Lowland Mill, Georgia. She came in with a brochure from the Peach Festival, where she missed you by minutes, and hasn't got enough money right now to feed herself properly. Her parents are dead and she has no other family. So, you see, there are many things this girl does not have and never has had. But what she does have is more natural ability than any girl I've ever seen. She's got the licenses, she's got ten times the flight hours of any other girl here, and she really should start with the next class," Meredith finished passionately.

"So you are here to see me to…" Ethel Sheehy began.

"To help push the paperwork through. Only you can give the approval for her to start with this next class. I'm asking you to admit her immediately to 44-W-1, because we need pilots like her and, frankly, she's got nowhere else to go," Meredith said.

Ethel Sheehy sighed. Meredith knew the woman despised circumventing normal channels. It just wasn't the army way of doing things, and she demanded that the WASP try so hard to adhere to the army standard. Their existence as an organization depended on it. However, Meredith knew how much Ethel Sheehy respected her. There were only thirty-nine women Ferry Service pilots like Meredith and her impressive record and genuine commitment to the WASP meant that she had Sheehy's ear.

"So, you feel so strongly about her that I should grant her a special dispensation?" Mrs. Sheehy asked. "Even though you know darn well that 44-W-1 is full up and due to report in only two more days?"

Meredith nodded. "Yes. And with respect, I do see a stack of no-shows there on your desk, so there has to be at least one spot open right now. If there ever was a girl who needed to be admitted to the program, she's the one. She's got guts and real skill, and her name is Sprite Shannon. I promise you won't regret it if you admit her, but all of us will regret it if you don't," Meredith said, fixing Mrs. Sheehy with a stare. Meredith then raised her eyes to a spot on the wall above Mrs. Sheehy's head, signaling Sprite's plea had been made.

"Well, do I at least get to meet her?" Mrs. Sheehy asked, almost smiling as she surrendered to Meredith's well-argued case.

"Right away," Meredith nodded. She turned smartly, strode to the door, and leaned out into the hallway.

"Sprite, come on in," Meredith said. Sprite entered, clutching her licenses and logbook against her chest.

"Instructor Lowe tells me you are a rare bird," Mrs. Sheehy said, looking Sprite up and down. "So, are those for me?" She pointed at the logbook and licenses.

Meredith gestured and Sprite handed over her credentials. Mrs. Sheehy repositioned her reading glasses and looked at the documents, making notes about them on a steno pad. "All WASP Trainees must be between the ages of eighteen and thirty-five to gain entry into the program. And how old are you, Miss Shannon?" Mrs. Sheehy asked.

"Eighteen," Sprite stammered. Well, she would be next February, she thought, justifying the fib.

Mrs. Sheehy said, "Uhm hmm, yes," as she flipped to the last pages of Sprite's logbook, noting the total flight hours Sprite had accumulated. After a short pause, she handed the items back to Sprite and shook her head in feigned exasperation.

Then Meredith smiled, for she knew she'd won Sprite a place in the next class. Ethel Sheehy opened her desk drawer and pulled a form, swiveled around in her chair to the typewriter, rolled the thick triplicate form into the typewriter, and clack-clack-clacked Sprite's orders out right then and there. When she finished typing, she ratcheted the form out of the typewriter, signed it, tore off a copy, and handed it to Sprite. Then Mrs. Sheehy turned to Meredith and said, "Well, Instructor Lowe, take her down to medical. Get her a physical. She has to report for training in two days. Get a move on."

⋉

Two long, hot days later, Sprite made her hotel room bed, showered, and put on a somewhat wrinkled short-sleeved pale green shirt and a pair of high-waisted cotton slacks the color of dry straw—school clothes from last year. Her shoes were the same loafers she had worn to her father's funeral, but they were all she had and she had spit shined them into what might be called a soft patina. She stood before the full-length mirror on the back of her door and checked that all her tags were hidden and her waistband was straight. Her hair, clean and brushed, was gathered into a low ponytail, secured by some twine she had stuffed into the pillowcase. She turned from the mirror, thinking she would do, plumped her pillow-case into a lumpy square, and shoved it under her arm. It looked a little more like a parcel than a pillowcase that way, at least from a distance.

Before she ever reached the ground floor, the chatter of a hundred girls filtered up the stairwell, and when she stepped into the lobby, the noise was almost overwhelming. *They sound like starlings*, thought Sprite. But they didn't look like starlings—they looked like birds of paradise. Feathered hats, white gloves, high heels, puffed sleeves, cinched waists, crinolins and expensive leather purses decorated the flock of giggling young women, and suddenly, Sprite became all too aware of how different and plain she looked among them. She almost stepped away and went back up the stairs, but she saw Phoebe across the room, and tentatively made her way over, if for no other reason than to let Phoebe know she that was, indeed, still there.

"Hi, Phoebe," Sprite said, a little more coolly than she had intended.

The dark haired girl turned around and looked at Sprite like she had never met her before. "I'm sorry—oh, Sprite, yes, hello," she said flatly. The three other girls Phoebe had been talking with looked at Sprite and then at each other, and another breath later, Sprite and Phoebe were standing alone. Phoebe frowned at Sprite, and said, "Why'd you do that? I was just getting to know them and they are really important girls here— all of them are richer than God and they seemed to like me before you came up and ruined it."

"Ruined what?" said Sprite, bewildered.

"Oh, never mind, you wouldn't understand anyway," snapped Phoebe, searching the room for one of her new friends. "Oh, Liesel!" she called,

"I'll be right over!" And with that, Phoebe flounced her big white skirt past Sprite and didn't look back.

Sprite was deciding she didn't much care for Phoebe when a small woman in her late twenties clapped her hands and stood on a chair amid the flock of excited young hopefuls. "Girls, girls, I need for you to be quiet and listen," said the smiling blonde woman. Sprite noticed she was dressed in the same uniform that Meredith had worn. "My name is Constance York, and I will be riding out to Avenger Field with you this morning, so everyone, let's go outside and form into three groups of about equal number. Your chariots await." Constance climbed down from the chair and the women parted ranks to let her lead them out of the doors. The girls followed and Constance took them around to the back of the hotel.

Where three huge cattle trucks were parked, their diesel motors running.

Sprite could not help but laugh aloud, breaking the stunned silence of the other girls when they saw the idling trucks, slats of wood broken here and there in the walls, sunlight and dust streaming through them. Dried mud and dust caked the vehicles and there were no steps up to the high beds. Every mascara-rimmed eye turned toward the laughter and immediately found Sprite, who was still chuckling, her hand over her mouth now, trying to quell her amusement. "What's so funny, farm girl?" shouted one of them from the middle of the crowd, "Surprised to see your usual transportation, *cherie?*" The angry voice sounded slightly familiar. Sprite looked over and saw that it was Liesel. Phoebe was standing right beside her, glaring back at Sprite.

Sprite flushed with embarrassment and stopped laughing, hoping everyone would look away, which they quickly did as they began to mutter and complain in outrage at their treatment. But they had all seen her, and all had heard Liesel brand her with that name, "farm girl." Among these debutantes and college girls, Sprite could plainly see that she was the only one without either money or higher education. She stared at her worn loafers and wondered if this group of women would ever accept her.

As each vehicle pulled away, the girls fussed about being knocked around and they worried over their expensive luggage and shoes, but quickly stopped talking when they realized that the sand kicked up by the trucks' tires blew into their mouths every time they opened them.

The convoy drove them to Avenger Field, an airfield way out from town and close to nothing else. Sprite had taken this trip a couple of days before with Meredith, but it had been in the comfort of Meredith's snazzy yellow Cadillac convertible.

The view was different from the cattle truck. Everything looked much bleaker and forlorn, and the truck beds didn't even have covers over them for shade. The sun beat down mercilessly and the wind buffeted them during the whole trip. By the time they arrived, almost everyone's hairdo had been wind-whipped into scraggles and a drenching sweat stained all of their beautiful dresses dark under the armpits and at the necklines. Worse still, photographers from a magazine snapped pictures of them as they passed through the gates.

"Don't mind them," said Constance, "They're here all the time. You'll get used to them and they help with public awareness for the program." Nonetheless, many a gloved hand hid frazzled faces as the cameras worked the crowd.

The girls climbed out and walked dejectedly to the Administration building, where they had been told to stand waiting until everyone had arrived. Sprite looked around, taking in Avenger Field's two runways, both longer than her lane at home by at least half again, and the few low-built, wooden structures which were probably to be their living quarters and classrooms. A tall, half-finished building with a lot of windows appeared to be a control tower, and there were ranks of hangars down past the other buildings. The whole place looked to have been slapped together overnight and Sprite felt the sense that it was all temporary, made to be ready to tear down and put up somewhere else, leaving the desert scrub to take over again one day.

But for now, the field buzzed with activity. Advanced trainees, their bodies toned and their faces tanned, ran wherever they went despite their bulky flight suits. Some of the flight instructors gathered to watch as Sprite's class assembled, and the air was alive with engine noise. Sprite counted thirty-five planes on the ground, which meant there were many more in the air. Meredith had said there were fifty at a time up for practice.

The last truck emptied its passengers and they were herded inside, where a short, broad woman of about fifty climbed up on a platform and waved her arms for quiet. "I am Mrs. Leoti Deaton, and you can call me Deidee. I'm your Establishment Officer. You will be living in barracks and you will find your bay assignments listed by alphabetical order. There are two Flights of you, eight bays in each Flight, and six girls in each bay. Your assigned bays are posted on the bulletin board. Leave your luggage here, find your bay assignment, and fall out on the parade ground—that'll be that big, empty place out back of this building. Don't make me tell you twice," Diedee said, hopping off the platform.

Sprite had no luggage to leave, so she was first at the board. Her assignment was to Flight 2, Bay J-6, and her baymates were Gertrude Schneider, Roberta Schneider, Ninette Sotheby, and… Sprite's face fell at the last name: Phoebe Summerfield. Another girl's name had been crossed out. *Well, at least Liesel isn't in with me*, she thought, trying to find a positive attitude.

A few minutes later, they had assembled on the hot parade ground, and mercifully, did not have to wait long for what came next. A sergeant, who Sprite thought must have the lungs of a hog caller, began to yell at them to line up in formation, four rows of twenty-five each, right arms touching the shoulder of the girl next to them, tallest girls in front. Sprite complied, automatically moving to the far corner of the formation since she was the shortest girl. She was happy with the position—it gave her claustrophobia to be in the middle of a lot of taller people obscuring her view. The Sergeant yelled for quiet when some of the girls started waving and chattering to each other. They stopped talking instantly—the Sergeant had a face that could curdle milk—and he was more than a little scary. Everyone paid full attention for the rest of the announcements, which had to do with a lot of rules and schedules, and then the Sergeant stepped aside as another man walked onto the field.

"I am the Base Commander, ladies," said the middle-aged officer. "Now raise your right hands, and repeat after me: I, having been accepted as a Trainee, in the Women's Airforce Service Pilots, do solemnly swear, that I will support and defend the Constitution of the United States…."

※

An hour later, after the luggage was either stowed in the barracks or sent to storage, Sprite sat on the edge of her cot and watched as the other girls, including what looked to be a pair of tall twins, put their things away. Each girl had an open locker, and Sprite's was bare but for the few things she had brought from home. Every other locker already looked full, and the Sergeant had told them there was regulation clothing still to be issued in the coming days. Perhaps it had served Sprite well to be without so much stuff. Where would all those fancy dresses be worn anyway? Certainly not up in the air.

Again, she had found the bathroom, or "latrine," less than ideal, but far better than her old outhouse. Her bay shared two of everything that goes in a bathroom with the bay on the other side. *God help us if we all get sick at the same time*, Sprite thought, already scouting for an answer to that dilemma.

"Hey, where is my mirror?" Phoebe asked, looking around at the bare, unfinished walls.

"In the latrine, where mine is. And hers, and hers, and hers. We all share one now, and it's an over the sink version, not a full length. So you'll have to take our word on whether your shoes match your outfit!" laughed the ice-blonde girl, who looked to be a little older than the others. "And my name is Ninette, by the way. Pleased to meet all of you. And you are?" She looked around the room, her bright smile inviting everyone to introduce themselves.

"Um, Phoebe," said the girl in need of the mirror. "My Daddy is in the oil—"

"You can call us Bertie—" one of the twins began, cutting Phoebe off.

"—and Gertie," finished the other identical twin, whose voice sounded exactly like her sister's. Sprite had been marveling at their great height earlier on the parade ground, and was amused to see them here in her own bay.

Sprite realized it was now her turn. "I'm Sprite," she said, "Pleased to meet everyone."

Ninette gave Sprite a long look, and then said, "Hey, I know you…

you're the girl who flew the plane under the bridge that day last week, aren't you? I thought your face looked familiar! Instructor Lowe told me the name of the girl who did that was Sprite, so that has to be you!" The others suddenly turned to stare at Sprite, who swallowed drily and blanched white.

"Yes, but how do you know that?" she asked warily, meeting Nin's friendly eyes.

Ninette threw her head back and laughed. "Because I was on the train that went over the bridge just as you zoomed through the supports and up on the other side! We all saw you coming right at us, and most of the passengers thought you were out of control and about to hit us—but I stayed at the window and watched and you flew that Stearman right under us, with what, how much clearance on each side of your wings? Had to be less than a yardstick. Then we all jumped to the other side of the train and cheered. I never saw such a thing! Did you hear us yelling? What a maneuver! Will you teach me that someday?" Ninette had moved over to Sprite as she told the story and now stood right beside her. "Girls, this is the best little pilot I have ever seen," said Ninette. Bertie and Gertie exchanged looks of awe and Sprite's face began to redden.

"Oh, Ninette, it wasn't that tough—sure, I'll teach you someday, and then you'll know that for yourself," Sprite said, secretly pleased. Maybe they had already forgotten "farm girl" and would think of her differently now. It seemed like everyone in her bay might possibly like her in spite of what Liesel had said that morning.

Well, everyone except maybe Phoebe, who now stood with her back to the group, folding yet another mountain of her clothes. Her shoulders bristled with tension.

"Phoebe, what do you think about our little aerobat?" Ninette said, forcing Phoebe to either respond or be rude to Ninette, who, by the strange phenomenon of silent consensus, had just become the natural leader of the bay.

Phoebe turned around slowly, her face composed into feigned pleasance. "Well, I think if she keeps that kind of recklessness up, we'll be getting a new baymate real quick!" She said it lightly, as though she were joking, but everyone in the room, especially Sprite, heard the jealousy in Phoebe's voice. After an awkward silence, Phoebe added, "You'll be pleased to know Sprite here is also a magician. She hocus-pocused her way right into our program without even getting any orders first. Just walked right up and said some magic words to Miss Meredith and now here she is, same as us."

Sprite felt her face flush and she began to rise from her cot, fists clenched. A firm hand on her shoulder gently pushed her back down as its owner said, "Well, Phoebe, I'd say anybody who could fly a plane under a bridge oughta be here, orders or not—same as us. You two agree?" The twins quickly nodded, and the note of warning in Ninette's voice and the ice in her eyes made Phoebe look down. Sprite felt the pressure on her shoulder ease as Ninette let go and patted it. "Now, we are all going to get along just fine, aren't we, girls? Let's be the best bay in this rodeo!" Anger set aside, Sprite smiled again, but Phoebe narrowed her eyes and mouthed "farm girl" to her when the others weren't looking.

CHAPTER 9

OVER THE NEXT few days, the Trainees practiced marching and filled out heaps of papers and had their arms mutilated by a series of inoculations given by overworked doctors who had abandoned all concern for their patients' comfort. By the end of needle day, Sprite had run out of places to be stuck. No one lifted her arms very high for a day or two after without a reminder that they were now completely safe from malaria, typhoid, tuberculosis, and a few diseases Sprite had never heard of.

Phoebe seemed to complain endlessly about the heat, the marching, the bathroom, and the remoteness of the airfield. "Miles and miles of ugly nothing," she had called it.

Sprite felt like complaining a bit too, but when she thought about her alternatives, she pushed the feeling back down. It was a shock, being there—people yelled at you and treated you just like you were in the regular army. That seemed a bit unfair to all of them at first. It was hardest on the girls who had lived easy lives. "But there are servants for that," was their usual bewildered response when asked to clean their own areas.

Day by day, life in Bay J-6 took shape. Bertie and Gertie had brought a radio and told their baymates they could listen whenever they wanted. Ninette had offered a typewriter for letters home. Phoebe kept to herself for the most part, but Sprite found friends in the twins and Ninette, who told her story one evening after evening mess, when they were back in their bay. Exhaustion and the love songs on the radio had put everyone in a quiet, pensive mood. Gertie finished typing a letter to her boyfriend, then turned to Ninette and asked, "Say Ninette, you got this beautiful typewriter here, but how come I never see you writing to your fella?"

"Well…there was someone, a long time ago," Ninette said, as a look of old pain contorted her patrician face. "He was killed in a car wreck just before we graduated high school. I…I was driving the car when a drunk man in a truck drifted into our lane and hit us head on. I wasn't even hurt, but Evan died. I guess I never really got over it. After that, my folks wanted me to go to college to find a husband, and I think I really disappointed them by finding a passion for art and design instead. I graduated from Vassar with honors, but they hardly gave it any notice. When I came home without an engagement ring on my finger, my mother took me into her sitting room and asked me if I had developed 'feelings' for other women instead of men." Ninette paused and looked around uncomfortably, but she was met with only sympathetic eyes. "Her question hurt me because it showed how little she really knew me. No, I had no 'feelings' for women instead of men—I like men fine, and had casually dated several while I was in college. I just never had brought anyone home for my mother to meet. I told her that I would surely meet the right guy someday, but for now, I had found actual love instead of 'the right match.' Mother couldn't understand when I told her it was love for the beauty I saw in color and form, or how a building reached for heaven or the way a coat draped on a man's shoulders. Most especially, I had learned to love the way airplanes are designed. Well, that was altogether too much for her. She told me I had let the family down and if I flew planes, I'd quite naturally crash, because that is what I was famous for. She said there had to be something wrong with me and she wished I would 'just be honest about it.'" Ninette dabbed at her eyes with a handkerchief. "So I took myself out of that room and out of that house and probably even out of that family, and came here. I want to be useful to the war effort if I can't be useful to my family. And someday, I want to design airplanes that fly faster than the speed of sound. Maybe then, when I fly one, I'll get away from the echo of my mother's words," she finished.

The room fell silent for a few moments, and then Bertie said quietly, "Wow. We understand, Nin. You can be yourself with us, right girls?"

"Of course," said Gertie, and Sprite nodded, thinking how blessed she was to have had a father who loved her for who she was, not who he wanted her to be. And one who wanted her to fly planes.

After a brief pause, Bertie began speak again. "Well, we come from Missoula, Montana.

"Which some people pronounce mis-oo-ry," said Gertie, and everyone laughed, breaking the tension in the room.

Bertie chimed in, "Yes, we are the eldest of twelve, the only girls, and there are two more sets of twins in our family," she said proudly. "We're the shortest ones!"

More laughter followed, and Gertie said, "We're nurses with the hospital, but we came because our brothers are in the air war in Europe. Our whole family flies because our parents are doctors, and they have to get to really remote places up in the mountains to tend to their patients. Flying just seemed the easiest way to do it, and all the ranches have big fields to land in."

"All of us kids just learned to fly from them," said Bertie. "We could fly before we could drive!"

Sprite knew her turn had come. She wondered how much about herself she should tell them, acutely aware that she should leave out the part about shooting Major Doyle. She decided to take a chance on a bare bones version of the rest of the story. "Well, I'm here because I had nowhere else to go," she said wistfully. "My father was a crop duster, and I helped him in the business and had my own plane. But then he died and the bank and the army came after the house and land, and my plane, too. So I had this flyer about the WASP. One day, I realized my life had changed, really understood what happens when all the old choices go away—I thought, well, I have some new choices about how to use the thing I do best—which is fly—and maybe I can be of some use to the war effort since my old life is gone. The WASP flyer said our country needed women pilots, and I thought, gee, I get the chance to help clobber Hitler and Tojo by being a pilot. That's the closest thing a woman can do to actual combat! I got on a train and here I am. That's all there is to it," she ended, feeling fervent in her newfound patriotism, but cringing in her heart at the lie she'd tacked on. There was far more to it than that. There was Major Doyle's bloody promise of revenge.

"That must have been tough, Sprite," Ninette said, compassion in her voice. "Were you mad at the army when they took everything?"

"You bet!" said Sprite. "And I still am, when I'm in a bad mood and think about it too much. But I realized that if the bank hadn't treated us wrong, then my Daddy would still be alive and the army would have paid us for the farm and none of it would have happened. So, I guess it's really the bank I'm the most mad at. It was the cause of all of this. So I try to do what Daddy always told me to—look past the cape and see the matador—he's the one with the sword!"

Ninette laughed, understanding, and then turned around. "Hey, Phoebe, what about you? Come over and join us," Ninette prompted, trying to bring the girl into the conversation. "What's your story?"

Phoebe, who had been sitting on her cot on the other side of the room, made no effort to move. Instead, she looked over and said, "Well, my Daddy's in the oil business, and I'm here because I'll be head of his company some day, and I want to get some experience flying bigger planes, so's I can shuttle clients around the world to the oil fields. I graduated from the University of Tulsa and then they sent me to a Douglas bomber factory, you know, as a kind of post-baccalareate thing for my program—not everybody got to do it—and I had to sort parts and so forth so I could learn all about the planes. This is really just sort of an extension of that study for me, another hands-on part. That's the only reason I came out to this God-forsaken sand pit and I can't wait to get out of this hideous room and this hideous countryside, if you must know. And now, I'm going to go and talk with Liesel on the other side of the bathroom. She's in J-5, thank God." With that, Phoebe got up and disappeared through the latrine's passage to the adjoining bay.

"Ah," said Ninette, watching Phoebe flounce out. "Well, I hope we all find what we are looking for here."

Sprite smiled at the little group at the table as Bertie tuned the radio to some Benny Goodman and pulled Gertie up to practice dance steps. *Maybe I will find what I'm looking for here*, Sprite said to herself, and got up to join the twins and learn the Lindy Hop.

CHAPTER 10

THE NEXT MORNING'S 0600 reveille caught Sprite already awake and lying in her cot while the other girls slept. She was practicing marching orders in her mind after waking up from dreaming about drill commands, her feet moving of their own accord, her head filled with the jody, or cadence song, Diedee had taught them. One by one, each of the others jerked awake and Bertie—she thought it was Bertie—almost fell out of her bed. That would have made the fourth day in a row, but her twin on the next cot over saved her with a waiting arm and pushed her back in. Sprite smiled and chuckled as she rose and stretched—and then beat it for the bathroom before the crowd arrived and she had to wait.

A few minutes later, she took up a broom and began to sweep their area, marveling at just how much sand accumulated in a day's time on the bare wooden floor. Ninette joined her and began to tidy the table and chairs, and when all of the girls had made up their own cots, they put on the uniform they had quickly learned to despise.

It was a "Zoot suit," as the previous classes called it, and it came in one size, men's 44, which, despite its label's promise, did not fit all, or even most. Sprite rolled up the sleeves of the olive drab material again and again, trying to make the rolls flat, but they were so thick it was impossible to get them to lie down neatly. The legs of the garment presented even more of a challenge for her. Sprite stood only about five feet two, and weighed somewhat under a hundred pounds. The Zoot suits were made for, well, made for the twins, apparently, who wore them like fashion models. Sprite began to roll material again and by the time she had succeeded in making the pants short enough not to trip over, she was the last one out into formation.

They marched to breakfast and fell out into lines for their oatmeal, eggs, and wonder of wonders, real coffee and real bacon. Every morning! Sprite had not eaten this well since the war started two years back and it looked like some of the other girls had gone a long time without some of these foods, too. They could have as much as they liked of anything and that, alone, would have been enough to keep Sprite at Avenger Field forever.

"Hey, Sprite, eat like that every day and you'll be picking up extra payload!" quipped Phoebe as she sat down across from her baymates. Sprite continued to enjoy her food, but Ninette gave Phoebe a sharp look.

"Phoebe, I am wondering why it is that you, in fact, eat so little. You know our days are about to gear up into extremely demanding physical work, right? Today is our first PT exercise, and our Flight Instructor, Mrs. Lowe, told me that we start flying the Fairchild PT-19's next week," Ninette said.

"Yes, I know that, Ninette, but I was taught that a lady doesn't eat like a horse," said Phoebe, eyeing Sprite and pushing around the eggs and toast on her own plate. She cut them into impossibly small pieces before taking them daintily into her mouth.

Ninette sighed and held Phoebe's gaze for a moment and then looked at the biscuit on her plate. As if there were a telepathic message sent to everyone at the table except Phoebe, Ninette raised her eyebrow, and she and the others picked up their own biscuits and shoved them whole into their mouths at the same time. The twins erupted in muffled giggles and Sprite nearly choked on the huge bite, but Ninette, cheeks bulging, simply continued to stare Phoebe down and slowly chew until she had swallowed the whole thing. With a final gulp, Ninette burst into laughter, but Phoebe just turned her face in disgust and shook her head.

Two tables away, Liesel gave an eye roll and a sigh and said, "What pigs!" in French. Phoebe nodded silently, and got up for more coffee. On the way back to her plate, she nudged Liesel, bent to whisper in French as she passed, "I have to get out of my bay. That Sprite Shannon thinks she is the 'Hot Pilot,' and so do the others."

Liesel grinned wickedly and said, "Oh, we can take care of that, *cher*! It might take a little time, but...." Phoebe broke into a smile. When she sat down again, coffee cup in hand, she looked at each of her baymates and smiled as though nothing had happened.

That afternoon, the girls met their PT instructor, a stocky, muscled army lieutenant who wore his cap pulled so low that his sunburned nose, wide mouth, and aviators were all they could see of his face. His given name was Alan, but everyone called him "Buzz" because of his haircut. Sprite waited for instructions at her rear corner and was thankful to be out of the Zoot suit for the exercises—doing them in that garment would have been impossible. Her pale blue button-down shirt and blue short shorts allowed for much more movement and were far cooler.

"Now, ladybirds, some of you out in this formation are looking like you've spent your young lives sitting on your young butts," said Buzz. "You are weak and flabby and unwell! And I am going to make you strong and fit and healthy! Do you hear me?!" he yelled, making some of the front row jump.

Everyone heard you, thought Sprite. *Letty, back in Georgia, probably heard you.*

"Alright, then! We will go for the entire hour with four three-minute breaks to start. I will call the exercise changes and you will execute them without stopping. Jumping jacks: give me a hundred and count 'em off. Ready – begin! One, two, three, one..." the instructor shouted, and the girls hopped to it. By forty, Sprite was feeling the drag in her muscles from the heat. By seventy-five, the entire group was noticeably slower. At eighty, Phoebe fainted.

"Do not stop your count!" Buzz yelled to the girls who had bent to help her. He walked between the rows of jumping women to Phoebe, shook his head and shouted, "Get up, Ladybird!" Phoebe, who had come around on her own, still looked fairly pale and ill. "Did you drink your water today? Did you eat your breakfast and lunch today? If you did not do those things, you will do them from now on, do you hear me?!" Phoebe put her hand over her left ear to shield it from the blast of words and got up, shaking and nodding. "Now go to the fountain and drink, sit down for five minutes, and then finish your jumping jacks while the others take a break and watch you. I believe you stopped at eighty," he said, getting right in her face. Phoebe obeyed, casting a jaundiced eye toward him as she walked to the fountain. Afterward, while everyone else rested, Phoebe did her last twenty jumping jacks, facing the group, counting alone, and feeling more embarrassed than she had ever been in her life. That night at evening mess, Phoebe silently ate everything on her plate and then went back for seconds as her baymates nodded their approval.

CHAPTER 11

A FEW DAYS later at the Auxiliary Field, Meredith called for Sprite to go up for her morning training flight, and when they had sailed into the air and practiced a few maneuvers, she said, "Sprite, there is no reason to prolong this—it's time for you to solo. Take me down and then go back up again by yourself."

Sprite gave her a thumbs up from the front cockpit, and said, "Yes, Ma'am!" as she banked the plane and set it down neatly, with no wobble or bounce.

Meredith climbed out of the plane, gave it a slap as if it were a horse, and sent Sprite back into the air. "You might be the first solo, Sprite— make it pretty!" said Meredith as she walked back down the flight line.

Then Ninette saw that Sprite was alone and going back up in the air. "Hey! Everybody look! Sprite's soloing! I think she's first!" Bertie and Gertie joined her as she craned her neck upward and waved at Sprite, who made a pass by them and tipped her wings in salute. Pretty soon, several girls had gathered and were watching. Three more planes took off shortly after Sprite's, and Phoebe thought Liesel must be in one of them, because she couldn't find her anywhere else.

An hour or so later, as Sprite's landing time neared, one of the advanced girls said to Ninette, "Say, is that your baymate rolling in?"

Ninette said, "Yes, it is! It's Sprite Shannon!"

The other girl looked back at Nin as she walked down the line to her waiting plane. "Then you better get ready to dunk her in the well when she comes down!" she laughed. "She'll be the first one in your class to solo and you know it's our tradition!"

Meredith, standing beside Nin and with her binoculars trained on Sprite, nodded her head in permission when she was sure Sprite was first, and Bertie and Gertie turned to each other and grinned, their twin noses wrinkling devilishly. In a few minutes, when Sprite had put the PT-19 down, they led the cheering and raced to meet her.

"What?!" Sprite said, pulling off her leather helmet and ditching her other gear.

"You have to come with us!" said Bertie, and they quick-stepped her back to the barracks, chatting about nothing in particular. Just before they reached their bay, the twins took a sharp turn around and each caught one of Sprite's arms to lift her onto their shoulders, hardly feeling Sprite's 90 lbs. split between them. They trotted her to the big stone Wishing Well that served as the only water feature in the entire compound, and threw her into the air over the fountain. The growing crowd of well wishers cheered.

As she splashed down, Gertie said, "That's your real solo flight! The one you take without the plane!" Ninette joined them as they dragged Sprite, sopping wet and laughing, out of the cool water to run dripping and squishing to the barracks to change her clothes. All of them, even Phoebe, followed her, whooping and laughing.

As Sprite turned the corner, Liesel unexpectedly met them from the other side, and she and Sprite bumped hard into each other, with Sprite taking the worst of it.

"Oww! Watch where I'm going, you little…! Hey…why are you wet, farm girl?" Liesel yelped as she pushed Sprite off and stepped back to find her own uniform had been soaked at the point of their impact. "You…? They dunked you in the fountain? But I just soloed…I just came down… that was supposed to be me!" That Liesel had missed first solo seemed to be slowly sinking in, along with the well water that was darkening her Zoot suit. "You. Farm girl. You got first solo," Liesel said, her voice full of venom.

Sprite nodded, unapologetic in her direct stare at Liesel's furious face. For weeks, talk of who would be first had made the rounds of every bay, with several girls neck and neck in the vying. After all, it was quite an honor for the chosen girl, and even for her bay mates, a glow of fame by association would always follow. Sprite hadn't known if she actually had been first or not until the dunking.

Phoebe, at the far back of Sprite's group, knitted her brows, knowing that Liesel would think she had betrayed her. She slunk behind the twins, hoping their height would hide her, but Liesel wasn't looking at Phoebe. She just stood her ground and continued to stare Sprite down. Then she walked around her and bumped Sprite again, hard, and whispered bitterly, "First solo was mine, farm girl. So get this: I'm gonna take something away from you someday. And soon!" And with that, Liesel disappeared behind the swarm of celebrating girls, leaving Sprite to wonder what had just happened.

X

That evening, Sprite went to bed with her hair still a little damp from her dunking. It had been a long, long day and she, like the others, was too exhausted to sleep well. She tossed and turned, her mind replaying the wonderful day—the dunking, her bay mates' pride in her accomplishment, and the beauty of the clear sky that was hers alone during the hour of her solo flight all felt better every time she thought about them. But just before she would fall asleep, her mind always came back to the ominous tone of Liesel's threat and she would jerk awake. Sprite knew she had two real enemies now—and one of them lived right next door. Liesel already had a reputation for keeping her cruel promises to girls who made her angry. Like any bully, she had both the intuition to see vulnerabilities in others and the meanness to manipulate them to her advantage. Two of the trainees had already been washed out of the program because Liesel, known behind her back now as "Liesel the Weasel," had reported them for having liquor or being out of their bays after lights out. Sprite knew that Liesel had meant those hateful words—"I'm gonna take something from you someday."

As for that other enemy, he had never been far from her thoughts since their set-to at her house. In that middle world that is neither sleep nor waking, tall, menacing Major Doyle always lurked, and it occurred to Sprite that Liesel's threat had sounded just like the Major's had that day he had stolen her ring and she had shot him. Over and over in her fitful sleep that night, Sprite saw Major Doyle's angry face and bleeding ear in front of her pistol and heard his bitter, determined promise to find and punish her. Sprite knew that somehow, like Liesel, he'd keep his promise of revenge.

She looked out the window to the sky. Amid the other constellations, Orion the Hunter wheeled overhead, chasing his prey, and the hours passed until dawn crept over the flat horizon. Unrested, Sprite opened her deep green eyes and saw fragments of her troubled dreams peopling her waking thoughts, and wondered when and how both of her enemies would strike.

CHAPTER 12

Late August, 1943, Northern Ireland

ACROSS THE ATLANTIC ocean, Major Doyle, his right ear healing but certain to be permanently notched, fell asleep to the quick huffing of the locomotive and the hypnotic sound of "roll-roll-roll-clack, roll-roll-roll-clack" the train's wheels made on the jointed rails. He lay back against the compartment wall, nodded off, and before he knew it, evening became morning, and the train had slowed.

At last, Doyle had arrived at Langford Lodge, County Antrim, more formally known as BAD-1, US Army Air Force Base 597. The supply and maintenance depot would soon become the busiest airfield in the United Kingdom and, just as Mattias had predicted, General Arnold had tasked Doyle with arranging for shipments of pigged chromium to arrive there for the top-secret British aviation project known only as "Archangel." Doyle sighed and sat down in a folding chair. It would be a long day.

And it was, as were the next two. Doyle sat through hours of soporific meetings, reviewed and signed countless forms, talked at length with supply sergeants and Quartermaster's Corps corporals, and then remembered hardly any of it. In his pocket, his hand nervously turned the Claddagh ring over and over as he thought of Coreen and where she was and how they were treating her.

It had been an easy choice back on Guernsey—agree to the Nazis' terms or die there and assure that Coreen would die as well. But Mattias had kept his word so far. He'd put Coreen on the ship when Doyle had sent notification that he had procured the Shannon farm in Georgia and the mining was underway.

That Shannon girl had been more than a bit of trouble and her face, now that he thought about it, was far too similar to Coreen's. The girl's snub nose and bright green eyes and long blonde hair, so like Coreen's features, had haunted his dreams since the day the girl had shot his ear. *That's the power of suggestion when the subject is under stress, and I was certainly stressed when she fired at me,* Doyle thought, attempting to scientifically explain his growing fixation on the girl. *Still,* he thought, a slight shiver running down his spine, *all that talk of Irish curses....* Doyle pinched the warm metal of the ring and shook his head, privately embarrassed at even entertaining the thought that the girl's heirloom really might be a curse to the thief who had stolen it. His fingers continued to trace the shape of the ring, a heart held firmly and protectively by two hands, but he forcefully pushed his mind into other thoughts.

Coreen was a day out from port, with four more to go until Greta would pick her up at the Azorian docks. The thought of Greta made his blood boil. Doyle hated her. She was everything he abhorred in women—severe, angular beauty, ruthless competency, and the self-confidence only a man should possess. And she was Mattias's woman. Mattias had been his friend, but now he was a Nazi, and Greta would kill Coreen without another thought the minute he told her to. That would be the minute Mattias believed Doyle had been or would be unfaithful to their bargain.

But maybe it wouldn't have to go that way. Maybe once Coreen landed in the Azores, he could rescue her and then tell his father about everything. Only three more days to wait until she stepped off the *Rowan* and onto British soil again. But what could he do to help her from that point on? From the accuracy of Mattias' information, Doyle knew that someone close to him had to be the German's agent, and that person would report Doyle's remarks and actions back to the Nazis with great efficiency. Mattias would keep the ruthless Greta on Coreen as well, so Doyle would have to be careful, take his time, and wait for his opportunity to help

Coreen. First, though, he needed to figure out who was secretly watching him. He had no time to ponder that further, because just then, a British Colonel, his face gray and agitated, burst into the room.

"We've a crisis brewing, gentlemen," the Colonel said. "A neutral cargo ship has sunk off our western coast. We think it's the *Irish Rowan*. No bad weather in the area, so our orders are to investigate immediately. Major Doyle, we won't be able to accommodate you further right now, but please express to General Arnold that we will arrange for reception of the chromium—most likely at the airbase in Scotland." The Colonel shook Doyle's hand perfunctorily and said goodbye, but Doyle didn't respond and sat unmoving in his seat. In truth, Doyle hadn't heard anything after the words "cargo ship has sunk" and "Rowan." His pulse thundered in his ears and his field of vision narrowed to the loudly ticking, phosphorescent hands on the wall clock as the Colonel withdrew from the handshake. The green glint of the timepiece brought Doyle back to the moment, and he realized he had been dismissed. But he still didn't move. There was something left to ask.

Doyle nodded and said, very quietly, "Sir, survivors of the shipwreck?"

"We don't know yet, Major," said the Colonel, "but it doesn't look good."

The *Rowan*. Coreen's ship. Sunk. The Germans? But why would Mattias order her death when he had cooperated—was cooperating? What now? How could he find out for sure? For a long moment, Doyle's mind seemed a roil of disconnected static, his thoughts coming to him "broken and stupid," as the Americans called it when the com connections were bad.

Then he had an idea. With two extra days now at his disposal, he could go back to the Residence and get his father to confirm what had happened. Diplomatic channels would be the most accurate because his father had a direct line to Ireland's Taoiseach. And then, if Coreen were truly dead, he would tell his father about Mattias and the Nazis after all. Straighten the whole thing out before reporting it to command and have his father's backing, no—his father's respect—for blowing up the German plot.

He set off at a ragged run for the motor pool.

CHAPTER 13

West Coast of Ireland, Look Out Post 38

THE EVENING TIDE at Roaringwater Bay had left an empty lifeboat and a slew of floating objects that lodged in the craggy rocks at the bottom of Coast Watcher Brian Alasdair's LOP. All day, he and his brother Diarmuid had watched the debris circle and bob while the rushing water ebbed away enough for Diarmuid to go safely down the cliff.

Brian knew before he saw the colors on the empty lifeboat what they were looking at. It was flotsam from the *Irish Rowan*, sunk just a day out of port. Brian also knew that his next job would be salvage and recovery, not rescue. He swallowed drily. They'd had to pull the dead from the water more than a few times since the war, and it never got easier.

When the war began, Brian and his brother Diarmuid, both in their late forties, had been recruited by the Irish Home Guard to do the same thing they'd done all their lives as fishermen, which was keep watch on their patch of the ocean. All around the island, the Coast Watchers built lookout posts with exactly one hundred thirty-seven blocks, sometimes brought up cliff sides by donkey, one block at a time, until the little bay-windowed buildings were complete. A lookout post, or LOP, housed a team of two men day in and out, and the only comforts of their twelve-hour watch were a small brazier that burned peat, and a telephone line to G2 for reporting any aircraft and vessels they spotted. Brian and Diarmuid watched five miles of Roaringwater Bay and had the day shift that week. Dairmuid was just finishing his walking patrol.

Up on the cliff and shivering from a cold, briny gust, Brian adjusted his binoculars, but he still couldn't make out the exact form of a particular bit of flotsam he was looking at. "Hoy, Diarmuid! Canya see what's snagged at the edge o' that whirly down there?" Brian called to his brother, who had climbed down the rocks beneath the cliff and was now picking his way across the slick, knife-edged granite spikes.

"Oh, an I will, Brian, keep yer shirt on, man," called Diarmuid, his amiable voice bouncing around the cliff walls, "These birds are hell-bound to have it before me, though." Angry gulls circled his head, diving at him, trying to scare him off from a possible dinner. Gulls would eat anything alive or that ever had been alive.

Brian panned the glasses across the wallowing lifeboat, shreds of clothing, and, there at the whirlpool—yes, that looked like the first of the bodies. He sighed. The Gulf Stream would be bringing them up and leaving them in the bay for days.

"Diarmuid! Bobber!" he shouted, and saw his brother wave in acknowledgment. Diarmuid pulled the lifeboat toward himself and checked it for damage, but the little craft had no water in it to speak of and one of the oars was lying in the bottom. He secured a line to a big rock and climbed in to began his grim fishing, and when Brian saw him wave again, he knew he'd called it right. He crossed himself and said the short prayer for those dying at sea.

They hauled them up by rope, one at a time, until all four of them lay stretched out on the grassy, weather worn cliff top. As they were required to do, Diarmuid had rung the priest and the local Garda, but their trip to the LOP would take them a couple of hours. It was a long, hard way up to their post from any direction. Meanwhile, Brian looked the poor dead fellows over, saw nothing but the unique pattern of their jumpers to check against the knitters' family records—the explosion had left their bodies shattered. He puzzled at the last body, the lone woman. The *Rowan* had been a cargo vessel. What was she doing on it?

Her long blonde hair tangled about her neck and shoulders and covered most of her face. Without touching her skin, Brian pulled a strand away and saw that sea and rocks had battered her face too badly for identification. She had been young, maybe twenties. He checked her body, burned as it was, for identity clues—jewelry, scars—but there was none of either. There was no way to tell who she had been.

Brian did discover something when he moved her hair back over her ravaged face. Edges of soggy paper protruded from her low neckline—the girl had been carrying some letters, kept in her bosom, tightly laced into her old-fashioned corset. Brian looked up at his brother, who nodded, and then Brian made to remove the parcel, laying aside the blouse only so much as need be, with long practiced tenderness and respect.

Diarmuid peeled back one of the envelopes, its writing, amazingly, still legible despite the saltwater. He read the names and addresses and then looked over to his brother and said, "I think we better be callin' Himself the Taoiseach this time, Brian. The letters are from the American ambassador's son to this girl. Seems she was his fiancée."

CHAPTER 14

Antrim to Dublin railroad route

THE TRAIN BACK to Dublin could not go fast enough for Doyle. He sat in his cabin, nervously tapping a foot or drumming his blunted fingers, watching the misty landscape drag by. All he could think about was Coreen drowning in the cold Atlantic waters, alone and without hope of rescue. Maybe she had died instantly in an explosion, which would have been better for her. Either way… his face grew hot again and the tears began to course down his cheeks. He couldn't stop them and didn't want to. She had been everything to him. Everything. With her, he had known who he was. But without her, his very sense of self had collapsed. All the beauty had gone out of the world. As the train rolled by, even the glorious greens of his beloved Ireland looked dull and dismal.

The porter came by checking tickets, and Doyle sat up. He decided to push the pain aside and work with the information he had. After all, he was a chemist, and his ordered, logical mind had always been a haven for moments when he felt overwhelmed, afraid, or vulnerable. He settled into figuring out how to tell his father George Doyle, American Ambassador to Ireland, about the Nazis' plot, for he was certain he must now reveal

Mattias' attempt to use him to divert the chromium that would soon be bound for England.

It would be a delicate discussion, because his father often heard only part of any sentence and then raced to his own conclusions before he got the entire story. Once those conclusions had been made, it was nearly impossible to get him to see otherwise, even with a strong factual presentation. Doyle would have to choose his words carefully and get it right the first time, or be considered a traitor for allowing himself to be kidnapped and shanghaied to Guernsey. But if the old man actually heard him out, Doyle thought, he would be astonished and thrilled that his son, the son he had never loved, had brought him the gift of his self-sacrificing courage—courage as worthy as his dead brother Parker's—and the information that could send George up the political ladder so fast that he would be Secretary of State once the war was over, provided the Allies won. That might still be possible—with the knowledge Mattias had given him about the Germans' lack of chromium, Doyle had the power to keep Germany's jets out of the air. Just one well-put word to his father.... Though it didn't take the pain of losing Coreen away—nothing would—it was some consolation that he might be respected, maybe even loved, by his family. And as for Mattias—well, it would make Doyle very happy to see the "old friend" and his Commandant pay for sabotaging Coreen's ship.

When the train pulled into Dublin Kingsbridge station, Doyle's heart leapt to his throat and a surge of pure adrenalin charged his veins. He ran from the train to the street, half expecting to find his father's head butler Liam waiting, because the man had always seemed to be clairvoyant about his duties, but the major domo was not there this time. Doyle hailed a cab and within a few minutes, was outside the Residence, knocking at the door.

Unperturbed, as and though he really had known Doyle was coming, Liam answered and let him in, saying, "Will sir be needing dinner? I am preparing your favorite."

Doyle shook his head warily. "No, Liam, what I need is to know if my father is back yet—" He didn't finish the sentence, because he could hear George Doyle speaking to someone in his study far down the hallway. "I'll be going on in now, Liam. It's very important."

Thick brows only slightly raised, Liam cast his gray eyes downward and gave Doyle a nod, then removed to the kitchen. "Then I'll include you in the tea service, sir. Your father has rung for it," said the major domo.

While he could murder that cup of tea—he was cold to the bone—Doyle ignored Liam and strode down the hallway, his speech prepared, his heart pounding, and then stopped outside the slightly cracked door just before pushing it completely open. It was an old, self-protecting habit. Before entering, he always listened for a lull or even an end to the previous conversation. George Doyle was always more likely to pay attention if he were not interrupted. Well, he had always been more likely to pay attention to Parker, Doyle's younger, smarter, better looking dead brother. But Doyle adhered to the old habit and, anyway, he needed to get his breathing under control before going in. He listened, also out of habit, to the words and tenor of his father's conversation. Whatever mood the talk had aroused in the old man would be an important factor in his willingness to give Doyle the time of day.

"Carrington, I got word of it this morning when I got back home. PR nightmare, this! Yes, I know it was the *Rowan*, not the Portuguese *Royale*. Yes, the courier arrived with the letters just a minute ago, and…. Umhm, umhm, yes, yes, very sad, but to tell the truth, the girl was a liability to me anyway, Protestant and all. Would have been blight on my family name. And what the hell was she doing on that ship? Hmm, perhaps we can use that. Leak that she was a collaborator. Probably was. And even if she wasn't, it can't be proved, right? So let's say she was a German collaborator, bound for espionage at your post in the Azores and the ship was just collateral damage to make sure she never arrived. What does it matter now?"

The voice on the other end shouted something through the receiver, and George replied, "When did a lie ever bother you, Carrington? I'm telling you, it can't get out that it was your boys and the Poles. This is war, man! It's either my story, or you'll have to find a way to blame it on the Germans, who were bloody nowhere near that ship, Carrington. We can't have this kind of thing dampening the morale of the troops and the people—the people, Carrington, would have far too many questions. Good men could lose their jobs. Yes, precisely like you and me." George paused while the voice on the other end spoke again. Then he made a sour face and said, "Oh, all right, it was only the Germans, then! Hell of a thing if anybody survived it and talks, though. Hell of a thing. It'll be all yours to explain then, old boy, and both our arses on the line for covering it up!"

Covering it up? Doyle thought, trying to make sense of the whole conversation while hearing only half of it. *Covering....* And then it hit him like a tidal wave. The Allies—specifically Commander Carrington's torpedo bombers from RAF Castle Archdale—had sunk Coreen's ship, not the Germans! Doyle recoiled in horror, backing away from the study door in several awkward, stumbling steps. Liam, appearing as usual at the perfect moment, caught his arm and righted him, and then looked him straight in the eye.

"Pardon me, sir, let me help you; wouldn't want you to fall," he said, somehow still managing to balance a full tray upon the fingers of his other hand. Liam's grip was astoundingly strong and Doyle winced at the increasing pressure on his brachial artery when Liam didn't let go. Doyle looked away and with some difficulty, broke the hold, saying, "Let me go, Liam!" It was the first time he had ever dared to speak sharply to the old servant.

Liam blinked slowly, serenely, and said, "Oh, very sorry, sir. But we wouldn't want you to be further bruising those cracked ribs you got during your excursion, now would we? I would also caution against talking too much or getting upset—strains the breathing, worsens the pain. I hear that certain volatile topics and names such as, for instance, Mattias, are known for causing terrible, sometimes even fatal, damage. Even to other people in the room. Please follow me into the study and have your tea."

Doyle blinked as Liam's words settled into his mind. How had Liam known about the cracked ribs? And "volatile topics and names such as Mattias"? And if he knew about Mattias, he knew...everything. So the person who had been watching Doyle, at least one of them, was old Liam, his father's trusted major domo for more than twenty years! Doyle had no more time to think about any of that because his father had seen him. Liam gave him a final warning look as he walked through the study door.

"Wallace?! What are you doing still here? Are things in Antrim finished already? Can't be! Something going on up there? Why aren't you back in the States? Or are you AWOL, boy?!" George huffed, his hand over the phone receiver. George removed his hand and spoke into the receiver, "One moment, Carrington, if you please," then replaced the hand. Liam entered, bowed slightly to his employer, and began to set the tea service out, a strange little packet of white powder secreted in the sleeve of his black jacket.

Still reeling from the appalling way his father had just spoken of his fiancée's apparent death, Doyle shook his head slowly and stood in silence for a moment in front of him. The old man didn't even have the decency to be ashamed or embarrassed that he'd been overheard trying to make Coreen into an official war criminal in order to use her in his cover-up.

"So it's true. Father..." Doyle began, his thoughts fracturing. Standing beside the tea table he had set up near the Ambassador, Liam slid the small cello packet of white powder out of his starched sleeve and turned his back on both father and son, flaring his jacket wide.

"Father, I have something to tell you. I mean, there is something you should know," Doyle stammered. Liam frowned viciously down at the tea service and the cello packet in his hand hovered for a moment over both of the cups.

"Well, then spit it out, boy! I don't have time for you to stand there gaping at me! Can't you see I'm in the middle of a crisis?" said George angrily, his big hand still clamped over the phone's receiver.

Doyle stood silent a tense moment longer. Liam stirred their tea and turned to gaze blankly at him. For a long moment, the sweet ringing sound of the silver spoon on the fine china was the only sound in the room. Doyle looked at his father, really looked at him, and saw that there was nothing in the elder Doyle's soul but vacant ambition and disgust for his remaining, incompetent son. George had already had enough of bothersome intrigue for the day and he was not in any mood to listen to his embarrassing offspring's bizarre tale about being kidnapped by Gallagher.

But it didn't matter now, because standing there, seeing the impossibility of ever impressing George Doyle, Wallace had just had an epiphany of sorts. His father's cold, sharp words about Coreen had stabbed their way into Doyle's already wounded heart, finally severing the tenuous, feeble bloodline holding him prisoner to this lying, self-serving old man and the ruthless, egocentric country he represented. Coming from somewhere behind his own eyes, blinding white light obscured his father's face as Doyle realized that he was free of that pain, free of that obligation, free of the starving need of his father's notice and approval. And he'd far rather be Seamus, the bloody rich traitor to a soulless country than be Wallace, the hero of George Doyle, but traitor to truth. His vision cleared, his heart rate slowed, and he took a deep breath.

"You know," Doyle found the words came easily now, "I had thought perhaps I needed to speak with you about something. On reflection, it is now astoundingly unimportant. I am sorry to have troubled you, sir. I should never have come."

George gave him a narrowed gaze, as though sensing a change behind Doyle's eyes, along with something fierce and feral crouching within the younger man's voice.

Oddly, now that it no longer meant anything to him, it seemed to Doyle that the old man had almost listened to him. But then, George Doyle did have a crisis to avert, so perhaps not. The Ambassador waved a hand dismissively in the air and turned back to his conversation. Yes, there it was—most certainly not.

Doyle lingered a moment longer, saying, "One last thing—I could not help but overhear," he said, watching Liam continue to stir their cups of tea, "that you have some things that belong to me. I'll take them now, please, and then be on my way." He didn't wait for George to hand him Coreen's letters. Instead Doyle stepped closer, his father seeming small now, almost as though he were cowering behind the huge oaken desk. Doyle gently lifted the envelope from the near corner pile and peered inside. His love letters, tied in Coreen's hair ribbon, smelled of salt and were still slightly damp.

"What happened to her body? I want to see her," said Doyle.

"Well, that's impossible, Wallace. She was drowned, for the love of God. They're burying her right about now," said George. Wallace closed his eyes for a moment and then continued.

"If I hadn't come back—if I hadn't seen these letters—were you ever going to tell me about her, father? Were you ever going to send these on to me?" Doyle asked, the pain in his voice making his words husky.

George just stared at him from his enveloping chair as though he couldn't wait for his son to be gone. "I have my answer, then. Right. I'll have my tea in the kitchen, Liam, if you please," he said crisply.

Liam smiled, and never having spilled anything within living memory, purposely overturned the two readied cups, tucked the arsenic's empty packet back into his perfectly pressed sleeve, and smiled approvingly at his nephew Gallagher's newest recruit.

"Oh, so very sorry, sirs. How clumsy of me! I shall make a fresh pot. Please follow me, sir," said the major domo to Doyle.

〤

Beyond the shadow of a dim streetlight, a white produce lorry idled at the curb in front of Deerpark. Inside, Greta, black overcoat collar pulled high against her pale, angular Aryan cheeks, waited to see which one would emerge from the Ambassador's Residence—Wallace Doyle, or Liam. If it were Wallace, all was well. If Liam, she would pick him up and transport him to safety, because he would have killed Doyle and the ambassador to protect the operation.

When Doyle's cab passed through the iron gates, she smiled triumphantly, threw the lorry into gear, and disappeared into the steady stream of Dublin's evening traffic.

〤

Mattias stood on the Guernsey quay, watching the tide change and the gulls wheel overhead as they dove for their supper. Sunset painted the skies with a few streaks of bright red. *The weather will clear tomorrow,* he thought. *And soon, I can get off this damnable rock out in the middle of wet nowhere.* The Commandant had been pleased with his new asset in Major Wallace Doyle, and now Mattias was bound for more glorious things than managing the brutes who managed the prisoners on Guernsey. Wallace had almost been too easy to manipulate—their old friendship from school days had given Mattias every bit of information he needed in order to press on Doyle's personal soft spots and, now, Doyle was his creature. Mattias lit a cigarette and blew smoke into the constant wind that buffeted the island. His U-boat, patrolling just off the island now, would leave tomorrow to patrol the Irish Sea. Greta would meet him after this was all over, when Wallace and his girl Coreen were of no more use to them. Greta would, of course, "tidy up."

"Sir!" said a guttural voice from behind Mattias' right shoulder. The click of boot heels followed instantly on the word as Mattias turned to see the Oberleutnant standing at rigid attention, arm in the air, his gray, flat eyes seeing nothing and everything at once.

"*Ja,*" said Mattias, returning the salute. "You have decoded Liam's report?" The Oberleutnant handed Mattias a folder and resumed his position while Mattias read through its contents.

Mattias' face darkened and he flicked the butt of the cigarette into the swirling waters below, but all he said was, "You have confirming knowledge of this?"

"*Jawohl!* Straight from Berlin," said the Oberleutnant as a small group of storm troopers gathered to meet the next boatful of Irish laborers.

"At ease," said Mattias, "Come with me to my office and we will discuss this in private." The Oberleutnant fell in behind his commanding officer and they began the descent into the dark, airless bunker. A long, damp stone staircase lead them to the tight little room where Doyle had been interrogated, and then onward to a much larger, warmer space, lavishly appointed with the riches stolen from wealthy Jews. An original Klimt hung on one wall, and a hundred year old, hand woven Turkish carpet covered the floor. Mattias pulled a lamp switch and flooded the room with bright light. He moved behind a huge mahogany desk that had once been a Berlin banker's and sat down. He motioned to one of the thickly padded leather chairs and the Oberleutnant lowered himself stiffly into it.

"This is troubling, to say the least, but not disastrous," Mattias began, looking again at Liam's intelligence report about the sinking of the *Rowan* and the recovery of several bodies, Coreen's among them. The Oberleutnant nodded.

"May I have permission to speak freely, sir?" he said, eyes meeting Mattias's.

Mattias nodded. "What are you thinking?"

"I beg your pardon, sir, but I am thinking that it *is* rather disastrous. Your Major Doyle has no reason at all to help us now, and he knows far too much to be left alive," said the Oberleutnant. "He could already have compromised us. Also, I think he is not trained or ready for this kind of espionage. It's too much pressure for an unstable person, even if he is a genius. I think he will 'crack up,' as the Americans say, and because we have no more leverage on him, he will be uncontrollable. He was not precisely fit even before this girl drowned, but when he learns she is dead? No, I think you have made a terrible mistake."

Mattias bristled at that, but then broke into a practiced smile. "I? I have made a terrible mistake? I think not. Watch and learn, Oberleutnant, watch and learn. Liam says that Wallace has assumed from his father's telephone conversation that the girl is dead, but has not seen her body, nor will he ever. Liam goes on to say that Wallace also knows it was the Allies who attacked Coreen's ship and that he overheard the Ambassador trying to conceal the truth about it. It is the idiotic British RAF commander's fault, not ours, that she is dead, and Wallace's father tried to cover it up. So better still for us—because of that, Wallace, even when he could have, did not share our information with the Ambassor, *richtig?* Where he once felt only somewhat detached from America, now he will viciously hate it and its Allies. The plan is all the same to us, you see. And that is good, because the Commandant is not happy that Wallace has sent only minimal amounts of chromium. We need to impress upon our Major Doyle that he must supply much more, and far more quickly."

"What about our leverage, sir?" reminded the Oberleutnant.

"Ach, still in place. We will make sure Wallace is cooperative by putting in his 'unstable' mind the idea that Coreen is alive—that it is all disinformation from the Allies. And he will then want so badly to believe it that he will convince himself of it, behave accordingly, and there is our leverage, more effective than ever."

The Oberleutnant frowned, but kept further thoughts to himself. His eyes wandered over the Klimt, glittering here and there with the gold leaf the artist was known for using.

He snapped his head back around when Mattias continued, "And so, Oberleutnant, send our contact in Archangel a message. Say that Wallace is to receive a packet at a dead drop, and include the following...."

CHAPTER 15

California coast, August 1943

CAPTAIN HALCYON "HAL" James, United States Marine Corps, was feeling a little silly. It wasn't even because he was sitting in his skivvies and t-shirt on this examination table, although that didn't help; it was everything that had happened from breakfast on. He had run six miles in the morning's PT session and physically, he had never felt better. That, in itself, was remarkable—six months earlier, they'd pulled him out of the Pacific after his squadron had gone down in flames. He alone had survived that air battle, having washed ashore after battling sharks and a searing sun for three days in a life raft. Then there was that month of near starvation on the nameless coral atoll before he was finally discovered and rescued. The effects of malnutrition and exposure were healed, but the sudden attacks of panic and the flashbacks had led to another diagnosis: battle fatigue. They had grounded him for that.

Now, after a few months of hawking war bonds and recruiting, he was back at San Diego, trying to get himself reassigned to flight duty. The process was endlessly circular, going from this office to that doctor and back to this office.

The silliness of his morning was compounded by the maze of ramshackle wooden buildings that made up Camp Pendleton. The base looked like it had been constructed overnight, which wasn't too far from the truth. Logical planning had clearly been scuttled in favor of speed. The wooden-framed buildings of the H-shaped medical complex sat too far apart and Hal had laughed out loud at the circus of nurses, corpsmen, and doctors riding bicycles, frantically trying to make their appointed rounds. *What am I doing here, he thought, don't they know there's a war I need to get back to?* If he passed this physical, it might happen. Then the old adage echoed through his mind in answer: Be careful what you wish for.

Nearby San Diego, despite its comforts, was no place for a Marine officer during wartime. He had resolved that if he couldn't return to flight status, he would request to be assigned to an infantry company, and he would spend the rest of the war as a ground-pounding grunt Marine. At least he would be in the fight and, because of that, he would be able to live with himself. Maybe the shellshock would stop, too.

The doctor's voice snapped him back into the present. "OK Captain, say out loud for me the smallest line you can read." The Navy doctor, a gaunt lieutenant commander wearing thick glasses, pointed to the eye chart on the far wall.

"Z-O-E-C-F-L-D-P-B-T," said Hal.

"Hmm," said the Doc, making a note in Hal's medical file, "twenty-ten. Nothing wrong with your vision." The Doc then placed his stethoscope on Hal's back and asked him to take a few deep breaths. After four times up and down Hal's lungs, he stopped the examination, removed the stethoscope from his ears, and sat down in his chair. An odd look passed over the doctor's thin face.

"Do you know why you are here, Captain James?" said the Doc. "Because there's nothing physically wrong with you."

"I've been saying that for months," Hal said.

"Classic shellshock," said the Doc, reaching for Hal's file and flipping through it. "Episodes of vertigo, panic, tunnel vision, fits of—"

"Doc, if you say 'fainting,' we're gonna have a problem," Hal said. Fainting, in Hal's mind, was what overly-dramatic Hollywood actresses did in Civil War movies while Atlanta burned, not the act of Marines who had pulled the body parts of squadron mates out of burning planes on carrier decks.

The Doc fixed Hal with a careful stare and finished his sentence.

"—blackout. I was about to say blackout. Captain, I've heard about your last battle. You've seen and survived things that would have killed most men. You've done your part. You've done your duty honorably. Now, you need to let yourself off the hook. There's no shame in that," he said, his voice easing into persuasive compassion.

Hal stared at his big feet dangling over the edge of the exam table and shook his head in mute disagreement. "Doc, are we done?"

The doctor sighed, reached in the pocket of his white lab coat and withdrew a pack of cigarettes and offered one to Hal, who declined. The Doc tapped one out of the pack and lit up. "Medicine is as much art as it is science; maybe more so. Physicians require judgment. A patient is not just some machine to be physically repaired and sent back to the front lines. You and I are more than flesh and blood, after all," he said.

But flesh and blood we are, Hal thought. He had seen plenty of flesh and blood, and it looked mighty different when it was smeared all over the deck, unattached to, or not contained inside, someone's body. The part of him that was 'more than'—his mind and heart—had witnessed all of that horror, and remained unhealed because of it.

"I could have you riding out the war here at Camp Pendleton, commanding a nice desk. You've already got your medals and war stories; your greatest dangers now should be sunburn and paper cuts. So just one more question, Captain James. Why do you want to be returned to flight status?"

Hal slid off the exam table and pulled on his trousers. He looked up and said, "Doc, I'm either going to fight 'em flying, or I'm going to fight 'em on the ground. So do what you have to do, but either way, I'm not sitting it out. I was the sole survivor of my entire squadron. I can't sit down when those guys gave all."

The doctor nodded slowly, ground out the cigarette, and scribbled some things on a form for Hal's file.

Minutes later, Hal stepped outside, feeling solid and sufficiently armored now that he had his uniform back on. As he strode between the buildings, he dodged a weaving bicycle, almost surprised that it hadn't been ridden by a clown. In the wake of the bicycle, a breathless young lance corporal with a bad case of acne hustled toward him. Hal was only twenty-three himself, but this kid looked like he hadn't gone through puberty yet. The corporal halted two paces in front of Hal, straightened to attention, and saluted. "Captain James?" the corporal asked.

"Who's asking?" Hal replied, grinning and trying to lighten the mood and the corporal's by-the-book manner. The confused corporal stood frozen like a statue, so Hal returned the salute, thereby releasing him.

"Sir, I have orders to take you to the Base Commander's office, on the double," the corporal said, his voice cracking.

Base Commander? Could this morning get any stranger, Hal thought as he watched a pretty nurse, cape flying behind her, ride by. "Barnum and Bailey," said Hal, "Where are the elephants?"

The puzzled corporal stared at Hal for several beats, unsure of what to say to the question. "Uh, no sir, no elephants, sorry. But my jeep is parked right over there," he stammered.

Hal shook his head and chuckled. "Lead the way, ringmaster!"

CHAPTER 16

SANTA SABINA HAD been a short flight from San Diego. After a quick, somewhat puzzling briefing, Hal discovered he had not passed the flight physical after all, and they had cut him new orders. As the army C-46 transport plane touched down at Santa Sabina Army Air Base, which was located somewhere north of Los Angeles, Hal took another look at those orders. They were intriguing, mostly because of their vagueness, which translated to secrecy. What he did know was that upon his arrival at Santa Sabina, he was to meet an Army Air Forces junior officer from the 412th Test Wing who would escort him to the wing's flight research compound—the "Angel's Roost"—which was separate from the main base. It had been made plain to him that this information, especially the location of the compound, was released to persons only on a need-to-know basis.

He folded the typed orders and placed them back in his breast pocket. From his briefing, he knew the army air base was a major port to the Pacific theater, and the Air Transport Command, or ATC, had seen fit to take over most of the base. The host wing was the 338th, and from what Hal could see from the plane's tiny window, it had to be one of the busiest air bases on the West Coast. Tons of materiel on countless pallets were being loaded and unloaded, and large cargo planes comprised the majority of the air traffic. The place looked like a huge supply depot.

Hal climbed down the ladder of the C-46 and stepped onto the tarmac. With a quick look around, he spotted his seabag, which had been carelessly tossed out of the cargo hold. As he retrieved it, a voice called out to him. "Captain James, sir?"

Hal turned to see a boyish Army second lieutenant standing next to a parked gun jeep, the type normally used only in a combat zone. "Lieutenant Pritchard here, and we have your transport waiting." A stout private jumped from the jeep to take the seabag.

Hal slid into the vacated passenger seat and the private climbed back in and stood to man the mounted Browning .30 belt-fed machine gun. *Why would the army be chauffeuring me around in a gun jeep on American soil?* Hal wondered as they took off.

At the edge of the base, facing east beyond the perimeter fence, a desert landscape opened up before them, reaching all the way to a mountain range on the horizon. The lieutenant drove them to a gate with a guardhouse and a red-and-white candy-striped boom barrier, both manned by armed MPs. Several posted wooden signs screamed out "RESTRICTED AREA" and "AUTHORIZED PERSONNEL ONLY BEYOND THIS POINT," and "USE OF DEADLY FORCE AUTHORIZED." On one side and to the front of the guardhouse, still inside the perimeter fence, two helmeted soldiers manned another .30 Browning machine gun. On the other side of the gate, still within the perimeter, two more helmeted soldiers in a second sandbagged fighting position manned an M18 recoilless rifle. *Holy smokes,* Hal thought, *that thing could take out a tank. What are they guarding out here?* Beyond the guardhouse, a road bordered on both sides by twenty foot, concertina wired, chain-link fences stretched into the distance.

At the guardhouse, the hard-faced MP examined their identification documents, checked his clipboard, then picked up the telephone and said "they're on their way." With his message transmitted, the MP then lifted the boom gate and allowed Hal's jeep to pass.

The lieutenant drove through and headed down the road. Hal couldn't help but feel somewhat trapped and nervous as he looked forward into the narrowing distance. The tall fences and razor wire formed an imposing silvery tunnel that was forcing them toward some destination within the mountains. *This road is a perfect kill zone,* Hal thought. *If someone were to attack us, our jeep would have nowhere to go but forward or back, and we'd be as vulnerable as we were when...*

Suddenly, the road dissolved as his vision blurred and he was flying a fighter over the Pacific, low on fuel, ammunition spent in a horrific dogfight. He had just given the order to turn back when seven Japanese Zeros, hiding in the brilliant sun, swooped into view. His men were flying right toward them!

Beside the lieutenant, in the jeep, Hal's breathing quickened, his palms began to sweat, and he clenched his hands around invisible weapons as he fought the vision for control of his body. For a brief moment, he thought he might pass out. *Count slowly backward; visualize the shape of the numerals,* he reminded himself, and began from twenty. By eight, his breathing had relaxed into normal rhythm and the adrenaline pumping through his veins had dissipated. *I am not in a plane over the Pacific. I am not in a life raft with no water. I am here on the ground in California, in an armed jeep, with two other military men.* The images of fire and flak over endless water subsided as he concentrated and looked past the fences to focus on the horizon. To his left, at the corner of his vision, Lieutenant Pritchard gave him an odd look, but said nothing.

They rode in silence as the road veered south, then looped back around north in the opposite direction, and Hal saw a vast complex of buildings and hangars on the floor of a small valley, ringed by a the horseshoe-shaped mountain range. The opening of the giant horseshoe was a large, flat area completely devoid of any vegetation or rocks. It was a salt flat, one of the many in the western states, where ancient oceans had once covered most of the land, but had dried up with the climate change. What had been the level sea bottom was now the perfect place to test aircraft.

"This is a dry lake bed, Captain," the lieutenant said, anticipating the normal question. "It's a perfect natural runway. We have several different landing strips marked off with painted lines, and we have a huge compass rose painted out there on the flats, visible for miles from the air."

"Why do you need so much landing area?" Hal asked.

"We fly experimental aircraft here and sometimes, you just gotta set 'er down wherever you can," Pritchard said. "Some of the new aircraft designs we're working on—they're not always so cooperative." The lieutenant blithely pointed to a pile of twisted wreckage radiating from a center starburst of blackened ground.

Hence all the secrecy, Hal thought.

"This little canyon is perfect for hiding our section of the base. We built this fence line topped with concertina wire running all around the base of these mountains. That way, no one can climb up to a vantage point and get a glimpse of what's going on out here," the lieutenant said.

"And the gun jeep? The sandbagged fighting positions?" Hal asked.

"More discouragement for the overly-curious. The airspace over this section of the base is restricted, too. It's usually not a problem since most of the air traffic is to the west. We have gun jeeps patrolling the inside perimeter also, mostly for show," he said.

As they got closer to the hidden canyon base, Hal noticed a posted sign with an ominous skull and crossbones declaring "DANGER – MINEFIELD!" Hal arched an eyebrow, and the lieutenant laughed, as though he had seen this reaction from newcomers many times.

"As best I know, the signs are decoys. It wouldn't do to have a mine-field near a runway now, would it? But we stoked the rumor, and no one has tried to run through it yet. The restricted airspace is no joke, though, and we've made it known that we have anti-aircraft batteries set up in the mountains. That has cut down on the 'lost civilian pilot' incidents consid-erably," he said.

Secret airbase, experimental aircraft, cryptic orders, and I'm a pilot. Maybe a stateside job won't be so bad, Hal thought, grinning.

At the end of the road, the jeep came to a stop at another guardhouse with a boom gate, manned by more MPs. This time, the MPs raised the boom and the lieutenant drove them through without challenge. Relieved to be out of the fenced corridor, Hal felt as though he could breath easy again. He looked around the sprawling complex. Someone had done a superb job of planning the Angel's Roost. There were several large han-gars and numerous one- to three-story cinderblock buildings laid out on a grid pattern, and there were more personnel moving about than he had initially guessed. The lieutenant slowed their jeep to a stop in front of one of the central buildings, engaged the parking brake, and they dismounted.

"Captain James, we'll take care of your bag, so if you'll just follow me, I'll show you where to report," the lieutenant said. Hal walked with Pritchard past a large open hangar that contained several unusual aircraft. One appeared to be a wing without a fuselage, but it had landing gear and several engines integrated into its low-profile shape. Hal couldn't be sure if the thing was a fully assembled airplane or still under construction. Another aircraft had large gaping holes on either side of its fuselage, but it wasn't wreckage. The holes appeared to be machined, and even stranger, the plane had no place to put propellers. Hal grew more and more intrigued with each craft they passed.

Eventually they came to a two-story block building with warning signs declaring "AUTHORIZED PERSONNEL ONLY," which they entered.

Inside, the lieutenant led Hal past the MPs at the front desk and through a set of double doors. They stopped in a workshop area that was as large as some small hangars Hal had seen; in fact, it looked very much like a Douglas aircraft assembly plant factory floor he had once visited. Yellow lines painted on the floor delineated several work areas and the air was alive with the hum and whine of power tools. With sparks flying from their grinding wheels, technicians in safety goggles welded, soldered, drilled, and otherwise fabricated parts. Acetylene torches blasted metal shapes into a red-hot glow, and the stink of machine oil and hot metal permeated the atmosphere.

A cluster of Army officers, remarkable because they were the only group not wearing lab coats or coveralls, had gathered around something on a test bench. The lieutenant led Hal up to them and waited politely.

When the talk stopped and one of the men turned to him, the lieutenant said, "General Arnold sir, Captain James is here." General Henry "Hap" Arnold, head of the entire United States Army Air Forces and member of the Joint Chiefs of Staff, settled his gray eyes on Hal. Hal snapped to attention and saluted, noting that General Arnold wore four stars on his epaulets. Rumor had it he was due for a fifth star. That would make him one of only a handful of men to attain such a rank. Even though General Arnold's reputation always preceded him, Hal was awestruck to be in the actual presence of the legendary aviation pioneer. He was a bit surprised at the man's appearance, though. Arnold was only in his fifties, but having suffered two heart attacks, he looked to be in his late sixties or early seventies. His hair, already going white, gave him a gentle, grandfatherly appearance.

Hal said, "Captain James reporting, sir!" General Arnold straightened, smiled at Hal, and returned the salute, apparently approving the cut of Hal's jib.

"Well, Captain James, welcome to our little program," General Arnold said, as he turned to a full-bird colonel on his right. "Clarence, why don't you 'read in' Captain James on what we're doing here," he said, "meanwhile, let me have a look at what we've got in Hangar Nine." And with that, General Arnold detached from the group and headed for the exit, several members of his entourage in tow. Hal followed the group with his eyes, still somewhat surprised by whom he had just encountered.

"Captain James, I'm Colonel Clarence Wesley, Army Air Force. What I am about to disclose to you is classified 'top secret,' and nothing you see, hear, or do here at Angel's Roost shall ever leave the confines of this base. Are we clear on that, Captain?" said Wesley.

"Uh, yes sir," Hal said, turning his attention to Colonel Wesley and one other officer, along with some technicians. Hal already possessed a top-secret security clearance and was well versed in how to keep mum on intelligence reports.

"I am the director of the project code named 'Archangel,' and I'd like to introduce to you another member of the team, Major Wallace Doyle," Wesley said. Hal nodded to Major Doyle, who had the pale, thin, somewhat scholarly look that reminded Hal of what he had seen many times in the British officer ranks. Brit officers were invariably Oxford or Cambridge graduates, of some dangerously inbred noble pedigree, long on brain power, courageous as all get-out, but too skinny and sickly-looking to inspire confidence in a fight. But this guy was an American, so Hal thought it best to put his prejudices aside. Doyle, in turn, regarded Hal with what Hal could classify only as a subdued sneer. With his small, darting eyes and his sour face, Doyle looked like a profoundly unhappy, deeply troubled man.

"Major Doyle is a materials scientist, and you are going to be working hand-in-glove with him... on this," Wesley said, as he directed Hal's attention to the workbench. The lab-coated technicians parted, revealing to Hal a cigar-shaped metallic contraption about eight feet long, bolted into brackets on the bench, with all sorts of metal tubes and wires and other components covering its outer surface. "This, Captain James, is a turbojet engine, and make no mistake—whoever figures it out first, Axis or Allies, will rule the skies, and probably win the war because of it."

Hal looked at the engine for a moment, then said, "Begging your pardon, sir, but why am I here? I'm not a scientist—and I'm a Marine, not army."

"Your background in engineering is why. I'm a West Point man myself, but I suppose an Annapolis graduate will do in a pinch," Wesley said, smiling lopsidedly. "But your experience as a combat pilot is where we need your input the most. That, plus you are alive and available. Men such as yourself are in short supply at the moment."

Yeah, they're all fighting the war or are dead from it, Hal thought ruefully.

"We know you have been attempting to be cleared for combat and that your heart is with your Division in the Pacific. So I'm asking you, can we count on your full commitment to this assignment, Captain? Or have General Arnold and I made a mistake?" Wesley asked, as he gestured for Hal to examine the turbojet. Hal stepped over to the engine and lightly ran his hands over the engineering marvel, noting its impressive multi-blade fan intake where a propeller would have gone, and the exhaust nozzle that looked like something from a rocket motor.

I bet this thing could top 350 knots, Hal thought. *"Rule the skies" is right. I've got to take a ride in whatever this beast is bolted into.* He turned to address Colonel Wesley. "Yes, you can count on me, sir," he said, now almost glad he had failed the flight physical.

Before Colonel Wesley could offer comment, a technical sergeant came up and interrupted them. "Colonel Wesley, we'll be ready to run the test for General Arnold and his group over at the blockhouse in about thirty minutes."

"Excellent," Wesley said, turning to Hal. "Well, Captain James, you're just in time for the show."

Half an hour later, Hal and a dozen other men had crammed into the ten by ten foot blockhouse on the test range. The blockhouse was a cinderblock bunker used to observe experiments, rocket launches, and anything else that might explode spectacularly. It was an especially important protective measure when men such as General Arnold were observing. In addition to the General and his staff, Colonel Wesley, Major Doyle, and a few technicians were jammed uncomfortably into the small space, and the ceiling brushed the heads of the taller members of the party. Hal, the tallest one in the group, felt his claustrophobia closing in again, so he jockeyed for position nearest the door.

Colonel Wesley quietly addressed the group. "General Arnold, gentlemen, as you well know, the Archangel program has been beset by performance issues. Higher temperatures for the turbojet mean more thrust, so what we're trying today is a new means of boosting that thrust: water injection. I believe we will see a large boost in power. Sergeant, you may begin the test."

The men in the bunker leaned to peer through the observation slits at a turbojet assembly that was bolted onto a rugged stationary steel frame about one hundred feet downrange. The technical sergeant barked, "clear the test area!" over the PA system, gave it a moment, then threw a switch. The jet engine powered up with a high-pitched whine. Hal could see the exhaust nozzle blasting an orange, then blue flame that gradually "tuned in" to its optimally efficient range. The engine continued to climb through its power band and the high-pitched whine of the turbine was soon accompanied by an almost musical, dulcet tone, like an orchestra of violins holding the same note. *This baby really sings*, Hal thought. Then suddenly, there was a deafening *crack!*, a huge ball of orange light, and a ferocious *ka-boom!*

As the shock wave from the explosion rocked the blockhouse, all the men inside instinctively ducked down below the observation slits, lest flying shrapnel tear their heads off. As clouds of dust rolled into the slits, Hal dove for the corner, his hands shaking, sweat suddenly pouring down his face. Gripped by the overwhelming need to escape, he bolted through the door as the technical sergeant screamed, "No, wait!" It was too late. Hal was already outside the blockhouse.

He bent double and gripped his knees for a moment, then began to count through his numerals and in a little while, he could breathe again.

Hal stood up and turned to the test range to see technicians descending on the burning test bench, their fire extinguishers blasting white clouds of carbon dioxide at the pieces of flaming wreckage. Thick black smoke rose into the air in great waves and billows. Hal composed himself, straightened his uniform, and tried his best to affect an air of nonchalance when the rest of the men filed out of the blockhouse. The technical sergeant sidled up to Hal discreetly.

"Sir, it's best to give it a few seconds before exiting. Sometimes there are secondary explosions," he said.

"Thanks Sergeant; just couldn't wait to see what went wrong," Hal joked as he looked over to see Colonel Wesley confer with General Arnold, who was frowning at the ruined engine in disappointment. Then the General and his staff gathered up and ambled away, leaving Wesley and the technical group, including Major Doyle, to clean up. Hal felt Doyle's eyes on him and looked up to see the Major intently studying him. Had Doyle noticed his panic attack? Hal smiled back at him as though nothing had happened, but Major Doyle just held his gaze and raised an eyebrow.

A second later, Colonel Wesley gestured for Hal and Major Doyle to gather 'round as he let out a deep sigh. "That, gentlemen, was a glimpse of the challenge that lies before you," he said.

"Well sir, I'd say it's a doozy," Hal said.

Wesley shook his head as he regarded the smoking, melted debris. "The General and I are expecting great things from you now, and as soon as last week. The free world is depending on you."

CHAPTER 17

A COUPLE OF weeks later, in one of the secure buildings not far from the hangars at Angel's Roost, Hal sat at his drafting table. The common work area, designed for promoting communication and the exchange of ideas among the design team, was the engineering equivalent of a chemistry laboratory. Besides other Archangel personnel, some civilian contractors, at least one Navy officer, and even the two Brits Hal figured were probably RAF, regularly came and went, scratched on the blackboard and discussed solutions to the day's problems. For the most part, the participants in Archangel had a free hand regarding their activities—only the aircraft dictated the tasks at hand. That was the usual order of the day, although Colonel Wesley popped in periodically throughout the workday, or night, to make sure everything moved forward.

Hal watched a heated discussion become an argument at the blackboard and then resolve itself with the erasure of a formula. Though he was the only experienced combat pilot assigned to the design team, he hadn't been asked to fly anything. All he had done for days was stare at scorched or melted components retrieved from the engine test explosion, measure their fractures with calipers, and doodle on his drafting paper, trying to look useful.

"So what do you have for me, Captain James?" Major Doyle said, suddenly speaking from behind Hal's shoulder, just out of his peripheral vision. *I hate when he sneaks up on me like that*, Hal thought, trying his best not to appear startled as he turned to face the Major.

"Well Major, not much, as it were. I mean, we obviously have catastrophic component failure, but I'm not sure that it's the fault of the alloys," Hal said bleakly. Doyle's face soured—well, soured a little more.

"Are you telling me my business, Captain?" Doyle asked, snapping out the words.

"No sir, but at this rate, if we keep increasing the weight of the compressor blades and the combustion chamber, we'll end up with an engine with such a low thrust-to-weight ratio that it will be useless as a fighter," Hal said, and then translated it to visual terms. "The thing will be a bumblebee. Too heavy to fly."

"Our job is to deliver a reliable, functioning aircraft. That means one that doesn't explode in mid-flight. Strengthening the components is the only way to achieve that," Doyle said. "So I don't want to hear what you *can't* do, Captain James. I want to hear solutions, for you can be assured that the Germans are finding solutions!"

"With respect sir, I'm suggesting that maybe there's another path—a way to achieve reliability without increasing weight," Hal said.

"Unless you have some new lightweight wonder elements from another planet, we're constrained by what is on the periodic table, so make do. Strength first, performance second. Are we clear?" Doyle said. He turned and stormed off without waiting for Hal to reply.

Hal massaged his temples for a moment. He picked up his drafting pencil, then put it back down. He'd been at it since 0600, before anyone else had come in, and it was now 1900. He smiled at the thought of his upcoming twenty-four hour liberty pass and when he saw Major Doyle leave for the night, he knew he was clear to go. He switched off his desk lamp and gathered up his gear.

A little while later, Hal strolled down Los Angeles's Hollywood Boulevard, trying to clear his mind and get a new perspective on things. Tinsel Town did a great job of carrying on with its business of manufacturing glamour and seemed almost unaffected by the war, he mused. That is, except for the so-called "Battle of Los Angeles" last year that he had heard about, when the panicky city declared a red-alert and went into total blackout mode. The gunners of the 37th Coastal Artillery Brigade went wild in response, firing over 1,400 anti-aircraft shells at phantoms in the night sky. The shrapnel and many unexploded shells had fallen back onto the city, causing untold damage and killing eight people. *What goes up must come down,* Hal thought.

Tonight, however, the war was a long way away from Hollywood. Servicemen in uniform strolled, stumbled, or staggered down the sidewalks, boisterously showing off for their giggling dates. The noticeably visible Shore Patrol and MPs kept order on the streets, while dance clubs blasted swing music and movie marquees twinkled their new offerings. *So much for keeping the lighting discipline*, he thought, as he watched twin spotlights sweep the sky for the sole purpose of drawing attention to a movie premiere.

Some street musicians tuned up for an impromptu jam session on the sidewalk and Hal stepped around them, then continued past a newsstand. He stopped when something caught his eye. Among the myriad magazines and newspapers, the latest *Look* magazine's cover featured a story on the Women's Airforce Service Pilots. Hal smiled to himself as he pulled a copy from the rack. He tossed the vendor a dime and tucked the folded magazine under his arm. When he spotted the inviting green and purple neon sign of the Frolic Room cocktail lounge next to the Pantages Theater, he decided it was time to sit down for a bit.

Inside, a haze of cigarette smoke and perfume filled the air, and the neon beer signs behind the bar flickered green and purple and blue. Hal found an empty stool at the bar under the best light in the room, a yellow neon flower decoration. One of his favorites, Glenn Miller's *Tuxedo Junction*, played on the jukebox. He ordered a beer, laid the oversized magazine on the bar, and flipped through the pages until he found the article on the WASP. He almost whooped out loud at the familiar face in one of the photos. It was a close shot of a petite, attractive—no, beautiful—girl, wearing a "Zoot" suit and aviator sunglasses, a parachute slung over her shoulder. The caption read, "WASP Trainee Sprite Shannon of Lowland Mill, Georgia, heads to the flightline." He smiled as he slowly traced his finger over her photo. *Well, fly girl, I guess you made it,* he thought. *Good for you, little Sprite....* Truth be told, Hal had often thought about the time he met Sprite Shannon. It was at the Atlanta Peach Festival. Something about her eyes...and hair...and smile. She had run after Ethel

Sheehy, and that was the last Hal had seen of her that day until he and his buddy had passed by her plane on the way to their own. He had seen Sprite sleeping under her Stearman, alone and so tiny in the darkness, and had just wanted to stand guard over her all night long. Hal mused at the photograph of the girl in his memory. She was training at Sweetwater. How about that!

Protecting the magazine from bar spills, he folded it closed and finished his beer. For some reason, he suddenly felt better than he had in a long time. A warm sensation grew in his chest, and with the smile lingering on his face, he decided he needed some live music to match his pleasant mood.

Five minutes and a few doors down the street, the Picador Nightclub's crowd seemed surprisingly mellow, but it was early yet—the band hadn't begun to play. Hal grabbed a seat at the bar and ordered another beer. He swiveled around and sipped as he watched an older gentleman with a red silk triangle in his dinner jacket breast pocket take a seat at the upright piano on stage and tickle the keys to warm up. Hal unconsciously matched the music's tempo with the fingers of his free hand. Eventually the other band members drifted onto the stage and began their warm-ups as well. The saxophone player leaned in to the piano player, who pulled out a tuning fork and thumped it on the piano cabinet. The sax player blew a steady note trying to match the resulting tone the fork produced… and Hal's restless, drumming fingers stopped.

Hal felt his focus narrow to tunnel vision and he almost fell off the stool. But this time, it wasn't a panic attack. He pulled out his pen, turned around to face the bar, and snatched up a cocktail napkin. As he scribbled some notes, he thought, *Are you kidding me? Could it really be that simple?* He slid off his bar stool and strode to the stage.

"Hey mister, would you mind telling me where I could get my hands on one of those?" Hal asked the piano player, pointing at the tuning fork.

"Willie's Music Shop on Sunset sells 'em for a coupla bucks," the piano man said.

"You think they'd be open tonight?" Hal asked, already knowing the answer. The piano man just chuckled and shook his head.

"Cap'n, Willie's done closed up and headed to the Blue Note by now," he said. "Is it a musical emergency?" he asked, and the sax player chuckled, too.

"More like a military emergency," Hal said, eyes sober and earnest.

Reading Hal's face correctly, the piano player picked up the tuning fork and held it out for him. "In that case, just take this one," the piano man said. "Gotta do my part, you know?"

Ж

The dawn found Hal back in the Angel's Roost common area scrawling equations and formulas on the huge blackboard. He put the chalk down and took a few steps back for an overview. He'd headed directly back to the base from The Picador and already had at least one pot of coffee in him, which was why his hands were shaking as he worked his slide rule. Concentrating intently, he didn't hear Major Doyle enter.

"Captain, what the hell are you doing in here? I thought you had twenty-four hours' liberty!" Doyle said, for no other reason than to be argumentative.

"You're just in time!" said Hal excitedly, without looking up, "I'm calculating iterations, using N.A.C.A. airfoils of differing cross-sectional area!"

"I'll remind you to address me as either Major or sir," Doyle said, standing on formality.

"Major, I just need to enter values for a few of these variables," Hal said, going back to the blackboard and picking up the chalk. "For E, I need the Young's modulus in pascals for the chromium alloy you've fabricated. And then for rho, I need the density of the chromium alloy in kilograms per cubic meter," Hal said.

"Captain James, you do not tell me what you need, I tell you what I need," Doyle said.

"Major Doyle, sir, if it wouldn't be too much trouble, sir, I could use your assistance in providing values for these variables, Major, sir. Thank you, sir," Hal said, figuring the terminally insecure Doyle would interpret the saracasm as respect. Doyle regarded Hal in angry silence for a moment, but Hal didn't care anymore. He didn't have time for it right now. He was about to achieve a breakthrough.

"All right, I'll get the figures," Doyle said, relenting somewhat as he evaluated the equations on the blackboard. "But first, tell me what you've got."

Hal picked up the tuning fork and thumped it on the side of a desk, making it reverberate with a precisely pitched ringing tone. While it held the vibrations, he plunged the fork into his cup of coffee and brown liquid sprayed out in all directions. Looking up at Doyle, he said, "I figured out why our engines are exploding."

Doyle sat down, the frown on his face deepening, but he was clearly interested. "And what will fix a vibrational explosion, Captain James?" he said, skeptically. "When you have actual blueprints, I'll look at them."

"Done," Hal said, and sat back down at his table. Four hours later, he had finished drafting the rotor designs into blueprints that Doyle could take to the floor.

"I don't know...I want to think about these a bit longer, Captain," Doyle said, peering down his long nose. "See if you have missed anything of import. I'll put them in the safe when I'm done."

Hal stopped erasing and stepped back, quite certain he had missed nothing, and that these were the designs that would solve their problems. He'd troubleshot it all night and it always worked. On paper, at least. But Hal had to have Doyle on board to get a prototype into production for testing, so he held his tongue. He knew better than to trust what he might say after a day without sleep.

It must have shown, because Doyle's next remark was, "You should go to bed now, Captain. You're no good to me too tired to think." Hal's left eye narrowed ever so slightly. Since when had Doyle cared about how much sleep Hal got? But he was tired, and Doyle waved a dismissive hand toward him, and he made his weary way back to his rack for a few hours of rest.

When the last set of doors closed behind Hal and the MP's were repositioned beside them, Major Doyle locked Hal's designs in the safe, put the carbons in the day's burn bag, flipped the switch on his intercom and said, "Mildred, I'll be going out for awhile. Please take care of today's burn bag."

Mildred pushed her horn-rimmed glasses up her big, bulbous nose, yawned, and gave Doyle the form to sign as he sealed the burn bag. Slipping on one heel, Doyle caught himself and began walking down the empty, freshly waxed hallway and out into the bright Santa Sabina sunlight, trying to think of ways to commandeer more chromium. Hal's designs were promising. Maybe Mattias would be pleased to have them and they might buy Doyle a little more time. The blades on Captain James' rotor designs also required a great deal of chromium. And Hal would have to order it. Maybe it was quite possible that somewhere along the chain of requisitions, a good bit of it could be diverted. And Captain Hal James would be on the hook for it.

CHAPTER 18

Avenger Field, Sweetwater, Texas

THE AUGUST NIGHTS in Sweetwater brought little relief to the daytime heat, and by the end of the month, the trainees were exhausted and cranky. Ninette, as one of the two newly appointed Flight Lieutenants, had just returned from today's discussion with Mrs. Deaton, the Establishment Officer, about the stifling temperatures in the barracks.

"Good news, girls," she said, as they waited for her nightly report. "Diedee says we can pull our cots out into the yard to sleep until the weather improves. It won't be much of a change, but maybe the breeze will help us get some rest."

Sprite had been lying in her cot, ready for lights out, but immediately jumped up and said, "Let's go. It has to be better out there than in here." The others voiced weak agreement and began to drag the army-issue cots into the area in between the barracks. They lined up the cots so that they were squared into formation and within a few minutes, the girls in the other bays joined them. Word had traveled fast.

"What do you think about this place, Sprite?" said Gertie, settling in to her cot and looking up at the vast sky filled with huge bright stars.

"Well," Sprite began, finding the North Star, then marking Orion,

"Sure is different from home, but I like it here. The work is no harder than farm work, and the food is so much better. Plus, I never got paid to do farm work—it just meant we got to eat! Can you imagine? We get $150 *a month*. My Daddy never made more than that a month in his whole life, and he was a man! Also, I'm beginning to see a great big purpose to what we are doing. Back on the farm, I had never really thought I could help with the war, but now that I'm here and I see all of us together training like soldiers, I kind of like knowing I'm part of the cause. Seems like I'm different from the person I was even two weeks ago. I've always had responsibilities with keeping our house and helping Daddy in the business, and school, of course—but this feels so different. This is maybe what my father called my 'destiny.' I remember when I asked him if I could fly his plane. He sat for a minute and then he just said, 'Alright then,' and the next day, I was in the air, taking my first lesson with him."

A little self conscious at her lengthy response, Sprite marveled at how she had opened up to the girls. She could hear the twin's smile when she replied, "Yeah? That's swell, Sprite. I like it, too, even if it's the hardest thing I've ever done. How about these dogtags?" She rattled hers on the end of their chain.

"Yes, they're kind of odd on us women, aren't they?" Sprite laughed.

"I heard it's because if we crash a plane and die, they'll know which one of us it was for sure, just like soldiers in the war. I mean, you know—when they're all messed up dead, not just dead," Ninette added.

"Yeah," said Bertie, a little less enthusiastically, "I hadn't thought about that. Makes sense, though."

"Don't think about it, Sis," said her twin. "Nobody should think about it." Sprite nodded her agreement, even though no one could see her.

"Say, I heard we get to move to another plane tomorrow!" said Ninette. "I'll be glad to get out of those little kittens they are making us fly first! I swear to you, my engine coughed up a furball the other day!"

"I'll be glad, too," said Gertie. "We can hardly even fit into those toys! Big girls need big planes! I can't wait!"

"And I can't wait to get to sleep," said Phoebe, her voice sharp with irritation. "Knock it off or I'll report all of you."

Sprite turned over and before her head settled into the thin pillow, she was asleep, dreaming of Orion the hunter wheeling overhead, watching over her all night long.

The next morning, somewhat before dawn, reveille sounded and startled Sprite out of deep sleep, and when she automatically rolled out of her cot, only half conscious, she shrieked hard awake with an "*Eep!*" when her bare feet hit the sandy ground.

It was a good thing she had. Coiled beside Phoebe's cot, flicking its tongue out to taste the air, was one of the largest rattlesnakes Sprite had ever seen—and Georgia had some whoppers. At her sudden commotion, the snake had apparently stopped crawling and was poised, head swaying, gradually winding up for a strike. Sprite thought she was still dreaming for a moment, and then she shrieked again. "Phoebe! Get up *right now*! Stand up in your cot and jump over the head rail! Don't put your feet down over here!"

Phoebe yawned and raised herself up in her cot and fixed Sprite with a sleepy frown. "What...?" she began, and then she heard the irritated snake join the conversation with its unmistakable rattle. Phoebe's eyes popped wide and she rolled up into a tight ball in the middle of the cot, screaming, "Is that a snake? Where is it? Is it in my bed? Oh, God, oh God, oh God!"

Sprite had frozen, her intense green eyes on the yellow, slitted ones of the snake. Its head had to be a handspan wide, and five fat body coils promised more than six feet in length. Its striking reach might be yards long. "Bertie, Gertie, go get Mrs. Lowe and tell her to bring her pistol," Sprite said quietly, thinking about just how close she was to the startled snake. "Phoebe, it's too late to move. He isn't interested in you. He was just wanting to get away, but if you move now, he'll strike, and don't you think he can't turn around and go backwards quicker than you can blink!" The snake's rattling had become faster and louder as Sprite spoke. She watched the reptile weave its head, searching for a heat target, drawing ever backward into huge coils that tightened like a massive spring. Sprite kept quiet and still for the longest thirty seconds of her life until she heard the crack of Meredith's pistol and saw the snake's head explode into pieces, most of them landing ten feet away from its writhing body.

A few landed somewhat closer. Tiny pieces of snakeskin caught in her thick dark hair, Phoebe leapt from the cot and onto Sprite, all her pent up fear spilling out in one big scream in Sprite's ear, "Oh my God! Oh my God! Oh *my God!*"

Who's making all the noise now? thought Sprite, untangling herself from Phoebe and the bits of dead snake.

Just then, Meredith shot the pistol again and, its coils twisting furiously, another long body separated from its triangular head and exploded into the air. All the girls leapt to stand atop their cots, searching in the glow of dawn to see if there were any more of the rattlers on the ground.

"Over here!" an unfamiliar voice from way down the line called. Meredith sighed, pushed her hair back behind her ears, checked her pistol, and walked down the line in only her t-shirt, underwear... and cowboy boots.

⚜

"I'm sorry. I should have told you about them last night," Meredith apologized as they waited in the ready room near the flight line for their turns in the air that afternoon. "Sweetwater is the rattlesnake capital of all the earth, I think. There is a big 'rattler round-up' here every fall, before the snakes find rocks and holes to crawl into for the winter. They don't exactly hibernate, like bears—it's called 'estivation,' and it means they are partly awake. Rattlers mate in the winter in those holes, so you can see why the round-up is held before then. I'm really sorry. That could have been bad. I didn't think about it—everyone here knows about them."

Sprite finished an Oreo and said, "Instructor Lowe, how do we keep from getting bitten? If the snakes are all over the ground at night—"

"Well, the best way is to stay in your cots. It also helps to use a flashlight and wear boots if you need to get up. Most snakebites happen on the lower legs, but those buggers can certainly go vertical, too. They can climb trees, come to think of it, but that's no issue out here," she finished, waving a hand at the treeless airfield. "Your cots have metal legs—and those get cold at night, so the snakes are repelled. They are hunting heat. Mostly, they want nothing to do with us. We're too big for food. Just don't provoke them, and be alert. Should be enough. Oh, and check your planes every time. They like to crawl up into them from time to time and snuggle into the warm cockpits."

Bertie and Gertie looked at each other, one the mirror image of the other, and mouthed, "Snuggle into the warm cockpits?"

Sprite, thinking beyond the horrors of flying with snakes in her lap, asked, "Instructor Lowe, could we maybe get some cowboy boots like yours?"

Meredith smiled and said, "Well, sure! That's a great idea—cowboy boots are the best to fly in as well, because if you have an engine fire, your feet won't be burned right away. And you're in Texas, girls! They'll custom make them here for you. How about you give me your sizes and we'll get you fitted up? Takes about two weeks to finish them, so by the time you get your first paycheck, they'll be ready."

Sprite smiled hugely from behind her Coca-Cola and the other girls, except for Phoebe, who was chatting with Liesel at the next table, looked at Sprite like she had actually invented Coca-Cola. "All right, then," she said, smiling as she heard her father's voice echo in her own.

X

A week later, another hot afternoon dragged by, leaving everyone exhausted and quiet. Sprite had drawn the last flight for the day, so the other girls had gone back to the barracks, leaving her to finish alone. Meredith sat in the rear cockpit again. Sprite revved her engine and stared down the long runway, then accelerated down the airstrip waiting patiently for the plane to reach takeoff speed. Piloting this PT-13 Stearman trainer was like flying a bus after her years with her beefy, souped-up Stearman, and it seemed like it was all the sluggish plane could do to find the power to lift off.

They were motoring down the strip when a huge, red spotted bull strode onto the landing strip and turned toward them, legs astraddle, horns lowered, front hooves pawing the ground. He waggled his head and began to run at Sprite's plane, picking up speed perhaps even faster than the Stearman, quickly closing the gap between himself and the plane with a thundering gallop.

"Oh, no!" shouted Meredith over the com, "I thought he had gone for good! Take us up right now! Right now! He's charging and he won't back down!"

"What? Who? Why is that bull on the runway, Mrs. Lowe? Is this some kind of new test?" Sprite yelled into her microphone as she slammed the throttle, jerked back on the stick and willed the Stearman into the air mere yards in front of the charging bull.

As they zoomed over the disappointed bull, Meredith said dismally, "No, that's just Chihuahua…. He's kind of a legend around here. Comes onto the runways and tries to fight the planes. The Base Commander has sent gunners after him time and again, but they are never able to find him. The Base Commander himself went out hunting him the last time, took a shot straight at him, and nicked one of his horns, but all he ever found were Chihuahua's hoof prints—the bull got clean away, which really powdered the Base Commander's nose. So our leader declared a personal vendetta against the bull, and even told the gunners to stop their hunting because he wanted the last word with that horned demon himself. We thought Chihuahua had been scared off because of the shot hitting his horn, because it's been awhile since he's been seen—the Base Commander thought he had won that bullfight. Guess not!"

Sprite laughed, now that they were safely in the air. "Well, that was a close one! Hey, why do you call him Chihuahua? He's enormous! And those horns! He's the biggest bull I've ever seen!" Sprite had circled over the strip again just to take another look at the bull, who was now forlornly bellowing at the plane, head tilted up and back so far that his horns, one of them clearly missing its tip, pointed downward.

"He came with the name. Well, he escaped with the name, more like. As that local legend has it, Chihuahua fought in a Mexican bullring once in the town of Chihuahua, and because he was so entertaining and smart, the matador honored him by asking the crowd if he could let the bull live, and they agreed. A bull fights in the ring only once, because after that, if he lives, he knows what's going on and he's really dangerous—as if being an angry bull with big horns isn't already dangerous enough. His owner brought him up here and put him out to stud on a ranch about twenty miles from the airfield, but the bull keeps getting out of his pasture. Chihuahua likes to fight and he thinks the planes are the only opponents worthy of his illustrious reputation!"

"Mrs. Lowe, is there anything else we need to know about the local wildlife?" laughed Sprite, thinking it would be good to get in front of any more surprise critter confrontations.

"Well," Meredith began, laughing. "There are the tarantulas, but they hide most of the time."

"Tarantulas!" Sprite exclaimed. The largest spider she had ever seen in person had been a wolf spider, and in Georgia, everyone let those live to eat the cockroaches.

Meredith chuckled. "They are, like everything in Texas, huge. But really, there is no venom in our variety here. The bites hurt, though. There are scorpions, too, and some of them are quite dangerous. Just shake your shoes every time you put them on and don't put your hands where you can't see first."

"I'll remember that," said Sprite, making a mental note to tell the others. Rogue cattle, snakes, spiders, and scorpions. It seemed that the only safe place at Sweetwater was in the air.

✕

An hour later, when Sprite circled the field as she finished her flight, she searched the vastness of the desert scrub for Chihuahua, but he was nowhere to be found. For miles and miles in any direction, there was no cover, nowhere a bull that size could hide. If Meredith hadn't seen him, too, Sprite would have sworn she imagined him.

She landed the plane, still musing about Chihuahua, but forgot the bull instantly when Ninette met them on the ground, a strained look on her face. Ninette fixed Meredith with a sympathetic eye. "Instructor Lowe…I'm sorry, but we just heard about a huge battle against the Japanese in the Solomon Islands, some place called Bella Lavella. A squadron from the 3rd Marine Aircraft Wing lost most of its men, and several others are listed as missing in action." A look passed between Meredith and Ninette that Sprite couldn't fathom, and Meredith ran for the Administration building. Sprite walked back in silence to the barracks with Nin, who finally said, "It's her husband, Sprite. That's his unit. She'll be trying to find out if he's OK." Sprite nodded and said nothing, and at evening mess, she noticed Meredith wasn't there.

Who was there, however, was the Base Commander.

CHAPTER 19

"SO, HE'S KINDA cute in that mature, Stewart Granger way," said Phoebe, watching the Base Commander as he sat down at the officers' table in the mess. Seated beside the Base Commander was the PT instructor, Buzz.

"Yeah," said Liesel slyly, "If you like older men, I guess. I have my eye on Buzz, actually, even if he is married."

"You and a hundred other girls here!" replied Phoebe. "We are surrounded by women all day and night, except for Buzz, the doctors, and the male flight instructors, which I never seem to draw for training. It's always Meredith or Constance in my backseat. Oh, Liesel, he's going to look over here!" Phoebe poked Liesel's arm and Liesel followed her gaze.

The Base Commander, a stocky, balding man of about forty-five and a full-bird colonel, had stopped speaking to Buzz and was scanning the room. When he found Liesel's table, his gaze lingered on her for a moment.

"Hmmm," said Liesel as the Base Commander stared at her. "I wonder what that's about." She threw back her shoulders and smiled back at him.

The next morning, at Saturday Morning Inspection, she found out. After a morning cleaning frenzy, the girls in Bay J-5 stood at attention beside their cots, ready for Buzz to make his usual rounds. If everyone passed, then the whole bay was free for the evening. If they didn't, everyone in the bay stayed there scrubbing the bathroom floor with toothbrushes while the rest of the Flights went to the Avengerette Club or the movies or did whatever they wanted off post. The bay was spic and span, the cots ready to bounce quarters on, and all the surfaces, so difficult to keep clean because of the windblown sand outside, had just been dusted.

However, something was odd about today's inspection. Buzz did not show up. Instead, it was the Base Commander himself who slid on the white gloves and ran his hands along baseboards and over chair legs. After a few strained minutes of breath holding, the others had passed individually, and Liesel confidently waited her turn so that she could join them for their night in town.

"What's your name, Ladybird?" said the Base Commander, turning to Liesel. He frowned at her as he looked past her shoulder at her locker.

Liesel said, "I'm Liesel Rongeur, sir." She stood at attention as he moved around her and kicked the trashcan by her bed.

"Trash in the can, two demerits, unfolded clothing, one demerit, dust on the baseboard behind your cot, one demerit. And that uniform is wrinkled at the seat, one demerit," he recited, drily. The other girls were now staring sidelong daggers at Liesel. More than five demerits meant they all stayed back, and the Base Commander was not finished. Liesel colored with rage at the Base Commander's assessment, but kept quiet. Then, to her shock, he put his hand under the waistband of her pants at the hip and said, as he stared into her eyes, "Your seams do not line up, Miss Rongeur. Two demerits." Liesel was so angry she almost didn't notice that he left his hand on her hip a little bit too long.

And then she did notice. She returned the Base Commander's stare with alacrity, and said, "Sir, I believe you have made a mistake. I th—"

The Base Commander cut her off mid-word. "Insubordination, three demerits. Actionable total, Miss Rongeur. The rest of you will report to work detail and I will expect you, Miss Rongeur, to report to my office at 1700 hours today after you have cleaned up your area. Seems we have some things to get straightened out," he said as he drew his hand very slowly over the seam of her tucked shirt, lingering at the place on her hip where the shirt met her bare skin. He turned on his heel and left her to the mercy of her baymates.

Who had none. Whatsoever.

"You idiot!" said the girl at the end of the cot line, once the Base Commander was out of earshot. The others fell out and joined her, lining up across from Liesel, their arms crossed over their chests and their eyes wide with anger. The girl who had spoken continued, "Look what you've done to us! We all passed and you have now wrecked our evening out, not to mention we will be on our knees under the plumbing for hours. Why didn't you clean?"

"I did clean. Look for yourselves. And my uniform is not wrinkled anywhere, and, yes, there is trash in the can, but that's on all of us—the can just happens to be closest to me. I don't know what's going on here, but I'll find out tonight," she said, breaking through the line. The others dispersed and began figuring out ways to get word to the boyfriends and the club that they could not make their dates. Liesel, however, gave her meeting with the Base Commander some long, hard thought, and by the time she was ready to report, she had figured out exactly what she would do.

X

At 1700 hours on the dot, Liesel walked into the Base Commander's anteroom, expecting to see his secretary sitting at her desk. But it was Saturday, Liesel remembered—Margie wouldn't be there. She sat down on the hard metal chair, but before she could even smooth her hair, the Base Commander opened his office door and motioned her in. He closed the door with a snick of the lock, lowered the blinds, tilted them closed, and then pulled a bottle of whiskey and two glasses from his desk drawer. He walked to the long red leather sofa that stretched out on one side of the office, sat down, and dragged over a coffee table burdened with several *Look* magazines and a thick trainee manual. A portrait of Franklin D. Roosevelt hung behind the sofa, almost matching it for length. The Base Commander beckoned again to Liesel.

"Have a seat," he said as he patted the sofa and poured two fingers of whiskey into each glass. "I saw your picture in the magazine last week," he said, holding one of the *Look* issues, its black and white cover photo showing Bay J-5 girls in front of a PT-19.

Liesel walked over to stand in front of him. He smiled up at her, not bothering to hide the leer in his eyes as he looked at the way her breasts strained the buttons on her uniform blouse.

Liesel smiled back. This was exactly what she thought might happen, and she was ready for it. She made a quick physical assessment of the Base Commander and decided that she would oblige him, provided there was something in it for her. Liesel was nothing if not practical, and the Base Commander was not the first important man who had noticed her. That had been the chemistry teacher back in high school, who passed her for the year after an afternoon in the lab, and then there was the banker with the invalid wife—he had "misplaced" a large amount of cash into Liesel's account—and just before she came to Sweetwater, there had been her civilian flight instructor, who had signed off on her license in return for a regular weekend summer tryst. Liesel made a point never to step down in her climb to power, and the Base Commander looked to her like the next rung on her particular ladder. Liesel had a plain face, but her body more than made up for it in the eyes of every man she had ever met. *This could be interesting*, she thought. *I'll have him dancing my tune in no time, and then, who knows where that can lead? Laissez les bons temps rouler!*

She dropped to the sofa beside the Base Commander, not waiting for him to make the next move. She placed her hand over his and said, an unmistakable huskiness in her voice, "Is there something I can do for you, sir?"

"I do believe there is, Miss Rongeur. I do believe there is," he said, drawing her mouth to his.

CHAPTER 20

THAT SAME EVENING in town, ready for some fun after the hard training of the past weeks, Sprite and the other girls of Bay J-6 piled into Meredith's yellow Caddy convertible and motored into downtown Sweetwater. Bertie and Gertie had put on their matching blue sundresses in spite of the Zoot suit tan lines across their arms from being outdoors daily. Phoebe had brought out a green party dress, and Ninette had chosen a close fitting black skirt and a puff sleeved red blouse. Meredith's long hair had been captured in a yellow scarf that exactly matched the color of both her car and her tailored suit, and Sprite, somewhat squashed into the back seat under Phoebe's flouncy petticoats, wore her best plaid shirt and green skirt. Not for the first time, she felt a bit drab next to the others, but didn't linger on the thought for long.

They parked in front of the Avengerette club and Meredith let them out while she put the top up on the convertible. Sprite waited for her, and they walked into the blaring music and neon lighting together. *This is like a foreign country*, thought Sprite, grinning ear to ear. Glasses clinked, the air smelled of Old Spice aftershave and cigarette smoke, and the jukebox played big band music. While it was overly warm in the larger room, it was still cooler than outside, and there were cold drinks to refresh them.

Ninette had crimped Sprite's long golden-blonde hair, so she wore it loose, and to her surprise, the twins had said she looked like a young Veronica Lake. She pushed back the curtain of shiny hair and saw that Bertie and Gertie, almost unrecognizable out of their Zoot suits, had already found dance partners in a couple of smiling soldiers who had been standing at the door, hoping for an escort inside. Phoebe and Ninette followed the twins through a door that said, "For Those Desiring Dates." Glen Miller's *Rug Cutter's Swing* was playing, and the room was hopping with exuberant swing dancers. That left Sprite and Meredith alone in the outer room. For a while they sat and drank their Cokes and munched peanuts, but then Meredith said, "Hey, Sprite, don't you want to go with Ninette and Phoebe? I'm married, so it's not Kosher for me to be in there, but that's where the party is, and I thought you would want to go."

Sprite blushed a little behind the sweep of her hair and said, "Well, Mrs. Lowe, I sort of already have a fella, and I really don't want anyone else, if you know what I mean."

Meredith chuckled and said, "I do indeed. May I know his name?"

"Well, I'd rather not say just yet...we—we've just met—but he's a Marine pilot, like your husband," she said shyly, remembering her day at the Peach Festival, and the way Hal had looked in his uniform at the recruiting tables. Not only was he the most handsome man Sprite had ever seen, he'd also been very kind to her that day, when others had not. Captain Halcyon James had been in her thoughts ever since then and she saw him often in her dreams. Sprite's face reddened momentarily and she fussed with her hair nervously. Respecting Sprite's privacy, Meredith just grinned and nodded, then quickly changed the subject.

"Want to see that new Gene Tierney movie tonight, then?" she offered.

Sprite almost jumped in her seat. "Do I ever!" she said over the lively, smooth notes of *In The Mood*. Meredith promptly grabbed her purse.

A few quieter minutes later, they sat in the Texas Theater, staring up at the newsreels that always preceded the feature films. The stentorian announcer from Movietone News narrated the progress of the war over grainy combat footage of US and British forces capturing the remaining areas of Sicily. President Roosevelt followed with his assessment of what this portended for the war in Europe.

Then, the images switched to the war in the Pacific. Torpedo bombers and fighters from the US Navy and Marines screamed through the flak-blackened air and battled the Japanese near some island called Kolombangara, in the Solomons.

Sprite could feel a change come over her companion. She turned to look at her and saw tears streaming down Meredith's face in the flickering light. Sprite remembered that Meredith's husband was still missing in one of those battles, but all she could do was wait for the images on the screen to change. Sprite closed her eyes hard and wished for the newsreels to be over, but when Meredith touched her arm lightly, Sprite turned to look at her.

"Sprite, no matter what, he chose to fly in the war, and I chose to support that," Meredith whispered, her voice catching in her throat. "Look at this...." She then drew from her purse a large gold pocket watch and showed it to Sprite. Even in the near darkness, the almost microscopic inscription glittered on the case, the tiny words as bright as if they had been written in diamonds. *For once you have tasted flight, you will walk the earth with your eyes turned skyward*, Meredith opened the watch and the inscription continued inside, *for there you have been and there you will long to return*.

"The quote is from Leonardo da Vinci, who was maybe the first engineer of human flight. It's my husband's watch, well, it's our watch, actually," Meredith said, looking at the words she had long ago memorized. "I gave it to him the day he was commissioned as a pilot and then he gave it to me when I joined the WASP. It's a twice given gift, the most precious kind."

"What do you mean?" said Sprite, knowing there was more.

"Well, I mean...the watch is a symbol of the freedom we gave each other to be ourselves, in whatever time we have together," Meredith said, smiling through her tears. "He's still alive. I feel his heart beating." Meredith watched the tiny second hand sweep silently once around and then closed the watch.

Sprite noticed she held it all through the movie.

CHAPTER 21

SOME DAYS LATER, Sprite sat in her ground school class twisting her pigtail ribbon and chewing the middle of her yellow pencil as the math instructor, Mr. Gibbs, explained how to use the sum of an infinite geometric sequence to convert repeating decimals to fractions in lowest terms. Beside her, Ninette wrote down the formula with ease and practice, and Sprite sighed, thinking she would never be able to understand the numbers like the others did. Phoebe, in fact, was an absolute whiz at math. When the test scores came back at the end of every week, Phoebe's was always the highest and Sprite's was always the lowest. She fought it daily, but Sprite's fear grew that math, always her weakest subject, would wash her out of training.

Later that day on the flight line, she struggled to get the figures for converting the quotient of two integers to standard decimal notation to work out. Phoebe sat across from her with Liesel, talking about boys back home, and Buzz, and even Mr. Gibbs, who they thought was having a little fun with one of the Flight One girls. The two giggled until they couldn't breathe, and then Liesel looked over at Sprite.

"Hey, farm girl, who's your honey?" she teased, a wicked look in her dark eyes. "I bet he's picking cotton in Georgia, barefoot, toothless, and too dumb to draft! What do you think, Phoebe?"

Phoebe didn't reply. She was looking at the math problem that Sprite had written out wrongly yet again. "That integer goes there," she said, pointing to it upside down. Oddly, she had said it helpfully and without rancor, like a good teacher would.

Sprite looked up, puzzled, but put the number where Phoebe said it should go, and then saw the problem unfold into its solution. "Wow, Phoebe! How'd you do that?" Sprite said, amazed at Phoebe's number magic.

"Oh, it's just how I see the world," said Phoebe, brushing off the compliment. "I feel better when there is a correct answer. I like rules. They make us safe. There are rules in math, they don't change, and everything has a right answer."

"Ah," said Sprite, "I guess I can understand that." She finished her figuring and sat watching the take offs and landings until her time in the air came.

"Sprite Shannon, next!" Meredith's crisp command echoed under the tin roof and Sprite hopped up to answer.

As she left, in answer to Liesel's previously ignored question, she called back over her shoulder, "Oh, and since you asked, my man is a Marine pilot, Liesel the Weasel!" The two girls left sitting at the table gaped at her in disbelief, and Phoebe had to hold Liesel back from going after Sprite and starting a cat fight right there in the ready room.

When Sprite had moved out of range, Liesel twisted out of Phoebe's grip and said to her in a low whisper, "Hey, let go. I'm OK. Let's not let it get to us—she no more has a Marine pilot for a fella than I do. That's just something to say back to us. And she thinks she's such hot stuff with that first solo! By the way, did you find anything we can use against Miss Perfect Pilot? I'm getting real tired of her."

Phoebe nodded, her face unreadable, but thinking that Sprite's remark actually had gotten to Liesel, and badly. "I looked through her things, like you said, and found out that she is underage to be here, if her baptismal certificate is telling the truth. She won't be eighteen until February of next year. What do you think of that?!" she finished, knowing her secret reconnaissance would impress Liesel, and maybe even make her forget Phoebe had cheered for her baymate Sprite's first solo.

"Great work, Mata Hari! That's just what we need," said Liesel, her eyes narrow black slits as she watched Sprite mount the plane, one of the

Stearmans. "I was starting to wonder where your loyalties lie. But this couldn't be any better. Now we just need for the 'right people' to learn about that, and I know some of them very well now. I told you I'd find a way to get rid of her! She took my solo, but I'll take her career! Until then, we'll tell her we know her little secret and then sit back and watch her squirm—that will be even better, don't you think? Make her do our barracks work and wash our uniforms?"

Phoebe nodded slowly, glad to finally feel Liesel's admiration and acceptance, but the way Liesel seemed to enjoy her plans for Sprite's suffering bothered Phoebe a little bit. In truth, all Phoebe had ever wanted to do was be better than Sprite at something, anything, and when she had seen Sprite struggling with the math for the last few weeks, she knew she already had her own superiority. And as she considered it further, getting Sprite washed out at this point seemed too mean, now that Phoebe had found her place at the top of ground school's grade list. Phoebe looked down at her new cowboy boots, their soft black leather stitched with plain black thread in the shape of a firebird unfurling its wings. Those boots reminded her that if Sprite hadn't kept her from leaping onto that snake with her bare feet that morning, she would have been bitten. Sprite had also proposed that all of them in Bay J-6 get the same boots. They were beautiful and perfect for snake country, and because of them, everyone knew the J-6 girls now as "The J-6 Gunslingers." Everywhere they went, people smiled when they saw those boots, remembering the day Meredith had shot J-6's two rattlers. Phoebe owed Sprite a lot, now that she thought about it. She sighed deeply and looked over at Liesel. The glow of Liesel's exotic French pedigree and East Coast schooling seemed a bit diminished by her need to see Sprite suffer.

"Liesel, let's forget it. I don't care anymore. I'll do my own laundry, and so will you. I don't want to get kicked out of here. So let her be," Phoebe said, suddenly rising from her chair to walk down the flight line. "And as for my loyalties, they lie where they always have—with the rules."

Liesel sniffed and turned away, a vicious, hungry smile stretching across her face, exposing the long, prominent front teeth that had gotten her the nickname she had so hated all her life.

CHAPTER 22

IN THE MONTHS that followed, Sprite marked time only with the transition of aircraft—November meant the BT-13 Vultee "Vibra-tor," and the end of Basic Flight Training. December finally brought Advanced Training and the North American AT-6, known affectionately in the WASP as the "Sweet Six." It was an honest to goodness combat air-craft, muscle-bound and sleek. It had retractable landing gear, bomb rails, and gun mounts. It was lightning fast and much more difficult to fly, especially on cross-country night flights.

Grateful for the bulky warmth of the Zoot suit and her shearling bomber jacket in the winter evening, Sprite climbed nimbly out of her cockpit. She smiled to herself. Flying the Sweet Six in her Army Air Corps gear had finally made her feel like a real military pilot.

The sun had just dropped below the horizon, and hers was the last bird to fly home to roost for the day. Brilliant reds and oranges and pur-ples streaked the sky behind her, and she paused for a moment on the wing of the plane to look at the beauty of the stark Texas landscape. *This is a place of extremes*, she mused, *burning hot in summer and freezing cold in winter.* There seemed to be no middle ground at Avenger Field. And that was true with their training there as well—you passed or you failed, and if you failed, you left. No second chances.

How many of us are left? she wondered, walking back to the barracks. *I'd guess about half*, she answered, taking count of the dark bays now scat-tered among the lighted ones in Flight Two, J Barracks.

As she neared her own bay, Ninette waved from the window, welcoming her in. The others had already dressed for evening mess, so Sprite picked up the pace in order to go with them.

A few minutes later, as they sat down to roast beef, peas, and mashed potatoes, Bertie said, "Hey, guess what I heard today?"

Phoebe picked a tresspassing pea out from her potatoes and said, "What?"

"We get to go to a big dance! Jackie Cochran herself set it up! It's called the Snowy Winter Dance, and it's formal! Jackie's gonna be there, and we can get dressed up and dance with *men* all evening!"

Sprite raised an eyebrow. "Dressed up?"

"Yes!" said Gertie. We'll have to get our dresses and shoes out of storage, Sis," she said as she turned to her twin. A matching smile broke out on the other girl's face.

Ninette had been watching Sprite since the topic arose and, now, in her subtle, caring way, said, "Sprite, I think I have the perfect dress for you, if you want me to hem it up for you, that is. I don't think I can wear it anymore, after putting on a little more muscle out here, but it would fit you perfectly, except for the length. I bought it at Macy's in New York City and it came all the way from Paris, and the green in it will match your eyes exactly!"

Sprite thought about it for a minute. While the selection of garments in the town stores was adequate, and she now had money enough to buy a new dress, she knew she probably wouldn't find a good fit there. Ward's clothing line was geared toward average sizes and average tastes, and Sprite was tiny and a little particular, given a choice.

Sprite remembered Ninette's dress from the first day when all of them were putting their clothes away. It was an off the shoulder, cinched waist sheath made of emerald green silk, with a side slit up to the thigh. Sprite had loved it on sight, thinking she would probably never have anything so beautiful and, even a few months ago, she would have been embarrassed to take the offer. But now, after all they had been through together and all that they knew lay ahead of them.... Well, Ninette wouldn't offer if she didn't mean it, and Sprite had to trust someone at some point. Besides, they were not only friends—they were sisters. *Sisters of the sky*, she thought, smiling to herself. *That's what we are now.* That felt pretty good.

Sprite said, looking up at Ninette, "I'd love to wear it to the dance!"

Unbidden but glorious, an image of herself swirled in that green silk and dancing with Hal came into her mind and her heartbeat quickened a little. She knew he wouldn't be there, but still…such a lovely thought!

"Done!" said Ninette, her blue eyes sparkling. "And I'll wear my cerulean cocktail dress with that pair of silk stockings I have been saving for something special. What about you two? And you, Phoebe?"

The twins spoke in unison without a moment's hesitation, "We'll wear our black gowns!"

Phoebe, who had been sitting quietly, added, "I think I'll just stay back here that night. I don't have a date or anything."

"Noooo!" a chorus of wails descended on her.

"You have to go with us! We're the only bay that hasn't lost anyone yet! It wouldn't be right to leave you behind. It doesn't matter if you have a date—there will be men there to dance with."

"Yes, come with us, Phoebe," Sprite pleaded, and remembering her earlier thought, she added, "You're… you're our sister, right girls? We can't leave you here alone."

Everyone nodded and agreed, but Phoebe just looked all the more miserable at Sprite's comment. None of them knew about Liesel's plans to get rid of Sprite and how Phoebe had helped her, but Phoebe's heart-eating guilt drew her face into a tight mask of pain.

"Well," she conceded, mostly to get them to leave her alone, "I'll think about it. And just who are these men you speak of?" she added, steering the conversation away from herself.

Ninette said, "Well! I know for a fact that General Arnold and his entourage are coming! And all the officer candidates from Camp Barkeley are invited."

"General Arnold?" said Sprite, amazed that their function would draw such a high-ranking officer.

"Yes—well, he's got to be there—he's the Commanding General of *all* Army Air Forces, and the head of our program, and the class before us is graduating the next day. The dance is sort of a send-off for them. The next day, he will formally address them as they leave to begin their service," Ninette said.

With that, each one of them except miserable Phoebe smiled and began to dream of the dance as they tucked into their cooling dinner.

CHAPTER 23

The Angels' Roost, Santa Sabina

MAJOR DOYLE, HIS eyes red and gritty from a long morning of paperwork, looked up with a jolt as Mildred waddled through his open door without so much as a respectful knock and casually dropped the late mail onto his desk.

"General says you have to go with him tomorrow. Wheels up at 0900," she mumbled. Doyle nodded. When she had waddled out again to sit down at her own desk, he began to open the envelopes with a sharp paper knife. When he got to the last one, it was empty. Doyle spread the envelope farther open, held it against the light, and finally saw that there were two words lightly written on the inside of it: "Park. Usual."

Doyle's blood ran cold for a moment, then he crumpled the envelope and put it in his pocket, took his coat from its hook, and walked out of his office just as the clock released him from duty. Mildred, her pleated lips pinched over her teacup, watched him go and then settled back into the romance novel she had concealed behind the sheaf of papers.

A short time later, Doyle sat on a bench in El Camino Park, pretending to read the *Los Angeles Dispatch* as he watched fat, purple breasted pigeons pecking at the sidewalk for crumbs. A little distance away, a man held a woman close as they walked through a copse of palms. Doyle watched them with wonder, thinking how much the woman, with her wavy blonde hair and her lilting walk, looked just like Coreen. He touched the little gold Claddagh ring on its chain. He wore that chain around his neck now, under his shirt and hidden by his tie, but defying regulations, even so.

He sighed, thinking that he saw Coreen everywhere now, on base in uniform, coming out of the movies, on the street. It could happen anywhere, anytime. He would walk up to the woman and look into her face, only to see that she was someone else and not his beloved. Disappointed, he would excuse himself, apologize and back away, unshed tears stinging his eyes. But he just could not, *would not*, let go of the feeling that Coreen was still alive. In this web of intrigue, in which he had been so easily caught, everyone lied. Everyone—himself included. *And I am going mad from it!* he thought, *I don't even know who I am anymore.*

Several groups of field tripping school children passed him on their way to their buses and, when the park lane had sufficiently emptied, he thought it might finally be safe to get up. He folded up his newspaper and ambled to a large bush in the middle of a small stand of trees.

Underneath the bush lay a large, flat rock. Doyle looked around once more, and finding himself still alone, lifted it up. In a shallow hollow under the rock lay a small brown package wrapped in wax paper and bound with twine. He retrieved the package, quickly stuffed it into his folded newspaper, replaced the rock, and walked to his car.

Filled with apprehension and curiosity as to what might be in the package, Doyle entertained several possibilities as he drove his official black U.S. Government sedan down La Fortuna Canyon Road. Could it be a new passport, identity card, or a key to a safe deposit box at the Swiss bank? Had his last shipment of chromium, small as it was, been enough to buy him out of this deal with the devil? Maybe the engine designs had done the trick! He could only hope. Mattias had promised…and he had, after all, seemingly tried to see to Coreen's safety. Maybe he was still a friend. Maybe his only friend. But everyone lied.

Doyle thought of that too-bright-for-his-own-good engineer Hal James they had assigned to help him at Archangel. What an unbearable chore to have to work with a man who so looked and acted like Doyle's dead brother, Parker. Doyle positively relished the thought of leaving golden boy Hal behind when this was all over. Perhaps he could even find a way to blame everything on him as well. He'd think about that. He pulled the car out onto La Fortuna Canyon Drive and drove until he found a scenic overlook, pulled over, and took a deep breath.

Doyle reached down and retrieved his attaché case off the floor. He placed it on his lap and opened it up. Retrieving a copy of his academic paper "Analysis of Superalloy Coatings in Critical High-Temperature Applications," he picked up the little package, pulled loose the twine knot, and then carefully removed the wax paper. Inside the package was a flowery envelope, the kind favored by women, and a small, note-sized stationery box. He opened the envelope and pulled out the folded paper, which contained a coded message hidden amid its gushy endearments. Had the package been found by someone else, it would have looked like nothing more than a secret love letter.

He took out his pen, and using the "Analysis of Superalloy" paper as a cipher key, began decoding. The published academic paper was a good choice as a cipher key, since it seemed natural that Doyle would always carry a copy with him. As recognizable Gaelic words began to take shape, Doyle felt his heart racing and his breathing become shallow. When he was finished decoding, he had to re-check the resulting message several times to believe it. It said:

Send much more chromium, immediately, not negotiable. Fail, deal cancelled. Deliver, bargain enhanced. Allies lied. Your woman alive, with us. Deliver, we pull you out, reunite. Fail, you both die. Proof in box

– Alberich.

Alberich was a character from one of Wagner's operas, and the code name Mattias used. Only the two of them knew about it, as far as Doyle had been told. The letter was real.

"Proof in box?" *What kind of proof?* A series of terrible images darkened Doyle's mind, but he summoned his nerve and slowly opened the box. To his great relief, it held a lock of dark blonde hair, a perfumed letter, and a very tiny photograph… of Coreen, the *Irish Times* newspaper in front of her blaring a headline from an event from *last week*.

The scent of Coreen's "Emeraude" perfume surrounded him like an embrace and he became lightheaded with possibility as he tore open the letter. It was written in Coreen's own familiar, distinctive handwriting. She told him that she was sorry that he had probably thought she was dead, and that she nearly had been, except she was hustled off the boat at the very last minute. Some kind of intelligence had come through to Gallagher about an Allied attack. But her "bodyguard" had already thrown her small bag of clothing down into the dark hole they called a berth on the *Rowan*. She had been shattered that their love letters had been in it, and now they were lost along with the rest of her belongings. She promised to be strong for him and urged him to hurry with what he had promised to do, and said that she loved him and longed to see him.

She is still alive! He closed his eyes on tears of silent joy.

And why not? Hadn't he known it all along? He began to laugh nervously, a little wildly, the tension he'd been holding in his jaw instantly released with the confirmation. He tucked the fragrant letter into the envelope with the lock of her hair, shoved it into his breast pocket, and threw Mattias' note and the box to the canyon winds.

In seconds, Doyle was back on the road and could barely keep his eyes on the highway as he careened around the hairpin turns and steep drop-offs of La Fortuna Canyon Road. More than one car blared its horn at him as he swerved over the centerline of the dangerous curves, but he didn't care. *Coreen is really, really alive*, he thought to himself. Giddy with joy, he thought, *Everything can resume, exactly according to plan, as long as Mattias doesn't harm her!* He resolved right then and there that he would not give Mattias any reason to hurt Coreen. He would do whatever it took, steal whatever he must, betray any oath, or eliminate any person that stood in the way of getting Coreen safely back. His beloved was alive, and he would get her back, and then nothing was ever going to take her away from him again.

I can do this, he thought, *I will do this.*

He touched the little pink and green gold ring beneath his uniform, and thought again of putting it on Coreen's finger. He broke into a smile so wide and unfamiliar that it hurt his face.

Back on base, when he passed the guardhouse and turned down the road to the Archangel compound, Doyle tried to will his features back into their normal sour expression, and found that to be much easier when he thought about what he had to do next.

How in the world would he get his hands on enough chromium to satisfy Mattias? And how much would be enough? Another question rocketed through his brain and he felt pain radiate into his entire body.

What if there would never be enough?

Would Mattias hold her hostage to keep him diverting the metal until there was none left, or worse, until he had been caught? And then what would happen to her? Suddenly, his mood plummeted again and he wept with deep, wracking sobs—he was so close to rescuing Coreen, and yet so very, very far away.

He needed a drink; no, he needed a bottle. But the General's plane to Texas was leaving in the morning and he had to be on it. Solace and sweet oblivion would have to wait.

CHAPTER 24

THE "SNOWY WINTER Dance" had been accurately forecast. Sprite stared out the window while Ninette knelt to pull the skirt of the wonderful green dress into its perfect drape. Against an iron gray sky, big white flakes drifted and blew in the cold wind, quickly adding to the two inches of snow already on the ground.

"There!" said Nin, rising. "You look so beautiful, Sprite. You wear that dress better than I ever did."

Sprite blushed under her face powder and mascara, feeling like a princess. "Nin, thank you so much…" she said, "You are so good to me." Ninette stood back, smoothed her own dress into place and grinned, satisfied with her work.

"You are so welcome, dear," she said, as she picked up a bottle of Emeraude perfume and carefully misted the air above Sprite with fragrance so that it settled gently on her hair. Bertie and Gertie came in from the bathroom after their turn at the mirror.

"Wow! You two look great!" Bertie said, approving. The other twin smiled her agreement and then Phoebe came in, pretty purple taffeta gown rustling, but there was no smile on her face. In fact, she looked like she was ill.

"Hey, Phoebe, are you OK?" said Nin, concerned.

"Yes… yes, I'm fine. Let's just go, alright?" Phoebe replied, not meeting Nin's eyes.

Ninette looked at her watch. "Yes, it's 1925 hours; time to form up," she said.

Without any more discussion, they gathered their wraps, checked their teeth for lipstick one last time, and filed through the door, ready to fall in for the swankiest formation Avenger Field had ever seen.

Outside, as the snowflakes swirled around them, Ninette took up her position as Flight Lieutenant in front of the formation area and ordered, "Flight Two – fall in!" The other J Barracks bay doors flew open as the Flight Two girls poured out, giddy and giggling, dressed to the nines, with more than one girl teetering unsteadily in her high heels in the snow as they fell into formation. "Fall *in*, not fall *down*!" Ninette said, prompting a ripple of laughter. Ordinarily, Ninette wouldn't have put up with laughing in the ranks, but this was no ordinary night, and the excitement was electric. She fought to compose her own face, but it was too much, and she grinned back at them and broke into repressed chuckles. Marching dozens of girls in their very best formal wear all the way to the rec room without a tumble or a twitter looked impossible, but she would try.

"Flight Two – riiiiight... face!" she barked, and the girls all snap-turned in unison, albeit with much wobbling and tossing of feather boas and mink stoles, prompting another round of giggling, which made Ninette realize she would have to make allowances. "OK, we obviously can't *march* dressed as we are! But, we will *promenade* in an efficient, orderly, ladylike fashion, understand?" she said loudly, to murmurs of agreement. "All right then, ladybirds! Route stehhhhp, march!" And with that, the coterie of begowned, perfumed ladybirds surged forward, like a gigantic chiffon, silk, sequined caterpillar. Somehow, it all worked, and they were underway. "That's it, ladies! Classy chassis, marching sassy," Ninette said, giving full face to her smile.

Once the girls arrived inside the rec room, the group separated into various clusters as they found friends and made over each other's gowns and shoes, so long abandoned for drab training gear. Diedee Deaton, dressed in a high collared, long sleeved matronly gown of a strange shade of pink, stepped on the riser and called for quiet. "I just want to remind you all that inside that gymnasium are over eighty officer candidates from Camp Barkeley..." she said over ooos and aaaahs and more than a few squeals, "but so is Jackie Cochran, and more importantly, from the Joint Chiefs, General Henry Arnold is in there." She let her words sink in and the mood in the room became more serious. "Do *not*, ladies—do *not* forget who you are. You are the women of the WASP. The very best this country has to offer. Conduct yourselves accordingly," she said, "I would also remind you to observe protocol and leave the room only after the General has gone, which is his signal of your dismissal. Now let's form two columns, according to height." The girls made two lines, tallest in front, shortest in back. Then Mrs. Deaton gestured toward the doors, and the girls began to file out toward the gymnasium, with Sprite, as always, bringing up the rear.

Even with salted paths, the walk to the gymnasium was a little challenging, but with careful navigation and a great deal of crunching, they all made it to the building without a fall. An enlisted MP, blue from the cold, stood waiting to open the door for them. Music drifted from within as the orchestra, an Army Air Forces band from Dallas, played the welcoming song *Don't Get Around Much Anymore*.

"You ladies are a vision of loveliness tonight!" he said, eyes firmly glued to Ninette's backside as she moved through the door like a sleek jungle cat. No one could walk in heels better than Nin, and the nearest girls broke into laughter at the goggle-eyed soldier's comment, knowing he hadn't even looked up to notice any of the rest of them.

As Sprite entered the huge room, the MP closed the door behind her. She marveled at the transformation the bleak gym had undergone. *Just look at this place tonight!* she thought. Silver, gold, and blue bunting hung from the rafters, and a huge Fifinella banner had been unfurled behind the food tables. The little Disney gremlin had been adopted as the WASP mascot some time back, and she looked down on the dance with an impish grin, clearly the belle of the ball. *Where did they get fresh flowers this time of year?* There were rows of white linen-draped circular tables, one reserved for each bay and marked with a tented piece of cardboard with the bay number written on it. *Every table has a little bouquet of yellow roses and a blue candle!* Sprite thought.

On the left side of the gym, past the left column of girls, Sprite could barely make out two rows of standing, sharply turned out brown-and-khaki uniformed Officer Candidates. Each one, rigid but for his slack jaw, looked on in wonder at the sight of dozens of tanned, toned, lovely females parading in.

As the musicians finished their welcome song, Jackie Cochran strode across the stage and took the bulky microphone. She welcomed them all, congratulated the graduating WASP class, and then turned the mic over to General Arnold. He began his speech, and although Sprite couldn't see him very well, she could see the effect his commendation had on the graduating girls—it was quite a thing to be honored as a WASP by the Commanding General of the entire Army Air Force. At the end of his remarks, he said, "Everyone enjoy yourselves! That's an order! You've earned it." The whole gym erupted in applause and Jackie Cochran made a step toward the microphone as if to resume control of the ceremony, but General Arnold did not yield. He went off-script, turned to the bandleader and said, "Hey, Charlie, you know the one I want to hear first! Hit it!" and the drum section launched into Benny Goodman's *Sing Sing Sing*.

In an awkward lapse of decorum, half the girls, unsure of what to do, tentatively strolled toward their reserved circular tables. However, the eighty plus Officer Candidates advanced en masse, shoving and elbowing each other as they descended upon the other half of the girls, grabbing wrists and yanking girls onto the dance floor. It was a good-natured moment of low-level pandemonium, with enthusiastic bumping and pushing, but within about eight bars of the song, it had sorted itself out. By the time the horn section kicked in, every Officer Candidate was twirling and spinning a dance partner to the lively tune, leaving the remaining girls to head to their tables, Sprite among them.

Sprite, Nin, and Phoebe sat down at the J-6 table and watched the dancers for a little while. A tall, blond haired soldier came shyly up to Phoebe and asked her to dance. She gave him a strained smile and obliged, and he whirled her off into the crowd. A few songs later, Ninette was next to be asked, and her partner took her to the center of the floor when the steamy tango began. The boy could dance—and so could Nin. Sprite watched, fascinated with the couple's intricate moves and the story the tango told. By the time the song had finished, Nin was dipped and gracefully arching inches from the floor, and the whole room broke into whistles and applause for them.

"I didn't know you could do that!" said Sprite, fervently clapping for her baymate as the girl rejoined the group at the table.

Ninette smiled devilishly and said, "I'll teach you when you teach me how to do that under-the-bridge maneuver. Promise!" and then collapsed into her chair, fanning herself.

It was a while before another young man came to their table, but when he did, he asked Sprite to dance. She rose from her chair as the quick music began, and surprised herself by not tripping in her heels. The soldier delivered her to the punch table afterward, and then, before he could fill a cup for her, another girl took him by the arm and he was off and gone.

Sprite didn't mind. As she filled her own cup with the punch, something mysteriously red and sweet, an army chaplain everyone was calling "Father Gabriel" discreetly emptied a large bottle of vodka in the crystal bowl. Unbeknownst to anyone there except General Arnold, "Father" Gabe was actually Archangel Gabriel of MI-6, traveling with General Arnold's group. He was accurately disguised as a US Army chaplain, down to the convincing American accent. With his fingers to his lips and a wink, Father Gabe begged her silence, and she nodded, smiling. Sipping her undoctored version of the concoction, she looked around the room from the table's vantage point. General Arnold, only yards away, stood talking with Meredith and another tall soldier, who had his back to Sprite. Several more of General Arnold's entourage had gathered into a tight knot, and when one of them moved a bit, Sprite noticed that it was Liesel standing in the center of the small crowd of soldiers, flirting madly with them all. *You can draw a crowd of men anywhere you go, Liesel,* thought Sprite, *especially in that luscious red formal, with that neckline. Or is it the waistline?* thought Sprite, and then instantly rebuked herself for being catty.

One of the men wore the dress blues of a Marine and stood out among the drab brown army uniforms in the group like a lone eagle among a flock of pigeons. Liesel kept touching his arm and laughing, and when the music changed, she sidled out from the group of laughing men, drawing the Marine away with her to the dance floor. As they neared Sprite, Liesel caught Sprite's eye and let the Marine sweep her around in the waltz.

A couple moved between Sprite and Liesel's partner, but Sprite felt a shockwave of recognition at her quick glimpse of his face.

It was Hal. No. Yes. She saw his face from the front and then Sprite stopped arguing with herself.

Geez! It's Hal! It's really him! What is he doing here? She thought, dumbstruck, her heart thundering in her ears. Then she realized that he must be part of General Arnold's group.

Liesel came a little closer on the next step and saw Sprite staring intently at the Marine, whose eyes were wandering over the room above Liesel's head, as though he were looking for someone. Liesel's sly intelligence missed nothing, and when she saw Sprite's face, she knew the look for what it was. Liesel realized instantly that she was dancing with not just any Marine, but with Sprite Shannon's Marine. Her eyes never leaving Sprite's, Liesel snuggled a little closer to Hal, letting her hand wander across his collar and then slip beneath it, where she drew her fingernail lightly across his bare skin. Hal jerked a bit and let her other hand go, absently swatting at his neck.

Sprite heard him laugh and say, "Oh, sorry, something got under my collar. It's gone now. Sorry!"

When he looked up, he saw Sprite... and he smiled the most breathtaking smile Sprite had ever seen, for the second time.

The music finished, Hal bowed slightly to Liesel and the orchestra began the opening strains of the slow, sweet *I Love You for Sentimental Reasons*. Hal pulled away from Liesel and made his way across the floor toward Sprite, who remained fixed as though her feet were nailed to the floor. Several other WASP girls reached out, grabbing at Hal's arms for a dance as he strode past, but he politely declined, and as he settled his gaze on Sprite, he said, "Pardon me ladies, but my next dance is with Miss Shannon."

In a second he had swept Sprite up in his arms. Neither of them spoke at first, but when he lifted her off her feet to correct their height difference, she giggled a little, and he smiled dreamily back at her. "Last time

I saw you, you were snuggled up under a plane in Atlanta," he said, teasing her.

"You saw me that night?" she said, amazed. "I didn't see you!"

"Sure did," he said, leaning in closer. "And you were sound asleep."

She colored in embarrassment, but was secretly pleased he had remembered her. In fact, could he have been looking for *her* over Liesel's head a moment ago? Because he had certainly stopped looking around when he found her.... She smiled at the thought and shifted a little, happily realizing that she was dancing on air. He shifted with her.

"Hey! You'll drop me!" Sprite laughed, tingling all the way down her body.

"Never," said Hal, looking into her eyes as if he really meant it.

He did. His strong arm held her steady through the entire dance, as though she weighed nothing, and then gently set her down. It was the best dance Sprite had ever danced and she realized that her shoes had hardly ever even touched the floor. She looked down at her feet to make sure they still worked.

Another song began, and when Sprite looked up, Hal had been captured by a girl from the graduating class. He winked at Sprite and before the other girl could pull him away, he said, "General's orders for my dance card. But I'll look for you after...."

'I'll look for you after...' Sprite had never heard such beautiful words. She sighed, realizing she had hardly breathed during the dance, and Meredith appeared next to her, saying, "So that's him. I am not surprised. Captain James is the best of the best. I know his family. And I think he is utterly smitten with you!" Sprite just looked at her and nodded, in her mind, still dancing.

The twins, arms locked and laughing, tumbled into their seats at the table for a breather and Ninette came back a minute later, a cup of punch in her hand.

"This...punch...packs one!" she said, eyes popping as she noticed the chaplain's additional ingredient.

"Yes, I do believe we have been hornswoggled into decadence, degeneration, and peccancy!" said Bertie, having had a cup or three of it herself.

Ninette laughed at the liquor's effect on the twin's vocabulary. Gertie and Bertie were full of surprises, and Nin never got tired of discovering them.

"Wherever do you get those twenty dollar words?!" she said, marveling at both the girl's memory and perfect elocution of them after drinking what amounted to several shots of vodka.

"I think she found them at the bottom of that cup," said the other twin, "Never fails. A few drinks in her, and the dictionary falls out of her mouth."

"For future reference," said Nin, "Which one of you is the lexicographer? I'm having a little trouble focusing right now."

"Bertie," said Gertie, patting her sister on the shoulder.

"Yep," said Bertie, "And I'm not the only one who has been hitting the sauce tonight. See that officer by General Arnold? I think he's trying to drink the rest of the entourage under the table. Just stands there by the General, looking unhappier by the glassful."

"Speaking of glassful, I think I have some catching up with you to do, Sister," said Gertie. "C'mon, Sprite—help me bring the table another round of that very fine red stuff."

Sprite rose, tossed her loose hair back, then brought it forward again like Rita Hayworth always did in her movies, and let it settle alluringly over half her face. She and Gertie made their way through the tightly packed crowd, and up to the punchbowl, and as they neared General Arnold, Sprite saw the soldier Bertie had been talking about. He stood beside the General, as if in attendance, but his face was turned toward the wall and his body language told a tale of misery, pain and overindulgence. Sprite shook her head, sad for him, in the middle of this wonderful party, looking so lost.

As if the tall soldier could feel her eyes on him, he suddenly turned to look and stood sniffing the air, searching the faces of the crowd as if looking for someone.

Sprite saw him quite clearly and knew him instantly once he had turned around, revealing the notch at the top of his right ear.

It was Major Doyle! The man who had requisitioned her property and plane from her, the man who had outright stolen her mother's ring. The man she had shot at her house that day in Lowland Mill. The man who had promised to find her, no matter where she went, and see her punished.

The man who was staring straight at her right now with something a little crazy in his eyes.

Despite her horror and shock, Sprite turned her head away from him, quickly drew back from Gertie, who had seen none of it, and began to thread quickly through the crowd, trying to lose herself among the taller guests. But Doyle had seen her, and the look on his face had told her he would be following. He would find her, just like he had promised. When Sprite reached the edge of the crowd, she broke free of it just as the band tuned up for a big, boisterous number. She began to run, slowed by her tall heels and tight dress. She felt Doyle's eyes on her and knew he couldn't be far behind.

With no idea of where to go, Sprite found a storage room and shut the door behind her. She fumbled with the lock, but it was broken. She couldn't hear Doyle's hard-soled footsteps for the music, but she knew he would walk through the door in a few heartbeats. She'd counted on that lock and now she was just trapped! Where to go? There had to be a window. In the almost total darkness, she pushed through tall metal shelves full of basketballs, volleyballs, and baseball gloves. Three rows over, the shelves ended at the wall, and a high, tiny window that had been bolted shut crushed her hope of escape. Her heels hindered every step and the window, she realized, provided a stronger light than it might have if the snow hadn't been reflecting a full moon. The long shadow she cast on the floor was startlingly sharp.

She jumped and whirled when she heard the door squeak on its hinges. She smelled liquor and the room suddenly felt much too warm. She could hear heavy breathing and a couple of footsteps and the sound of the door closing again. Major Doyle was in the room with her.

She barely breathed, pushed herself against the wall under the window, and thought of the other time she had hidden under a window from this man, outside her house in Georgia, seemingly so very long ago. She'd made her escape then, and she could somehow make it out now. But how?

Doyle walked slowly down the shelves, step by swaying step. Sprite held her breath and tried to listen. She could hear his hands reaching for support and finding only the balls and gloves, which tumbled and bounded down from their racks, bumping and bouncing as they rolled to a stop in front of her. A short stack of wrestling mats to her left captured one or two of them as well.

"Coreen? Coreen, my darling, where are you?" Doyle's low, plaintive voice called in the shadowy darkness. "Are you playing hide and seek with me like you did on the beach that time? And the other day in the park? How smart of you to leave the dance and hide in here, where we can be alone!"

Coreen? Sprite thought. *Who is Coreen?* She realized Doyle was terribly drunk, and the smell of the liquor was getting much stronger as he got nearer. In fact, the reek of him was strong enough to mask even the cloying rubber and sweat odors in the room that had marinated for months in the Texas heat.

Sprite bent over, her tight dress making that more difficult than she had thought, and took off one of her heels to use as a sort of spiked hammer. Thin and only three inches long, the heel might be good for only one strike, but she could make that count and at least get away. The whiskey smell suddenly became overwhelming. She froze behind the drape of hair that covered most of her face. She looked up to see the reflected moonlight on Doyle's tear-streaked cheeks. He was grinning.

"Found You! I win! Coreen, darling, you are alive! I knew it! My father didn't let me see your body because there was nothing to see! And now you are here and I have found you again…however did you get away from Mattias? I knew I had seen you over here in the States! You were trying to find me, weren't you?" Doyle reached out to Sprite and clasped her free hand in his, causing her to twist on the other heel, throwing her off balance. As she tried to catch herself, she dropped the shoe, and Doyle brought her hard against his chest, almost smothering her in a desperate embrace.

"Oh, Coreen, Coreen, I have so missed you, so missed the fragrance of your perfume, so missed the feel of your hair in my hands. And how ever did you get away from Gallagher and Greta?" He ran his fingers through Sprite's hair, and when he got to her neck, he forced her face to his, closed his eyes, and began to kiss her deeply and hard. She sputtered and resisted and tried to scream, but he kept his mouth over hers and became the more ardent for her struggles. "Shhh, my little wild one, you can tell me how you did it later, when there is more time. But do listen carefully, because I have a plan for our future, now that I have you back," he said, coming up for air and clamping a hand over her mouth. "My friend Mattias has given me a lot of money and when I have delivered the last load of chromium to him, we can run away from the army, from this country, from the Nazis and the whole Third Reich, and just be together anywhere you like. You would like that, wouldn't you, my dear? Oh, yes," he continued drunkenly, his eyes trying to focus, "let's celebrate right here, right now!"

Sprite tried again to scream, even though she thought no one would hear her over the band. Doyle's hand tightened over her mouth as he shoved her against the wall, pinning her there, as his other hand wandered ruthlessly over her body. He started to lift her dress, tearing it at the slit as his fingers groped her thigh. Sprite's hand blindly searched the equipment rack to her left, feeling for something, anything, that could be used to fight this man off. She found the cold, smooth, taped handle of a baseball bat and gave it a hard tug, but it was wedged, immovable, under more equipment.

Now panicked, she shifted her eyes to search for another weapon, but suddenly... she saw a man's left hand clamp down on Doyle's right shoulder. The interloper cocked his right fist as he spun Doyle around a quarter turn, and then with a powerful overhand right, he socked Doyle on the chin with a *crack!* that sent Doyle backpedaling into a wheeled rack of basketballs. Doyle tumbled into the rack, knocking it over and spilling the balls everywhere as he collapsed on the floor. The interloper stepped into the shaft of moonlight that shone through the window, and Sprite saw that it was Hal. She could only gape at him in wonder.

"Sprite, you've got to get out of here before someone sees you!" Hal said. Sprite threw her arms around him as hot, painful tears began to form in her eyes.

"Hal, he was hurting me..." she sobbed.

"I know, I saw the whole thing, or at least the last few seconds of it," he said, trying to calm her. He brushed the hair away from her face, looked her over to make sure she was OK, and gently wiped a tear from her cheek.

"What are we going to do? I think you killed him," Sprite said, looking down at the twisted body by her feet.

Hal shook his head. "I think he's just out cold. But you need to get back to the dance, because this is more trouble than the two of us could ever possibly explain," he said as Sprite looked down at Major Doyle's prostrate body and sniffled. "Quickly, Sprite," Hal urged, "Someone might have seen you."

"OK," she said, hugging Hal tightly, afraid to let him go.

"Let me clean this up, and I'll find you later, all right?" Hal said. Sprite nodded, then reluctantly let go of him and found her shoe. She hurried out the door into the hall, and then made her way back to the gym.

As she slowed her walk, Sprite smoothed her hair, composed her face, and stepped back into the dancing crowd.

"Hey, where did you go?!" said Gertie, balancing a round of punch on a tray like a roller skating carhop. "Took them forty forevers to fill the order and then I had to ask the caterers for a tray," she chided, leading Sprite to the table where the others sat watching the dance.

"I…" Sprite began, looking down, her hand wandering to the huge rip in her dress. "My dress…I ripped the seam when someone bumped into me. I ran to the storage room to fix it, but I couldn't find a pin."

Gertie set the tray down and looked where Sprite was pointing. "Ah. OK, we have to mend that—can't have Diedee seeing it. You're almost indecent. Bertie? Give her the emergency safety pin." The other twin obliged with an enormous spare pin, the kind used with babies' diapers, retrieved from the hem of her dress. Gertie sat Sprite down at the table, and behind the cloth, Sprite pinned the ragged part of the slit closed as neatly as she could. The distraction gave her a chance to calm her breathing and regain a bit of emotional balance after Doyle's attack.

Trying to settle her mind, she began to think it through. The Major hadn't known who she really was, Sprite realized, amazed. But then, she didn't look the same as she had a few months back, not to mention the difference in her clothing that day and now. "Coreen" must be his sweetheart; that much was clear, she reasoned. But who were Gallagher, and

Greta, and Mattias, and what did Doyle mean about money and the Nazis and chromium? There was no time to wonder further. Across the room, she glimpsed Hal leaving the little storeroom, but Doyle did not follow. Hal looked for her, held up a hand as he caught her eye, and appeared to be coming over to her when the General took him by the arm and dragged him into a group where Jackie Cochran was holding court. Hal looked over his shoulder at her, mouthed "Sorry," and then he was gone. Sprite would have to wait for the dance to end before she could see him again.

"Hey, anyone seen Phoebe since the dance started?" said Ninette, looking around the floor.

"No...wait, there she is—with the... chaplain?!" said one of the twins.

Across the room, Father Gabe danced with Phoebe, keeping her close to the edge of the crowd.

"Father, I need to confess," said Phoebe, tears forming in the corners of her eyes. Father Gabe gave her a puzzled look, but let her go on. "I have done a terrible thing to a person who has done me only good," she said, her voice almost disappearing from pain at the end of the sentence. Father Gabe just nodded and kept dancing.

When Phoebe looked up at him, pleading for absolution, the MI-6 agent knew he would have to hear her out, even though his chaplain's uniform was merely a costume for his cover identity, and meant to help him blend in. But at Avenger Field, a unique base populated by mostly women, the disguise was drawing more attention than he had bargained for.

"You want to confess right now?" said Father Gabe, "As we dance?"

Phoebe nodded, saying, "I can't stand the guilt any longer. I'm not a person who usually breaks the rules and when I do, it's like my world stops. Would you please help me?"

Gabriel smiled down on her, looking wistfully past her head at the empty doorway where the girl named Liesel—the girl who had brazenly propositioned him with an irresistible litany of sins—had been waiting for him when Phoebe had tugged on his arm to dance. "Well, I cannot hear a formal confession on the dance floor, but of course, my dear, do unburden yourself and we'll see what I can offer as a counselor in these very few minutes."

Several eternities later for Father Gabe, with Phoebe's story of betraying Sprite told and her sins of jealousy and back-biting revealed, the dance ended. Gabriel, searching his mind for an appropriate comment, could manage only, "Of course, our Lord forgives you, but you must ask the girl's forgiveness as well before you will feel completely relieved." Phoebe lifted her head, wiped away her tears, and smiled for the first time in weeks.

"Thank—" she began, but Gabriel gave her a quick, chaste hug, and then made a dash for the door. Liesel wouldn't wait for him in that empty bay forever.

An hour later, as Nin, Gertie, and Bertie slow danced with the seemingly inexhaustible men from Camp Barkeley, Sprite sat alone at the table, still waiting for Hal.

"Hi, Sprite," said a small voice from behind. Sprite turned a bit in her chair to see Phoebe standing there. "Mind if I sit down with you?"

Sprite was mildly surprised that Phoebe would want to, but said, "Sure, Phoebe. I'm just waiting for Hal." Sprite didn't add that she was also watching the storeroom door for Doyle's exit.

"Oh, are you sure you don't mind?" said Phoebe, uncharacteristically concerned for Sprite's feelings.

"Of course not. Phoebe, are you all right?" Sprite had to ask. Phoebe had been acting oddly for a few weeks now, and this desire to keep company was certainly out of character.

"Yes. I'm all right. Really all right—now, anyway," said Phoebe, smiling. "And, I wanted to say... to say sorry for the way I've treated you since the first day we met. You know, I was always the top of my class, the most popular, the best at whatever I wanted to do. But I came here, and it's like it's a different world. And from that first day, it was clear that you were the best at most of what was going to happen here. I... didn't know how to handle that, and I took it out on you." Phoebe dropped her eyes to the empty table and traced the pattern of the cloth with her finger. She couldn't look Sprite in the eye.

Sprite sat still for a moment, taking in what Phoebe had said. Sprite knew Phoebe was close with Liesel, and Liesel hated her. Could Phoebe be trusted, or was this just part of another ploy to later embarrass Sprite for Liesel's entertainment? Sprite decided to take a chance. The girl really did look contrite, and she *had* been talking with that chaplain....

"Phoebe, I forgive you," Sprite said quietly. "I don't understand you most of the time, but it doesn't matter. We're baymates. We're sisters. Sisters forgive each other." Sprite found herself tearing up a little as she extended her hand and put it over Phoebe's. She hadn't realized how much of a burden the constant, low frequency fear of Phoebe's mockery had been for her. Sprite felt much lighter in her heart when Phoebe looked up at her and smiled her gratitude through her own tears.

A moment later, an officer took to the stage and announced that the next song would be the final number of the evening. On behalf of General Arnold, he bade them all a good night and remarked that the General would see them at graduation tomorrow.

Swallowing hard, Sprite looked around the emptying room again for Hal, but he wasn't there. Some minutes later, the music ended and the band began to break down their stands and put their instruments away. Sprite knew Hal wouldn't be coming back to the gym.

With one last hard look toward the storeroom door, Sprite said, "Phoebe, let's go home. We have only half an hour before lights out and it seems Hal has been delayed." Phoebe nodded and got up, helped Sprite to her feet, and they moved toward the exit, where the MP on duty bid them goodnight and closed the doors behind them.

Ж

Across the way, in a dark, cold, empty bay, Liesel had run out of hot water in the shower as she waited for the chaplain. And she was feeling a bit woozy as well. The punch she had drunk earlier had not set well with her. She ran her hands down her body, noticing her swelled breasts were a bit sore, and her abdomen a little rounder than usual. Nothing that would be noticeable to a love hungry man, though. Not yet, anyway. And the Commander... well, he would have to take care of her if need be. Stepping out into the chilled room, she looked around and saw the door had blown open and snow was drifting in, already piled a couple of inches high in places. Where was Father Gabe? She had told him exactly which of the empty barracks she had chosen. Unless… Liesel frowned, a terrible suspicision growing in her mind. Had he actually *stood her up?*

No man had ever rejected Liesel before. She didn't know quite how to feel about it. Then she heard footsteps coming toward the room and she bolted back into the bathroom, pulled the door to behind her, and peeked through the slit. But it was not Father Gabe standing in the open doorway. Instead, the Base Commander dusted the snow from his shoulders and said quietly, "I know you're in there, darling." An odd note of anger colored his voice.

Liesel eased the door open a little to give him a glimpse of her naked body, conjured up her most sultry voice, and said, "Oh, sir, I've been waiting for you…."

"Oh, I don't think you were, darling," said the Base Commander. "I think you were waiting for that chaplain. And by the way, Father Gabe won't be coming. General Arnold's aide came for him just before he reached this barracks. You see, I followed him after I saw your little seduction on the dance floor…."

Liesel hung her head, closed the door all the way, and said through it, "Could you please hand me my gown, Colonel?"

He coldly obliged her and in a minute, she came out of the bathroom, hair damp and bare arms prickly with goose bumps. She adjusted her dress and waited.

"Liesel, my darling, there are two things you should know about me," he said, looking her up and down.

"What are they, sir?" she said, not meeting his eyes.

"I always get what I go after. And I do not share. Consider your services no longer required. Do you understand? I don't want to see you any more," he said, and turned around, letting his last sentence trail over his shoulder.

"Liesel's eyes widened and she took a step toward the empty doorway. The Base Commander had already disappeared when she said, very softly, "But, sir… I think I'm pregnant… with your baby."

Doyle's head felt like it would explode. Or maybe it already had. He opened his eyes in the dimly lit storeroom to see that he lay stretched over a pile of wrestling mats, with basketballs and volleyballs as his sole companions. He sat up, then fell back down and tried it again after a moment, this time much more slowly. He squinted down at his watch and discovered about an hour had elapsed while he'd been unconscious. What had happened? The details came back in a rush as he saw the baseball bats in their stand.

The girl... the girl he had thought was Coreen. She had looked so like her under the low lights, wore the same perfume... he had been so drunk and miserable... he still was, but now he knew she had been someone else. Her dress had been a shade of green Coreen had always favored; that much he was soberly sure of.

That and that she had bloody well clocked him with a baseball bat! The bitch could have killed him! He touched his jaw, already hot and swollen, moved it a bit, winced, and realized it wasn't broken. *If she'd had a better aim or more strength, I'd be dead*, he thought. Doyle felt a burning, embarrassed anger redden his face.

And then he thought about something else, something perhaps worse than being dead. In his drunken delirium, he had told the girl about Mattias and the chromium! Doyle jumped from the mats and stumbled to the door of the storeroom to find that the gym had been closed for the evening and all the lights were out. Everyone had gone. How could he ever find her now? She had to be at Avenger, but hundreds of women were at Avenger!

He sped to the double doors of the gym and pushed through them, slipping a bit on a patch of ice as his feet hit the pathway. He caught himself before falling, shook his head to clear it a bit more, rethought that move, straightened up, looked around, and then walked crisply toward the barracks area. Though the snowfall had become heavier and the only light was the full moon, he could make out a couple of small forms ahead on the path. They had to be WASP girls and if he could catch up with them, he could ask them where he could find the girl in the green dress.

Then, with sobering shock, he realized one of them *was* the girl in the green dress.

❌

"You go on ahead, Phoebe," said Sprite. "You are already sniffling a bit and I can't walk very fast in the snow with these heels and my ripped dress, and besides, maybe Hal will still be looking for me."

"Are you sure?" asked Phoebe, blowing her nose delicately. "The snow is getting heavier and it's colder, too. You've just got that little wrap, and it's really dark, and—"

Sprite thought about what had nearly happened to her only an hour earlier and decided she had to keep it all a secret for the moment. "I'll be fine, Phoebe, but thanks for looking out for me," she said as convincingly as possible. It was cold and dark, and she was still a bit in shock, but she had to give Hal every chance to find her.

"Well... alright. But if you're not back before lights out, I'm coming after you, even if your Captain James *does* find you!" Phoebe said as she drew away, shivering violently as a sharp gust of wind caught her in the face.

Sprite watched her friend disappear into the sparkling darkness. Then she began stepping slowly and carefully through the snow, which was coming down so thickly that the salt on the paths couldn't melt it fast enough to prevent accumulation. Her concentration was so intense that she never heard the footsteps behind her.

She felt the hand clamp her mouth closed before she could make a sound, and a strong arm around her waist stopped her in her tracks. The reek of liquor from the hot breath on her neck flooded her nostrils, and she knew instantly who had seized her. Major Doyle was not quite dead after all.

"I will say this once, girl," he whispered harshly in her ear. "If you tell anyone what happened tonight in that storeroom, I will not only make sure you are cut from this program, I will put a word in General Arnold's already WASP-weary ear and the whole thing—the whole program, d'you see—will be gone before lunch the same day. Do you understand? I'm going to turn you around so I can see your face and know that you do understand. But make a sound and I'll break your neck and say you fell on the ice before I could catch you." He slowly eased his hand away from her mouth and spun her around.

"*You!*" said Doyle, astonished, as he looked her up and down, seeing her clearly for the first time all evening. The dress was the same, the perfume as well, but her hair had been swept over her back by the wind, and in his sobering state, Doyle realized just who she was. "The Shannon girl? Of all...." One hand automatically went to the scarred ear where Sprite had shot him long months ago.

Sprite jerked free of him and stumbled, trying to run, but he caught her arm again and quietly said, "Just because of our delightful history, I'll also make sure it won't end with you or with the WASP. I saw my assistant dancing with you tonight. I saw how he looked at you. He is one of my least favorite people in all the world, by the by. And he has some trouble with battle fatigue, did you know that?" Sprite shook her head in denial. "Oh, but yes," Doyle continued. "He's kept it quiet so far, but his record could be... re-examined, and 'new' things might come to light. So unless you want him drummed out and dishonored by what I would interpret and then be duty bound to submit to the brass, just stop right there."

The mention of Hal did make Sprite stop right there. While she could tell herself that Doyle was bluffing about her and the WASP program, and that she could testify that he had attacked her, there was nothing she could do if he took it out on Hal.

"That's better, Miss Shannon," Doyle cooed. "I hold all the face cards in this game. And speaking of faces, then there is the matter of this." He pointed to his swollen jaw. "You realize I cannot let your newest insult stand. You hit me with a bat, you little bitch. Wasn't shooting me enough?" Doyle snarled, his anger twisting his voice into a low growl.

"But—I di—" Sprite caught herself just before she said *I didn't do that—Hal punched you.* Better by far if Doyle thought Hal knew nothing about this. Hal had to work with the man and Sprite could not bear the thought of Hal being discharged from his duties—or the Marines—because of her. If Doyle thought she had hit him, it would keep Hal safe from a court martial. Hal had struck a superior officer and it was a criminal offense, no matter what the circumstances. Doyle already hated her, so if he thought she was also the cause of this new pain, then Hal would be protected. She closed her mouth and waited for him to go on.

"So here's what you will do. You… you will go back to your barracks and forget everything that happened in the storeroom. You will tell no one, especially your boyfriend, about anything I said concerning money, chromium, or a man called Mattias. Not that…" he smiled crookedly, looking down at her, "anyone would believe you. You're just a girl. I'm an army major. What do you think? I think your Base Commander would think you had propositioned me and when I refused you, you made this story up. Happens all the time."

Sprite boiled with rage at the thought that Doyle would get away with what he had done to her a second time. She clenched her fists at her side and ground her teeth.

Doyle laughed bitterly, seeing the effect his words had had on her. "That's the spirit. Now go home. I'm done with you… for the moment." He stepped back from her and turned to go, leaving Sprite shivering and alone in the blowing snow.

CHAPTER 25

BEFORE THE MIRROR the next morning, Sprite yawned as she drew the hog bristle brush through her hair. She had lain awake most of the night, thinking about what Doyle had almost done to her. There was a big, spreading bruise on her thigh and one in the shape of a large handprint on each upper arm. She knew Major Doyle had meant to rape her right there in the storeroom. If it hadn't been for Hal… she turned it over and over in her mind, thinking of ways she could have done things differently. Maybe she should have run to the table instead of the storeroom, gone toward her baymates instead of away from them. Safety in numbers. It was a good thing she hadn't, though, she told herself. Doyle would have seen them with her, and there is no telling what he might do to them, just for being her friends. Doyle's threat toward Hal had opened her eyes to just how much her next actions might mean.

Then there was the problem with what Doyle had told her when he thought she was the girl he called Coreen. He had mentioned that mineral he'd wanted on her farm in Georgia again—chromium—and someone named Mattias, who Sprite thought must be a German, with that kind of name. And Doyle had said "Nazis," so there had to be a connection between them and this Mattias and Doyle.

With so little information, she couldn't work it out, and if she couldn't work it out, she couldn't tell anyone—yet, anyway. Doyle had threatened to make sure that the entire WASP program got shut down if she accused him of anything. That was unthinkable! And there really was no proof for her story—and no witness but Hal. If she told anyone, Doyle would accuse her of hitting him with a bat and she knew Hal would own that he did it to try to keep her out of trouble. And for striking a superior officer, Hal could be court-martialed.

She couldn't have that. She set the incident aside for the moment.

Sprite pulled her long sleeved white shirt on gingerly, trying to keep from touching the bruises on her arms. She smoothed her khaki pants, tied her brown shoes, and pinned her cap into her hair. The morning would be spent with both Flights of her class and then there was the wing review on the flight line. It would be a long day, but at least Major Doyle would have no opportunity to find her alone again.

"C'mon, Sprite," said Ninette. "We have lots to do—say, what's the matter? You look a little pale."

"It's nothing, Nin," Sprite said, managing a smile. "It's nothing."

The hours passed quickly, and soon Sprite and the other girls looked on while the families, guests and trainees found their seats in the center section of the gymnasium. The band from Camp Barkeley played the Army Air Corps song while the graduating class filed in. After opening remarks by Jackie Cochran, General Arnold addressed the class, and he personally pinned WASP pilot wings on each graduating girl. Next was the review, held outdoors on the parade field. Fortunately, last night's snow had melted into puddles in the bright sun, and the day promised to be milder, though there was still a cold wind blowing.

Sprite eased into her A-2 flight jacket, tied her long white flight scarf into an ascot, and made her way outside to form up. Bleachers for family and friends of the graduating class were set up facing the field, with a dais in front for General Arnold and the rest of the top brass. The trainer planes had been arranged to provide an impressive background and the graduating class, followed by the underclasses, would march by in formation between the bleachers and the array of aircraft.

In a brief moment, the 44-W-1 formation was complete, and she was marching in her usual place at the end in the far right file. Every girl in that file had to act as "right marker" for the rest of the formation. This meant that when they passed in review in front of the bleachers, the right marker girls maintained a proper interval between rows to keep everyone marching straight ahead. From many hours of practice, Sprite knew her duty well.

The parade began, and as they passed in front of the bleachers, the parade leader gave the command "eyes – *right!*" The other girls turned their heads 45 degrees to the right and saluted General Arnold and the brass on the dais. Sprite fought the temptation to turn her head to look at Hal. She knew that Major Doyle had to be up there as well, undoubtedly painting her with his menacing gaze. She could almost feel his eyes burning holes in her back, but she kept her eyes fixed dead ahead until the command for "ready – *front!*" came. Everyone turned their heads forward again, and each girl resumed responsibility for keeping herself in step and in line. Their formation marched on, leaving the flight line, the reviewing stand, and Hal behind in measured steps.

Meredith had said that the General and his group were due to fly out in less than half an hour, so there was nothing for it. The few wonderful, magical moments she had shared with Hal the previous evening would have to sustain her until their next meeting. If there would be one—could be one.

And then there was that other reason she needed to see Hal. She needed to tell him about Doyle's threats after the dance. Hal needed to know that he should watch his back now. She suddenly felt very sad and very afraid. Major Doyle might well be planning something that would be devastating to her country and she felt helpless to stop him. *Well, at least Hal knows where I am for a couple more months, so there is no reason he can't write*, she thought.

The formation halted, the order to fall out was given, and the girls dispersed to assume their duties. Sprite had been assigned train station duty, helping the departing graduates and their families board the trains at the Texas & Pacific depot in Sweetwater. It would take the rest of the day. She sighed and made her way to the barracks, where she could see a line of suitcases already waiting to be hoisted into the trunk of someone's Daddy's Oldsmobile.

⋊

Oddly, Liesel had not found her own assignment on the duty roster for the day. She stood next to Phoebe, scanning the page on the bulletin board, but there was only the single sentence next to her name, "Report to Mrs. Lowe directly after the ceremonies."

"Well, that's perfect," Liesel said, "Whatever I'm to be there for, it can't be good." Then a slow smile stretched across her crooked front teeth and her dark brows pinched together.

"Liesel, what are you going to do? I know that look," said Phoebe, frowning.

"I still think we shoulda made her work for us first, but I think now's time to pull the wings off of little Miss Perfect Pilot," said Liesel, grinning wickedly. "C'mon with me, *cher*. You can be my witness."

"No, Liesel. I have a duty post and I told you I was done with your nasty plans, and I still am. I don't want to hurt Sprite anymore. Why can't you just drop it?" said Phoebe, fear rising in her voice. She knew Liesel the Weasel would never drop it—true to her nickname, she wouldn't pull her sharp little teeth back in until her prey was dead. It just wasn't in her nature.

"Well I think I won't drop it," said Liesel casually. "Whether you help or not, she's a dead *oiseau* after I tell Meredith about her baptismal certificate." She pointed to Meredith, making her way to the Administration building. "There's my date! See you later, 'fraidy lady."

Phoebe watched helplessly as Liesel unhurriedly followed after Meredith. Phoebe had just last night apologized to Sprite, and it would be the end of their new friendship if Liesel implicated Phoebe in Sprite's exposure. "Fraidy lady," Liesel had called her. And Liesel was right. Afraid, that was her. Afraid of everything that broke the rules. Maybe just afraid of everything in general. Phoebe thought for a moment, blanched white, and then ran for the barracks.

"Sit down, Liesel," said Meredith, her face dark with controlled anger as she opened her office door. Liesel sat as Meredith settled behind her desk. "Do you know why you are here?"

"Well, *I* know why I'm here, but I'm not sure *you* know why I'm here," Liesel replied brazenly. Meredith's eyebrows slowly raised to full fury position. Liesel continued, pretending not to notice. "I'm here because of what I have discovered about one of our group. Before you get your-self in trouble with the General when this comes out—and it will come out—I thought you should know what I've known for sometime now. Sprite Shannon is not yet eighteen. She must have lied on her application, which I'm pretty sure is grounds for her dismissal," she said triumphantly. "Maybe yours as well."

Meredith's eyes widened in shock at both the information and at Liesel's tone. She pursued the information issue first. "What? How do you know this? What proof do you have? And why would you wait to tell me at this point if you have known all along? Why now, Liesel?"

Liesel sat back, relaxing into her chair, but said nothing.

"In order to level such a charge formally, you will have to produce proof of it," said Meredith crisply. "But let's get to why I think you're here, shall we? You are here because I saw that you were sick directly after our lesson day before yesterday, and that wasn't the first time in the last few weeks. And I have noticed that your clothes are not fitting quite right anymore, are they? Liesel, you are pregnant, aren't you?"

Now it was Liesel's turn to be shocked. For six or seven weeks, she had thought she'd hidden it so well—she hadn't had morning sickness—her nausea came in the afternoon, when it was easier to hide, but that day after the lunchtime lesson, she had climbed out of the cockpit and it had hit her low and hard. There had been no way to disguise it. She had taken one step away from the plane and then lost her lunch. But all of that still didn't clear Sprite, Liesel thought, quickly regaining her balance in the discussion.

"Maybe. But even if I was and I'm not saying I am, that doesn't mean Sprite Shannon magically turned eighteen today," Liesel said smoothly.

"Before this discussion goes further, Liesel, I am going to tell you two things," said Meredith, fighting to keep her cool. "I need rock solid proof of your charge against Sprite, and you *will* have the good sense to speak to me with respect. I am about one more of your high-handed comments away from escorting you to the gate right this minute."

Outside the office door, shaking in her shoes, Phoebe stood listening, a piece of old, yellowed paper in her hand. When the door opened and

Liesel stormed out, Phoebe ducked behind the corner into another hall-way and watched the girl charge out of the building. Phoebe knew she didn't have long, so she gathered her resolve, took a deep breath, and knocked on Meredith's door.

"What!?" shouted Meredith, still incensed with Liesel's lack of comportment.

"Mrs. Lowe?" Phoebe flinched, but pushed the door all the way open. "May I come in? I have something that you might want to see. I saw Liesel come in here and I know what she is trying to do. I think I need to give you this." She unfolded the piece of paper, and Meredith could see from across the room that it said, in bold, fancy lettering, "Baptismal Certificate" at the top of the page. Meredith gaped, and beckoned Phoebe in.

After a brief confession of her early complicity in Liesel's plan, Phoebe nervously watched at the door while Meredith perused the paper. Phoebe's heart raced at the thought of Liesel bursting through and finding her there, but she sat glued to the chair, bravely sticking it out.

Meredith picked up a pair of reading glasses in order to see the fine print on the paper. "I see what you mean, Phoebe," said Meredith, picking up a pen. "This certificate is faded and very old; I'd say at least eighteen years old, wouldn't you? No wonder this date is illegible. There! That's bet-ter. What do you think? Can it be read now?" Meredith handed Phoebe the paper.

Phoebe looked at Sprite's birthdate, and her mouth fell open. Mer-edith had lightly marked over the entire original date, 1926. The final numeral, 6, now appeared to be a 5. "But...you..." was all she could get out. She just looked up at Meredith and smiled wanly, and then said, "Oh. Yes. Perfectly legible now. I am sure I read it wrongly before, Mrs. Lowe, when I made mention of this to Liesel. My mistake." She gave the certificate back to Meredith.

"Yes, it was your mistake," said Meredith, meaning so much more than her agreement. "I hope you never make such an error in judgment again, Phoebe. I can't forget it. But thank you for bringing this to me. I won't forget that, either."

"Now get back to your duties, Phoebe," said Meredith, as her eyes drifted to the view of the parade ground out her office window. "And use the back door of the building." Phoebe sprang from the chair and was gone before Meredith got the entire sentence out.

Slowing to a walk, Liesel cautiously entered the J-6 bay, one eye out for anyone who might have returned from her duty for some random reason. When she saw she was alone, she found Sprite's shelves and began to pull everything off of them, frantically shaking every notebook and book for the baptismal certificate. She was tossing the mattress on Sprite's cot when she noticed Meredith standing at the door.

"This what you were looking for?" said Meredith, holding up the baptismal certificate. She came closer to Liesel, who stared at it, saw the birthdate, and winced. "How about we take you down to medical to get a pregnancy test when you have put everything back like you found it?" said Meredith.

Liesel looked at the floor, hot, angry tears welling in her eyes. "No, how about we don't? I'm leaving this useless, ridiculous program. I'll pack my things and go out with the other girls on the train today."

"Liesel, that is the first good decision you have made since coming here," said Meredith. "I will get your discharge papers in order. But you're still going to put Sprite's things back, understand? And I mean inspection perfect. While I watch." Meredith waited for that to happen, and then turned around to go.

"Liesel, you are a really good pilot," she said, stepping out of the doorway. "You could have been such a credit to your country. Instead, you have spent your time here trying to take down your competition and seduce men, and have done your best to damage the program. I can't really understand why. Your application papers say your family has money, so you come from privilege, and you have an enviable education. What more could you want? Did you think that with Sprite and the others out of the way that you would shine all the brighter? And why would you even need to?"

"You wouldn't understand," said Liesel, her voice cracking on the last word. "You have no idea."

Meredith shook her head. "And you're not going to tell me, are you? You're just going to get on that train and disappear into ignominy like so many of the other washouts and we will never know why." She stood silently for a moment, and when Liesel nodded her head, Meredith walked away.

When Meredith's back was turned, Liesel made a vicious, feral face at her and ran back to her own bay to pack her suitcase, leave her uniforms and zootsuit crumpled on her stripped bed, and try to find a ride into town.

"Liesel?" Phoebe's trembling voice came from the doorway of the shared bathroom.

Liesel jerked her head around, red face glowing with fresh tears and anger. "What the hell do you want, you little traitor?!" she snapped.

Phoebe shrank further beyond the doorway. "I just wanted to say I'm sorry things had to be this way. I hope we can still be friends," she said quietly, her gaze on the floor.

Liesel shook her head slowly. "No, *cher*, we cannot be friends. Now, if you will leave me alone, I am packing, and I don't need your help."

Phoebe raised her head and looked Liesel squarely in the eye. "Liesel, I'm sorry for that, too. I liked you very much."

Liesel winced, turned her back on Phoebe and laughed ruefully. "Well, *cher*, I hate to break it to you, but I never liked you, OK? You are nothing and no one, and you are scared of your own shadow. So now will you just go?"

When Liesel turned around again, Phoebe was gone.

X

The sun had almost set, which meant her shift was almost over. Sprite looked up to see a too familiar form standing in the corner by a phone booth. "What are you doing here, Liesel, and, Geez, you're out of uniform!" said Sprite as she shut the last train's door. Liesel, intently rummaging through her purse, looked up sharply at the sound of Sprite's voice.

"Not that it's your business, but I'm going home," she said huffily. Tearstains had caked her face with a few rivulets of fine dust. "I'm done with this place and everyone in it, especially you, farm girl!" She continued to prowl the bottom of the big purse, but came up empty for change.

"Need a dime?" said Sprite coolly.

Liesel choked back bitter bile, the product of both her rage and her pregnancy.

"Yeah, you got one?" she sniped. "Well, of course you do—you're Miss Perfect."

Sprite frowned at the hurled insult, but held out a coin anyway. "Anything to help you on your way, Liesel."

Liesel snatched it. "Now go on, Sprite. I need some privacy here," said Liesel, rattling the booth's door, which was off its rollers and wouldn't close.

Unthanked, Sprite turned around, but then stopped and listened, not believing her ears. She clearly heard Liesel speaking loud, animated French into the receiver. But it was not Parisian French, nor was it even Canadian French. It was…Cajun! Sprite's high school French teacher had told her Cajun French was spoken in only one place—swamp country. Liesel, the supposedly wealthy Bryn Mawr graduate with an east coast family pedigree was asking her father for train fare to come home. To Louisiana. To the family… farm.

CHAPTER 26

Santa Sabina Air Base – Angels' Roost – California

THE SMELL OF acetone permeated the darkroom as Gabriel gently shook the photograph through the developing solution. The darkest parts of the picture appeared first and then the details, but he still didn't know exactly what he was looking at until the timer dinged and he took the wet paper out, let it drain for a moment, and then clipped it to a line. The red light overhead showed him something he was pretty sure he didn't want to see, but he put the magnifying glass to the photo to be sure of it. A cold sweat broke out on his brow and he said to himself, "No wonder they killed Valois for taking this." A few minutes later, Gabriel clipped up the rest of the developed photos and charged out of the revolving darkroom door.

In the outer office, he snatched up the telephone and dialed. "General Arnold? It's Father Gabe," he said, peering around the room and into the hallway. Only Mildred, Major Doyle's dowdy old secretary, putting on her coat, stood at the far end of the corridor. "Sir, I have something in the darkroom I think you'll want to see right now, before you return to Washington," Gabriel whispered.

✕

Major Doyle turned up his collar to ward off the chill of the cold night air blowing off of the ocean and tugged the serge overcoat tighter at his waist. Wandering along a dimly lit street near the beach in the area of Los Angeles called Venice, he walked carefully around the piles of drifting trash and stepped gingerly over the wino sleeping in his own stinking filth.

The Venice of LA had been named for the canals dug to drain marshes, thereby creating drier land to build the community upon. There was truly no other correspondence to the beautiful Italian city of the same name. With its three amusement piers, their carnival lights and Ferris wheels aglow in the foggy evening, the place had been aptly tagged "slum by the sea."

Doyle fumbled at the little gold Claddagh ring on its chain inside his uniform, thinking of Coreen. She was the only reason he continued to obey Mattias's orders, continued trying to keep his fragmenting mind together, continued living at all. And continued walking down this dangerous, dark alleyway.

The hasty message he had just received carried two bits of information: the first was that the General possessed damning evidence of Doyle's treachery if they ever figured it out, and the second was that Mattias wanted him to go to this Godforsaken bar in the worst slum of Los Angeles, this very night.

Finally, he spied what he was looking for: the Blackehart Irish Pub, featuring the rather imposing head of a yellow-eyed black stag painted on the swinging sign. Doyle composed himself, took a deep breath, and then stepped inside.

The pub interior reminded Doyle of an aging burlesque queen—it had been once attractive and comely, but after decades of cigarette smoke, hard liquor, the effects of gravity, and the grimy pawing of thousands of customers, it was now well past its prime. The oak-paneled walls hadn't been polished in years and numerous patrons had gouged their initials into them. Tarnished, fingerprint-smudged brass rails stretched down the bar and the smell of soured beer and body odor lingered in the air. All in all, it was the least inviting pub Doyle had ever seen. In fact, it did not even deserve to be called a pub. It was just a dive trying to look like a pub.

A few obvious regulars hung over half empty beer glasses and there was no music besides the grating cackle of the whores in the corner as they chatted up a drunk sailor before they robbed him later in the alley. Doyle sidled up to the bar, gritted his teeth at the thought of making contact with the dirty, cracked leather seat of the stool, and sat down. The bartender, his back to Doyle, began humming a low tune...a tune Doyle instantly recognized as *Im Märzen der Bauer*, the same German folk song that Greta, Mattias's girlfriend, had sung to signal her companions out on the cliff top. That was the day Doyle had been kidnapped and taken to Guernsey. The last time he had seen Coreen.

Of course, thought Doyle. It had to be you. "I got your message," he finally said to the bartender, who was busy wiping out pint glasses with a greasy cloth.

"You'll be needin' a pint and a shot then, boyo," the bartender said as he turned around. It was, of course, the IRA man, Gallagher. Gallagher placed one of the glasses he had been wiping under the tap and began filling it with beer.

"Just a bottle of tonic water, please," Doyle said, knowing that if he started drinking, he wouldn't stop. He still had a sore jaw and bruises from the last time he had not stopped.

"Only I'm not askin' you, I'm tellin' you. Have a drink to calm yerself," Gallagher said, as he poured a towering shot of murky whiskey into a lowball glass and slid it down the bar. The glass came to a stop in front of Doyle, and half the contents sloshed out and onto his sleeve before settling. *Of course,* thought Doyle, *I knew I'd not leave here without damage.* Gallagher brought the beer over to Doyle and then poured a whiskey shot of his own.

"I didn't exactly expect to see *you* here," Doyle said, as he the sipped the beer.

"Just doin' a bit of fundraising for the Cause. Once Irishmen become Americans, it seems their wallets grow as fat as their bellies. But then, as long as I found meself in the neighborhood, our good friend Mattias thought I should be havin' a word wi' ya," Gallagher said.

Before Gallagher could deliver Mattias' latest message, Doyle leaned over the grimy bar and hissed, "Well, I have a word for him, too! You have to get me out of here! They're going to find me out soon! I can't do this forever without getting caught, and Mattias needs to set a limit on what I have to deliver."

"Now Seamus, you've not yet lived up to your end of the bargain," Gallagher chided, *sotto voce*.

"I gave you the plans and more chromium! When is it going to be enough? Is it ever going to be enough?" Doyle said, drawing a long, delicious swallow of the beer. The alcohol warmed him and he forgot all about his vow to stay sober.

"True, ye've sent the blueprints. But as you already know, that pittance of chromium wasn't enough to make a set of earrings. You'll have to do better than that, boyo, before we can deliver on our end," said Gallagher.

"Deliver on your end? I want to see Coreen!" Doyle said fiercely. "I *must* see Coreen!"

Gallagher downed his shot of whiskey and poured himself another. Then he filled Doyle's whiskey glass to the rim. "Drink your whiskey, Mary," Gallagher said with a bit of menace in his voice, "and settle yerself. And then listen sharp."

"There is only so much I can do," Doyle said a bit too loudly as he downed the whiskey in one practiced gulp. "Mattias has to understand that."

"Oh, but he does. Which is why I'm to offer you an additional 200,000 francs...a dirty great pile of money, *when* you deliver him his dirty great pile of that metal. Just one more big, big load of it, and it has to come well before the air war hots up, so there's time for manufacture. Gerry's running factories around the clock, but ain't nothing getting' made without that stuff. Remember, Seamus. After the German victory, you'll be a rich, important man, prized for your knowledge, feted all over Europe, in *gloria infinitum*, forever, amen...." Gallagher said sarcastically. "Now do your bleedin' job, or I'll personally see to it you and your fair Coreen are found...in the drink, as it were," he finished, lifting and draining his glass.

🜨

General Arnold, already unhappy to be summoned by the MI-6 agent at such a late hour, looked where Gabriel indicated on the photo and frowned stolidly. "We need to get an engineer's perspective on this. Is Captain James still here?" General Arnold said.

"Perhaps. Can he be trusted, sir?" Gabriel asked.

"I know his family. If we can't trust *him*, then there is no such thing as integrity in this country anymore," he said.

"Very well then, sir," Gabriel said, as he placed four wet photos into separate trays and stacked them one atop the other.

With Gabriel carrying the trays, they strode to the engineering work area marked AUTHORIZED PERSONNEL ONLY. A sleepy MP leapt to open the door for them.

"No one disturbs us," said General Arnold, as he passed the MP.

The rest of the research team had all gone home for the evening. The General and Gabriel headed for the only light, a gooseneck lamp, which outlined Hal's angular silhouette as he drew at his drafting table.

Hal looked up at the sound of footsteps and saw the General approaching, so he rose to his feet and stood up straight. When he noticed Father Gabe, Hal casually slid a large blank piece of drafting paper over his work in progress.

"Captain James, stand easy. I'd like your opinion on something," General Arnold said.

"Yes sir," Hal said, eyeing Father Gabe with some curiosity. Hal watched as Gabriel placed the stack of trays on a nearby desk, removed the top tray and handed it to Hal. In the tray lay a damp black and white photo of a piece of mangled machinery. Despite its damage, Hal immediately recognized the object for what it was.

"Begging your pardon General, but isn't this a conversation we should be having… alone?" Hal asked.

General Arnold turned to Gabriel. "Guess it's time we read the young captain in," he said. Hal arched an eyebrow, puzzled. "Captain James, what we are about to disclose to you is classified 'Top Secret,' do you understand?" said the General. "As of now, only we three are aware of this information. Now, is *that* understood?"

"Yes sir," Hal said, baffled but obedient.

General Arnold nodded toward Gabriel and Gabriel began, slipping back into his native British accent. "Well first, I'm not *Father* Gabe, I am not in the US Army, and I am not American," he said, smiling. "I am an agent from British Military Intelligence, Section 6, and your team's liaison to the British Archangel program."

Hal chuckled, "Well, *Father*, I have to say you might drink like a priest but you sure don't dance like one!" Gabriel grinned and nodded.

General Arnold gestured impatiently toward the stack of trays, trying to move things along. "Gabriel, show him the rest." Gabriel brought the other trays over and unstacked them, spread them on a desk, and then switched on a lamp so that Hal could view them. Hal picked up a magnifying glass and examined each tray's photograph carefully. *I can't believe what I'm seeing*, he thought to himself. One photo showed a single turbine blade attached to a piece of broken rotor. Hal grabbed a set of calipers and took some precise measurements of the width and height of the blade, then made a note of them. He did a quick calculation and scribbled out a ratio.

A second photograph showed the cross-section of the same blade. It had the characteristic semi-teardrop shape of an airfoil, exactly like an airplane wing. But it wasn't just any airfoil; it appeared to be N.A.C.A. Airfoil #154. Hal hefted a thick binder off the desk and flipped through the pages until he found a chart cataloguing all of the N.A.C.A. airfoil designs by number and cross-section illustration. When he compared the photograph with Airfoil #154, he whistled softly.

General Arnold and Gabriel turned to each other and exchanged a look as Hal continued his measurements. *These airfoils are an exact match,* Hal thought. He looked at the next photo, which was the cross-section of what was called a "stator blade" on a jet engine compressor's stationary ring. Hal flipped through the N.A.C.A. chart and located Airfoil #137. Just as he suspected, the stator blade was another exact match. Hal jotted down the airfoil numbers next to the final ratio.

"Well, Captain, what can you tell us?" Gabriel asked, when it appeared that Hal had finished. Hal held up his index finger to signal he was in the middle of a thought and didn't want to lose it. He strode to a large floor safe by the wall, knelt down, and began spinning out the combination. He then torqued the metal handle downwards and the safe's heavy door swung open. Hal brought out some blueprints and hurried over to a flat worktable to spread them out. Gabriel switched on another light. Hal searched the blueprints, drawing his index finger across figures and notations until he finally found what he was looking for. He then slapped his handwritten notes down on the table. The ratio he had calculated and the two airfoil catalogue numbers he had written down matched the blueprints of a turbine rotor's blade design.

"Captain James, please don't keep us in suspense," General Arnold said, mildly irritated.

Hal took a deep breath, unsure of how to put his conclusion, so he just said it. "Our engines were exploding, General Arnold, because of blade resonance in the engine's operating range. Enough resonance and vibration to cause the blades to break off and be ingested, causing catastrophic failure. We reconfigured the rotor and stator blade designs to eliminate that vibration. *These* blade designs, precisely." Hal pointed to the photos. "And these specs have been locked up in that safe until now."

General Arnold pulled a chair out and wearily folded himself down in it. He loosened his tie, leaned forward, rested his head in his hands, and massaged his temples. Finally, he looked up and said, "You are sure?"

Hal nodded. He was positively sure.

"Then you both know what this means," said the General, quietly.

Gabriel looked at Hal's notes and then at the blueprints. He confirmed that the data in question did indeed match, sighed deeply, and said, "Yes. It means we have a mole in the Archangel program."

CHAPTER 27

Old King Cole was a merry old soul
and a merry ol' soul was he, uh huh.
He called for his pipe, and he called for his bowl
and he called for his privates three, uh huh.
Beer! Beer! Beer! cried the private.
Brave girls are we
There's none so fair as they can compare
to the flying WASP trainees, uh huh.

EVERYONE BUT PHOEBE sang, as the group of twenty trainees bounced around in the back of the cattle truck. Sprite collapsed into laughter as the twins hit the last note in harmony. "Phoebe," said Sprite, still giggling, "you will do fine. Stop worrying."

Phoebe shook her head, distress written all over her face. Ever since morning mess, Phoebe had made Sprite go over the procedure for their check flight again and again. Today was the day they would all fly for the check flight instructor and if he passed them, they would be allowed to graduate from the program and get their wings. Sprite hadn't thought much about the check flight, but they all could tell that Phoebe couldn't take her mind off of the test. She seemed sure it would wash her out of the WASP at the very last possible minute.

"You know they try to make us fail up there, don't you, Sprite?" said

Phoebe as the twins and Ninette began another jody behind them. Sprite looked into her friend's troubled brown eyes.

"Why are you afraid of this, Phoebe?" she asked. "Nothing they have thrown at you has made you curl up and play dead like this test. You have topped our class in ground school, you can fly anything, and if you are concerned about that night flight last week, you do realize that we figured it out and that's all we needed to do. Plus, look—broad daylight! The instructors won't be asking you to fly this one at night!"

Phoebe dropped her gaze and stared at the dusty truck bed as though she were reliving the incident in her mind. Sprite said nothing, but the memory of last week's cross country night flight was very fresh in her own mind and it made her smile.

Phoebe's assigned night flight, with Sprite assigned as copilot, had meant they would be returning to Sweetwater after sunset by five hours.

"What's up with you, Phoebe?" Sprite had asked as they soared over the desert. The moonless night was the darkest they had ever flown in. Besides the control panel in the cockpit, the brightness of the stars was their only light, and they had been flying by instruments for most of the trip.

"Nothing. I just get tired sometimes. And I hate flying at night. Where are we? What are our coordinates again?" said Phoebe, rubbing her eyes.

Sprite read them back to her from the map. According to Sprite's calculations, they were somewhere over the flat, empty landscape of west Texas, with just a little longer to go before the lights of Avenger Field would come into view. "Just a little farther and you can rest," said Sprite. "I know it's hard to fly in such a blackout of a night."

As if on cue, the control panel sparked once and went dark. "Uh-oh. Something must be wrong with the circuits," said Sprite, as calmly as she could. "We'll just have to land, I guess." Sprite could barely see her hand in front of her face.

"No! No! Not now!" cried Phoebe, panic rising in her voice. "We're almost there!"

"Now, let's keep our heads, Phoebe," said Sprite, as much for herself as for Phoebe. "I think there are matches in the survival kit." She fumbled beneath her seat and came out with the kit. Opening it by touch, she fished around until she found the waterproof matchbox. "Here! I can light these to show the instrument panel until we… run out of them," she finished dismally as her fingers felt exactly four matches left in the kit. Sprite struck one of the matches and it sparked, but refused to catch fire. She struck it again on its other side and it still wouldn't light. The smell of burnt sulfur permeated the cockpit.

"Sprite, I can't read the instruments! If you don't get those things to work, we are gonna crash, do you hear me?!" Phoebe yelled.

"I know, Phoebe, believe me, I know!" countered Sprite as she dropped the useless match and took out another. This one did light, and Phoebe breathed relief as Sprite held it to the panel. Apparently, the problem was with the panel light, not the instruments. Phoebe read them quickly. They were still level, but had lost some altitude and their bearings looked odd to Sprite. "Phoebe, weren't we on a heading of 190 degrees when we lost the panel lights?"

"Yes!" Phoebe nodded just as Sprite had to drop the match, "And now we are at 160 according to that. It can't be right! How can we stay on course without looking at the instruments?"

"Hmmm," said Sprite. "I think it can be right. But look up. We have some help up there."

"What?" said Phoebe, totally startled at the absurdity of Sprite's words.

"I said, 'look up.' The stars…"

"What about them?"

"People have navigated by them for centuries. They'll get us pointed toward home, and these last matches will get us down," said Sprite. "See the biggest star?" Phoebe looked out of the Plexiglas canopy. The North star blazed brightly.

"Yes. North star. Polaris. What about it?" said Phoebe, clearly irritated.

"We have to keep it on the starboard side of the plane, just about there," said Sprite, pointing to a rivet on the canopy. "I'll watch it as you fly."

Phoebe sighed and said, "OK," as she turned the yoke to put the star where Sprite had pointed. "But I really don't know how we can do this. I think we should get ready to bail."

"No. You can do this, Phoebe. You can bring us home safely. We have two matches and the end of the first one left. Avenger should be coming up really soon if we keep this course. Let's see if we're in range." Sprite flipped the radio switch to hail the control tower at Avenger Field. "Avenger Field, this is four-two-one, over," Sprite said.

"Four-two-one, this is Tower, go ahead," answered the controller.

"Tower, four-two-one requests that you clear the pattern for emergency landing. Mechanical failure; instrument panel light shorted out. We are flying blind, over," said Sprite.

"Roger, four-two-one, Tower acknowledges; clearing the pattern," came the reply.

For two more long minutes, Phoebe flew on, big tears rolling down her fear whitened cheeks, and when Sprite spotted the runway lights of Avenger, she said, "There it is!"

"Not on the ground yet, Sprite!" shouted Phoebe, beginning to breathe too rapidly. "How do I get this thing down now?"

"I'll strike a match, but it needs to burn longer than I can hold it. Give me one of your bobby pins." Phoebe pulled at her hair and produced the little hairpin and Sprite carefully took it. "Now you look at the altimeter. Lose as much altitude as we safely can until the match burns out. If they burn the same as the last one, that's about ten seconds, and this pin will get us another three or four for each one. But that probably still puts us a couple of miles from the landing strip," said Sprite. "Ready?"

Phoebe flexed her hand on the stick. "No! I really…Sprite, I just can't! You have to take the yoke or we bail."

"Yes, you can," said Sprite softly. "Slow your breathing and look at me." Phoebe gurgled a measured breath and looked over at Sprite, who was smiling at her as if they were sitting in the mess hall or at the Avengerette Club and not about to hit the ground at 100 miles per hour in a winged, wooden crate. "Phoebe, just do the next right thing and we'll be alright. I believe in you. Now, again, ready?" she said.

Phoebe levered the landing gear down. In a weak, but steadier voice, Phoebe said, "Ready." Sprite struck the match. It flared brightly, illuminating the instrument panel. Phoebe checked her altimeter and artificial horizon, then dropped the plane quickly, causing Sprite's stomach to lurch, but by the time two of their matches had smoked out, they had descended 200 feet and were only 100 yards from landing.

"OK, that was good," said Phoebe. "But I'm not gonna make the airstrip. Landing gear down and locked! Light the other one! There's the ground!"

Sprite sparked the match into light, then clipped it into the bobby pin. When it had burned down to the metal, she dropped the match, just as their wheels slammed down on the runway. It was harder than recommended, but it was a solid landing. Phoebe powered down to reduce their speed and blindly guided the plane to an eventual stop.

"Well," said Phoebe, her hairline damp with perspiration. "I'm wide awake now."

"You were great!" said Sprite, watching the whirling lights of the emergency vehicles charging toward them. "That landing was a bit scrambled, but still sunny side up."

Ж

The truck bounced along and Sprite looked over to Phoebe, who was staring out at the bleak, featureless landscape. The long ride to the airstrip was almost over, and Phoebe had seemed to grow paler with each passing mile. "Phoebe—it really will be OK today for you."

"You don't know that. I'm still shaken up by that emergency landing and I don't see how you can be so calm about it. Sprite, I panicked up there when the lights went out and we almost died getting that plane down! I...I never thought I'd face anything like that and when I had to, I choked," Phoebe muttered, "You know I choked. If it hadn't been for you—if I had been up there alone...."

"Yes, but you weren't and we didn't crash and die. You managed to land us safely even though you felt panic. That's what matters—and you learned that you can function up there even if you get a bad surprise," said Sprite, keeping her voice low. She knew Phoebe hadn't told the others everything that had happened in the cockpit that night. "Phoebe, I once had to land a plane before I'd ever flown one when my father passed out in the Stearman. I know how you felt. I also know you came through and did your job."

Phoebe smiled a little at that. "Right," she said softly.

The truck lurched to a stop and they waited for a minute while the dust clouds swirled and then settled before they hopped out. No one could afford to have grit in her eyes today.

"Awwwwright, ladies," the tall, lanky Captain called to them as they walked toward him. He stood looking at his clipboard and counted them off. Aviator glasses hid his eyes, but not the bored expression on his sunburned face. "My name is Captain Cullen. And you are the J-6 Gunslingers, eh?" he said, looking down at their cowboy boots. "Yeah, I've heard about ya'll. So let's see what you can do…Miss Soth-e-bee?" He searched for an answering face.

Ninette stepped forward and said, "Sotheby, sir," pronouncing it "Suttabee."

The Captain fished around in his mouth with his tongue like he'd lost something in his teeth and then said, "Uh huh. Come with me, Miss Soth-e-bee." Sprite noticed that, to her credit, Ninette didn't even blink. They'd been told the army check pilots were a disinterested, tough group whose job it was to uncover any weakness, bad attitude, or lack of preparedness in the WASP. It seemed they'd been told right.

When Ninette and the Captain had walked far enough to be out of earshot, Phoebe said, "Sprite! He's the one they call 'Captain Cull 'em!' He washes out more of us than any other check pilot!"

"Phoebe," Sprite sighed, "the only thing that's gonna get you washed out is if you show him any fear! Remember what Henry Ford said? 'Whether you believe you can or cannot, you are right.'? You can do this—just believe that. I do," Sprite said, facing Phoebe and looking her straight in the eye. "I believe you can."

Phoebe smiled shyly and said, "Really? You do?" Sprite nodded, smiling. "OK, then. If you believe it, so do I," Phoebe said, taking a deep breath.

Ж

One by one, their names were called and Captain Cullen took them up in the plane. Phoebe was last, and when she finally climbed down from the wing of her plane, her check flight passed, she had a big smile on her face. "See? Told ya!" crowed Sprite as she followed Phoebe into the truck bed for the ride home. "We all passed, and we're all gonna graduate day after tomorrow!"

"Yes. You were right," Phoebe said, grinning. The tension in her face had been replaced with relief and joy.

> *Cheer up, and the same to you!*
> *Good luck, in every thing you do!*
> *Cheer up, the skies will clear up!*
> *America's boys will come home once again!*

... sang Phyllis, one of the J-5 girls in the front of the truck bed, as she began Diedee Deaton's jody to the tune of the "Colonel Bogey March," but no one sang along until Bertie and Gertie exchanged a look and rose simultaneously to take over the song.

Bertie conducted the time signature and Gertie sang the harmony to:

> *Hitler! He's only got one ball!*
> *Goering! His are very small!*
> *Himmler! Has something sim'lar,*
> *but then Goebbels, has no balls, at all!*

Pretty soon, the entire truckload of newly flight-checked girls had joined in with full voice.

CHAPTER 28

TWO DAYS LATER, in her brand new Santiago Blue uniform, Sprite sat in the corner seat of the auditorium's last row—the spot in the formation she had occupied for the entire six months of her training at Avenger Field. Scattered in front of her, according to height, the other J-6 girls also sat listening to General Arnold's graduation speech to their class. What a strange feeling it was to be leaving. If still felt like she had just arrived. But then, no. So much had happened, so many changes had occurred, and so many memories had been made in those six short months. Sprite had come to Sweetwater as a lonely, orphaned country girl on the run with nothing but a sock full of change and her skill and determination. Now she was leaving as a fully-fledged WASP with a healthy bank account and a group of loyal sisters, each one of them someone special in her own right.

The general began his speech, but it was the same one he had given to the previous class at their graduation, so Sprite began to unconsciously tune out the words she had already heard only a couple of months ago.

Her eyes wandered over the crisp blue uniforms around her and settled on Ninette. Nin's face was partially visible from Sprite's angle and she saw a deep, satisfied smile on her friend's face. She had never told Nin, but Sprite had liked her from the beginning and thought she was the most elegant person she had ever known. Though it had taken some time for the others to get to know each other, and even more time for Sprite to trust their friendship, Nin had treated her like a little sister from the start. Nin's courage in the face of her wealthy family's narrow ideas of her life had given them all courage to be themselves, to grow in themselves. *I wonder where you will go for your posting, my wonderful friend,* Sprite thought as she saw Nin feel Sprite's eyes on her, look over, and wink. Sprite smiled back and looked away, suddenly sad and shy, and then caught sight of the twins.

Bertie and Gertie sat exactly diagonally to Sprite at the very front of the formation since they were the tallest of the group at somewhere close to six feet. Those two lived and breathed for each other, and danced so gracefully and in synch that they seemed to share the same mind. *You probably do share the same mind,* thought Sprite, silently chuckling. *You share the same everything else!* The twins looked and sounded so much alike that, early on, Sprite had asked one of them to mark herself in some way that they could know for sure who they were talking to. Bertie had obliged by cutting her hair three inches shorter than Gertie's and wore it in a long pageboy rather than a ponytail, like her sister. Still, when the hair was pinned up to fly, no one could tell which twin was which. Though the twins didn't seem to need anyone else, they were still very social, full of surprises, and the life of any party or night out. Sprite liked them very much and was a little unhappy that she wouldn't get to know them even better. They were the kind of "deep water" souls that her father had told her it took more than a little while to understand.

Right above the twins, Meredith sat on the dais, proudly surveying her newly fledged WASP girls. Meredith had been really good to Sprite from the beginning, sharing her lunch and her time with her when she didn't have to. Sprite would never forget that. Meredith had put herself on the line to get Sprite accepted into the program, again, when she didn't have to. But that was Meredith all up and down. Always there, always supporting her girls despite the heartache of missing her husband, who was God knows where in the Pacific, if he was even still alive after being shot down. Meredith was more than a mentor—she was a friend and sometimes, almost like the mother Sprite had wished for all her life. Meredith had finished her time at Avenger as an instructor and would be going to Santa Sabina in California in the next few days to join the WASP as a pilot. Sprite almost teared up thinking about that. *I had lost everything, even my father, and then, here, with these girls and Meredith, I have found a new family. Now we will scatter and fly away on the four winds and might never see one another again.*

Then she saw Phoebe's curly brown hair in the middle of the group, a little to the left. Sprite was especially glad Phoebe had earned her way to graduation—though Phoebe was a whiz at ground school, she had trouble with confidence in her flying. But she had made it. They had shared some intense and harrowing moments in that forced landing last week and there was something about that kind of experience that binds people together for life. Sprite was glad of that. They were real friends now. Only six months earlier, they had met on that train platform in Sweetwater and Phoebe had talked nonstop until they had reached the hotel. Sprite now knew that had been Phoebe's way of trying to hide her discomfort and fear, but that day, it had just annoyed Sprite, who had been tired and hungry and worried. Very, very worried.

The thought of why she had been so worried that day passed through her mind then and she suddenly lost her smile and all the warm feelings she had been enjoying. All the way from Georgia to Sweetwater, Sprite had thought about what Major Wallace Doyle said to her that day he had stolen her ring and taken her farm. He had promised her he would find her and see that she was punished for shooting him and sure enough, he had found her even here in the west Texas desert. How close he had come to raping her the night of the big dance, just a couple of months ago, still sent a shiver up her spine. Only Hal had stood between her and that evil man's drunken attack, but Hal hadn't been there when Doyle found her later and threatened her. She'd had a hard choice to make then—accuse a senior officer of misconduct, take the chance of him getting her washed out or even shutting down the WASP program, or keep quiet, knowing that he had a potentially dangerous secret that might impact the entire war. She had decided to keep quiet until she had more proof than his slurred, one-sided conversation, but it was still hard to think about what Doyle might be up to. Thank God for Hal, though.

Her smile came back at the thought of him.

Applause broke out all over the room at the same moment and Sprite realized the General's speech was finished. The pinning ceremony was beginning. The first row of graduates stood in unison and walked to the dais, where they waited to hear their names. One by one, they climbed the several stairs and received the wings of a trained, fully certified, WASP.

Row by row, the chairs emptied in front of Sprite and then it was her row's turn. She rose, felt a thrill or expectancy run through her body and could not keep from beaming. When the General pushed the pin through her uniform and locked the wings in place, she almost burst into tears. It was done. Finally, and forever, Sprite Shannon was a WASP. She was the very last one to be pinned, so the applause began again, this time with a deafening roar. She shook the General's hand and someone with a camera called, "Smile for the cover of *Look*, honey!" as a flashbulb popped in her eyes.

※

Meredith picked up the photograph frame that held her favorite picture of Frank, her husband. The photo had been taken in the Hamptons, at their beach house, two years earlier. Frank had come back for a week of leave and surprised her by appearing on the beach during her early morning walk. She frequently went out to see the sunrise, making photographs of the moods of the ocean and the shore birds, a life long hobby. Meredith had studied flight since she was a small child, watching the gulls bank and wheel overhead and hang in the air before snatching a crust of bread from her hand. She'd never lost her wonder of birds and the miracle of flight.

The day Frank had come back, she'd had her camera aimed at a rare, white tailed sea eagle that had been hovering at the shoreline, fishing. She'd been deep in concentration, never hearing Frank approach in the soft sand, and he had simply walked into her shot. Meredith had startled badly and pressed the shutter. The result was a photo of Frank smiling and holding his arms wide, as if in flight, with the disturbed sea eagle caught in the air just above his head, wings spread to exactly follow the lines of Frank's arms. She could never have hoped to set up such a perfect shot.

She hugged the photo to her chest and said, "Frank, my love, I know you are still there. Please, please, hang on until they can find you.

I miss you so much." She wiped at the tears the words brought forth and then sniffed hard to stop them. The girls would be coming in any minute to give her their assignment requests. She needed to be presentable. She wrapped brown paper around the photo frame and pushed it gently into the box with the few books and other personal items from her office. Her orders to report to Santa Sabina in California lay to the side on her empty desk.

"Hello?" A knock came at her door, Sprite's voice behind it. "Instructor Lowe? May we come in?"

Meredith smiled widely and said, "Yes, of course."

A parade of Santiago Blue uniforms filed into Meredith's office and spread out in front of her. The five girls in them didn't look like girls anymore—their faces were tanned and more angular, their bodies thinner and more muscular, and their bearing far more confident than that of the eager recruits they had been only six months earlier. She was proud of this group like she had never been proud of any other. All of them had amazing gifts, and she had been privileged to discover and develop them. It had been a rewarding job and she was suddenly overwhelmingly sad at the prospect of them flying off into their individual futures, far away from her.

"Instructor Lowe, you wanted to see us?" prompted Ninette.

"Oh, yes," said Meredith, "I did. Do you have your requests ready to turn in?"

The newly graduated pilots traded looks. Now was the time to reveal their choices for duty and, even though they all had an idea of who wanted to go where, it was about to become a firm choice. Sprite stood by Phoebe, who had earlier told her that wherever she wanted to go, Phoebe would go with her. Sprite had considered Delaware, thinking that Hal might be close there, so both girls had written it in the blanks. Bertie and Gertie wanted only to go together, so they might be sent anywhere. Ninette had thought about someplace close to Manhattan and had marked her request as such. They all held the papers behind them now, waiting for Meredith to ask for them.

"Before you hand the requests in, I have something I'd like for you all to consider," Meredith began hesitantly. "As you know, I'll be leaving to join the WASP as a pilot, just like you, since my work here is done. I… I was wondering if you might like to come with me to Santa Sabina, in California, as a squadron under my command. I would really like it if you wanted to come," she said, hopefully smiling at them.

The five girls exchanged looks once more and without another word among them, began to tear up their requests and toss them into the trashcan. "Um, I think we'll need new request forms, Meredith," said Ninette, laughing.

"And I just happen to have some right here!" said Meredith cheerfully, holding up the blank forms.

The forms filled in and signed, and their lots thrown in with each other, Sprite, Phoebe, and Nin decided to go back to the barracks to rest for a bit, while Bertie and Gertie went off with their parents for a long overdue visit.

The three ambled along in the cold February sunshine, enjoying the vast blue sky and thinking their own private thoughts until Sprite said, "Say, Phoebe, who is that man over there waving at you?" She had noticed a wiry, middle-aged man in a threadbare suit coat that looked like it belonged to someone larger. "See him?"

Phoebe had seen him. In fact, she had seen him before the graduation ceremony and ducked behind another girl to keep him from seeing her. The man caught sight of her then and came over, his right leg dragging a bit, a huge, gap-toothed smile lighting up his weathered face.

"Honey! I been lookin' for you all over!" he said gleefully, catching Phoebe up in a bear hug. "Look at you! All dressed up like a bluejay! I shore was proud when they pinned you up with those wings!" He let Phoebe go and she immediately backed away from him, her face flushed with embarrassment.

"Um, hi, Dad," she said quietly, forcing a weak smile.

Sprite almost betrayed her shock—Phoebe had told them her father was in the oil business, but this man looked like a day laborer with his gritty, dark rimmed fingernails and rawboned face. Sprite managed to hide her surprise with a big greeting. "Hello, there, Phoebe's Dad, I'm Sprite, one of her bay mates!"

"Oh, hey, little girl," the man said, but his sparkling blue eyes never left his daughter. "Phoebe, your Mom had to stay back with the boys, but I couldn't let you graduate without comin' to see you. Say… you don't look too happy to see me," he said, disappointment erasing his smile.

"Um, Dad, no, it's just that—" Phoebe began, but Ninette was extending her hand.

"Hi, I'm Ninette. Proud of your girl, sir?" she said, giving him every bit as much respect as if he were really the savvy businessman Phoebe had bragged that he was.

Phoebe's Dad nodded vigorously. "Hello, I'm Marshall Summerfield, Phoebe's father," he said, taking the hand and shaking it roughly. "Pleased to meet you." Phoebe's color deepened and she suddenly grabbed her father's arm and pulled him aside, leaving Sprite and Nin standing alone, puzzled looks on their faces.

"Why are you here, Dad? I wrote and told you not to come! You are embarrassing me in front of my friends!" she whispered angrily.

Mr. Summerfield drew back and gently disengaged his daughter's hand from his arm. "Embarrassing you? Really? Because the last time I checked, my permission was the reason you got to be here at all," he said. His white forehead, the only part of his face that his hard hat usually covered, creased in deep, oil stained wrinkles beneath his dark, curly hair.

Sprite and Nin could hear every word the two said, but politely began a meaningless weather conversation a couple of feet away. Phoebe sighed deeply. "Yes, Dad, I am grateful for your support. Now please let me go with my friends and I will find you in an hour or so." She looked expectantly to her father's hurt face.

"OK, honey. If that's what you want," he said, fatigue and pain in his voice. He tipped his imaginary hat to Sprite and Nin and then turned to walk away, standing straight in spite of the obvious limp.

"Phoebe? Why did you send him off like that?" said Sprite.

"Because, that's why. Just because. Now let's go," said Phoebe, trying to close the conversation.

"I know why," said Nin. She smiled gently at Phoebe, putting her arm around her. "Because your father 'in the oil business' is not a landowner or an oil baron; he's a roustabout, isn't he, Phoebe?"

Phoebe began to sob. "Yes. He is. And I am so ashamed of it, so just don't tell anyone else, alright?"

"Why?" said Sprite. "Why are you ashamed of him? He does honest labor despite that limp that no doubt kept him out of the war. Apparently, he's humble and patriotic enough to let his only daughter serve in his place. And Phoebe," she said, her voice trailing off, "—be glad you have a father."

Nin slowly added, "And one that's here to see you on your big day." Nin's parents had not bothered to come.

Phoebe dared to look up at them then. "Are you mad because I lied to you about him? Can you ever forgive me?" she asked, sniffling.

Sprite and Ninette stood silently for a long moment, their arms crossed over their chests. At length, Sprite said, "Oh, we're plenty hot about that, Phoebe, and the way you just treated him was pretty low." Then, managing a crooked smile despite her irritation, she added, "but you don't ever need to pretend with us. Ever."

"Phoebe, of course we forgive you," said Nin, looking to Sprite and receiving a nod, "but please don't ever lie to us again, OK? Too much now depends on our trust of one another. We're going to be a squadron. Someday, up there, it might mean the difference between life and death." Phoebe nodded, shame washing over her face as the possible import of her behavior sunk in. Nin saw and quickly added, "I think you could begin to make up for this, though. Why don't you go find your Dad and make him feel better?" Nin's suggestion sounded more like penance to Phoebe, but she nodded and went after her dad.

※

"So, riding with me?" said Ninette, tossing her bags into the boot of her two seater aubergine Jaguar convertible. A few days had passed since graduation, and all the newly fledged WASPs were on their ways to all parts of the country.

Sprite looked up from the automotive marvel and said, "Nin, this car… really something else, isn't it? I've never seen one like it."

Nin laughed and waved a casual hand, "It really is. I just love it. High school graduation present from my grandmother, who was a 20's flapper! Sometimes I can't believe it's really mine. Just look at those Art Nouveau lines! C'mon, hop in." Sprite grinned and put her suitcase next to Nin's two others, noticing that her belongings had increased to the point that her old pillowcase would never have held them now. Still, she had only the one case while Phoebe had kept her five, which were now stowed in the back of Meredith's larger Cadillac. The twins would be riding with Meredith also, and had already claimed the back seat. Meredith and Phoebe put the top down and when Sprite had taken her seat in the Jag, Meredith sang, "Well! Off we go…"

The girls finished the phrase, shouting, "Into the wild blue yonder!"

And the J-6 Gunslinger WASPs pulled out of Avenger Field, leaving behind the dusty barracks, the training planes, Deidee, the Base Commander, the snakes, the tarantulas, and Chihuahua. Ahead lay California, Santa Sabina airbase, and a new life of service.

And though she had told no one, it was Sprite's 18th birthday.

PART II

CHAPTER 29

THE FIRST FEW weeks of active duty for Sprite, Meredith, Bertie, Gertie, Ninette and Phoebe at their new duty station of Santa Sabina Air Base, California seemed to entail a lot of time spent *away* from the base, at various flight schools, learning to fly other aircraft in the US arsenal.

Sprite, to her disappointment, discovered she was physically too small to qualify for bomber pilot training, but learning to fly "pursuits," or fighter aircraft, helped make up for that. Her favorite course, the training for the North American P-51 "Mustang" fighter, was conducted just outside of Palm Springs, California. Sprite felt a keener appreciation for her new duty, when at the conclusion of flight training, all of the pilots—male Army Air Force pilots and WASP pilots alike—were ordered to the armory, where they were issued .45 automatic pistols. The newly-trained Mustang pilots who had not already qualified with the .45 sidearm, mostly the WASP girls, were then marched down to the base firing range for several hours of weapons instruction.

"At present, the P-51 Mustang is the hottest plane in the sky. So you are being issued these sidearms as a precaution," said the weapons instructor, an army captain. "In the event of a forced landing in the Mustang, you are to prevent any unauthorized personnel from taking control of, or even *approaching*, the aircraft. If necessary, as a last resort, you are to use your sidearm to shoot the fuel tanks, which will cause the aircraft to explode, preventing it from falling into the wrong hands. Are there any questions?"

Sprite thought long and hard about those words and when she glanced over at the other girls, she saw very serious looks on their faces. The war, the one being fought overseas, with real bullets and real blood, had just stepped a little closer to them. They spent the rest of the day dutifully learning to disassemble, assemble, clean, load and fire the Colt .45 pistol, and by late afternoon, the WASP J-6 Gunslingers were living up to their name. They all stood on the firing line blasting away, punching holes in paper targets and wondering what it would feel like to have to use those pistols for real, when the targets were human.

Eventually, Sprite and the girls settled in and began to consider the sprawling, busy Santa Sabina airbase their home. Although they traveled far and wide delivering all types of military aircraft to bases all over the country, Sprite always felt happy when she touched down on the familiar runway.

"A new assignment has come down," said Meredith one afternoon, breezing into the common room in the Officers' Club, where the rest of the girls had gathered to listen to the radio. President Roosevelt was about to speak. It was a few hours later on the East Coast than in their time zone, so the "Fireside Chats" came to them in the late afternoon rather than at night.

"Where are we going?" said Sprite, lifting a cup of coffee to her lips.

"Canadian Forces Shilo base in Manitoba," said Meredith as she flipped through the pages of the orders. "We are to deliver some Airacobras to…oh, wow, to the Night Witches!"

"The who?" said Bertie, pushing the last of a roast beef sandwich into her mouth.

"The Night Witches!" said Meredith, excitement lighting up her face.

"I've never heard of them," said Gertie. Sprite appeared to be puzzled as well.

Nin smiled, knowing what was coming next, and pushed a fresh cup of tea toward Meredith. Still an instructor at heart, Meredith happily sat down and began. "The Night Witches are sort of a Russian version of us," she said. "But they fly combat and drop bombs on the Germans, and that's how they got their name. They figured out how to sneak in over their targets and cut the engines on their little biplanes and then by the time the Germans know they are there, it's too late. The name is from the word '*nachthexen*,' literally, German for night witch. They call them that because all the Germans hear when the biplanes pass overhead is the whoooosh! the cables on their Po-2s make as they glide over, and the men think it sounds like a witch on her broom."

"Wow!" said Sprite, transfixed.

"The Germans automatically give out an iron cross for every Night Witch shot down—that's how afraid of them the troops are," Meredith continued. "There is even a rumor among the German troops that the Night Witches take special pills or injections that give them the kind of night vision cats have, but that is just rumor. I think it helps with the intimidation factor, though."

"And we are going to bring them new Airacobras?" said Phoebe. "Quite a step up, then. Those planes are big and loud."

"We are. Looks like they are finally, well, at least this elite group of them, getting better equipment. They have flown their old planes just about to death. Sometimes, they do twenty or more missions a night and come back all shot to pieces, but they go out again and again. Eventually, there are more holes than plane left, I guess." Meredith added.

"Who does their mechanical work?" asked Ninette, who had been quiet up until then, her face a study in thought.

"Why, I think other women do it," said Meredith. "Yes, they must do. Because the 588th is made up exclusively of women, from the pilots to the ground crews."

"The WASP should be like that, too," said Nin, laughing. "Then, maybe our training planes would actually have gotten serviced!"

With that, they all heartily agreed and began to clear the table. The President's voice crackled over the radio and they fell silent as he told the nation about the battle of Anzio. In other news, the Germans had declared victory in the fight at the Russian front, losing an estimated 68,000 men to the Russian's 100,000 estimated dead, with possibly many more to come. Germany measured victory in bodies, apparently. No doubt, the Night Witches had been part of those battles.

The President signed off and the girls looked at each other soberly. Sprite said, "Meredith, when do we leave? Let's give them some help over there."

"In three days," said Meredith.

"I wish we were going tonight," said Sprite, and the others nodded in agreement.

X

"You have to go tonight, Captain James," said Major Doyle, looking up at the puzzled face of his engineer. "In other words, right now."

"But, Sir, I should be there to test the new blade design tomorrow, and—" Hal protested. He didn't want to go to Detroit to meet with the contractors. While vital, it was a job any number of other men could have done, and he should be there when they fired up the next test engine to see how well his blade design—the one in the photos of the German wreckage—worked. Doyle was simply taking the project away from him, just before it came to fruition, not to mention using the mundane meeting as a way to keep Hal in his proper place, which was, apparently, under Doyle's thumb and somewhat in the dark. If the test went forward without him, the data he could have harvested would go unassimilated, the engine might have to be rebuilt and the test done again, and that took far too much precious time. The delay would be weeks and no one but he and Doyle would know that. Why was Doyle so keen to keep him from progressing? He knew he had it! He had a working jet engine for the Allies and here was his boss, telling him to take off right at the point of success! Was Doyle trying to claim all of the glory for himself, or was…. Hal swallowed hard at his next thought. *Or was he the mole in the Archangel operation?*

Before Hal could chase that thought any further, Doyle raised one dark eyebrow and drew his thin lips into a sneer. "You should be," he replied, waggling his head a bit, "wherever I say you should be, Captain James, or perhaps you would like to take it up with the General, whereupon I might need to inform him of your ongoing issues with battle fatigue?"

Hal's mouth fell open. So Doyle *had* seen his reaction for what it was that first day when the engine exploded and Hal had reacted badly and run out the bunker door.

"Oh, yes, Captain James, I know all about your little problem," said Doyle. "Your doctor didn't report your condition as such, but I can read between the lines of his summary. And he *didn't* clear you for combat, now did he? What happened? Did you survive something you shouldn't have? *Cause* it?" Hal said nothing, but he did not deny any of it.

"Ah. Yes, you caused it," Doyle smiled bitterly. "As I thought, then. So if you don't want anyone else knowing about your psychological problems, especially anyone who might permanently ground you just when our jets are going to need flying, then I think you will be waking up tomorrow in Detroit. Are we clear?"

Hal dropped his eyes, and said, "Sir. Yes, sir!"

Doyle cocked one eyebrow and went back to his papers. "That is all," he murmured and Hal turned on his heel, maybe a little too sharply, and marched out of the office to go and pack his bag.

Less than an hour later, Hal was aboard a C-46 transport plane to Detroit to speak to some experts in the art of metallurgy. He sat watching the tops of the moonlit clouds, thinking Doyle had just blackmailed him into disappearing and wondering why that had been so necessary. Doyle had not given him time to contact anyone and had sent an MP with him "to see him onto the plane." Hal had tried stop at his desk to make a quick call to the General or Gabriel, but the MP had shaken his head and said, "Sir, there really is no time for that. Major Doyle specifically told me to get you on that plane by 1900 hours." The steely glint in the eyes of the hard faced soldier told Hal all he needed to know about resisting.

Now Hal stared out at the surreal cloudscape and thought about the viable possibility that Major Doyle was the mole in the Archangel program. What came to mind first in support of that idea was Doyle's secrecy about himself. What did anyone know about him, anyway? Hal had no clue about the man's life outside the narrow confines of the interaction they had over the engine problems. Hal had never seen Doyle leave the base and knew no one who socialized with him. The Major was a sour, unhappy man who always seemed to be pushed just slightly beyond his tolerance and might wingnut off into the wild blue yonder at any minute. Perhaps he already had.

Hal sighed and wondered what the next step might be. He had no proof at all about Doyle—just that gut level intuition that told him he was right. Whatever else happened, he should tell Gabriel and the General about his suspicions, though that news would not make either of them very happy. Doyle was privy to a good many state secrets and if he were indeed the mole, then not only had Archangel been compromised, very likely, so had much more.

Hal landed and immediately tried to call the General and Gabriel, but the base operator said both of them were out of their offices, due to the late hour, so he left messages for them. He found his quarters, slept badly, and awakened to find a group of grumpy civilian engineers waiting for him on the assemblage floor at the plant. They showed him design after unimaginative design and offered too much advice that had nothing to do with Hal's mission at Archangel. There was a tour of the facilities and a sampling of materials to be approved but otherwise, the morning had seemed a total waste of time. When they handed him a four-inch stack of orders to sign for Doyle's materials requisitions, he almost couldn't believe it. All of it could have been done from the Angels' Roost.

He finished his paperwork at last and tossed the pen onto the desk, his hand cramping and his mind spinning. It was now past noon. He stared at the silent phone, picked it up and tried the General for a third time, but there was no dial tone. *What is going on?!* Hal thought, slamming the receiver down in frustration.

"Sir?" A polite corporal stood waiting for Hal's acknowledgment. Hal nodded as he started to put his overcoat on. His flight was scheduled to leave in a few minutes. "Oh, no, sir, I'm not here to collect you. Really bad weather coming in quickly from the west. Big blizzard already knocked out a bunch of phone and electric lines. Looks like you'll be with us for another day, at least. You can get out then with the WASP pilots taking the bomber back to Santa Sabina. Sorry, sir."

Hal closed his eyes in fatigue and frustration, and then they popped open again. Would Sprite be on that bomber? Maybe. Very possibly. Hal's face lit up at the thought, but the corporal never saw it because the room went suddenly dark.

"Correction, sir," said the efficient corporal. "Really bad weather has just arrived."

CHAPTER 30

"LET'S GET IN the jeeps, girls," laughed Meredith, turning to hand the last of the paperwork over to a Canadian RAF officer. "We are overnighting, so there's time to meet the women who will be flying the planes we just brought up here. Apparently, there was a vodka shortage on the base, so they have already gone into town. We'll just have to find them there." Before Meredith turned back around, the jeeps were full of tired, thirsty, curious girls.

In the winter, evening came early anywhere in Canada, but it seemed to arrive pretty much right after lunch in the small town of Brandon, Manitoba. With two solidly packed feet of snow underfoot, the WASP girls made their way in blue semi-darkness toward the neon lights of a dozen different Canadian beer signs which hung in the same window of every night spot on Brandon's "main drag," as Ninette had laughingly called it. Canada was, after all, the land of lumberjacks, beer, and places lumberjacks went to drink beer. This particular establishment was called "The Big Moose," and Bertie had made mention of how the name seemed redundant. But then Gertie reminded her they were in Canada, and a big moose in Canada likely meant something that should be called "ugly raging death with antlers the size of a bomber's wings." Bertie conceded the point, noting there still had to be a better single descriptor than "big."

"Oh, look!" cried Meredith, pointing through the window at the long bar behind the overlapping beer signs, "They're here!" The five other parka hooded heads behind her tilted like a flock of geese looking skyward, and the girls quickly funneled into the door of the little pub and began to stamp the snow from their boots.

Sprite let her hood down and when the toque-clad heads in front of her parted—because there was standing room only—she saw three red cheeked, blonde women in flight suits dancing precariously on the bar to a Russian folk song. The whole room was clapping time to an accordion player's ever quickening tempo until finally, the women raised their hands, linked arms, gave a shout, and jumped to the suddenly cleared floor where they landed awkwardly, but were quickly steadied by three more of their group. The song ended, the handclaps turned to applause, and someone shouted, "Drinks for the dancers on me!"

The middle dancer laughed heartily, took the small, tube shaped glass of vodka she was offered, and tossed it down in one swallow as if it had been a drink of water. Sprite's eyes widened in wonder and she felt a bit queasy at the thought of chugging a shot of straight liquor like that. Who were these women? And what were they drinking?

Meredith, as though reading her mind, said, "Come on. Let's meet the Night Witches!" The girls shed their parkas, smoothed their uniforms, and threaded through the clusters of beer-hoisting Canadians to find the dancers at the far end of the bar, now talking amongst themselves.

Upon seeing Meredith's wings pinned to her uniform, one of them raised her arm in greeting and said, "Hallo! You are WASP persons who bring us new planes, *da*?"

Meredith stepped forward and smiled, offered her hand, and the woman took it with a firm grip. "Yes, my name is Meredith Lowe, and I lead this squadron of WASP. Meet Bertie, Gertie, Ninette, Phoebe, and Sprite, she said, sweeping her other hand over the girls at her side.

"I am *Starshij Lejtenant* Olga Vladimirovna, and leader of this squadron from 588th night bombers," the woman replied, "and this is squadron, Katya, Marina, Oksana, Nazdeka, Trinka."

The girls all nodded to each other and shook hands. "Do you all speak English?" asked Sprite.

"No, only Katya and me," said Olga, "We will translate. Please sit. We talk."

Phoebe and Katya took drink orders and went to the bar while the others moved toward a big horseshoe shaped booth by the far wall, where it was a bit quieter. They had all just settled in when two barmaids brought trays laden with various lagers and a flight of vodka chilling in some ice that had no doubt come freshly from the yard in back of the bar.

"First is this," said Olga, eyeing the drinks. "We are thanking you for meeting us here. Is always better to begin friendship over vodka." She took one of the tubes of vodka, raised it, and her crew instantly, simultaneously, followed suit, then waited for the WASP girls to join the toast. Meredith found the lone glass of pale ale, and the others took what was closest to them, not waiting to sort the orders out.

"To new friends in high places," said Olga, laughing at her own joke, and glasses clinked all around.

Sprite took a sip of something called "shandy," and made a face at what surely was half beer and half lemonade, but decided it must be better than the dark, opaque lagers that were in the other glasses. Sprite's taste in alcohol had been limited to her Daddy's yearly batch of peach brandy they used as a tonic for croup. Everyone laughed as she tried the shandy again and had the same reaction. Glasses clinked, names were repeated, the music began again, and Ninette scooted out to find the "washroom," as they called it there.

Sprite studied the lined, weathered faces of the Russian women, remembering that Meredith had said most of them were not even twenty yet. Olga and Katya seemed a little older, maybe Meredith's age, and also fared better in the looks department, with interesting, angular faces and striking blue eyes. Sprite realized they must be sisters. All of the Night Witches wore their hair chin length and severely cut. Wisps of pale blonde hair straggled out from behind Olga's ear and when she pushed them back with a practiced gesture, her sleeve slipped up to her elbow. When Olga's arm came down to the table, the sleeve stuck, and the neon lights revealed great patches of puckered red and pink skin on the woman's bare forearm and hand. Sprite almost gasped. *Burns!* She thought, *whatever caused them?* Olga saw her looking and smiled ruefully as she met Sprite's eyes.

"Is scarring from mission," she said, matter of factly. "Not so pretty, *da?*"

Sprite, embarrassed to have been caught looking, just dropped her gaze and mumbled, "Sorry, I didn't mean to stare."

"Is no problem," said Olga, her eyes half closed. "I lived." She pulled up the other sleeve and stretched her other hand and arm out to show Sprite a matching group of burns on them. The hands looked stiff and Olga's left pinky finger appeared to be useless. "You want to hear about it?" she asked.

At that, she had the whole table's attention, and with the art of a natural story teller, she began. "Here is happening," Olga said. "On *feef*-teenth mission of the night, we got shot down six months ago—six months, Katya?" she looked to her stolid sister, who nodded. "Katya is navigator," Olga explained. "She drops last bomb and I did restart engine when beeg German fighter came out of clouds from above, shooting to us! We dive through tall hedges, low and slow to stall the fighter which is following; this works, big German plane starts to fall from sky and, heppiness!, we are almost out of range! But German shoots one last round and lucky shot hits our nose before he creshes in huge exploding. We think, '*Da*, we have still made it!' But then, engine catches fire, plane begins fast burning, is just wood and cloth, you know, flames coming into cockpit, all over my gloves and jacket." Olga took a sip of vodka and lowered her volume for emphasis. "I am thinking we hev maybe terrible future. I am pilot, so I hev choice, you see. If I choose burning arms but steering plane down, because we are already so low to ground, maybe we live, but we are behind German lines and maybe I never fly again even if we make it home—or if I choose take hands off stick to save arms from terrible pain, we die in cresh for certainly because is no parachute. I choose enduring fire, land plane almost good in beeg snowbank, and we live. I am burned, but Katya is OK. Hunters pick us up next day, take us home, I go to hospital for next month to recover. But now, is scarring on hands and arms to remind me to always watch above as well as below. Sometimes, a German gets lucky, *da*, Katya?" Katya grunted her stone-faced agreement and threw back another shot of vodka.

Sprite nodded in respect, thinking that she was glad she'd never had to make such a pilot's choice, and then wondering if she ever could. All around the booth, the other WASPs sat wide-eyed and silent.

Olga and Katya told several more of their tales while their companions sat by and drank in amenable silence. They spoke of how their leader had been driven off course and killed, crashing on the frozen Volga River just recently, and how they'd had to fight government, family, and the male pilots every step of the way to be able to fly. Sprite knew she would never forget any of those stories, especially the one about a terrible blizzard.

One winter, there had come such a snow and windstorm that the ground crew for the Night Witches had been ordered to stretch themselves out over the flimsy canvas wings of their planes to keep them from being blown away. Hour after hour they lay there, colder than Sprite could imagine, and then the shift would change and new girls would take their places, until a day later, the wind stopped. Katya said the last shift of the crew were so covered in snow that they looked like mythical frost giants when the others pried them off the wings. Oddly, the heavy blanket of snow had kept them from being any colder than the snow itself, and had added to the weight on the wings as well. Even so, many of the women had suffered frostbite and one had died from hypothermia when she had fallen asleep. But every plane was still there at the end of the storm.

The evening stretched into almost morning, the women comfortable enough by then with each other to trade jibes and jokes, and finally—promises to stay in touch—when the publican shouted for last call. The time had flown by. Ninette paid for their last round, which was black coffee, and they all walked together to the jeeps, then formed a convoy back to the base.

Snow began to fall and as they bumped and slewed along on the packed ice on the roads. Sprite thought about the bitter, stinging, frozen wind blowing in her face in the open jeep, and how the Night Witches flew missions in open cockpits, sometimes nearly twenty times a night. These women were so much more than delivery flyers—so much more than the WASP.

When they got back to CFB Shilo, the Russians bade them a formal, amazingly sober, good night and good-bye before they went to their quarters. The WASP girls were abnormally quiet as they, too, found their rooms, so Meredith stopped in to say good night to each of them. It had been an unusual evening.

When she got to Sprite and Phoebe, who shared a room, she asked, "Why so pensive?" Phoebe looked up and sighed.

"The Night Witches... I think we are all really amazed and a little embarrassed," said Phoebe. Sprite nodded her agreement.

"I get the amazed part, but why embarrassed?" said Meredith, although Sprite could see she had an inkling already. Meredith always wanted them to shape their own answers.

"Because we... we are just bus drivers compared to them, aren't we?" said Phoebe. "We don't fly combat, or have to fling ourselves onto frozen wings to keep planes from disappearing in snowstorms. No one is shooting at us when we fly. We seem to have this war really easy, from what they said. It makes me feel grateful, but also like I'm not doing enough. And Olga called us Powderpuffs when we told them what our duties are!"

Meredith laughed and nodded. "Yes, she did, but you know she was joking with you. Russian humor, you know. If she'd had no respect for us, they wouldn't have talked to us at all. The Night Witches are rising to their particular challenges, but then, so are we. Those challenges are just different. Well, maybe only some of them are different—you heard them talk about their obstacles in the course of their training. Their barriers sounded much the same as ours."

In fact, they had been, and in comparing those obstacles was where the real friendship with the Night Witches had begun, in Sprite's estimation anyway. All of the WASP had their own version of those barriers to relate, and the shared oppression of constant resistance by mechanics and male pilots and family had drawn the two disparate groups together.

"They seem larger than life, yes," said Meredith. "And I suppose they really are. But we could match them, given the need."

Given the need? wondered Sprite, thinking she'd like some elaboration on the comment, but before Meredith had left the doorway, Phoebe was asleep. A minute later, Sprite closed her eyes as well, the thought undiscussed.

Sprite did not sleep well. In her recurring dream, Sprite battled horrible images of engine fires and impossible choices, and Major Doyle's angry face repeatedly flashed over deafening explosions while a huge storm raged all around her. She awoke to darkness and Phoebe's hand shaking her.

"Wake up, Sprite. We have to fly in an hour. Let's get some breakfast." Sprite rolled over on her back and tried to clear her head, which happily, did not throb with a hangover. After the hideous shandy, she'd opted for straight lemonade for the rest of the evening. Phoebe's tired face sharpened into focus and the dream faded.

"OK, thanks, Phoebe," she mumbled, and then sat up, swung her feet onto the cold wood floors of the barracks, and took a deep breath as she remembered where she was. They were going home, back to Santa Sabina. Their mission had been completed and the Airacobras were probably already in the air, flying toward Russia, piloted by the bravest women Sprite had ever met.

CHAPTER 31

"NEXT LEG, BACK to Romulus, Michigan," said Meredith, as she set her empty coffee cup down, "then we'll be hitching a ride on a bomber back to Santa Sabina."

The girls rose from their metal chairs and stretched one last time before boarding.

The trip to Romulus passed quickly and the girls filed out onto the tarmac, where the big B-17 bomber they would fly home was being serviced. Sprite stood for a moment, just taking in how big the thing was. It took a minimum crew of five in combat and it had a huge Plexiglas nose that normally positioned a bombardier for a panoramic view of the sky.

"C'mon, Sprite, shake a leg," said Phoebe, pushing her friend gently along. "We have only a little time to take care of the necessaries and get some lunch. It's a long haul back to California. Sprite grinned and fell in behind Phoebe and, pretty soon, they were all sitting down to a bowl of some kind of stew and a loaf of bread. The hot food made Sprite feel better after the cold flight, and she began to feel her hands and feet warming. In a few more minutes, they boarded the bomber, with Meredith as pilot, and Ninette beside her as copilot. Bertie and Gertie shared navigation and radioman duties, while Phoebe and Sprite settled into their jump seats and waited for the take off. They would rotate duties later in the flight.

Sprite heard the metal hatches slam and lock. The engines started, the props whirled into invisibility, and then the big bird rolled toward the runway, lifting off flawlessly in the cold cloud cover. Sprite's ears closed up momentarily and she clicked her jaw open and closed to clear them. Then the roar of the bomber filled the air and conversation was impossible without radio headphones.

About ten minutes into the flight, just when Sprite was nodding off, Phoebe unbuckled her harness, stood up, and shook Sprite awake for the second time that day.

"Whaaa?" said Sprite, as she opened one eye. "Leave me alone, Phoebe!" She had just dropped into deep sleep, and this time, had been dreaming about Hal.

Phoebe stepped aside and let the person behind her come forward.

Sprite thought she was still dreaming, because right there in front of her stood Captain Hal James, in the flesh, smiling from ear to ear.

"Hi, Sprite," he said, over the noise of the engines.

Sprite sat bolt upright in her seat and frantically smoothed her uniform as she broke into a big smile. Phoebe was sure she was fully awake at that point, so she strapped herself into her seat again and pretended to read. There was nowhere for Hal to sit, so he beckoned Sprite to follow him, and he led her through the convoluted handholds and hatch down into the nose of the bomber. Meredith winked at him as they descended. It had taken a little wrangling, but between them, she and Hal had managed the surprise.

When Sprite stepped into the Plexiglas nose of the plane, she gasped in wonderment. Forests of bare trees and evergreens covered in virgin snow stretched out below them and reflected the red glow of the low winter sun, and little towns and farms dappled the cleared land. Hal closed the hatch and threw a blanket around her shoulders. There wasn't a lot of spare room in the bomber's nose, so Hal sat down and invited Sprite to squeeze in beside him. She did, and then shared her blanket with him, wrapping them up in scratchy olive drab warmth. To sit that close to Hal, to feel his body heat and have his arm around her again—it was the happiest Sprite had felt since the Snowy Winter Dance a couple of months before. For a long time, they were silent, just looking at the spectacular scenery and thinking their own thoughts.

Then Hal said, "I bet you wonder why I never came back for you that night at the dance... I want to apologize for that... I had to go with the

General and Jackie Cochran. I felt so bad about leaving you after what happened. I tried, I swear I tried," he said a little desperately when she made no reply.

Then Sprite smiled again and said, "Hal, it's alright. I knew what had happened and I knew it was your job. But I did wonder why you never wrote to me!" Her green eyes sparkled in a sudden ray of sunshine as the plane banked into a slight turn.

Hal's face colored beneath his tan. "I... couldn't," he said slowly, choosing his words carefully. "They have me working on something very secret and our communications are monitored. They don't want us talking to anyone, even family."

Sprite cocked her head to the side and said, "Not even a letter? Just to tell me where you were and that you were alive and well?"

Hal shook his head sadly. "No. Especially about where I am. And I couldn't be more sorry about it. I wanted so much to write to you, to put down on a page what I have been feeling..." he stopped there, looked deeply into the green wonder of her sunlit eyes. He touched her face, then closed his eyes and kissed her gently, then more deeply.

A sweet spark of electricity went through Sprite's body and she melted into Hal's arms as if she had been made to fit them. He held her for a long time, both of them savoring what had just happened, knowing that there is only ever one first kiss. Just one. And it had been the most glorious moment of Sprite's life. She wondered if he had felt the same thing—that electric connection between them—and decided he must have, because his eyes had gone wide in surprise after she had finally opened hers, and now his full lips swept upward in the smallest of smiles.

"Was that too awkward and forward of me—?" he said softly, but she shushed him and met his lips with hers again.

"No," she said at length, "it was a perfect landing, Captain James. But even experts can never practice enough, so why don't you try it again," she whispered, and he obliged her.

⋊⋉

Later, much later possibly, because Sprite noticed they were over the flat heartland with its winter-brown corn and wheat fields now, she sat back in Hal's arms. As he hugged her to himself, she felt him breathe a sigh of peace. But then his face contorted as though a painful thought had just entered his mind.

"What is it, Hal?" she said.

He sat quietly for a moment and then said, "I need to talk out my thoughts about something. I'm thinking about how much I can tell you, but since we were both in on what happened with Major Doyle at the dance… I can trust you, can't I?" he asked.

Sprite said, "You can trust me no matter what, Hal. I was raised by an honorable man." Hal smiled at that and took her hand in his.

"Sprite, I think Major Doyle is working for—"

"The Nazis!" Sprite finished vehemently, her eyes popping wide. Hal, startled she had guessed what he was about to say, let her go on. "That night, when he almost—well, he was so drunk that he started telling me stuff about someone called Mattias, which is a German name, right? And how this Mattias was going to give him a lot of money and how we—he thought I was his girlfriend, I think—could get away from the Nazis and the army and go off where they couldn't find us. He said other names, too—Greta and Gallagher."

"What?!" said Hal. "Do you mean to tell me he said who his contacts are?"

"I think he must have. Mattias, Greta, and Gallagher were the names he said; I'm sure of it," said Sprite.

"What else did he say, Sprite? Did he tell you anything more?" Hal pressed.

Sprite's face lit up. "Yes! He said that he had a job to finish, and it was about shipping something to Mattias, and I think, yes, it was chromium! I remember because that was what he told me was under my farm when I first met him, and how it 'would win the war….' Her voice trailed off. "I thought he meant win it for us, not for the Germans!" she said, horrified.

Hal said, "Anyone would have thought that, Sprite. I think Doyle is a master manipulator."

Sprite nodded, but said, "Now I maybe wish I had aimed a little lower and to the right when I shot his ear!"

At that, Hal burst into laughter and hugged her again. "And she's funny, too, folks!" he said to an imaginary audience. "Wait, *you* shot his ear?! He said he got that in 'action' in the field. He lets everyone think it's a war wound!"

Sprite threw her head back and giggled so hard it brought tears to her eyes. "Yes, I shot him. But it was in my parlor, not the field—not even the cornfield. The Snowy Winter Dance wasn't the first time that man came at me," she said. "I had to shoot him to keep him from hurting me."

Hal sobered instantly. "What?"

"Yes, he wouldn't give my mother's ring back. I caught him stealing it when he was there to seize my farm and he just laughed at me. I had him backed up at the door with my father's pistol. Then he lunged at me and tried to take the gun out of my hand. And I did warn him twice," she finished, coming out of the vivid memory. "Daddy taught me to shoot. But only when I had to. That day, I had to."

Hal listened closely, then said, "Well, I had no idea about any of that. I'm so glad you were all right, both times. He won't get a third chance, I promise you."

Sprite nodded. "No, he won't," she agreed, one eyebrow arching with conviction.

"But what now?" he said. "I think he's the mole in our top secret operation for sure, now, but there is absolutely no proof."

"Yet," said Sprite. "No proof yet. He'll make a mistake. I'm pretty sure he's got a drinking problem and looks to be about that far away from becoming unhinged. But there's more, Hal. He threatened me after the dance when he sobered up. He said if I reported him, he'd make sure I got washed out of training and that the whole WASP program would be terminated and that you—"

"Me? What about me?" said Hal, surprise in his voice.

"He said he'd make sure your career was over if I told anyone about what he'd said to me, because he says you have battle fatigue," she finished, looking down. This wasn't the way she had wanted to talk to him about this part of it.

"Well, I suppose that's how my medical record might read," Hal allowed evenly. He had already decided he would never hide that from Sprite. "I didn't get reassigned to flight status because of it. It's why I'm on the ground and not in the air again after my squadron was lost. It was bad for a while, absolutely. But I have it under control."

Sprite looked at him and said, "Do you think he could make a case against you? Ruin your career? Get you discharged?"

"Maybe, but more likely, he could just get me permanently grounded, and that would really put a monkey wrench in the works of our current project. I'm just glad you have graduated and are out from under that part of his threat. Still, the WASP program is at risk, so I see why you have kept all of this to yourself. It must have been a terrible burden for you to bear. Especially alone. But no more. I'm here and I think that together, we can find our proof that Doyle is a traitor. It sure would explain a couple of things..." Hal looked into the distance below. The terrain had become mountainous. They were approaching the Rockies, and Sprite knew she needed to take her turn at the radio, much as she just wanted to stay right where she was. Forever, if possible.

Hal sensed the tension in her body at the thought of her duty. "You need to go back up, don't you?" He said.

"Yes. I do. I don't want to go, but I do need to," she replied, straightening her uniform again.

Hal kissed her once more, they let it linger between them, and then she drew away, a bittersweet smile on her face.

"Don't be sad, Sprite," said Hal. "I will always find you again. I will keep that promise." She nodded, edged out of the tight hatch, and left him alone to greet the mountains looming in front of them. After a few moments of thought, Hal followed her, and stayed close the rest of the way home.

※

Sprite finished out the flight home at the radioman's table and thought about what had just happened to her. And what *had* just happened to her?

She felt feather light and free and every time she thought of Hal, a delicious thrill ran through her body and settled happily over her heart. *Is this what it's like to be in love? I have never felt like this before, not with Jesse or any of the other boys in school I kept company with. Could it be I have fallen in love with Hal?* she wondered, then checked the thought. *Do I even know him? We've had only a few stolen moments and a lot of time apart....* But yes, she did know him on an intuitive level, that "knowing" place in herself she had learned to trust as a pilot. She could feel Hal's goodness and courage and honesty. He radiated confidence and humor and there was nothing she wanted more than to learn all there was to know about Captain Halcyon James. He was asleep now, but still at her side.

A few hours later, they landed, Hal awoke and stole one last kiss as he stepped off the plane, and Sprite turned to pick up her gear and go back to her quarters. The other girls came alongside her and chattered about the trip, the Night Witches, and what would come next, but Sprite kept quiet, thinking about where Hal might be going. He'd said his next ride was a quick connection, but he'd seemed a little surprised when Sprite had told him that Santa Sabina was home base for her and the other girls. He seemed to think she would have been flying on with the bomber to its next destination.

As Hal strode quickly away from the tarmac and towards his waiting jeep, he looked over his shoulder and said another silent good-bye to Sprite, happy in his heart to know she was so close now, and achingly miserable that he could not see her at will. Hal would shoulder the burden of that longing without placing it on her, just as she had shouldered the burden of keeping quiet about Doyle's possible treachery to keep him from a court martial. *She is quite a girl*, he thought. *A tiny package of beautiful skill and bravery.* Hal knew he was falling in love with her and that thought gave him a warm happiness he had not felt since before the disaster with the squadron. Despite the war, he felt all right again when he was with her.

His posting had to be kept secret, both for her sake and his, and most certainly, he didn't want Major Doyle to see them together or to know that she was here. Hal couldn't get their conversation about Doyle, and all the questions it had raised, out of his mind. Exactly how had Major Doyle leaked Hal's engine designs to the Germans? And if Sprite's information was correct, how was he also stealing chromium for them?

"Sir?" the baby faced corporal said, still holding a salute he had snapped off a good five seconds ago.

Hal noticed him for the first time and returned the salute, saying, "Deep in thought, corporal. Anything blow up while I was gone?" He threw his bag into the back of the jeep, careful to place the toss beyond the gunner's feet.

"Um, no sir, not that they would tell me, anyway," the corporal laughed as he started the jeep. "Also, I have been assigned to the gate after today, so I won't be driving you anymore."

"Oh, sorry to hear that, soldier," said Hal, and he was. The young corporal and he had struck up a bit of a friendship during trips back and forth from the Roost, talking of fast cars, the corporal's woman troubles, and action in the war.

"Yes, sir. I will miss our discussions," said the corporal, pulling into the long, wire spiked tunnel to the Roost.

A few dusty minutes later, Hal disembarked and made his way to the General's office, not stopping even to stow his bag first. As he rounded the last corner on the top floor, he made a pleasant observation that the tunnel hadn't bothered him as badly as it had at first. He definitely had his battle fatigue under control.

Hal knocked and waited. In a moment, an aide opened the door and ushered Hal before the big walnut desk of General Arnold.

CHAPTER 32

A FEW DAYS later, Meredith knocked on every door down the hall from her quarters and called a meeting of her squadron. In less than two minutes, all the girls had assembled in the ready room and Meredith told them that Jackie Cochran had asked to see them in ten minutes. There was a new assignment.

Exactly ten minutes later, Jackie Cochran, admiring Meredith's squadron, stepped in front of the group and said, "Ladies, I want to personally commend you on the outstanding job you are doing. You are a credit to the WASP and to all women serving in, and in support of, the military everywhere." She paused for a long moment.

"But things are changing," she continued. "With the Allied advances in Europe, the need for pilots in that theater is lessening, and those men are coming home, and they expect to have piloting assignments waiting for them." Jackie let her words sink in. "Therefore, the WASP needs to be more flexible. I have personally promised General Arnold that we will be available for *any* assignment, *anywhere*, including those assignments that the men might find distasteful. I know that you girls will do your duty and support me on this, because the justification for our continued existence as an organization depends on it," she finished, her unhappy news delivered. That news hung in the air for a long moment as the girls processed her request. Jackie raised her dark brows and waited.

Meredith, sensing Jackie's unspoken question, coughed and said, "You can count on us, Director Cochran. We are ready, willing, and able."

Jackie smiled and continued pacing back and forth in front of the group as she spoke. "Outstanding, Mrs. Lowe. I'm pleased to hear it. That brings me to my next point—a new assignment, which other members of the WASP will also perform, on a rotating basis. Your squadron is being tasked for tow target duty with the 35th Tow Target Squadron at Camp Winder Aerial Gunnery Range. You will be piloting the target tugs. Are there any questions?"

The WASP pilots looked at each other uneasily, then Ninette spoke up. "Ninette Sotheby, Ma'am. Do you mean we will be flying the targets while soldiers are *shooting* at them?" she asked.

Jackie nodded. "You pull the targets with a 3,000 foot cable, so there will be around a half mile of distance between you and the target. It's not as dangerous as it sounds. But make no mistake—this is an important job. For the men who defend us, who defend our nation, this training is vital. I know you girls will acquit yourselves admirably. Commander Lowe?" Jackie said, raising her eyebrows in a gesture meant to signal the end of the discussion, and the end of the briefing as well.

"Squadron—a-ten-*hut!*" Meredith barked. The squadron came to attention. Jackie took one last look at her brood, then turned and walked out the door. Meredith commanded, "Squadron—dis-*missed!*" The girls fell out of formation and then huddled around Meredith, peppering her with questions.

"So we fly through the air, pulling a target behind us, and they try to shoot it down?" Gertie asked.

"Are they really gonna shoot at us with *live ammo*?" Phoebe asked.

"If they're still in training, then how accurate are they with those guns?" Bertie said. "How do we know they won't blast *us* out of the sky?"

"All right, girls. I understand your concerns. I'm going to do my best to find out more. But we have an assignment and we're going to complete it," Meredith said. The room fell silent, leaving all the what-if questions unanswered.

The following week, at Camp Winder's airfield, Sprite bounced around in the back of a jeep and tried to see around Gertie's tall upper body. She decided there wasn't much to see and sat back again while Meredith drove them over the desolate desert base, located far inland. There was more than enough to hear, however—the air constantly reverberated with the sound of anti-aircraft artillery and bombers practicing runs.

The WASP had a few days to "check out" on the target tugs—obsolete Douglas TBD "Devastators"—old, slow torpedo bombers that the Navy had sadly discovered were no match for the Japanese Zeros in combat.

Sprite turned around and waved at Ninette, who followed in another jeep with Bertie and Phoebe. In another moment, they all pulled up and stopped at the flight line where the aircraft were parked in a row. Sprite and her squadron sisters climbed out of the vehicles to inspect the planes.

"These things look like old nags that were 'rode hard and put up wet,' as my Daddy used to say," said Sprite, running her hand over a battle-scarred wing. "Have they seen any recent maintenance at all?" The aircraft fuselages needed to be painted, and on one plane, Sprite saw a wavy string of circular repairs that were probably carelessly patched bullet holes.

"My stars, this thing looks like it was already shot down over Midway," Bertie said.

"Yeah, maybe a couple of times," Gertie said as she peered back at Bertie through a gaping hole in the rudder.

"Well, they're not going to win any beauty contests, but look on the bright side: if you ding one up, no one's going to give a happy damn," Meredith said, as she manually moved the squeaky rudder back and forth on one of the planes.

Sprite backed away and watched as Ninette stood, arms crossed, staring at another of the planes. *She's figuring something out; probably calculating the odds of pilot survival,* Sprite thought, only half-joking. Ninette walked around to the starboard side of the plane and tapped gently over the wing surface, listening for the flat tone of invisible cracks. Sprite made her way around and underneath the plane's other wing and inspected the landing gear.

"You know, girls, I think I should fly the 'forlorn hope' for this one.

If it's okay with you, Commander Lowe," Ninette said quietly, her brow furrowed.

"No, Ninette, it's Sprite's turn at 'forlorn hope' duty. You'll all get your chance; I know you're champing at the bit," Meredith said, drily joking. "Forlorn hope" was the term used by soldiers in previous wars for the first group of men to engage the enemy. They took the brunt of the conflict and had little chance of survival, but they also won the greatest glory. Forlorn hope duty, for Meredith's girls, meant being first at whatever unpleasant new assignment they got and they all took turns at it.

Ninette wiggled the aileron of the plane she was inspecting. "No, really. I think this one is different—not like our regular duties. So as squad leader, I should go first."

Meredith shook her head, "No, if we go out of order, then I should do it first, since I'm squadron commander."

"The colonel wants you at the range with him for the reporters," Ninette reminded her. "Besides, I want the bragging rights, and Sprite can't take her turn because she is about to crash right now anyway," she said as she shoved the starboard aileron up, which snapped the port aileron down, gently tapping Sprite on the bottom to send her sprawling under the plane!

"Ninette!" Sprite shrieked. Then, without warning, she rolled from under the plane and playfully chased Ninette around the landing gear, bobbing-and-weaving until they both collapsed on the dusty ground in laughter.

Meredith sighed. "Alright, Nin. But I don't like it."

"You don't like whut?" said a deep voice behind them. They all whirled to see a mechanic standing there, his rotten-toothed smile interrupted by a huge, unlit cigar. "Nuthin' for you to like or not like here," he said, spitting a few tobacco fragments out with the words. "You don't get to have opinions! You're just a bunch of women drivers," he continued. "So these planes are just right for you—expendable and ready to scrap. I'm chief here and I ain't gonna give you anything you might actually destroy."

Meredith had waited patiently for him to stop talking. She put on her best smile and said, "'Ready to scrap, you said?' Well, then what are you going to do to make them skyworthy, chief? That's your job, isn't it?

To make them safe and keep them running well? That part's on you—it's your job to service these planes for us, right? Because that's what the Colonel told me. Unless the Colonel was somehow… wrong." Meredith had a way of turning the conversation on its head.

The chief mechanic looked like a man who had come to a gunfight with a spoon.

Ninette, usually the paragon of propriety, could not help but giggle, and that started a chain reaction among the others.

"I'll remember you," said the chief, pointing his chewed cigar at Meredith and then at each of the girls. "I'll remember all of you. But especially you, Blondie," he said as his eyes lingered on Ninette.

꘎

The day of the first mission, the base commander, a colonel, offered the Santa Sabina WASP squadron the opportunity to observe and even fire some of the weaponry used for anti-aircraft defense. Meredith had jumped at the chance, even though they would have the audience of the newsreel reporters. All of the girls, especially Sprite and Phoebe, wanted to know exactly what they could expect when the anti-aircraft gun crews fired deadly exploding flak at the target drogues they'd be dragging on a cable only 3000 feet long behind their planes.

While Ninette prepared to take to the air in a retired torpedo bomber, Meredith, Gertie, Bertie, Phoebe, and Sprite rode to the gunnery range with a bunch of grinning, accommodating young soldiers in a convoy of jeeps. Cruising through the desert, long clouds of dust extending behind them, Sprite and her WASP cohorts wisely wore their goggles and had wrapped their flying scarves around their noses and mouths. The poor soldiers had to squint, hack, cough, and find other creative ways to endure the sandblasting on their desert commute.

꘎

Over on the flight line, Ninette searched for the crew chief. She finally found him, tinkering around with the landing gear on one of the Douglas TBDs. "Chief, which ship am I flying today?" she asked the greasy boots protruding from beneath the plane.

"So it's you up first, Blondie? This one right here," the chief said, not bothering to come out and face her. Ninette checked the tail numbers on the plane, then looked at her clipboard.

"Chief, isn't this the one that needed the hydraulic lines flushed? Is that what you're doing now?" she asked.

"Nope, Blondie, but she'll do just fine until you get her back here. I been fixin' these things since before you were doin' kindergarten tea parties," he growled, clearly despising the need to further converse with her.

"What about ship 37-188143?" Ninette asked politely.

He looked up from his work and pointed at her with a dirty wrench. "That one's due for a total engine overhaul. And in about five minutes, I gotta get the Commander's bird ready for him. He's regular army, and you ain't, so don't even *dream* you're gonna pull rank on me. I say *this* is the ship you're flying today, so this is the ship you're flying today," he said, tapping the plane's already dented skin. "Or did I just say something technical that your little female brain can't understand?"

Ninette turned away, frowning. She had half a mind to go check the maintenance records on the other ship herself. She had done quite well in Engine Maintenance during ground school back at Avenger Field, earning the highest scores in the class, and knew her way around the moving parts of almost any plane. She sighed. Everywhere she had been based, these old-timer mechanics bristled at having to service planes for *women* pilots, as if somehow caring for a female pilot's plane was an indictment of their importance—or even their masculinity.

Meredith had been right about the mechanics' job description—it was their duty to make these planes skyworthy for the women—but being right didn't mean much to these guys—being a man did.

They would have to rely on these men for the condition of their planes, so Nin decided it was best not to make further waves on the very first mission of her WASP squadron's new assignment. Ninette put her better judgment aside and began her pre-flight check on the plane the chief had assigned to her.

Ӿ

Sprite waited for the dust cloud to blow away when the jeep convoy finally stopped near a cluster of small buildings and some gun emplacements. Then she and the large group dismounted from their vehicles.

"I thought you ladies might try firing the 50s first, then we'll work our way up to the bigger guns," said the colonel to Meredith, gesturing expansively at the weapons arrayed on the firing line. The multi-barreled guns required the gunner to sit in a metal seat in the carriage to operate them, and the ones that amounted to big cannons pointed at the sky.

"This one'll cut through a cinderblock wall," said the colonel as he motioned toward the huge, powerful .50 caliber M2 machine gun, or the "Ma Deuce," as the soldiers called it. Sprite believed him. The Ma Deuce fired five and a half inch long cartridges linked in belts and the cartridges contained bullets bigger than her thumb. "This is the same machine gun mounted in our bombers, and modified versions of it are mounted in the wings of many different fighter planes. This particular gun is used to familiarize bomber crew trainees with the firing characteristics of the weapon, since the B-17 employs twelve of these guns for its defenses," the colonel continued.

The girls looked the weapons over and Sprite saddled up in the gunner's seat of the Quad Mount—four .50 caliber guns on an electrically operated swiveling trailer mount. With her feet working the firing pedals, she blasted away at the sky as she used the controls to elevate and traverse the guns via electric servos. The brute force of the weapon nearly brought her out of her seat and it took a minute for her to master it. *That's a lot of firepower for one person to control*, she thought to herself, *I hope the men have lots of practice at it.*

Bertie and Gertie chose the Bofors guns. Fittingly, the Bofors was an arrangement of *two* twin 40mm guns with characteristic conical flash hiders mounted in a carriage that fired two-pound high explosive shells pre-set for various altitudes. The gunners operated the Bofors by sitting in two gunners' seats, one on either side of the carriage, and the guns swiveled, elevated, and traversed using electric servos and handwheels. It would have seemed like a carnival ride, except they all knew it was deadly serious business.

Upon climbing out of her seat on the Quad Mount, Sprite felt a new respect for what combat pilots did. These anti-aircraft batteries could wreak a lot of destruction on low-flying planes. *Could I face off with these*, she thought, shuddering, *if it ever came to it?*

When they had all taken a turn on the Ma Deuce and burned through several yards of belted ammo, they relinquished the guns to the soldiers training with the targets and gathered at the line to watch Ninette fly her pass.

Ninette sat in the cockpit, idling on the flight line, ready to go, and tried to slide her canopy shut. It wouldn't budge. She looked down to her left at the impatient chief. "What's with the canopy, Chief?" she yelled over the engine noise, pantomiming the canopy's resistance for him.

"Billy, get up there with a rubber mallet!" she heard the chief yell at a young mechanic. "Blondie can't get her lid to fit." Billy fetched the mallet and then climbed up on the wing to stand next to the cockpit. He gave the canopy's metal frame a couple of really hard whacks on the rear to dislodge the Plexiglas cover. It jerked raggedly forward in its tracks.

Ninette just shook her head and sighed as Billy jumped down and away. *Like it needs another kink in that track*, she thought as the canopy locked in place, *but that's the best they're going to do for me, I guess*. She nodded to the ground crew marshaller, who stood in front of her plane at a safe distance from the propeller, both hands on his sides. Catching her eye, he then flapped his arms with palms up—the signal to pull wheel chocks. Ninette smiled to herself, thinking of at least three new ways to design a plane canopy. She'd draw them when they got back to barracks tonight.

Back at the gunnery range, the range officer barked orders over the PA system for the gun crews to load weapons and prepare to fire. Sprite, Meredith, and the girls clustered around the colonel, who invited them to listen as he took a seat at a table next to the radio operator. "The operator will be coordinating with your girl as she flies target passes in front of the guns," explained the colonel.

A minute later, the radio crackled as Ninette's voice came through. "Tow pilot to ground, commencing target pass, altitude twelve hundred feet, over," she said, an odd note in her voice. Sprite looked to the other girls, but they seemed not to hear it.

"Roger, tow pilot. Commence your run, over," the radio operator said, calmly.

Within moments, Ninette's plane came into view, flying east to west, towing a white target sleeve behind on its 3,000 feet of cable. Somehow, to Sprite, it didn't seem like nearly enough air between Nin and the target.

Then the firing line erupted with the massive booms of anti-aircraft artillery, the rhythmic bam-bam-bam of the Bofors guns and the rat-tat-tat-tat of the machine guns. Black puffs of smoke appeared around the target sleeve—some behind, some on target, but some in front of the sleeve. *Far* in front, Sprite thought. Ninette finished her pass and slowly began her wide turn to come back around, west to east.

Minutes later, Sprite could hear the drone of Ninette's plane coming back within range. "Tow pilot to ground, commencing second pass, altitude two thousand feet," said Ninette's transmission over the radio. Again, the guns boomed in a deafening cacophony. Sprite looked down the firing line at the various weapons rocking and recoiling sharply on their mounts, a testament to the massive power of the shells they were firing. Ninette's plane completed the pass and once again made a wide turn to come around east to west.

"Tow pilot to ground—third pass, altitude three thousand feet," Ninette said. This time, Sprite put her fingers in her ears to help block out the next round of deafening artillery fire as the firing line erupted once again.

Suddenly, Ninette's frantic voice came over the radio. "Tow pilot to attackers—I'm *pulling* the target, not *pushing* it!" Sprite and the other

WASP girls watched in disbelief as little black puffs of smoke began appearing in clusters all around Ninette's plane!

"Gunners, watch your leading interval!" barked the range officer over the PA system, but everyone on the ground knew that his order had come too late. A ball of orange flame burst out of the engine compartment of Ninette's plane and gushed a stream of thick black smoke.

Eyes wide in horror, Meredith turned to the colonel and screamed, "Dammit, *do* something, Colonel! Tell them to stop! Tell them to cease fire! They're shooting down my pilot!"

The colonel gave the order to cease fire, which the range officer picked up and relayed over the PA system. "Cease fire! Cease fire!" echoed the order over the PA speakers and up and down the gunners on the firing line.

"Tow pilot to ground, have taken a hit to the engine! Recovery impossible. Disengaging tow line and target," was all Ninette could manage to say before Meredith practically shoved the radio operator out of his seat to grab the radio mic and headset.

"Ground to tow pilot!" Meredith shouted, "Ninette, bail out! You've got to invert and bail out! Bail out now!" she cried. The white target sleeve suddenly billowed up on itself as Ninette cut the towline loose and then she slow rolled her plane upside down.

The colonel, face red with bluster, stepped over. "Commander Lowe, get hold of yourself! This is an army exercise and I am in command here! Relinquish that radio to the *RTO*!" he bellowed. Sprite pried her eyes away from the sky, ready to protest, but she didn't have to.

"I will not! Colonel, that's my girl up there, and you are *not* a pilot!" Meredith screamed, venom in her voice. Stupefied, the colonel shrank back and they all turned their attention again to Ninette's damaged plane. "Nin, bail! Bail now! Over!" Meredith pleaded.

"Tow pilot to ground—negative. Canopy is stuck, over," Ninette said.

"Ground to tow pilot—Ninette, can you make it back to the airfield? Over!" Meredith said, pleading into the microphone.

"Negative, ground. Will attempt emergency landing. I'll have to put her down right on the range, over," Ninette said. Sprite and the others watched Ninette's smoking plane bank, turn, and descend.

"Okay, you're looking good," Meredith said, regaining some of her cool. "Your approach is good. You can do this, Nin." Sprite reached out and grabbed Meredith's free hand. It was cold and tense. Phoebe, Gertie, and Bertie also joined hands as they watched, completely lost as to what else to do.

"Tow pilot to ground—Commander Lowe…" Nin's voice faded and cut out, "—gear—not extend. I—to—belly land—."

Meredith bit her lip. "Don't worry about that. Just get 'er down sunny side up, Ninette," she said, "You're a J-6 Gunslinger, the hottest pilot in the WASP. This is just a day at the beach for you."

Sprite watched breathlessly as Ninette came in low, but with entirely too much airspeed, her engine smoking furiously and streaming orange flames from the vents. Sprite fought to keep her eyes open when she heard the horrible scrape of shearing metal on rock. The plane bounced back up in the air for a brief second, then came down hard again. Ninette's left wingtip clipped a huge rock and folded back on itself like it was made of paper.

All of them watched helplessly as the shattered wreck containing their beloved squadron mate cartwheeled through the scrubby desert and blossomed into a gigantic ball of flame, tumbling and bouncing, flipping and rolling, disintegrating more on each succeeding impact. It stopped only when there was nothing left of the burning aircraft that was large enough to fall apart.

"Get in the jeeps! Get in the jeeps!" Meredith yelled as they clambered in and sped to the crash site, which seemed to Sprite to be so much farther away than it had a moment ago.

Sprite and Meredith found it first. Ninette's impact trench, just a long black line of charred debris awash in aviation fuel, had ignited the sparse brown grass and scrub. Meredith leapt out into the smoke and began running from burning patch to burning patch, crying out Ninette's name, searching, hoping, but finding nothing.

Then Sprite's heart sank when she spied Ninette's parachute, half ripped from its canvas bag, shredded and burning. Sprite had to turn her back when she recognized something else.

Amid spent shells and smoking debris, Ninette's broken body lay just beyond the useless parachute.

Meredith saw Sprite react and charged forward blindly. "*Oh, Ninette! Nooooo!*" Meredith cried, voice disappearing into the silence of wordless grief. As Meredith ran toward Nin's body, Sprite leapt in front, grabbed her by both arms, and spun her around.

"Don't look, Meredith," begged Sprite, "You know she wouldn't want us to look." Meredith collapsed to her knees and wailed uncontrollably. Hot tears coursing down her own face, Sprite fell to her knees beside Meredith as Phoebe and the twins gathered closely around them. Though Sprite had saved Meredith and the others from the sight, the image of Ninette's fire ravaged, torn body was forever burned into her memory. Sprite turned and looked back toward the firing line, knowing that the young soldiers who had manned the guns would never see anything but the desert wind blowing the white smoke of Ninette's funeral pyre high up into the air.

✕

"No, I do not have anything to say to the press at this time," the colonel said stonily. "We have things to deal with here, so please just pack up and I'll give you a statement later, after we have notified the family of the pilot."

Protests from the press corps ceased at that, and by the time Meredith and the girls returned to the firing line, the reporters had gone.

Sprite and the twins helped Meredith out of one of the jeeps and sat her down on a folding field stool. "Phoebe and I will get you some water," said Sprite, "and Bertie and Gertie will keep you company." Meredith looked into space with unseeing eyes, but nodded slightly.

"Over there," Phoebe pointed to a canteen on the table several yards away. She and Sprite made for it. "I… I can't believe…" she started, and then began to cry again.

Sprite shook her head miserably, "It should have been me up there, Phoebe. It was my turn at the forlorn hope."

"Nin knew what she was doing," Phoebe said, unable to offer much more.

"No she didn't," said Sprite, picking up the canteen. "None of us did!" The sudden vehemence in her voice startled Phoebe and she stopped walking.

"What are you saying, Sprite?" she demanded.

"I'm saying that this time, they gave us the most dangerous duty and the least competent aircraft and mechanics! It's almost like they wanted us to fail," she said. "Or maybe they wanted us to do worse than just fail, she added, remembering the chief mechanic's promise, "*I'll remember you. All of you. But especially you, Blondie.*"

Phoebe began to walk again and took Sprite's arm in her hand. "I know. You're right. I think we should talk about it with the others later. Let's get Meredith back to the infirmary. Bertie says she's in shock."

Sprite nodded as they approached Meredith and opened the canteen. "Here, Meredith. Take a few sips. We're going back now," she said gently, casting a dark look at the colonel a few paces beyond as he mounted his jeep. The soldiers on the guns had been dismissed. Just like any other day.

X

"I say we quit," whispered Phoebe, seated with the others at the evening mess table. "They are for sure trying to kill us! I heard the chief mechanic isn't even going to get a reprimand for sending Nin out with a messed up canopy! So you know he'll just do it again!"

Bertie and Gertie exchanged a look. "We have to think about this some more before we make any decision about it," said one of them.

"What about you, Sprite?" said Phoebe. "What are you going to do? We are scheduled to go back to tow target duty tomorrow!"

Sprite chewed a bite of roast chicken longer than it really needed and then said, "I'm going to talk to Meredith after mess," and with that, she got up and left the table.

A little while later, Sprite knocked at Meredith's door.

"Who is it?" came the tired voice.

"Sprite. And I need to talk to you if you feel like it, and yes, Meredith, right now."

The door opened and Sprite stepped into Meredith's quarters. "Have a seat, Sprite. I think I know why you're here, but tell me anyway," Meredith sighed.

"We...have been talking about it," Sprite began, "and I think some of us want to quit after this. We haven't ever felt wanted, but now we don't feel safe, and we can't control what happens with our planes," she said.

"Umhm," Meredith said softly, looking her straight in the eye. "When could we ever control what happens with our planes, Sprite?" Sprite nodded, conceding the point. "But what about you? Not the others, you? You want to quit?"

Sprite held Meredith's gaze. "I want to do this job, Meredith, more than anything. But I need to know I've got the mechanics behind me. If they aren't, then..." she looked away as her eyes filled with new tears. "If they aren't, then sooner or later, we all follow Nin," she finished. "I'm afraid to die, and that might seem cowardly, Meredith—"

"Stop right there," Meredith cut in. "Afraid to die, 'cowardly'? Maybe or maybe not. Only you know. But it's never cowardly to want to live. In fact, it's extremely courageous to want to live. It's how we survive anything—everything," she trailed off, her mouth beginning to quiver.

"You are thinking about him, aren't you?" Sprite said softly. "Your husband."

Meredith nodded. "I know he's alive. I know he wants to live. I know he endures and as long as he endures, so will I," she said, reaching for the pocket watch Sprite had first seen at the movies the night of their first leave in Sweetwater.

Sweetwater, like Georgia, seemed so long ago and far away now. Sprite looked down and wiped her eyes. "So you think it's OK for me to want to quit?" she asked.

Meredith said, "Of course it's OK, if that is what you really want. If you can do it for the right reasons."

Sprite puzzled over that for a moment. "You mean, if I can quit without fear making me do it?" she asked, finally bringing forth the argument she'd been having in her own mind all afternoon. Sprite never liked the idea of doing anything out of fear, but Ninette was…dead.

"That's exactly what I mean. Whatever you choose, do it because of the best and highest motives. If you can't say you are quitting for those reasons, then what's left?"

That stung a little! thought Sprite. But Meredith was right. She'd never be able to live with herself if she left the WASP out of fear. She'd have to stop flying altogether if she did, because "Once you let fear rule part of your life, it rules all of your life. We can't fly afraid. Pilots are dangerous when they're afraid," she said aloud softly, repeating the words she'd heard first from her father and then again from Meredith so many times in the ready room.

"Yes," said Meredith, hearing her. "Yes."

⋇

"Phoebe, you can go if you want, and you two as well," she motioned to the twins, "but I have to stay on," Sprite said matter-of-factly as they ate breakfast the next morning.

"Oh," said Phoebe, disappointment in her tone. "Well…"

"We are staying, too," said Bertie. "Our brothers are still over there, flying missions and risking their lives. We can't go home until they can."

Sprite smiled, grateful that she would still have their company. "If all of you are staying, then I'm staying, too," said Phoebe, "I want us to stick together as long as we can."

⋇

Meredith stood before the neat pile of Ninette's things as she waited for the family to come for them. It had been a week since the accident and the memorial service had already been held back in New York. Only this little heap of personal possessions remained to be collected, and then Ninette would be truly gone.

"Are you Commander Lowe?" a raspy voice, heavily accented with

Northeast vowels, startled Meredith out of her reverie. She turned to face a woman of medium height and superior attitude.

"Yes, I am. And you would be Nin's mother?" Meredith noted the family resemblance in the woman's clear blue eyes and Nordic blonde hair.

"Indeed," said the woman frostily. "I suppose those are hers?" She pointed to the little pile on the stripped cot.

"They are," Meredith said, "I will help you carry them out if you like."

"Not necessary," said the mother, who still hadn't introduced herself by name. "All I want are the clothes and jewelry and, of course, the car. The rest of it is rubbish. Throw it away." She pointed to the sketchbooks and WASP photograph album.

Meredith dropped her jaw. "Rubbish?" she said, "You think her work and her friends are rubbish?"

"I do," the woman chirped, "Her friends, you among them, got her killed, and her work, if anyone could call it that, was just a ridiculous diversion." Mrs. Sotheby wiped a diamond encrusted hand over her eyes and said, "Ninette was such a disappointment." She picked up the clothes and the jewelbox, and without so much as a goodbye, marched toward the door.

Meredith sank to the cot, stunned. "Wait. I can't let you go without saying this. You had a beautiful girl in Ninette," she said. Mrs. Sotheby stopped at the doorway and turned, a frown on her pinched face.

"Look, just look at these," said Meredith. She opened a sketchbook and showed Mrs. Sotheby Nin's wonderful pencil drawings of Sprite, Phoebe, and the twins dancing. She turned another page, and there was Meredith's own portrait smiling up at them. Nin had perfectly captured each of them in the sketches, but Mrs. Sotheby hardly even glanced at the work.

On the last pages, Ninette had drawn aircraft designs. "Look at these, then, if you don't think much of her candids," Meredith tried again, marveling at the sleek wings and bodies of the airplanes, rendered to scale and detailed in colored pencils. Exploded engineering drawings showed the planes' interiors, engines, and landing gear. The very last page offered Nin's masterpiece—a supersonic aircraft, drawn from all angles, with a spec list at the right margin. "These are incredible, don't you think?" she murmured.

"Incredible? Incredible? Yes, I would agree," hissed Mrs Sotheby. It is quite incredible that she wasted her precious time and the family reputation on cartoons! She should have stayed home and found a husband and started a family! I ask you, what real woman draws airplanes? Or flies them?" she added, narrowing her eyes at Meredith.

It was too much. Meredith squared her shoulders and fixed Mrs. Sotheby with a commanding glare. "I am sorry beyond belief for your loss, which, please understand, is also my loss. But you—her own mother— you didn't even know her. You never saw her value or her courage, and now you shame her sacrifice and her legacy! Maybe you lost a disappointing daughter, but we lost our beloved friend and sister. So yes, take the car, the jewelry, the things that she wore. We will gladly keep the things that she was!" Meredith snatched the sketchbooks and photo album and her eyes forward, stormed out of the room, leaving Mrs. Sotheby in her angry wash.

By lights out that night, Nin's portraits had been proudly framed and placed on each of the J-6 Gunslingers' nightstands.

"Rest in peace, Nin," said Meredith, writing "To General Hap Arnold" on the envelope that now held the supersonic aircraft sketch.

CHAPTER 33

FOR THE NEXT few months, everyone went about her job with a sense of hollowness that gradually diminished only when daily routine had overtaken the lingering fear left by Nin's accident. But flying would never be the same for Sprite—never be as carefree as it had before. Sometimes, she heard the artillery practice at the far end of the base and the image of Ninette's flaming plane diving for the earth and cartwheeling across the rocky desert flashed in her mind. It affected Phoebe, too, and Sprite became worried that her friend might someday find herself unable to overcome her renewed fears of making a mistake in the air. Meredith tried to keep morale up, and for the most part, succeeded. The twins were helpful, making sure they all had something fun to do when the group was together. But everyone missed Nin.

Sprite missed Hal, too. One Sunday autumn evening, a cool breeze wafted through Sprite's window, and she took up her pen to write a letter to him. Watching the sunset turn the sky purple and orange and pink, she turned on her radio and caught her breath at the song that was playing. *I Love You For Sentimental Reasons* drifted from the speaker, and almost as if the music had conjured him, Sprite closed her eyes and could see Hal's wonderful smile beaming down at her. *Where are you, Hal? Where on earth are you? I so wish you were here with me now....*

Across the base, high in his small room at the Angels' Roost, Hal was listening to the same station as he sat trying to work out an equation. The beginning notes of "their" song, as he now thought of it, made him put down his pencil and stop to listen. The song filled him with longing and he looked out over the mountains, feeling the evening peace, wishing he could share it with… her. *You are so close, Sprite. But it might as well be that you are half a world away. I so wish you were here with me now….*

The last red glow of the sun winked out and the song softly finished, leaving both of them alone in silent darkness.

CHAPTER 34

S PRITE WAS BESIDE herself with excitement as she pushed forward on the stick to descend in her Republic P-47 "Thunderbolt" fighter plane. Happily, since there were plenty of pilots on hand, she and Phoebe had been left behind at Santa Sabina, while Meredith and the rest of the WASP squadron, mixed in with some male ATC pilots, delivered several B-17 bombers across country.

The Flight Commander of Santa Sabina Air Base's host wing, the 338th, had suggested that Meredith send Sprite and Phoebe over to get some experience doing strafing runs at ground targets over on the bombing range, with real fighter planes and live ammunition!

Now, two days later, Sprite found herself zooming in low over the bombing range, lining up for a ground attack, just like the combat pilots did. She had an assortment of ground targets in view: four railroad cars strung together on the desert floor, a scattered half-dozen rusted out deuce-and-a-half army trucks, and two burned-out Sherman tanks. Several huge piles of fifty-five gallon drums, randomly deposited on the range as well, simulated fuel depots.

This is going to be spectacular, Sprite thought. *I'll start with the railroad cars—they're the largest targets. Then, I can "walk" my fire up their length and get some hits for sure!* When she judged the cars to be within range of her guns, and she was sure she was properly aligned, she depressed the trigger on her joystick. The "double quartet"—eight .50 caliber machine guns, four in each wing—opened up, rat-tat-tat-ing in unison, and an impressive barrage of tracer bullets streaked forward and struck the desert floor, stitching the ground with several lines of tall eruptions of sandy dirt. The sand strikes walked their way up to the railroad cars, where they transformed into big puffs of dust as the .50 caliber slugs punched huge holes in the metal skin of the old train. Some large chunks of sheet metal even fell off the cars. *That's right! If you were a real target, you'd be my duck now! Scratch one Nazi train*!

She pulled the nose up, and began scanning for her next target, thinking that a Sherman tank might be a challenge worth going for.

Suddenly her radio crackled with the voice of the tower operator. "Base to two-six-seven, come in," it said.

"Two-six-seven to base, over," Sprite replied.

"Base to two-six-seven, emergency, emergency. You are instructed to cease training mission, and proceed immediately to grid one-one-seven-zero for search and rescue operation. Navy pilot has disappeared off radar. One-one-seven-zero is area of last transmission, over," the tower said.

"Roger base, two-six-seven proceeding to grid one-one-seven-zero, out," Sprite said. She listened closely until she heard Santa Sabina tower give Phoebe, using call sign "two-six-five," the identical instructions.

It was a short leap to the ocean from Santa Sabina and the WASP squadron had been tasked with search and rescue missions before. Sprite knew that every second counted, and it was a good for the Navy pilot that at least two aircraft, hers and Phoebe's, were already airborne and proceeding to the search area. *Not that any crash is a 'good' one,* thought Sprite.

Sprite sped to the search area as quickly as she could, watching the desert and mountains below her gradually give way to deep blue ocean stretching all the way to the horizon.

As she arrived in position, Sprite said aloud, more to herself than to the missing pilot, "Well, where are you?" Banking the P-47 in a wide, lazy turn over the calm waters of the Pacific, she peered out the starboard side of her canopy at the endless, hazy blue below. She adjusted her Rayban aviator sunglasses and then held her left hand over her eyes in an attempt to further cut the glare from bright, sunlit water. She could see nothing but miles and miles of featureless ocean below. She clicked the radio mic switch on her joystick with her right hand, and said, "Two-six-seven to base, beginning search pattern, out."

Sprite knew that even with clear weather, finding a downed pilot in such a vast expanse of ocean would be next to impossible, so instead, she would look for a piece of wreckage or an oil slick. And even those would do little good if the pilot hadn't managed to parachute out of his plane. Sprite knew the odds of surviving a water landing were less than 20 percent. She said a silent prayer asking that if the pilot had managed to bail out, she would find him before hypothermia or the sharks could claim him.

About twenty fruitless minutes later, Sprite saw the glint of sunlight reflecting off of something in the water at her two o'clock low. Her heart began to beat a little quicker as she dropped her altitude to get a better look. "Maybe..." she whispered, but then her hope sank as she realized it was only a floating wing fragment and a trail of debris behind it. The navy plane had evidently crashed into the ocean and disintegrated on impact, leaving little chance of the pilot's survival.

She clicked the radio switch once again. "Two-six-seven to base, have spotted wing fragment and crash debris at coordinates... one-one-seven-zero, three-four, over," she said, then added, "two-six-seven to two-six-five, suggest you converge on my grid coordinates to assist in search for pilot, over."

Sprite knew that rescue was still a long shot, but there was no point in Phoebe continuing to search her own grid. The plane had been found.

"Roger two-six-seven, two-six-five proceeding to grid one-one-seven-zero-three-four. What do you think, over," came Phoebe's reply.

"Not good, but still searching. Poor fella... over," Sprite said. Suddenly, Sprite caught a glimpse of what looked to be the white silk of a parachute bunching and stretching on top of the waves. "Wait! Two-six-seven to base, I see something! Could be a parachute! I'm dropping down for a closer look, over!"

Sprite descended to about one hundred feet in altitude and headed toward the floating silk. A few hundred yards farther out, she spotted the bright yellow of a Mae West life jacket wrapped over the bobbing figure of a man. It was the Navy pilot, and he waved frantically at Sprite's approaching plane. "I see him! I see him! Two-six-seven to base, have spotted pilot, alive in water, grid coordinates one-one-seven-zero, three-four, over!" Sprite waggled her wings as she zoomed over the pilot in the international signal that every downed pilot prays to see: *I see you. Am sending help.*

Sprite climbed and banked into a pylon turn. She would fly circles around the pilot's location to provide an overhead aerial visual cue for the rescue ship to follow, and then it would just be a matter of time before the sailors were able to pluck the soggy aviator out of the drink.

Sprite knew it was great comfort for stranded pilots to see a plane circling overhead—a kindred spirit providing overwatch. "I'll stay with you; just hold on Buddy," she said softly.

Sprite checked the gyroscopic pitch-bank, or artificial horizon, on her instrument panel and tried to maintain a steady degree of bank in order to lock herself into a circular flight pattern. Being locked into a canted position meant that she could view the ocean and the pilot's location out of only the starboard side of the canopy. The port side showed just clear blue sky. The white underbelly of her plane faced outward, clearly visible to the downed pilot.

And clearly visible to someone else—glowing *tracer bullets* suddenly streaked by from underneath her plane! She instinctively broke out of the circular pattern and banked into a Chandelle. Someone was shooting at her!

Sprite could hardly believe what she saw on the water. It was a submarine, its conning tower now clearly visible. Several crewmen scrambled, swinging around the twin-barreled anti-aircraft guns to aim at her! Another hail of glowing 25mm rounds streaked past her plane. Sprite immediately began a flat scissors maneuver, dodging to and fro in a zigzag pattern, which would force the crew to swing the unwieldy, hand-cranked guns back and forth to try to hit her. *One of our subs thinks I'm an enemy fighter plane,* she thought, *I've got to make them break off their attack!* As she closed the distance to the sub, she dropped down as low as she dared, practically skimming the waves as she zoomed past the conning tower.

Then that she saw the unmistakable red sun disc and its sixteen rays against a white background—the ensign of the Japanese Imperial Navy! *A*

Japanese submarine! How can it be patrolling right off the coast of California? she wondered as she climbed, gaining altitude quickly. Breaking into the flat scissor maneuver once again, she frantically keyed her radio. "Two-six-seven to base! Two-six-seven to base! Have spotted Japanese submarine! Repeat, have spotted Japanese submarine and am taking fire, over!" she screamed, trying her best to calm her voice. Sprite knew she'd have to come around again to confirm the sub's speed and position, so she took a deep breath and banked to turn, knowing the glowing tracers would soon be greeting her again. Thoughts of the downed pilot also hammered at her mind. "I promised to stay with you and I'm still here," she breathed, "but I have a situation up here, so just keep holding on."

"Base to two-six-seven, say again your last, repeat, say again your last, over," came the incredulous reply from Santa Sabina tower. Sprite took a deep breath, keyed her mic, and prepared to transmit the message again as she looked toward the horizon. Another P-47 flew directly on line toward the sub.

"Phoebe, no!" she said aloud as she watched the sub's crew swing around to bring their guns to bear on the new aircraft. The twin-barreled Japanese AA guns tracked Phoebe's trajectory and began spewing red-hot tracers on full-automatic at Phoebe's plane. "Two-six-seven to two-six-five! Take evasive maneuvers! Phoebe, get out of there! Two-six-five, take evasive maneuvers, or you're gonna get yourself killed!"

But Phoebe, being Phoebe, did not vary her path. Sprite felt utterly helpless as she watched her friend make a beeline for the submarine. *She's flying straight into the gunfire,* Sprite thought. Suddenly, Sprite saw flashes of light winking from the leading edges of Phoebe's wings and geysers of water shot up from the surface of the water around the sub. Could it be? Yes....

Phoebe was shooting back! At a Japanese submarine!

Sprite's radio crackled and she recognized Phoebe's voice, an octave higher than normal, saying, "two-six-five to base, am engaging the enemy! Am engaging the enemy, over!"

But how? Sprite wondered, but then she had it. Of course—our planes are still armed from the strafing exercise! Sprite watched Phoebe's plane zoom past the submarine, climb high in the sky, and make a slow turn to come around for another strafing run. "Well, Phoebe, if you're gonna do this, you will need some help. That sub is 'one huckleberry over your persimmon,' as my Daddy used to say. So I'm your huckleberry," Sprite said aloud, swinging into a position that would afford a firing solution. She fumbled for the red safety cover on her joystick, flicking it up with her forefinger, exposing the trigger.

Scarcely believing her own actions, Sprite spotted the sub at her two o'clock low position and fixed her eyes on the churning white water at the bow of the sub. She would have to lead the sub if she were to going to score a hit on the conning tower, the best target. She keyed her mic once again. "Two-six-seven to base, two-six-seven to base. We are taking fire from enemy submarine at grid coordinates one-one-seven-zero, three-four. Am preparing to engage, over!"

"Negative, two-six-seven! Do *not* engage! Repeat, do *not* engage! Break contact! Acknowledge, two-six-seven, acknowledge! Retur—" crackled Santa Sabina tower on the radio, the last words breaking up.

Just as Sprite began to take the slack out of the trigger, the submarine started to disappear beneath the waves. In a few seconds, only the antennae on the conning tower remained visible as it cut small wakes into the ocean's surface, and then those, too, disappeared. Within a few more seconds, no trace of the submarine remained. It would take the sonar of a Navy destroyer to find the sub now.

Sprite exhaled, then drew in a few deep breaths to calm herself. She flipped down the safety cover over the joystick's trigger and locked it in place. Too late on the draw, she had missed her chance. She keyed her mic again. "Two-six-seven to base, affirmative, out." Then after a few seconds' pause, she keyed the mic once more. "Two-six-seven to two-six-five, come in. Phoebe, are you okay? Over," Sprite said.

"Weeeee-heee!" came the reply. "Two-six-five to two-six-seven, did you see what I did?? I wasn't even the least bit afraid! Sprite, did you see *what I did?*"

"Yep, I saw," said Sprite dispiritedly. "I'm going back to find our pilot again, if he's still there. I made him a promise." She banked her plane toward the coordinates where the pilot had been floating, saw him wave at her again, and circled until the ship came.

✖

"Just what in the *hell* did you think you were *doing up there*?" the Flight Commander screamed, as Sprite and Phoebe stood, braced at attention, on the small carpet in front of his desk. Just minutes ago, Sprite and Phoebe had landed and the MPs had brusquely escorted them both into the Flight Commander's office. He was livid.

"Well, sir, they were shooti—," Phoebe began.

"—It's a *rhetorical question*, Summerfield! I know what you *think* you were doing—you *think* you were up there being *fighter pilots*, for God's sake!" he said.

"Sir, what were we *supposed* to do?? It was an enemy submarine, and they were *shooting* at us!!" Sprite said.

"You were supposed to be searching for a downed pilot! And Shannon, if you speak out of turn again, I swear on my great grandma's pretty pink bonnet, I'll have your *wings*…" he said, his eyes burning holes in her as he let his warning sink in. He sank heavily into his chair and placed his face in his hands.

Sprite watched the veins in the Flight Commander's temples throb rhythmically for several moments, then the moments between throbs gradually grew longer and the throbs gradually faded. Eventually, he drew in a deep breath, and then muttered, "If word of this gets out, General Arnold is going to have my jewels in a Tiffany giftbox. I'm the one who *authorized* you to be flying armed combat aircraft…. Good Lord, female pilots, exchanging fire with a Japanese submarine, right off the coast of California! The press is going to go ape! When the public finds out, there's gonna be pandemonium in the streets…."

Sprite glanced over at Phoebe, but she was just as bewildered as Sprite was. Sprite opened her mouth to say something, but Phoebe shook her head 'no,' vigorously. Sprite went ahead anyway. "Permission to speak, sir?" Sprite asked.

"Denied, Shannon!" he snapped back.

"Yes, sir!" Sprite said. "But, just so you know sir, *we're* not going to say anything…." Phoebe's eyes opened wide, as she looked at Sprite.

The Flight Commander looked up. "You're damn right you're not gonna say anything! You're not gonna say anything because this *never happened!* The WASP are *ferry* pilots! Women do *not* go into combat! You will leave the combat sorties to the *men*! Am I making myself clear??"

"Yes, sir!" Sprite and Phoebe barked in unison, keeping their eyes fixed on a spot on the wall.

The Flight Commander stood up behind his desk. "This whole episode is now classified. If either one of you so much as *peeps* about this, the closest either of you will ever get to a plane again will be in Long Beach, riveting sheet metal in the Douglas bomber factory. Understood?" he said.

"Yes, sir!" they both replied.

"Shannon, you are grounded for one week," he said. Sprite started to protest, but then thought better of it.

"But sir, she didn't even *do* anything!" Phoebe said.

The Flight Commander came around from behind his desk, and got nose to nose with Phoebe. "And *you*, Summerfield. You are grounded for *two*. Now both of you, get outta my sight. Dismissed!"

Sprite and Phoebe fumed as they walked back to the hangar to retrieve the rest of their gear.

"Sprite, how could you say that back there? I should have gotten the Air Medal for what I did to that submarine!" Phoebe said. "Now, no one will ever know about it!"

Sprite stopped in her tracks, and turned to Phoebe. "When are you gonna figure out we're playing against a stacked deck? We're not gonna get any medals! We're not gonna get any recognition at all for what we do here! Only the men get that. We are invisible. And if we happen to die for our country, doing our duty…" Sprite said, as her thoughts turned to Ninette, "then that's just the way it goes.…

"And, Phoebe—There's something else about this that we need to talk about—you really could have been killed. You got your shots in, but you presented yourself to that sub as an easy, predictable target and it was only pure chance or grace or whatever that they didn't hit you. You can't lock your pattern into a straight line in a real fight."

Phoebe stared sullenly at the ground. "I should have gotten the medal.

I scared off an enemy sub, Sprite; no matter how I did it, I did it. So save the lecture, OK? I've had enough of those for the day."

"Sorry, Phoebe," Sprite said, "I didn't mean to lecture. I...just don't think I can stand to lose anyone else."

CHAPTER 35

DOYLE SAT AT his cluttered desk, drumming his fingers. *Every-thing should work now,* he thought. *If the plan is discovered, everything should point toward Captain James. He has signed the requisition forms for the chromium, and when it's delivered to the transport for Blackpool, it'll be his name on the paper, not mine, if everything goes pear-shaped. We'll see then who is the golden boy. But if it all goes right, I'll be there to unload and count the crates and Gallagher will send his "fishermen" to row them out to Mattias's U-boat and bring Coreen back to shore. Then, after I get Coreen back, we will quietly disappear. Almost done, Seamus, almost there! Keep yourself together just a little longer....*

Doyle peered out the open office door and saw only Mildred at her desk, doing crosswords. It was 1000 hours by the clock, but Doyle pulled his desk drawer open and took out the silver flask, turned it up and drained its vodka, then ate several wintergreen Lifesavers and replaced the empty flask.

⋊⋉

A crisp November afternoon found Sprite and the girls performing their own maintenance checks on a group of Douglas A-24 dive bombers they would deliver to Gray Field, Ft. Lewis, Washington, later that week. Even though the planes had already been checked by the mechanics, after the

Camp Winder tow target incident, the Santa Sabina WASP Squadron no longer took anyone's word for an aircraft's flight worthiness. It was a good thing. More than once, the girls found overlooked mechanical issues of exactly the same sort that had killed Ninette.

Sprite finished her checklist, the plane passing, when Meredith strode into the hangar, came to a halt and drew herself up even straighter than usual. "Squadron—briefing room in five minutes!" she said. Sprite and the girls, surprised, looked up from their clipboards at Meredith, then toward each other.

"Yes, Ma'am," said Phoebe, answering for all of them.

Five minutes later, in a separate administration building, the girls filed into the briefing room. Meredith stood in front of a large wall map, and to their surprise, Colonel Clarence Wesley was sitting beside her, shuffling some papers into order. The Colonel stood and casually said to the group, "Ladies, please come in and be seated."

Sprite and the girls obeyed. Meredith began. "Squadron, this is Colonel Clarence Wesley, commander of the 412th Test Wing here at Santa Sabina," Meredith said, as the Colonel nodded in acknowledgment. Meredith surveyed her squadron and measured her words carefully. "Ladies, we have just received orders...to perform probably the most important mission any WASP squadron has been tasked with to date."

The girls all looked at each other, wondering what that meant. Meredith picked up a pointer and turned to the large map depicting the United States, the Atlantic Ocean, and Europe. "We are being tasked to deliver a specially outfitted B-17 bomber and two pursuits—P-51 Mustangs—to Blackpool, England," she said as she tapped the destination on the map.

"We're going to fly...across the Atlantic?" Phoebe asked, marveling. "But no WASP unit has ever left the United States, well, except for one or two trips into Canada."

"That is the plan, yes," Meredith said, pausing to let them take it in. "And, yes, Phoebe, it will be a first for us. "The war still rages in Europe, so I know you appreciate the gravity of this mission."

"What's so special about that particular bomber?" one of the twins asked, wanting more details.

Colonel Wesley stepped over to an easel and flipped the cover sheet, revealing a blowup of a black and white wing camera photograph of some type of aircraft. To Sprite, it looked like a kind of winged bomb with a rocket engine of some sort bolted on the top. "Since the week following D-Day, the Germans have been terrorizing Britain and Belgium with a new 'revenge' weapon. It is called the *Vergeltungswaffe 1*, or V-1 for short, but the Brits have their own name for it: the 'Buzz Bomb,' because of the sound it makes. Thousands of them have been launched on England, causing tremendous damage. However, in the interest of protecting the British public's morale, that has been kept as quiet as possible," he said.

"It looks like some kind of torpedo," Bertie said.

"It's a flying bomb, basically. This apparatus on top here," he said, as he pointed to the motor, "is what is known as a pulse jet. It puts the bomb's average speed...at about 340 mph. It can top 400 in the right conditions."

Sprite looked at her squadron mates in disbelief. "So the Mustang is the only thing that can catch it, sir?" she asked.

"Well, it's one of a very few fighters that can. Which brings me to the B-17," he said. Colonel Wesley flipped to the next photo on the easel. "What the 412th Test Wing has developed is a type of airborne radar—an early warning system. This specially modified B-17, equipped with this radar, will fly off the British coast over the Channel, monitoring the German's V-1 launch sites in Holland. It will give our British friends time to scramble their fastest fighters to intercept the bombs over water well before they reach land targets. If this technology works, it will save countless lives. Ladies, it is imperative that we deliver this bomber."

"Begging the colonel's pardon, sir, but why the WASP?" asked Sprite. The mission had "army" written all over it.

"Because our country has asked," Meredith interjected, her tone low with warning. The Colonel held up his hand and smiled at them.

"It's a good question, Commander. To answer, it's because when it comes to ferrying service, the WASP is the best," the Colonel said, "but there's more to it than that." He smiled as he measured his thoughts. "I'm sure you have had your share of run-ins with male ferry pilots, right?"

All of the girls nodded wanly.

"I'm going to let you in on a little secret. If a male pilot is not deployed in a combat theater, if he's assigned to stateside duty, that usually means he is the bottom-of-the barrel," the Colonel said.

All of the girls, including Meredith, chuckled. The Colonel's honesty was refreshing. "Frankly, ladies, they're scared," the colonel continued. "And I'm hoping that your successful, quick delivery of these aircraft will embarrass them back into doing their duty. It won't be the first time the WASP has performed that function," he said, smiling bleakly.

"What's our route to be, then?" Phoebe asked. "The Azores to England?"

Meredith answered, using the pointer to tap the map. "We'll take delivery of the bomber and the pursuits in New Castle, Delaware. Then, we'll fly to a Canadian RAF base in Labrador. We'll refuel, proceed to the US Army base in Greenland, then it's on to Keflavik, Iceland. From there, we stretch our legs, fuel up, and make the final push, 800 miles to the coast of Scotland and on down to Blackpool." she said.

"We've never flown a mission that long before," Bertie said, a bit of trepidation in her voice.

"Bertie, Jackie Cochran delivered a B-17 to England, flying this exact route, in '41. If our WASP Director could do it, then other WASP can, too. So don't worry, Colonel, my girls are ready," Meredith said, turning to the colonel.

"I appreciate that, Commander Lowe. Well then, I'll leave you to finish this briefing. More information to follow later," he said.

"Squadron—a-tehnn-*hut!*" Meredith barked. The girls leapt to attention. The Colonel smiled, nodded to them, and then strode to the exit.

After he had left the room, Meredith said, "Listen up, ladies. The Colonel told you the men were afraid to fly. But here's what he didn't tell you—the Germans still occupy Norway, and you know what that means," she said.

Phoebe, her voice wavering, said, "It means there's a good reason why the men are scared."

Meredith nodded. "Yes. The men are afraid because the Nazis prowl that corridor like wolves."

X

Three days later Meredith, Sprite, Gertie, Bertie, and Phoebe disembarked from a C-47 cargo plane at New Castle Army Air Base, Delaware. They shouldered their gear and Meredith led them into a hangar where the modified B-17 sat waiting. From most outward appearances, everything about the plane looked normal.

A technical sergeant carrying a clipboard saw the WASP squadron enter and headed over to welcome Meredith and the group as they dropped their gear.

"Commander Lowe? Welcome to New Castle," he said. Meredith took a moment to stretch, then she ambled over to the aircraft.

"Yes, thank you. All right Sergeant, what can you tell me about her?" Meredith said, running her hand over the bomber's riveted metal skin as the other girls spread out to examine the craft from nose to tail.

"Most of the radar equipment has been placed in the bombardier's station, in the nose," the Tech Sergeant said.

"Oooo, you mean the 'Love Nest,'" Gertie whispered, nudging Sprite in the ribs. Sprite recoiled from the tickling but maintained an admirably straight face for the benefit of the Sergeant, who carried on as though he were reading to them. Sprite ducked under the plane to look at the belly of the beast.

"So all the equipment that would normally go up there, the navigator's table, bomb sight and so forth, has been removed, including the guns," he said.

"How will the changes affect the longitudinal stability?" Meredith asked.

"We've spread the cargo in the bomb bay as best we could to keep your center of gravity the same," the Tech Sergeant said. "It should be about the same as flying with a full bomb load."

"Cargo?" said Meredith. "What are you talking about? This is the first I'm hearing of any cargo."

"I don't know, ma'am, and I was told not to ask. All I know is that your plane is filled with a bunch of crates marked 'Top Secret,' and that they're real heavy," he said.

"Who authorized a Top Secret shipment?" Meredith asked, disbelieving.

"The manifest was signed by an officer from the 412th Test Wing. It says his name is Captain Halcyon James," the Tech Sergeant said.

Meredith relaxed a bit and shook her head. 'Top Secret' was code for 'above your pay grade,' and the Test Wing was famous for surprises.

Sprite rose from the floor and whirled sharply at the mention of Hal's name, but said nothing, waiting to see if the Sergeant had any further information. He didn't.

"Okay, so we've lost two of our nose guns, but we've still got the top turret guns that can face forward," Meredith went on, head cocked to the side as she evaluated, "and we probably can't make use of the ball turret, but we've got the waist guns." The Tech Sergeant laughed out loud, causing a mocking echo in the huge hangar. Meredith turned to face him and fixed him with a dark stare. "Did I say something *funny*, Sergeant?" Meredith said too politely, "Please do tell me."

"Well, ma'am, about those guns—even if you could shoot them, a lot of good they'll do you," he said, still grinning.

"What the hell do you mean?" she said, her voice low and menacing. Sprite, Phoebe, Bertie and Gertie eased from their positions on the plane and formed a semi-circle around Meredith, the same affronted look on all of their faces.

"No offense Ma'am, but I thought you already knew," the Tech Sergeant stammered.

"Knew *what*?" she replied.

"I was instructed by a Colonel Wesley from the 412th that you were forbidden to carry any ammunition. I mean, you're just the transport team and all. The delivery girls. You're not supposed to shoot at anything anyway, right? So why would they send you out with ammo? The boys need all of it they can get." With that, the Sergeant backed up, snapped his clipboard under his arm, and almost ran across the hangar floor.

✺

"He didn't have to laugh at us," Gertie said, removing her web pistol belt and holster from her duffle bag and fastening it around her waist. After a few adjustments, her Colt .45 automatic hung down her right hip.

"Same old story, sis. We're just the transport team; we're *just the delivery girls*; we can't possibly know how to shoot," Bertie said, also strapping on her pistol belt.

"Well, we delivery girls have other problems, too," Phoebe chimed in, "Anyone remember that the B-17 needs a crew of at least five? I count only four of us who can fly it. And I'm pretty good at math."

Meredith answered, "We will make it work. I'll take the pilot's seat on the first leg. Gertie, I want you in the cockpit with me as copilot. That means Bertie, we'll need your skills as navigator, and you'll have to fill in as radio operator and flight engineer, OK? Phoebe, I want you flying pursuit along with Sprite. We'll switch up again when we leave Labrador."

"Three jobs for one person, Commander?" Bertie said, wondering how she would fill all those positions at once.

"It won't be for the whole run. The colonel told me that we'd pick up another crew member in Labrador. I suppose he's a qualified pilot from one of the Allied air forces because the big brass want this to look like a joint Allied effort," Meredith said, as she shrugged on her A-2 jacket over her flight coveralls. "Good for the newsreels."

Phoebe muttered, "Sure, but we all know it's because they want a man to chaperone us because we're—"

"—Whining will not change anything," Meredith said, cutting her off, "Doing our jobs with distinction will. So get your faces right. As long as the man can fly, I'll take him, and so will you."

✕

Eight hours later and five thousand feet above a darkening sea, the red brilliance of the setting sun suddenly struck their tight three-plane formation, seeming to light the wings of each plane on fire. The beauty of it took Sprite's breath away and for a small moment, she felt like she was back home in the skies of Georgia, watching the sun dance on her father's plane in that golden hour before dark when they flew home together, tired after a long day in the air.

I wish you could see me now, Daddy, she thought, *you'd be so proud of me.* Stinging tears welled in her eyes, threatening to spill, but she smiled them away. *So much has happened in such a short time*, she thought, not for the first time. *Less than a year and a half ago, I was a crop duster in Georgia and I thought I always would be one. Now I am part of an elite group of amazing women on a secret mission. Together, we know we can fly anything, anywhere, anytime.* "I miss you, Daddy," she whispered aloud as the sun sank lower in the sky, its brilliant reflection on the formation gently fading. Night was coming.

They had flown north 1,200 miles without incident and Sprite could now see Happy Valley, Labrador, below. Despite growing darkness and a thick curtain of sea mist, the eastern Canadian coastline looked ragged and rocky even from this high up. Sprite lifted her gaze from the land formation to peer out the canopy of her P-51 Mustang. She checked the positions of the B-17 bomber and Phoebe's own P-51 as she listened to Meredith radio the tower at Canadian Forces Base Goose Bay.

"*Alkali Tower, this is Juniper Flight 227 on the base leg, requesting permission to land,*" Meredith's tired voice crackled over the radio.

As they went through the landing clearance procedures, dropping altitude, Sprite marked the position of the winking runway lights and readied her craft. A large, triangular shaped base, CFB Goose Bay belonged to and was commanded by the Royal Canadian Air Force. All Allied traffic on the North Atlantic route to Britain used it as a refueling station, but the British RAF and the US Army Air Forces had staked out sections of the base for their own particular, sometimes secret, needs.

First step accomplished, Sprite thought to herself, *we're out of the United States and landing at an Allied air base.* When the tower gave her clearance to land, she flipped a switch and the hydraulic system hissed as her landing gear lowered, ready to touch down on Canadian soil.

The next morning, after a restless night's sleep in some vacant and rather spartan officers' quarters, Sprite and the girls headed to the Goose Bay base canteen for hot food and coffee. A heaping tray of eggs, croissants, and some kind of hot grain cereal in hand, Phoebe settled down beside Sprite at the long tables and said, "So where's our mystery man pilot? He'd better get here soon if he plans on joining this wagon train. We're wheels-up in less than an hour."

"I told the ground crew to send him over here whenever he shows up," Meredith said, "He'll want to chow down before we leave."

"Better hurry. Won't be anything left," Sprite said between bites of bran muffin.

Suddenly, a loud, brusquely accented voice cut through every conversation in the room. "This is to be kidding!" it rang out, commanding the girls' instant attention. They turned around instantly, and then relaxed into laughter when they saw *Starshij Lejtenant* Olga Vladimirovna of the Soviet Military Air Forces, standing behind them, ready to go. Olga's usual dress uniform neatly trimmed her narrow frame and she had added a big gray fur hat that obscured her blonde hair. Her dancing blue eyes peeked from beneath the mink as she sipped from a steaming cup.

Olga smiled back, laughing, "Delicate American girls are *transport pilots*? You are my crew? Big surprise on me, but also funny."

Meredith stood to greet her. "Well, starchy Lieutenant, I guess the joke's on us as well," Meredith said, laughing as she gestured for Olga to sit with them. "We thought you'd be a man."

Still smiling, Olga glowered fiercely at that and then said, "Hyello, everybodies. Is good to hear you," she waved a long-fingered hand to each of them as they greeted her. "But no time is for chatting, so I will say problems. As I study mission, Commander Lowe, I hyave beeg concern. We are flying through Nazi airs. There is needing more fighters escort," Olga said, folding her tall frame into a chair.

"Ah, yes. We noticed that as well. And even worse, Olga, we've been forbidden to defend ourselves," Meredith said.

"What is this meaning? You have two fighters planes! And guns protrude from every surface of bomber," Olga said, pronouncing it "bom-burr."

"True, and not the problem. We don't have any *ammo*," Sprite said, draining her coffee cup.

"*Nyet!* Olga does not fly two hundred seexty combat sorties to be killed on boos driving mission," she said, chopping the table with the side of her hand. Coffee jumped out of every full cup.

"Well what shall we do about it?" Meredith said, dismally.

Sprite watched Olga think for a moment as the Russian's ice blue eyes drifted over a room she wasn't seeing. "Is easy. I am officer in Russian Air Force. I will command soldier to do loading of fighter plane guns. Tall trees," she motioned to Bertie and Gertie, "will procure ammunition for bom-burr," she said.

"How will we do *that*?" Bertie and Gertie said in unison.

"Figure out," Olga said, the matter settled. "Pass pastry, please," she said, taking Phoebe's last croissant.

An hour later, back in the hangar, Sprite looked on with admiration as Olga barked orders in Russian-peppered English at two bewildered and highly intimidated American privates. They hurried to winch belts of .50 caliber ammo into the wing magazines of Sprite's Mustang, trying to move as fast as the Russian officer wanted.

Meanwhile, across the hangar, Gertie had cornered another young private. She stood leaning with one hand against the wall, listening as the overly enthusiastic, red-headed private responded to her queries about last month's World Series. He apparently found Gertie's seeming confusion between the St. Louis Cardinals and the St. Louis Browns to be endearing. As the private launched into a diatribe about the inferiority of American League pitching, Bertie crept up from behind and sank gracefully against the wall on his other side.

"Hi," she purred, catching him off guard. He spun around to see the mirror image of Gertie, instantly delighted to find himself in the middle of a twin sandwich.

"Hello ma'am," he stammered, suddenly red-faced.

Gertie, behind him, brushed some non-existent lint off the private's shoulder. "Soldier, wouldja point us to your ammo dump? Much as we'd like to stay and talk to you, we've got to load up and get going, right Bertie?" she sighed as the private wheeled around once more.

"Yeah, but Sis, those ammo cans are so *heavy*," Bertie said. "I don't think I can carry them, let alone lift them into the bomber."

Ziiiiiiiiiiip. Gertie unzipped her flight coveralls down to her waist, revealing her white a-shirt, and said, "I know, but let's peel these hot suits and get going anyway." She pushed the flightsuit over her shoulder, pulled her arm out of the sleeve, wriggled out of the other sleeve, and tied the two sleeves around her waist like a belt. The private, mesmerized, heard another *ziiiiiiiiiiip* as Bertie followed suit.

"Well, gosh, ma'am," he stammered, "I mean, *ma'ams*, you know, I could load ammo for you."

"*Really?*" Gertie and Bertie said in unison, their eyes huge and inviting, "That'd be... *swell.*"

"Yeah...I'll just grab some of the fellas, and we'll have you squared away in a jiffy," he said.

Ten minutes later, Gertie and Bertie smiled and waved at the three grinning privates seemingly unable to keep their minds or their eyes on their business. Sore toes and bruised shins would remind them of the girls' trick tomorrow but they wouldn't mind a bit. The redheaded private managed to bonk his head on an open hatch at every single pass as he waved back at the twins, but he never felt a thing.

"Heh, heh, heh," chuckled Olga, as she sat in the bay door and watched the ammo cans stacking up in the bomber. "I see you figure out," she smiled at Bertie and Gertie as they waved at the privates for the final time.

Across the hangar, Sprite and Meredith stood waiting for the Mustangs to be loaded. When the first one was done, the crew removed the magazine panels from the second Mustang and discovered there were no guns to load. The plane the girls had been given was a photo reconnaissance craft, meant only for taking aerial photos.

Sprite looked at Meredith in bewilderment. "How are we supposed to defend with this?" she said.

Meredith chuckled, but was not amused. "We aren't supposed to defend with anything. We aren't supposed to shoot back! And I think this is the 'joke' the Tech Sergeant was laughing about back at New Castle."

Sprite said, "OK, then this one is mine."

"No," said Meredith firmly, "I am commander. It's mine. Don't argue—you'll lose in the end anyway."

Sprite knew she was right. Nothing could move Meredith once she had set her mind on the matter. But Sprite still didn't like it one bit.

CHAPTER 36

I N A SECURE area in the Angel's Roost Administration Building, Gabriel and General Arnold inspected two packing crates. Gabriel used a crowbar to pry the lid off of one of the crates. He removed the cushioning straw, then pried off the sides of the crate to reveal a large metal box about twenty-four by eighteen by twelve inches in size. The box had a tube protruding from it and the tube had a lens cap over it. General Hap Arnold eyed the object with frank curiosity. "So what is it?" he asked.

"It's called an orthicon camera, used for closed-circuit television systems. MI-6 got the idea from the Germans. They use similar cameras to monitor their rocket experiments. They can watch from a safe distance in case of an explosion," the MI6 agent said.

"So it's German?" General Arnold asked.

"No sir, this is actually made here in America. The technology just isn't well known as of yet," Gabriel said.

"So what do we do with it?" General Arnold said, his brow furrowing.

"Well sir, from the attic, we can bore a hole in the ceiling of the document incineration room and then position this camera's lens to shoot through that aperture to provide a wide angle view. What the camera sees will be transmitted via a cable to a monitor, which is packed in this second crate. We will set up the monitor in a secure viewing room, and we'll have men watching it around the clock. If something fishy is happening with document incineration, we'll be able to remotely and secretly observe it," Gabriel said.

"And also see who is doing the fishing," General Arnold said. "Whom can we trust with this? Captain James?"

"Yes, but he has departed for Blackpool with Major Doyle. I suggest we bring in several men from the Military Police unit for the duty," Gabriel said.

The General pondered this for a moment. "No. We must keep this as quiet as possible. I'll request some manpower from the FBI as soon as I arrive in Washington, but until then, bring only Lieutenant Pritchard in on this, and no one else. You and he are to personally monitor the camera feed in alternating shifts. Only the three of us will be aware of the surveillance," General Arnold said.

"Those will be long shifts, sir," Gabriel said.

"You won't have any help getting set up, either," General Arnold added. "We have to keep a tight lid on this. If the mole becomes aware of this camera, we'll never catch him."

Gabriel sighed, and picked up the crowbar again. "Unfortunately, I agree that you're quite right, General," Gabriel said, as he pried the lid off the second crate.

X

The next morning, Gabriel carried two steaming cups of coffee into a small control room. Inside the room, Lt. Pritchard sat in a wooden chair directly in front of the closed-circuit television monitor. The black and white image on the screen never changed. Gabriel could see the young officer was straining to keep his eyes open.

He handed one of the coffees to the Lieutenant. "Not much to look at, eh?" he said, nodding his head toward the monitor screen. He threw a leg over the edge of a table and sat.

"I've been watching the hands move on that clock on the far wall. That's the only action so far," the Lieutenant said as he sipped the coffee. Gabriel chuckled wryly, less than happy about having to relieve the Lieutenant and pull his own twelve-hour stint in front of the monitor in a bit. Intelligence work often involved mundane tasks, and he hated the mundane. He pulled up a chair, sat down, then propped his feet up on the monitor table, turning his attention back to his coffee.

Suddenly, the monitor flickered with new shadows and movement. Lt. Pritchard sat up and leaned in closer to watch as Gabriel rose and peered over his shoulder. On the monitor, Major Doyle's secretary Mildred carried a canvas bag into the document disposal room. Gabriel noticed Mildred moved a little faster than usual and the slump in her shoulders had disappeared, but maybe it was just the odd camera angle. She tossed the bag onto a table and walked over to the document incinerator to turn on its natural gas-fed flames. She deftly pulled the "burn bag"—a sealed paper bag treated with chemicals to facilitate quick burning—out the canvas bag. The treated bag, as per usual, was stuffed with documents slated for disposal. Mildred stood back from the incinerator as far as she could and gingerly opened the small fireproof door on the incinerator, revealing the intense flames inside.

Gabriel swallowed hard and tried to chase a sudden dire thought from his head. The archangel operative Michael—who had been missing in action since the beginning of Operation Archangel—had been very recently seen just before being captured by the Germans. Was Michael still alive? If so, the agent might have been taken to one of the Nazi POW or work camps. Camps where ovens just like this incinerator provided the Nazis with "the final solution."

Gabriel shook his head, took a breath, and willed himself to pay attention to the scene unfolding on the screen. Mildred smiled a peculiar smile and tossed the burn bag in. It immediately caught fire and she closed the door.

"This is the most excitement I've had all day," Lt. Pritchard said, taking another sip of coffee as he watched the screen.

"Unfortunately, there's no other way a—," Gabriel said, an odd note in his voice now.

"What in the—" Lt. Pritchard interrupted. Gabriel's head jerked over to the monitor. Mildred was now quickly tearing open another burn bag, pulling out its documents and shuffling through them on the table. Then, to their great surprise, she produced a small object from the voluminous folds of her skirt. Gabriel immediately recognized it for what it was—a tiny Minox camera, of German design, but one that MI-6 spies also favored for covertly photographing documents. Mildred, the harmless old secretary, was spreading out classified documents on the table and then carefully using the camera's attached 18-inch chain to measure the proper focal length to snap photos of each page.

Gabriel leapt to his feet. "Call your MPs! Arrest her immediately and secure that camera!" he said. Lt. Pritchard snatched up the telephone and dialed as Gabriel bolted for the door.

Twenty minutes later, in a small office at the end of a convoluted hallway, Gabriel sat on the battered edge of a desk as he supervised Mildred's interrogation. With her hands folded in her lap and her face a study in fearful innocence, she sat in a stiff backed metal chair as Lt. Pritchard paced back and forth in front of her. An olive-drab web pistol belt sagged slightly on his right side under the weight of the .45 automatic in the holster. An MP, also armed, stood at ease in the corner, and appeared to be rather bored by the proceedings. Upon noting the MP's relaxed attitude, Gabriel's left eye twitched and somewhere in the back of his highly trained mind, a tiny warning bell sounded. But the old girl seemed hardly any real danger and he had more to think about at the moment than rebuking the man.

Gabriel watched as Lt. Pritchard held up the subminiature Minox camera. "So Mildred, what can you tell us about this?" he said, tossing it up and catching it in his hand.

Mildred began to cry a little, saying, "Wh-wh-why are you interrogating me? I'm just a secretary and I have high blood pressure, you know. It's so cold in here. Please, what have I done?"

Gabriel nodded to Pritchard, pointed at the camera, and the Lieutenant tossed it over to him. He deftly caught it in one hand and began to examine it. He snapped the shutter button, and then pushed the telescoping halves of the camera together until it clicked—the tiny camera's means for advancing the film.

"Not exactly for sight-seeing, is it, Mildred?" Gabriel said, but again,

Mildred remained implacable, shifting a bit in her chair, shivering and putting her hands in her pockets as if to warm them. Gabriel sighed deeply, then continued. "This could go very badly fo—"

Suddenly, Mildred lunged upward out of the chair, stooped over, and drove her shoulder into the Lieutenant, tackling him to the floor in one fluid motion. Gabriel could scarcely register what was happening and he whipped his head around to see that the MP stood frozen, mouth agape, hand glued to his holster. The man was clearly in conflict about shooting an old lady, and couldn't move.

Instantly understanding he was on his own, Gabriel launched himself toward the scuffle on the floor. Just as he reached to pull Mildred off Lt. Pritchard, she rolled over and brought up the Lieutenant's pistol in her hand. For a split second, Gabriel was looking down the gun barrel. He pulled back with a practiced twist hard on his right foot and dove behind the desk just as Mildred began firing. *Bang! Bang! Bang! Bang!* The shots rang out with deafening force in the small room. Gabriel felt a round hit the part of the desk where his head had been a second earlier and he hunkered lower still. Then he saw bullets striking the stunned MP in the chest, spraying his blood across the drywall behind his slumping body.

Good Lord! She got the drop on us! he marveled. Now on his hands and knees, Gabriel took a deep breath and summoned the nerve to peer around the side of the desk. *Bang!* Another shot splintered the wood millimeters from his face and he instantly recoiled.

A second later he heard the door open. Gabriel peered out and caught a glimpse of Mildred's support hose pooling around her ankles and over her orthopedic shoes as she ran through the door into the hallway.

Gabriel jumped to the MP's crumpled body to render first aid but the two bloody holes perfectly placed over his heart and his vacant blue eyes told the story. *Damn it! You let your guard down! How could you be so stupid?* Gabriel chastised himself, and yanked the dead MP's unfired .45 pistol from its holster. Gabriel clicked off the safety, eased the slide back a half inch, saw the brass casing of a round in the chamber, and cocked the pistol with his right thumb. *I'm ready to deal with you now, old girl.* He scrambled for the door, but a sound from the floor made him stop. Lt. Pritchard rolled over and groaned, "What happened?"

"That old crone just overpowered you and took your weapon! We've one man down! On your feet!" Gabriel barked as he pulled the Lieutenant up with his left hand.

Moments later, Gabriel and Pritchard burst out the door of the building as Mildred fired two more shots. They ducked down and sought cover behind a car. Gabriel quickly scanned the company streets and then heard the peal of spinning tires just four cars over. He turned toward the sound and saw Mildred, low in the seat, behind the wheel of the Colonel's staff car, burning rubber and making a huge cloud of smoke. She gunned the engine again as she ground the car into gear and caromed off another parked sedan with a crunch, then sped away. Up ahead, Gabriel watched the MPs from the guard gate wave wildly for her to stop, but she slammed through the boom barrier, splintering it like a toothpick, and kept going. "We've got to cut her off!" Gabriel yelled.

"Sir, the gun jeep!" Lt. Pritchard yelled, as he pointed over to a parked vehicle. They sprinted for it. Gabriel dove headlong into the rear of the gun jeep with a *thud* as the Lieutenant jumped in the driver's seat, cranked the engine, and floored it.

As the jeep sped toward the opening in the fence near the airstrip, Gabriel put his pistol on "safe," then handed it butt first up to the Lieutenant, who reached over his shoulder to take it. Gabriel then stood up, grabbing the pistol grip of the mounted Browning M1919 .30 caliber machine gun in order to steady himself. He swiveled the machine gun around into position and yanked rearward twice on the weapon's charging handle, loading a round in the chamber, making it ready to fire. "Get up alongside her! Get right up to the fence!" Gabriel yelled.

"But that's straight through the minefield!" Pritchard yelled over his shoulder.

"You told me the minefield was fake!" Gabriel shouted.

"Well, I *think* it is! Nobody's ever tried to drive through it!" the Lieutenant yelled.

"Just bloody go! We have to stop her!" Gabriel said, as they zoomed past the warning sign that declared DANGER MINEFIELD. Gabriel gritted his teeth as they plunged headlong into the field and said a silent prayer of thanks when, after several seconds, nothing had exploded under the jeep's bumping wheels. "We're clear; now speed up! Get alongside her!" he screamed.

A minute later, the jeep came up behind and to the left of the staff car at a 45-degree angle. As Gabriel bounced up and down in the rear, he trained the machine gun on the speeding car as best he could. He slowly pulled the weapon's trigger and let loose a short burst with a *Rat-tat-tat-tat!* Ricocheting bullets sparked as they bounced off the staff car's trunk and the road. *Damn*, Gabriel thought, *Steady on, man!* He adjusted his point of aim toward the front of the car and fired another quick burst. This time, bullets punched holes in the car's rear fender and door. *There's the sweet spot!* He smiled and pulled the trigger again, and… nothing happened. He tried again. Nothing, again. *Blast it! Jammed!* he thought, as he grabbed the charging handle and yanked it backward, attempting to eject the misaligned cartridge.

Through the curling fence, Gabriel could see Mildred looking over her left shoulder at him. *Are you smirking at me, you old Nazi bitch?* He drew a bead on the space just ahead of the car and pressed the trigger. He heard the *Rat-tat!* of only two rounds and then the jeep lurched wildly. Gabriel felt the bizarre sensation of sudden flight as he was launched gracelessly into the air. The jeep had struck a large pothole, and since he was so focused on Mildred, Gabriel hadn't braced for the jolt. As Gabriel hit the ground, he tucked and rolled, letting his forward momentum dissipate along with the cloud of dust his tumble had kicked up. Lt. Pritchard quickly circled back to retrieve Gabriel.

The Lieutenant pulled up, slammed on the brakes, and skidded to a stop. "You all right??" he yelled.

Gabriel dusted himself off and jumped back in the rear of the jeep. "The MPs will stop her at the gate!" he said, as he watched Mildred's car roar away down the fenced corridor, "but if not, we cannot let her get past them!" Gabriel said. The Lieutenant nodded and resumed the chase.

As the jeep rumbled toward the end of the road, Gabriel suddenly realized that the MPs would shoot at Mildred's car and he and Pritchard needed to be out of their line of fire. "Swing out wide!" he yelled at the Lieutenant, who was already doing so. The words had barely come out of his mouth, when up ahead, Gabriel spotted the fiery rearward flash and giant puff of smoke of the big recoilless rifle. The soldiers in the sand-bagged position had let loose an anti-tank round at the car. The round rocketed toward the vehicle with a scream and slammed into the engine, exploding it. Somehow, the car kept rolling. Engine compartment now aflame, the car careened to the left and smashed into the chain link fence with a rending rattle. The burning vehicle, now also entangled in concertina wire, dragged several yards of shredded fence behind it as it rolled to a stop just as Gabriel's jeep approached.

Gabriel and the Lieutenant jumped out of their jeep and raced to the flaming wreck, and Pritchard reached through the barbed wire tangles and tore open the door to drag Mildred out. Gabriel, right on his heels, spotted a small canvas bag lying on the floorboard of the passenger side. He braced himself for the blistering heat, thrust his hand into the wreckage, and quickly snatched the bag from the flames. Beyond most of the wreckage and the burning car, the Lieutenant lay Mildred down and stooped over her. Seconds later the flames reached the car's fuel tank, and *ka-boom!* Gabriel dove to the dirt as a huge fireball engulfed the staff car and thick black smoke obscured the clear sky.

And then it began to rain paper. The blast had blown documents out of the car and now they fluttered down like fireflakes around the crash area. As the MPs from the guard gate came sprinting toward them, Gabriel yelled out, "Secure those papers! Secure them! Stamp out the fires! Do *not read* them!"

Mildred lay watching them and smiled. Though her arm was broken and she had taken a bullet in the back, she seemed fully conscious and alert. As the Lieutenant mopped blood from a huge gash in her lip, Gabriel dug through the singed canvas bag, reading snatches from its documents, and then he pulled out a small codebook. He quickly flipped through it, wincing at what he found. He turned to Mildred, who was now bleeding freely from the nose and ears.

Gabriel shook the codebook in Mildred's face. "So the mole *is* Major Doyle! You've been helping him pass the information to the Nazis!" he shouted.

All pretenses abandoned, Mildred looked Gabriel in the eye and said,

"*Jetzt ist es zu spät.* It's too late. The chromium is already on its way to the Fatherland...."

"But you'll not live to see it fly," Gabriel said coldly.

Mildred, with her last breath, opened her ruined mouth wide into a rictus grin and rasped, "*Heil Hitler.*"

Gabriel let her head fall, walked away, and stood for a few moments, thinking. Then he called over to the Lieutenant, "Where is Captain James, Pritchard? I couldn't find him earlier and he needs to be here."

At the mention of Hal's name, the corporal that had been Hal's driver snapped his head up and yelled, "Sir, are you Father Gabriel?" Gabriel nodded as Pritchard walked over and brought the corporal to Gabriel. "Sir, Captain James tossed a gum wrapper out the window when he and Major Doyle left this morning. It ain't like him. I went over and picked it up and shoved it in my pocket to put in the trash later. We got no can up here. Just now, picking up all this paper reminded me, and I took it out of my pocket to throw away 'cause I'm going back to the barracks. I'm off duty now. But then I saw the gum wrapper had a message on it. He handed Gabriel the flattened Wrigley's wrapper. Written in tiny print, it said, 'For Father Gabriel, find Sprite asap. Cr on bomber.' That didn't make any sense to me, but maybe it does to you. Captain James didn't even speak to me as they passed the gate, and that ain't like him, either. We're friends."

"Thank you, Corporal, you may go." Pritchard waited for the boy to be out of earshot. So he's already gone," said Pritchard to Gabriel, "and if it's Sprite Shannon's squadron that's bringing the bomber with the chromium as cargo, they're well under way, too. In fact, they'll be taking off from Iceland in about thirty-seven hours. There is no way to get in touch with them."

Gabriel was already moving toward a jeep parked by the gate. "There's one, Pritchard," he called, "but I'll have to grow angel wings to pull it off."

CHAPTER 37

Meeks Field – Keflavik, Iceland

SEATED IN THE cockpit of her P-51 fighter, Sprite looked at the darkening sky and thought about the thunderclouds in Georgia that could form out of clear blue nothingness, and within minutes, rain down hail the size of goose eggs. In the near distance, large flocks of sea birds wheeled and dove toward the low mountains and rocks, leaving their fishing grounds for safety. *"When the birds act like that,"* her father had said, *"that's the time for you to put 'er down right smart, too."* Every instinct that had kept her safe back home now told her to go back to the hangar and wait this out. Weather control had warned of a huge storm forming off the coast of Scotland, and the clouds she was looking at were part of its outlying squalls, now threatening her takeoff. The last thing she wanted to do was try to dance with such a storm, but she had just watched Phoebe, Olga, Bertie and Gertie, crewing the B-17, followed by Meredith in the other P-51 Mustang, do exactly that. It would be close for her, the last plane up, but she could make it. She had to.

Her radio crackled, "Fox two-two, your runway is clear and ready for take off." Sprite acknowledged and began to taxi away from the flight line toward the runway, grateful that Icelandic Base Command had done a good job with the WASP squadron's maintenance and refueling. She gave it a little gas just as the first icy drops hit her windscreen. She shook her head and pushed the memories of the deadly Georgia weather away. There was no room for doubt now. The mission had come down to this final leg from Iceland to England.

Sprite's plane wobbled toward the runway as she throttled up, but out of the corner of her eye, she thought she saw—no, she *did* see—a man running alongside her plane, waving marshaller's flags, signaling her to stop. Sprite, confused, slowed the plane carefully, lest the Mustang nose over and damage the prop, causing even more of a delay. When she had all but stopped, the breathless man clambered up onto her wing. Sprite slid open the canopy to find out what could be the matter, and then she saw that she knew this man—he was Father Gabriel, General Arnold's chaplain. She had met him at the Snowy Winter dance at Avenger last December.

"Father Gabriel? What are you doing here?" she shouted above the noise of the Mustang's engine.

"Sprite—urgent intelligence from General Arnold and Captain James!" he said.

"What are you talking about??" she said. "And what's with the English accent?"

"Oh, sorry! You see, I'm not *Father* Gabriel. I'm a British MI-6 agent and I've flown for 36 hours straight to bring you this information, so I need you to listen sharp. The radar system that your bomber is carrying and the cargo cannot fall into the hands of Major Doyle," he said. "We have proof that the man is working for the Nazis. Do you hear? Cargo *must* be delivered to the British!"

"Yes, those are our orders, to deliver it all to Blackpool," she said above the noise. "Major Doyle, you say? I just knew it! But he won't be there, so why are you here? Unless he *will* be there...." Her voice trailed off as the realization hit her.

"He's *already* there! And he has Captain James with him. James got word to me, but just barely. When you arrive at Blackpool, you must find Captain James before Doyle gets his hands on the cargo! Catch your squadron and tell them to keep the cargo safe. I'm trying to alert my agents on the ground there now, but if I can't, you and James must stop Doyle! And on the QT, or we'll never bag the rest of the spy ring! No one outside of you and your squadron mates can know," he said, batting at the icy drops hitting his face. "Trust no one but them, James and me! Stop Doyle!"

"How do we do *that?* Shouldn't we just call the squadron back to base?" Sprite asked, thinking that the sky was making that option look ever more attractive.

"No! The delivery of that bomber's radar system and the crates is crucial to the Brits! Just be prepared to support Captain James's play, whatever it may be. That's all I can tell you now. Be careful, and Godspeed!" Gabriel said. He jumped down from the wing and disappeared into the shadows of one of the hangars.

Gabriel had decided not to give Sprite his other piece of news, which had been for Meredith. The prison camp where her husband Frank had been held had been *shelled* early that morning. There were no survivors.

Sprite sighed, her heart pounding, and throttled the engine again. *Sorry, Daddy, I know better but I can't do better. Too much depends on me.* "So move out of my way, storm," she yelled to the swirling clouds. "This time, I'm coming through!"

✕

Half an hour later, Sprite had caught the others and made radio contact. "That's what Gabriel told me," she said. "He flew 36 hours straight, all the way from Santa Sabina to catch us. I don't think he was winding us up."

"We'll have to find out what Hal's take on this is," Meredith replied. "He'll know what to do. And when he does, like Gabriel said, we need to be ready to back his play."

Olga broke in on the frequency. "*Da, da.* But first order to business – we deliver bom-ber safely. We have 1400 kilometers on final leg, and Nazi airspace to be crossing. Eyes sharp!"

"The starchy Lieutenant's right," Meredith said, "let's keep our heads in the game. We've got a lot of foul weather to deal with here, and it's enemy territory, so lets do our jobs. We'll think about Major Doyle once we're on the ground."

"Roger, out." Sprite said, signing off. This was about the furthest thing possible from flying crop dusters for Shannon & Sons back in Georgia, Sprite mused to herself. But she had wanted to serve, and now here she was in the thick of it. At least Hal would be waiting when she finally touched down in England.

※

Two hours in, the cloud cover grew thick, but here and there, the sun still shone brightly through and it seemed that everything was humming along perfectly. Sprite flew abeam with Meredith in what was called a "combat spread," with the bomber beneath them. So far, the flight had been uneventful, and her thoughts had wandered back to Major Doyle. She thought about having notched Doyle's right ear with that shot from her Daddy's pistol, and for the second time, truly wished she'd aimed a just little farther right.

She was replaying that moment over and over, when blobs of glowing light began streaking past Meredith's plane. It took Sprite only a split second to recognize that she was looking at the same thing she had seen when she and Phoebe had happened upon the Japanese submarine off the California coast. *Tracer bullets*, she thought, *someone's shooting at us!* She swiveled in her seat to look back over her shoulder, thankful for the 360 view afforded by the Mustang's clear bubble canopy. There was nothing....

Then she saw him! Zooming out of the sun, one German Luftwaffe Ju-87 Stuka finished its high-side guns pass and dropped in behind the WASP formation, his guns trained on Meredith's Mustang.

"*Germans!*" Sprite screamed over the radio. "Meredith, you got a German fighter on your tail!"

"Sprite, *sandwich!*" came Meredith's immediate reply. Sprite and Meredith immediately broke off in unison at a 90 degree angle, each toward her nine o'clock. After Meredith and Sprite had both turned the full 90 degrees, they came into single-file alignment with each other, "sandwiching" the Stuka in the middle. Meredith had no guns—all she could do was lead the German a merry chase and line him up for Sprite—but most importantly, away from the Bomber. Like a wounded dove, she wobbled her wings a bit and tried to look slow. It worked. The German roared after her.

Oh, no, I'll have to shoot, Sprite thought, *No way around it.* With an index finger, she flipped up the red safety cover on her joystick's trigger and made ready to fire the six .50 caliber machine guns mounted in her wings.

And waited.

And waited.

Then the Stuka fired a burst at Meredith, who broke into a snap roll to evade, then dove away. *There's my shot!* Sprite thought, and fired at the Luftwaffe fighter in a sustained, sizzling burst of tracer bullets that she was sure would put the fear of God into him. *Oh my Lord, I'm in a dog-fight with the Luftwaffe,* Sprite thought, *I should feel afraid, but I don't. Maybe later.*

Before she could figure that out, she realized the German now knew that Sprite was on his tail, which made her his next target! He "broke" to the right, turning sharply across her flight path, trying to increase the angle off tail. Momentarily, he exposed himself to Sprite's guns, and she fired a long burst again. *OK, girl, easy on the ammo,* she thought, remembering her very limited supply, *I've got to fire short bursts, or I'll eat it all up.* Sprite knew what the German was trying to do. Moving in front of Sprite at such a high crossing speed made him extremely difficult to hit because Sprite's bearing to her target was changing so abruptly. *Ah, you're trying to make me overshoot you! Well, You big ol' fat turkey vulture, I'm little, but I'm quick! Now watch this wild horse fly a "high yo-yo"!*

As the German fought to turn his plane in a flat half-circle, Sprite reduced the angle of her banking plane as she turned. She pulled back on the stick and brought the fighter to a different level, slowed to conserve her airspeed, and rolled into a steeper pitch turn to momentarily climb above the German. The trade-off between airspeed and altitude gave Sprite's nimble Mustang a burst of increased maneuverability, so she was able to make a smaller turn, avoiding an overshoot, and once again drop down in behind the German. When she got back down on his geometric plane, she gunned the throttle and picked up speed.

Sprite gritted her teeth as she bore down on the German pilot. *Now you're getting the idea!* she thought. *That's right, fly away from our bomber; we'll dance way over there… I've almost gotcha!*

"Meredith!" Sprite called into the radio, "I'm on him!"

Meredith, her heart pounding, began circling in "overwatch" when she heard Sprite's last transmission. But she had no time to recover from the violent, bone rattling aftershock of the adrenalin rush, because she saw two more German planes materialize from the clouds ahead: one was another Stuka, which made enemy fighter #2! That Stuka appeared to be escorting its companion plane, a Heinkel 111 bomber. Meredith took a deep breath and started to close the gap, but the Germans performed a Defensive Split. The Heinkel plane veered one way, while the Stuka broke in the opposite direction.

"Well, then, here we go, Meredith thought, *look out, Stuka 2!* and began dogging him once again. The B-17 bomber, Phoebe at the yoke, zoomed straight onward, radio-quiet, and Meredith desperately hoped that Bertie, Gertie, and Olga could hold off the Heinkel if it engaged them. She took a little comfort in that Olga had some combat experience. *Are there any more of you blighters?* she wondered. No matter, she knew she had to get the second Stuka out of range from the Bomber. The B-17 was just too slow and sluggish to fight, and she thought about the radar, and all the Allies' lives it would save. She immediately began working hard to get on his tail. *Ah, I have fooled you, too! Good!* Stuka 2, rather than employing the sophisticated tactics of Sprite's opponent, panicked and started "jinking," or randomly changing speeds, dives, pitch-ups, and rolls into "Guns Defensive, or "Guns D." *Oh, well look at you now! Very impressive,* Meredith laughed grimly, *Well done indeed, sir. I cannot possibly keep my aim on you, just as your textbook promised. Too bad you are wasting all the effort. Don't you think I might have shot at you by now if I had anything to shoot? OK, then around we go again!* Flying a Chandelle turn as she chased her prey, Meredith looked out the side of her canopy, and to her horror, she saw the Heinkel 111 bomber move to attack the slow, unmaneuverable B-17. *So your friend has come to the games after all,* she thought, *and without being invited. How very gauche, but that's no surprise. He brings his three guns and his many stations to line up on our B-17 bumblebee, with just*

girls for its crew and hardly any ammo. Then Meredith caught herself and laughed aloud. "Just girls." She had thought, "just girls." *You can do it, my darlings. No matter what, I know you can. In fact, I'm going to believe you've already beaten them!* She laughed aloud again, thinking of the Germans' shame should they learn they were dogfighting with "just girls." That is, if they even lived through this encounter to find that out.

Meredith decided to risk a call to the bomber. "Fox two-one to Baker-niner-four—make ready. You're about to be engaged, over!"

"Fox two-one, we read you," came a twin's voice back, "and we know, over!" Then the radio crackled as one of the Germans broke into their frequency. Meredith grimaced and went back to her own fight.

Inside the bomber, Gertie stood in the radioman's dorsal gun station, pulled back twice on the charging handle, and trained her .50 caliber machine gun on the approaching Heinkel. She held the gun's spade grips tightly and when the German plane aligned itself in her gun's crosshairs and blade front sight, she depressed the butterfly trigger with her thumbs. With a *Brrrrat-tat-tat-tat-tat!*, she let loose a furious fusillade of bullets. Her sister Bertie simultaneously blasted at the Heinkel from the right waist gunner station. As the Heinkel passed over them, Gertie tracked it over the top of the bomber with her gun, firing unrelenting bursts. The twins moved in what looked almost like a beautiful dance. Each silently anticipated the other's moves as Bertie smoothly jumped across to the left waist gunner position to pick up the crossing Heinkel's path. As the Heinkel passed from Gertie's field of fire, Bertie picked up and rained fire on the flying target again, never missing a beat. Gertie then jumped from the dorsal gun station and climbed into the top turret's twin, swiveling machine guns, and blasted away at the German bomber until it was out of range. Something crackled in their ears.

Gertie, still monitoring the radio, put her hand to her headphone to make sure of what she thought she was hearing. The Germans were now monitoring her frequency, apparently not bothering to hide their own conversations.

"Hey, I can hear them! She translated quickly. "They said the defensive fire is too fierce. The Heinkel was ordered to retreat to a safe distance!"

"Maybe it's heading for a bombing run, protecting its bomb load!" Bertie said.

"Careful. The Germans can also hear our coms," Gertie said, "and our voices." She climbed down out of the top turret and moved back to the radioman's table and worked the dials on the radio panel, adjusting the squelch. "They just figured out that the WASP squadron is female. They're laughing at us."

Olga frowned and narrowed her icy blue eyes at that, but Phoebe, though somewhat more pale, seemed to be pretending she hadn't heard the conversation or seen anything except the sky ahead of her. Stuka 2 then appeared in her line of sight and she slapped her leg in frustration.

Across the sky, Meredith began to perspire, even with the cloud cover making the air much colder than normal. Since early morning, when she had startled awake out of a bad dream, she hadn't felt well at all, but had kept it to herself…maybe a touch of flu, but she'd deal with it later. For now, she was hot on Stuka 2's tail, matching him move for move.

"That guy is pushing in on my line, Commander Lowe! Get him!" Phoebe's voice suddenly shrieked in Meredith's headphones.

"What else do you want me to do, Phoebe? Take pictures of him?" came Meredith's unnaturally quiet reply. Then, with instant, crushing regret, Meredith realized she had just told the Germans she could not shoot at them. In the bomber, Olga, Bertie, and Gertie closed their eyes in pain, and Phoebe sat mute, watching the sky, flying onward and frowning.

All of them could hear the sudden yelling of, apparently, the Heinkel's radio operator. The German radioman declared to his compatriots in English, "She is unarmed! The wasp has no stinger!"

Then came what had to have been Stuka 2's reponse. "*Ja?* Hahaha!"

Meredith watched in horror as he suddenly stopped his evasive maneuvering and came back around in a huge, sweeping turn, directly into Bertie's fierce defensive fire from the right waist gun. Stuka 2 then launched a vicious beam attack, laterally raking the B-17 bomber with machine gun fire. A glowing stream of German bullets blasted the Plexiglas of the B-17's top turret station, exploding the gun emplacement into flying chunks of plastic and aluminum framing. Then the line of streaking bullets walked up the wing and hit the number one engine as well. "Oh my darlings!" Meredith murmured, her face white with shock, "Please God that none of you was in that turret!"

Way beyond Meredith's position, Sprite finally closed the distance on Stuka 1. When she was within firing range, he abruptly inverted and dove in a Split S maneuver, changing direction. *No, I'm not going to follow you! I have another tactic in mind!* Sprite thought, climbing into the half-loop of the Immelman Turn. Reaching the top of the loop, she flipped over again erect. Heading in the same direction now as Stuka 1, she used her altitude advantage and, picking up speed, dove toward him as she prepared to do a high-guns pass.

As Sprite came into range again, her opponent also jinked into "guns-D." *So you're out of tricks! But Guns-D doesn't help you much, either! I'm still right here on your tail and you're my duck now!* Sprite thought.

Jinking madly or not, the German could still accidentally fly into Sprite's bullet stream. He couldn't outrun her and they both knew it. But Sprite had to aim ahead of the Stuka to hit it, and as long as he could keep up his haphazard, random maneuvering, she'd never find a firing solution.

Sprite exhaled as she felt a growing sense of a "knowing" moment coming on. *"You're my duck now..."* the phrase brought her a memory of learning to shoot waterfowl on brilliant fall day, Randall Shannon's big shotgun in his work-gnarled hands, a golden retriever named Bringer waiting stock still for the shot. "Sprite, honey, you cain't aim where they *are*—you gotta aim where they *will* be," her father had whispered. Then a big flock of mallards had broken cover from the cattails and taken the air. Randall had pointed his gun well beyond a cluster of them, as though knowing exactly where they would fly, and had brought two of them down with one shot. Bringer had leapt into the cold pond... and then the memory dissolved as quickly as it had come.

Sprite smiled, pictured a spot in the sky relative to the German fighter's 11 o'clock position and patiently waited. When she somehow just knew it was right, her trigger finger acted on its own, firing a long burst of glowing tracers and the German flew right into the bullet hose. Her red-hot shots tore into the Stuka's metal skin, ripping off chunks of panels. The plane's engine exploded and destroyed the left wing and then the entire German plane disintegrated in a slow-motion blossom of fire....

"Wooooo!" Sprite screamed, partly in triumph and partly in horror that she had just killed a man. There was no time to absorb any of it, though. She banked and climbed in a Chandelle turn to avoid the flying debris and zoomed back to help Meredith and the girls in the bomber.

Coming headlong toward the remaining Stuka and the Heinkel flying behind and aside it, she fired a raking burst at them, but after only a second or two, her guns fell silent, even though she had her finger still on the trigger. *Nooooo! Not now! I can't be out of ammo now.... Ah, but you don't know that, do you? Let's see if you scare.* There was no room to fit between the two German planes, so she did a quarter roll onto the "knife edge." With her wings aligned vertically, she squeezed between the flight paths of the two Luftwaffe aircraft and tried to send them running.

But they didn't scare. Instead, the Heinkel gunners trained their guns on Sprite and as she roared by, presenting her Mustang's white belly to them, they blasted away. She heard bullets plinking off her plane's belly and possibly her drop tank, but they missed the cockpit. Sprite brought her wings back to level and then banked to turn. She squeezed her trigger to test her guns but again, nothing happened. Her guns truly had gone dry. *OK, girls, looks like all the shooting is on you now,* she thought as she searched for the bomber's position.

Back inside the B-17, Bertie couldn't get a bead on Stuka 2 from the left waist gun and from the dorsal gun, Gertie couldn't either. Bertie leapt across to the right waist gun and swiveled it rearward, her sights searching the sky for it. No good. "I think they know we haven't got a tail gunner!" Bertie called to her twin, "Damn! All that radar equipment is back there instead."

"And our top turret is shot to bits, so that leaves us with no guns facing rearward except the radioman's dorsal," added Gertie. "But that one can't rotate low enough to hit the Stuka!"

"As long as he stays in that pocket behind and below us, he's got us where he wants us!" said Bertie.

"Yeah...and it can't be long before he rises up and chews us to pieces with those wing guns. Wait! Listen..."

The twins shared a look as they heard the German repeat the same basic plan over the radio to his Luftwaffe compatriots. The cold glee in his voice chilled the twins. "He's already enjoying his kill," said Bertie.

"Not yet, he won't!" shouted Gertie, firing a final burst in his general direction, using the last of her ammo on the dorsal gun. "Bertie, bring me more ammo from the top turret!" Bertie let go of the right waist gun, ran past Gertie, and then grabbed ammo belts from the damaged top turret guns. Some of them were damaged, but the whole nine yards of one of the belts was intact. She stumbled back and handed the belts over to Gertie and they frantically tried to reload the functioning .50 caliber machine guns.

Gertie pinched her throat mic for the intercom and said, "Girls, we can't just let him have us. We've gotta *do* something! Phoebe, *move* it! Don't present such an easy target! Do some evasive maneuvering before this guy blasts us out of the sky!"

Meredith broke in with her radio mic. "Yes, Phoebe, snap out of it! Get some deflection! If you drop down or scissor, maybe the twins can get a shot at him!"

But Phoebe, frozen with terror, knuckles white on the yoke, continued to fly on the beam, doing it all by the book. She seemed not to have heard Meredith at all.

Olga had seen this kind of shock before. She had also seen what kind of damage it could cause. She snarled a Russian curse and took the controls, leaving Phoebe in her powerless trance. "Tall trees, you hold *on*!" Olga warned over the intercom, "We are now rolling bom-burr!"

Gertie and Bertie grabbed whatever solid purchase they could and held on for dear life, tumbling around like rag dolls inside the bomber's fuselage. Dozens of empty shell casings, debris, flight manuals, and every other bit of detritus that wasn't bolted on or strapped down flew around in the cabin. A large gash opened above Phoebe's brow when she hit her head against her side window, but she seemed not to feel it. Her eyes remained locked onto space somewhere outside the plane. Olga angrily ripped paper away from her face, and the twins twisted and dodged the shell casings, finally finding each other's arms and locking them to keep their perches.

Despite Olga's ingenuity and skill, Stuka 2 seemed to have had no problem sticking to the B-17 bomber like it was flypaper. He laughed over the radio again and fired a few bursts but the laughter ceased when he found that the angle of deflection was far too great for him to properly lead his target. His fusillade passed harmlessly beneath the bomber. Olga had outwitted him after all.

"Sprite, switch to channel two!" came Meredith's urgent voice over Sprite's headphones.

Sprite switched to the new frequency and said, "Meredith, you read me?"

"I'm here. Is everyone alive? What's your situation?" Meredith asked.

"Yes, we are all alive! Olga dodged him, but I'm out of ammo," Sprite said as she banked into a Chandelle turn. "I'm coming around for a pass. Maybe they don't know I'm out yet and if I start bird-dogging this guy's tail, maybe he'll break off his attack."

"It's worth a shot. My God, I hope this works," Meredith said.

But Stuka 2 matched Olga's moves again, followed her inverted dive, and stayed with her as she came out of the dive and climbed in the opposite direction in a "corkscrew evasion" maneuver. The determined German moved into his firing solution.

There was nothing for it. If Meredith didn't do something in the next few seconds, the girls in the bomber were dead for certain. Meredith closed her eyes for a breath, trying to slow time. She pulled the gold pocket watch from her jacket, clicked it open, and stared at it in wonder. It had stopped, hands frozen on 0300 hours.

She had known it even before she looked. Her startled awakening that morning…then the ill feeling…the watch's ticking had always been like another tiny heartbeat against her body and in that place where only the spirit sees, she had known since morning takeoff that its time had stopped short.

Actually seeing it, though, caused a strange, awful rending in her chest.

So this is what it feels like. This is what a broken heart feels like. You're really gone, aren't you, Frank?, she thought, sensing nothing where Frank should be. *Yes, I know you are; have been…since 0300.* She switched back to channel one, keyed her radio and said, trying to keep her voice level and calm, "Phoebe, listen to me. You can do this. I'm counting on you to bring it home. Everyone...I...love you all," and killed the radio before anyone could reply.

Meredith set her jaw, took a deep breath and pulled back on the stick, then ascended into a quarter loop, slowing to near stall speed, turned on her wingtip in a wingover and dove sharply. *I match my heartbeat to the engine's, then count it out, one, two, three...," you said. Sprite, my little sister, thank you for that lesson...Frank, darling, I'm coming to you now...*

Her Mustang screamed downward and with absolutely precise timing and a smile on her beautiful face, Meredith slammed right into Stuka 2.

The cloud cover exploded into sparkling mist and flames as both planes blazed into an enormous, perfect fireball.

They all saw it. One by one, it dawned on them what Meredith had done for them. For a long moment, no one could speak. Blood dripped down Phoebe's face and as though she felt the wound on her forehead for the first time, she began to wail uncontrollably. The twins touched hands and shared a single, private thought, and tears formed in Olga's brilliant blue eyes, but she flew on, ignoring their spill down her angular cheeks.

And Sprite sat in her cockpit, disbelieving what she had just seen. But then, no. She had seen it before. It was part of the recurring dream, but she had never known what it meant until...now. "Meredith... oh my God," Sprite tried to blink away the last moment, but it was now engraved forever in her mind and heart. "Meredith..."

Sprite flew through the flaming debris cloud and thick black smoke, her pounding heartbeat accompanied by the drone of her Mustang's engine humming in her ears, but the radio hissed with only static. She shook her head to clear her mind and swallowed hard as she fought the tears. *"Whatever you do, do it for the best and highest reasons." That's what you said, Meredith. And I am sure that's what you just did. You quit the fight, but only because it saved our lives. All of our lives.* She wanted to be angry, but when Meredith's words came back to her, Sprite knew she just had to let it be. It had been Meredith's choice to make.

But that doesn't mean I can't cry, she thought and the tears, blinding in their fierce heat, filled her eyes again and again until she thought they would never stop.

But they did stop, and Sprite was surprised that only a couple of minutes had passed as she watched Olga come out of her climb and settle back into level flight, the bomber damaged but still more or less intact, and most importantly, still flying. Sprite switched her radio back to channel one, but all she could hear now was Phoebe's unintelligible shrieking. She tried to tune it out as she labored to concentrate on what came next. Meredith had disappeared in a split second, a split second when all time seemed to have stopped, but now Sprite was back in the moment again, and that meant back in the fight.

Sprite looked down at the Heinkel 111 flying well below her now at her 7 o'clock low. It suddenly stopped its evasive maneuvers and settled into straight, level flight. *I guess they figured out I'm out of ammo,* Sprite thought, *but they can't possibly be out, too. That's very odd…why…did they break off the fight?*

Within seconds she had her answer. A long, winged torpedo shape fell gracefully from beneath the German plane and a smaller cylinder, affixed to the top of the torpedo, suddenly fired up its pulsing blue flame. Then the contraption literally rocketed forward with speed like nothing Sprite had ever seen. *A V-1! So that's why the Germans are up here! They're launching a V-1 at London,* she thought with alarm. Sprite watched the Heinkel, its mission now complete, roll and dive into the classic "bug out" maneuver intended to put as much distance between it and Sprite as quickly as possible. Sprite was powerless to stop it, so she pulled back on the stick and began to ascend.

Back inside the B-17 bomber's cockpit, Phoebe's hoarse voice yelled into the radio, "Sprite, what are you doing?"

"I'm gonna catch that buzz bomb," said Sprite evenly.

"No! Meredith just blew herself up! And now you're leaving us up here all alone and defenseless! You can't!" Phoebe screamed.

"You've still got guns, and ammo too, right? That's more than I have," Sprite replied.

Phoebe grew even more frantic. "Sprite, what are you gonna *do* if you catch it? I mean if you're out of ammo?" Phoebe cried.

"I don't know, but the whole reason we're bringing the B-17 over is to stop those things! How many civilians will that thing kill if I don't do *something*?" Sprite asked.

Then Gertie chimed in on the radio. "Sprite, you're not thinking of doing anything crazy too, are you?"

Phoebe interrupted again. "You can't! You'll never reach it anyway! If you dive at full throttle, you could tear the wings right off your plane!"

Sprite's voice crackled back in aggravated reply, "Look, if the paint starts peeling off, I'll slow down, OK?"

Phoebe's voice rose by an octave as she yelled, "Sprite, get back here! Don't leave me! You—"

"—Enough, you silly little crying-baby!" Olga barked from the bomber copilot's seat. She reached over on the panel and snapped off Phoebe's radio switch.

But then Olga softened a bit when she tasted the salt of her own tears. She lowered her voice and said, "You...are no help, Phoebe. Meredith made hard call, bought our lives. Let Sprite do what she must, honor Meredith, save more lives. Let us all do what we must. Is pilot's choice." Phoebe sniffed and rolled her swollen eyes, but said no more.

In her Mustang, Sprite pulled back on the stick a bit more, raising the nose of the plane as she applied full throttle to climb. *All right, time to prove Phoebe's fear wrong again*, she thought, *or at least I hope it is.* When she gained what she figured was enough altitude, she dropped the nose and the Mustang screamed and rattled as it picked up speed against the extreme wind resistance. She clenched her teeth as she pushed the plane's performance envelope to its outermost edge. After a few long moments, she saw the vapor trail of the buzz bomb's pulse jet, squirreling right up to the flying bomb itself. *Dang, that infernal thing is fast*, she thought, *but I can catch it!*

Sprite leveled off from her dive and the screaming of the wind diminished a bit, but her engine still roared at near full power and maximum velocity. She pulled up alongside the V-1, the bomb's wings wobbling slightly from turbulence, and Sprite adjusted her throttle to match its speed. *Okay Daddy, I remember what you used to say*, Sprite thought to herself, as she eased her own right wingtip under the left wing of the buzz bomb. "The probability of survival…is equal to…the angle of arrival," she repeated aloud.

She dropped slightly and jerked the stick to the left, popping up her right wing, which in turn popped up the bomb's left wing. The shudder of the quick contact moved through Sprite like a bolt of electricity and she dove out of the way as the buzz bomb, never designed for such a sudden change in attitude, flipped over, spiraled wildly out of control, and then resolved into a near-vertical spinning dive.

It plummeted toward the sea and Sprite circled and banked, keeping her eyes locked on its descent until she saw a huge geyser of water erupting from the ocean's surface. The bomb had exploded on contact with the sea. It could do no harm now. *And that angle of arrival was perfect for you, you little bugger*, Sprite thought as she breathed a sigh of relief and leveled off to begin her ascent and rejoin the B-17 in formation.

Coming back, she asked no more of the Mustang than normal speed, and the few minutes it took to find the others gave her time to settle her jangled nerves a bit. The veils of cloud before her parted on a serene sky. It looked like nothing at all had happened out there.

Sprite slid into the escort position to the port side of the American bomber and was instantly dismayed to see that the outermost engine on the bomber's left wing spewed trails of black smoke. "Olga, your number one engine is smoking like a Texas barbecue and number two looks like it took several hits as well! You're on your way to a major engine fire," she said.

"Acknowledged, using fire extinguishers, I shut engines down," came Olga's reply on the radio. Sprite watched as carbon dioxide streamed from the bomber's disabled engines, smothering any nascent flames, and their propellers slowly stopped spinning as Olga expertly feathered the props to lessen drag. The bomber dipped a little on its dead side, but the other engines kept it perfectly aloft. "Ha! Is actually better flying now," she said, "I am not having to fight pull so much if I keep broken wing in good place."

Then it was Sprite's turn to get a warning. Gertie's voice came over the radio. "Do a slow pass over us, Sprite—I think you're leaking fuel. Your drop tank probably took a hit." Sprite slowly crossed above and in front of the bomber, and Olga confirmed the suspicion.

"*Da*, drop tank leaking and no thanking you for black liquid spraying onto bomber's windscreen," Olga advised evenly.

"It must be my landing gear's hydraulic fluid," Sprite said with more than a bit of concern. She flipped the switch to lower her landing gear to test the system. Absolutely nothing happened. "Looks like my landing is going to be a little tricky," she said, unable to quell the sudden flash of memory of Ninette's failed belly landing in the desert. *That was only a few months ago,* she thought. *Seems like ages.*

Olga came back on the radio. "With planes damaged and storm front building over Scotland, we divert."

Bertie chimed in with, "Vagar airfield in the Faroe Islands is socked in, so it's either onward or downward."

"I set new course for Antrim, Northern Ireland. We cut 120 miles off flight path. Tall Tree, inform Blackpool," Olga ordered.

"Roger that, I hope we can make it," Bertie's voice said.

Sprite checked her fuel gauge again. *Me too, Bertie. Me, too.*

CHAPTER 38

ALMOST TWO HOURS later, Sprite could see the Giant's Causeway on the coast of Northern Ireland looming on the horizon, fierce waves foaming white around the odd, hexagonal columns of it rock formation. She checked her fuel gauge for the fiftieth time. *This will be close. It's maybe enough fuel to make the coast, but you* always *have too much fuel to crash land,* she thought. Regardless, she would have to jettison the drop tank to belly land. Then she had a sobering thought. She figured it would be best for the wounded bomber to land first, lest she... possibly create a burning debris field in the landing zone. She keyed her radio mic, and said, "Olga, you're gonna have to land fir—"

"—I understand," Olga curtly replied. "Am losing power now, cannot maintain airspeed and altitude. I must drop some cargo even to make coast, much less find runway at Antrim."

Fighting for control of the now underpowered, overloaded B-17, Olga glanced over at Phoebe, who was staring blankly into space again and mumbling to herself. Below them, the deep blue of the North Sea was turning into the brown, rocky cliffs of Giants' Causeway, and they were losing altitude quickly. Olga pinched her throat mic for the intercom, and said, "Tall Trees, remain clear of bomb bay. I dump boxes of chromium, try for rocks, not sea." Olga reached over the panel and flipped the switch for the bomb bay doors. As the servos whirred to open the doors, the bomber got a bounce in altitude as tons of crated chromium began falling out and crashing onto the rain-whipped Giant's Steps below.

The rocky coastline gave way to green fields, and as the last of the cargo fell out of the nets, Olga snapped the switch to lower the landing gear. She adjusted the flaps and searched for a clear spot large enough to put down a heavy, crippled bomber, but she realized there was no choice. It was here or nothing. She pinched her throat mic. "Prepare for possible creshing landing," her terse order came over the intercom.

Olga touched the B-17 down on the grassy field, which had more than a few big fieldstones in it, but the huge balloon tires of the bomber bounced with forgiveness, perhaps a little too much for Olga's liking. The big aircraft hopped and sprang a few times, and when the bomber settled down onto the ground for good, Olga judiciously applied the brakes before they ran out of open field and ran into a fast-approaching rocky outcropping. Angular jaw clenched in determination, she held on tight as her entire body shuddered with the effort to stop the bomber's headlong charge. Finally, as the outcropping grew larger and larger in the windscreen, the bomber slowed and, mercifully, came to a stop.

Olga shut down the engines, exhaled deeply and then removed her headphones and detached the wires to her throat mic. She reached over and shook Phoebe, still in her semi-catatonic state. "Wake up, flight is over, no creshing. Get out." When Phoebe didn't move, Olga unbuckled her harness and pulled her up to drag her to the hatch.

Bertie and Gertie made their way to the hatch, took the bar and swung gracefully out of the bomber like gymnasts. When it was her turn, Phoebe fainted and Olga had to hand her down to the twins, swinging down after her.

While the twins saw to Phoebe, Olga walked away from the plane and watched Sprite circle the area. A large, metal teardrop shape detached from the bottom of Sprite's plane signaling that she had jettisoned her drop tank over the sea. Olga then surveyed the trail of debris behind them. The crates of chromium were scattered all over the Giant's Steps and the field, but the airborne radar equipment in the bomber was intact. The bomber, although damaged, would fly again. Olga sighed and made her way up the rocks to scout the area.

With her engine sputtering, and starved for fuel, Sprite made her final approach to the field. *There's my best angle, away from the bomber. Just in case…* she thought bleakly. As she lined up, the engine coughed again and wheezed into a death whistle. *I'm about to ruin this perfectly good propeller, but at least it won't be a fiery crash. Still, what a waste…* Then she quickly thought of Hal, instantly conjuring up his handsome face, and her friend Letty from back home, and all the girls from Sweetwater, Meredith, and especially Ninette, who had tried—and fatally failed—to land in exactly this same way. But she paused on the thought of her father. *Well, Daddy, what do I do now?*

The sky roiled blackly above her, and the waves white-capped beneath the descending plane. The storm was close now. Then, oddly, the wind quieted and the sun broke through, shining a beam of pure gold across her dark path.

She caught her breath at the beauty around her. The raging sea shone with blinding brightness, and she thought about the day she had left her home in Lowland Mill. *"What do I do now?"* she had asked then, and gotten no answer, just a sudden calm of the wind in the pines. *"Is that all I'm gonna get, Daddy?"* she had said, irritated. The words echoed in her mind from that day so long ago. But then she had realized she already knew exactly what to do.

And she knew now, too.

Sprite came in fast, dropping quicker than was advisable for her airspeed, and the propeller's blades became visible again and froze in position. As the plane made first contact, the rocky ground tore at its belly, then tossed it back up in the air for a brief second, turning it almost completely over. Sprite saw the ground from the top of her canopy and thought of how Ninette had begun her cartwheel at just that point, where gravity and inertia had made their fatal agreement. But the rocks, or the rising wind under her plane, or maybe God Himself pulled her back over and Sprite came down hard again, holding her breath, her hand glued to the joystick as she plunged forward. The leading edges of her wings lopped off spent gorse blossoms and clipped tangles of tall heather like a gigantic scythe as she passed over them.

First she realized she had no brakes. Then the stick wouldn't even steer, so she just let go of it and took the ride. Finally, friction gradually overcame forward energy, and her Mustang bounced, slid, and skidded sideways to a halt.

Sprite exhaled and said a quick prayer of thanks, unbuckled her harnesses, removed her flying helmet, and disconnected her headphone cables, all while shaking like a twig in a tornado. She pushed back the bubble canopy and climbed out of the plane quickly, hoping nothing would catch fire, and saw that without the landing gear, her wings now almost touched the ground. She slid onto the wing and then stepped off directly onto the green grass of Ireland.

Olga, waiting only a few yards away, motioned to her to be quiet and then crawled over and whispered, "*Da*, you make it fine. Tall trees are helping Phoebe, way behind rise of rocks by leetle road. From top of rocks, I see Major shove gun into blonde Captain's face. They are coming over hill soon. Something wrong here. We hide."

"Yes, very wrong. The Captain is my sweetheart Hal and the Major is the one Gabriel warned us about. Hal's a pilot. Doyle must have made Hal take him here when he heard we were diverting. I'm staying here, Olga. I have to try to help Hal," Sprite whispered.

Olga nodded her understanding and mouthed, "I go back, tell them be quiet. We wait. Help when we can, *da*?"

Sprite nodded and smiled. You could do worse than having Olga and the twins behind you.

CHAPTER 39

HAL STEERED THE jeep up what served for a road in the rough sheep country of Northern Ireland, but apparently was not doing it fast enough for Major Doyle. "Faster, James," Doyle said, laughing a little at how that sounded to him.

"Sir, all due respect, I'm not your chauffeur," said Hal quietly.

"You are today!" said Doyle, crowing a little in the seat beside Hal. Doyle brandished his service weapon at Hal. "Today, the best of all days, the day I see Coreen again, the day I get paid, the day I say 'bugger off' to the US Army and all that it stands for—today, you, golden boy, are most certainly my chauffeur!"

Hal gritted his teeth and tried to keep his mind on the duty of every prisoner of war—finding a way to escape. When they had boarded the plane at Blackpool, Doyle had pulled his gun on Hal to make him fly them to Antrim and despite the massive amounts of whiskey Doyle drank during the flight, had kept that gun on him every second of the way.

At least I know I can fly again, thought Hal. *Even at gunpoint!* He savored that thought for a moment, and then slowed the jeep as they followed the sheep trail to the crest of a big hill. The air stank of burning.

"I said faster!" Doyle demanded.

"Major Doyle, we seem to have arrived," said Hal, keeping his tone neutral. "Look." Down the hill lay bits of wreckage and several small, heavily smoking grass fires. Hal searched the rugged landscape for signs of life as he motored carefully through the debris, but he saw nothing but the hulk of the bomber and what looked like the tail of a Mustang almost swallowed by tall gorse bushes. *There should be two Mustangs,* Hal thought. *Where is the other one? And why have these two planes come in so hot and broken? Are those…bullet holes?!* His next thought was too painful to bear, so he pushed it aside. Sprite had to be alive and all right. She just had to be. But there was no sign of any of the girls.

Then, from the corner of his eye, Hal saw the familiar curve of a pixie face peeking from amid a tangle of gorse and gooseberries. He winked, and she ducked quickly back into her cover before Doyle could notice her.

"What?!" Doyle shouted frantically as he stood up in the jeep and looked around. "Nobody said they had crashed!"

"Looks like they didn't actually crash, Major. Just came in hot and damaged. I'd say they've had a dogfight with some Nazis on the way, by the holes on that bomber's side. Look at the bullet lines.…" Hal wanted to bolt out and run to Sprite, but he didn't move from his seat. Doyle still had the gun.

"Then where the hell are they? Get out. We have to get my chromium!" Doyle ranted, getting out of the jeep himself. He waited for Hal to park and then walked him toward the smoking bomber. Doyle motioned for Hal to go around the back. They waded through the thorny gorse and saw that the bomber's bay was hanging open. Doyle lost all color in his face as he peered up into the bomber's belly. Not a single box of chromium remained.

"Where…?" he began under his breath, staring in disbelief. He brandished the gun in Hal's face again. "Let's go," he said, and they began to walk toward the rise of the Giant's Steps, Hal in the lead.

From the thick cover of another copse of trees, Sprite pressed herself belly down to the grassy ground and watched Doyle and Hal moving away from the bomber. Hal had seen her, she knew, but Doyle had not! Sprite backed farther into her thicket and waited to see what they would do next, taking note of Doyle's gun at Hal's back as they walked toward the cliff. She was about to follow, but she heard an odd, mechanical sound, like a big motor, somewhere in the distance. She froze in her tracks.

Then the sound gradually became louder until Sprite could tell where it was coming from—the road beside where the other girls had gone to hide. Sprite hoped it was help, but judging from its direction, that was not likely. Anything helpful would be following Hal and Doyle, coming from Antrim base. That lorry was probably full of Doyle's friends. After all, he had expected to hijack several tons of chromium and would need some muscle to load it.

Her theory proved out when the green lorry, its sides announcing Guinness Stout as the pride of Eire, lumbered to the end of the rutted road, which was still some distance away from her. The lorry's diesel engine puttered to a stop and Sprite saw Doyle break into a smile when he noticed the vehicle. She began to circle around again, putting herself between Doyle and the other girls. She drew her side arm and checked it quietly, flipping the safety off as she tried to figure her best position. She would need some rock cover, and the Steps, curving raggedly down the coastal cliffs, had plenty. *If I can sneak up that ridge and hide at about Hal's 3 o'clock, I might get a clear shot at Doyle,* she thought, slowly creeping up the ridgeline of the odd, hexagonal rocks.

Below her, Doyle whistled a little tune as he marched Hal to the edge of the cliffs. "Gallagher, you are right on time!" Doyle shouted as he saw the lorry, "Good man!"

Hal took note of the big lorry, but kept most of his attention on Doyle's eyes and hands. All along the path, rubble and debris from the torn up planes lay scattered in the tall grass and rocks. If he could just find a heavy tool or pick up something with an edge on it....

As though Doyle had overheard his thoughts, he stopped Hal and walked in front of him, peering sideways over the cliff to the Steps below. Broken boxes of dull chromium pigs lay in heaps here and there, some of them already threatened by the roughening waves.

"This is far enough, James," he said, his mouth quirking into a bitter smile as he leveled his gun at Hal's face, "I can kick you the rest of the way over myself."

Then Doyle's smile dropped as he heard a door slam. He glanced back at the lorry and shook his head. "But wait; lucky you, as always," he moaned sarcastically. I see my new wardrobe has just arrived. Time for me to change. Wouldn't want your blood to spoil this wonderful uniform!"

Hal looked to his left and saw a very tall, blonde woman with red lips and a newsboy cap slung over her forehead. She carefully approached them, a bundle in her arms, and dropped it at Doyle's feet.

"As you asked," she said coldly, stepping back to reveal her Walther pistol.

"Ah, Greta. So glad you have joined us. Train your gun on Captain America here while I shuck this Halloween costume," said Doyle, not really so glad at all that Greta had joined them. He hated Greta. But she was Mattias's woman, and he needed Mattias to keep Coreen alive. Mattias had said Coreen was waiting for him "somewhere out there in the sea," no doubt moving along the coast in a U-boat with Mattias's men, who were supposed to exchange her for the chromium.

Hal stood passively, observing the sharp-faced woman. Her eyes were cold and a little bit sly—as though something reptilian lived behind them instead of a warm-blooded woman.

"Don't tell me what to do, Seamus, or my gun will be pointing at you. Now dress and hand over the goods. How long have you been here and where have you put the chromium!" she said, narrowing the chilling eyes at Doyle. "It had better still be here…."

"It is," Doyle said hastily, "but the chromium… is scattered down there." He pointed to the Giant's Steps. "Those bitches dumped it. And the storm is about to hit! We have to hurry!" he urged. Greta glanced to where he pointed and rolled her eyes when she spotted the broken ore boxes.

The seaward sky had darkened to a steel gray, with patches of bright green light breaking through, casting hard shadows on the chromium littered rocks. Greta snarled something in German, making Doyle screw up his face in disgust.

With Hal watching his every move, Doyle tugged off his shirt, but the top button seemed to catch on a chain of some kind. Then Hal saw the pink and green gold of Sprite's ring wink in the stormlight as Doyle carefully freed it from the button and let it drop back to his chest.

Sprite saw it, too. *Well, I'll be…! There's my ring! There's my Claddagh ring!* She hadn't seen it since the day Doyle stole it, and now…there it was.

When Doyle was fully dressed again, Greta turned her back on them both and sauntered off to the lorry to bring the loaders.

Doyle smoothed his clothes, pulled his flask from his pants pocket, and said, "So Hal, meet Seamus," he said in an overly polite Irish lilt. "I'm going to be killin' you now, boyo, and rather enjoyin' it."

Hal's jaw clenched, but his gaze never left Doyle's deranged eyes.

Doyle took a huge swig from the flask, came right up to Hal's face, and breathed whiskey fumes into his nose. "I been waitin' for this since yer stupid little bitch of a girlfriend clocked me with that baseball bat at the dance. And wherever she is, I'll be findin' her, too. I made her a promise, ya see, that I would hunt her down and make her pay for the damage of my ear, and then I'll be adding that knockout to her tab. So you can take that little thought with you to your grave, Parker."

Parker? thought Hal, and then he remembered Gabriel saying that Doyle's file mentioned a brother named Parker who had died at Pearl.

"I'm not Parker, Seamus," Hal said evenly. "Put the gun down and let me help you with your chromium. I doubt you have either the men or the time to get it all." He pointed over Doyle's shoulder at the gathering storm, lightning now flashing through the dark clouds.

Doyle just grinned and chuckled. "You don't know Gallagher. He's probably brought all of County Down with him. Cheers!"

Doyle cocked the pistol and smiled, but Hal had begun to run like he was stealing third before the bullet ever left the gun. Hal kept low, but Doyle fired again, this time hitting Hal in the side. Hal dropped to the ground, began to crawl toward a shamble of rocks, and Doyle presented sideways and drunkenly, carefully, aimed at Hal's head, thereby putting the third bullet through his leg. Then Hal lay still, face up beside a fissure of the rocks.

Doyle stood alone at the top of the Giant's steps and laughed insanely into the wind, shooting his pistol at the man-high columns looming up at him accusingly. "And here's one for you, Father, and you, Mattias, and you, General, and some for all of the rest of you!" The ricochets bounced and zinged around Sprite's head, pinning her to the remarkably inadequate back side of one of the larger of the hexagonal pillars as she tried to get a bead on the madman.

Hal stirred at the echoing noise of Doyle's revel and tried to stand, but it was too much. Though it wasn't deep, the side shot was bleeding, but the real problem was the leg, and it crumpled instantly under Hal's weight. At that moment, Doyle turned and came striding back, gun still in hand, shaking his head. "Ya just don't stay down, do you Parker? Ya just won't stay dead!"

Hal saw two of Doyle resolve into one and felt around the ground for a weapon, anything, and found only a loose, roundish rock about the size of a baseball. *I'll not die like a cornered beast, you coward!* he thought, praying that his fastball was still major league material. Timing would be everything... Doyle came closer, and Hal waited until he stopped and raised the gun. Hal then brought his pitching arm around with everything he had.

The rock struck Doyle squarely in the chest and he stumbled, raising one knee in futile reflex and screaming in pain. But then Doyle bore down on his agony, snorted through his nose, steadied his hand, and aimed again. Hal dove aside into the fissure, and the flintrock caught the bullet and sent it flying wild. *That should be your last shot, you Nazi bastard! Now let's do this like men!* thought Hal as he pulled himself up onto the rocks at his back.

"Ooops!" said Doyle apologetically, "I seem to be out of ammunition! But look!" Doyle grinned crazily and snapped open the ammo pouch on his web belt, pulled out another magazine, and smacked it into the .45, training the barrel once again on Hal. Before Hal could react, a woman's voice cut through the rising wind.

"Over here, Seamus. I'm here! It's Coreen! I'm over here!"

Startled, Doyle fired wild and high, and Hal dove for the ground. Doyle shot again, this time grazing Hal's thigh, and with that, Sprite stood up and fired her gun, hand steady and heart pounding.

Doyle tottered at the edge of the Giant's Steps, his face contorted with pain and surprise as his throat gushed blood.

Sprite had aimed a little to the right this time.

He dropped the gun as a gust of wind tumbled him over the cliff, and he fell without a sound.

Sprite darted out of her cover and checked Hal's pulse. "I'm OK," he whispered to her. "I'm hit, but it's nothing fatal. The others, in that lorry—they will have heard you—hide, quick!"

Sprite looked up, considered his words, saw no one coming from the direction of the lorry, and made a different choice. She bolted for the Giant's Steps, looked over and saw Doyle, his back twisted in an impossible angle, a bubbling wound at his throat, caught on a small outcropping about half way down. Without thinking, she jumped, landed badly, slipped on the trailing seaweed and cut her hand, ending up just below Doyle. A breaking wave licked hungrily at her feet, threatening to take her out to sea.

Marveling at the water's force, Sprite held on against the churning pull, and when it lessened, she looked up and saw Doyle's eyes on her, her ring dangling out in space from his ruined neck. He was still alive!

"I told you this ring always comes back to its rightful owner," she said, grabbing the gold chain and snapping it from his throat. He stared at her and smiled faintly as she held the ring tight in her bleeding fist.

"Coreen?" he moaned. The last thing Doyle saw what the fierce green of Sprite's eyes. Another, higher, wave covered his face and then dragged at her back, flooding into her eyes, the salt stinging them into blindness for a long moment. When she had blinked it away, she saw that Doyle was dead.

She began to climb upward slowly and carefully, dingy red and purple bladder wrack entangling her waterlogged boots, her good hand bearing all her weight. Her cold-whitened fingers had gone numb, making their grip untrustworthy. With every step, she saw the next six-sided column present its flat platform. She shoved the pointed toes of her heavy boots as far into the cracks of the rocks as she could and pushed upward, each step a fresh agony for her tired muscles. Slowly she rose up the Steps, the top within reach, just one more push....

Her fingers failed and she slipped one step backward again and sprawled across the lower column, her face toward the raging sea.

This time, a seventh wave, always the largest in the tide's implacable pattern, rose up before her and towered ten feet above her head, its translucent brilliance lit by a flash of lightning that struck so close to her that the sound deafened her and she felt the heat crackle through the rocks beneath her knees. The magnificent wave held for long seconds, caught in time, the force of its power defying gravity, bits of flailing, spinning kelp inside it backlit by the lightning's flash. Then it crested and the first drops of what had to be tons of water began to shower lightly down on her. She closed her eyes and held onto the ring. With nothing in her mind but the thought of Hal, she waited for the next, awful second.

But the next second was all Hal needed to grab her by the jacket, haul her up and over the edge of the Steps and hug her to himself as he rolled over onto the ground to dodge the icy claws of the enormous wave.

Sprite, shocked and cold, began to shiver uncontrollably, sobbing deeply as she looked at Hal—Hal who had been shot three times himself, who could not walk.

But who had still somehow crawled to the edge of the Steps to save her.

His face was blanched white and pinched with pain, but he looked down at her with pure love in his eyes, and it warmed and quieted her. She settled in his arms and stopped shaking. After a long moment, they sat up.

"I…thought I'd lost you, Sprite," said Hal softly. "I really did."

"I know…but I couldn't let him take anything else from me. I had to get this back." She opened her hand and showed him the Claddagh ring, its gold bright against the welling blood in the palm of her hand. She dropped the chain, wiped the ring clean on the lush grass of Ireland and placed the Claddagh on her own right hand ring finger.

Hal nodded. "Help me up, Sprite," he said. "I think I can stand if you don't drop me."

"Never," she smiled, remembering his promise to her at the dance when he had picked her up. She rose and gripped him under the arm as he pushed off from the slick grass, wobbled a bit, and found his footing.

Then he kissed her hard, his arms encircling her tiny frame, shielding her from another thundering blast of icy water that had crashed over the Giant's Steps. They parted lips and Hal turned her face to the sea, saying, "Look down now, Sprite. Between the waves. See that he is gone. He can't hurt you anymore." She did look, and saw that the place where Doyle had lain broken on the rocks was empty.

She nodded and shivered again. "I know," she said. "Hal?"

"Mmm?"

"Thank you," Sprite whispered, and he hugged her again. It was over.

Only it wasn't. At the edge of the road, the lorry's engine suddenly started. Hal drew Sprite behind him protectively and as the lorry began to creep forward, Hal quickly looked around for Doyle's dropped gun. Sprite saw it first. "Let me," she said, kneeling and reaching for the weapon. Sheets of cold rain began to pelt them, obscuring their view of the lorry, but also obscuring the driver's view of them.

"Give it to me and get back behind me," said Hal. As the lorry slowly approached, Hal waited calmly for whatever came next. It didn't matter. Sprite was behind him and safe as long as he could shoot.

Then the lorry stopped, its engine gearing down to a low idle, and the driver's side door cracked open. The tall blonde woman, her newsboy cap slouching over her eyes, her jacket collar turned up against the driving wind and rain, walked steadily toward them, her hands raised in surrender, but Hal didn't relax. It could be a trick. These were Nazis, after all.

Then the woman stopped and shouted over the storm, "Hallo, plis don't shoot me!" Hal felt Sprite relax at his back, and then she stepped forward.

"Olga! It's *you*! How? Wh—" cried Sprite, relieved. She had all but forgotten the other girls.

Olga broke into a run and reached them in a few seconds. "Is short story," she huffed, "Idiot Nazis drive up and stop, woman gets out and leaves lorry, tall trees and I sneak up on men in back, take care of booznez, and wait. Woman returns, she fights me in the booshes, I snap her neck and take her clothes in case I have to fool Major. Worst part was having to put on her trashy leepsteek," she added, wiping it off of her mouth with Greta's jacket sleeve. "But I see you take care of Nazi traitor yourselves," she finished, waving a hand at the Giant's Steps.

Sprite smiled and shook her head. "I should have known. Olga, meet Hal. Hal, Olga."

"*Da!* We do this part in warmer lorry; I am now soaked and you two are shakink and blue," laughed Olga, moving to Hal's other side.

They helped Hal aboard the lorry and through the pass window, he saw Bertie and Gertie standing up in the back, their matching German MP-40 submachine guns pointed purposefully at six bound and gagged, angry faced "fishermen." One of them—the one with the cracked front tooth—was much older than the others. Phoebe hunched in one corner, mute and solemn, and would not meet Hal's eyes.

Hal frowned. "Where is Commander Lowe?" he asked, and then he remembered the missing Mustang. "Oh," he breathed, and squeezed Sprite's hand softly as she closed her eyes, fresh tears starting down her cheeks.

"Captain James?" one of the twins called from behind the partition. "You'll want to keep pressure on those wounds, and there is a church key and a bottle or two of Guinness in the cab to help with the pain." Hal nodded and found the beer, opened it, and took a long, long, swallow.

With the rain lashing the windscreen, Olga knocked a warning on the cab for Bertie and Gertie, who sat down at opposite ends of the double line of captives. Olga carefully backed down the gravel road until it curved into the straightaway to Antrim. When the lorry found pavement and began moving faster, Sprite dropped instantly, deeply, into sleep on Hal's shoulder.

CHAPTER 40

Guernsey Island, English Channel

THE KNOCK CAME far too softly for it to be anything other than what Mattias expected. He sat smoking and playing chess with himself on the board in his office, a half empty bottle of schnapps at his elbow.

"Sir!" The Oberleutnant clicked his heels together and waited for Mattias to grind out his cigarette.

"Oberleutnant, I wondered when you would come," Mattias said, his voice a little thick and slurred. Mattias already knew what the Oberleutnant had come to tell him. Liam, his eyes and ears in Dublin, had relayed the failure of the chromium mission and the death of Wallace Doyle almost as immediately as the American Ambassador had received the news, which was less than an hour after Olga had driven through the gates at Antrim. Liam had told him something else, as well—something even more troubling. Greta was dead.

And so Mattias had waited. The U-boat that should have taken him to the mainland had left after Doyle failed to make contact and now, instead of arriving triumphant back at Berlin, a vast quantity of chromium ready to present to the Fuhrer and a promotion to accept, Mattias waited for the inevitable.

The Oberleutnant cleared his throat and said, "You are an officer, so I am granting you a choice." He put a clear packet with one white pill in it on the desk and slid it toward Mattias. "I will come back in an hour. I trust this is goodbye." With that he clicked his heels again, raised his arm to the Fuhrer, and walked out. Mattias noticed that the Oberleutnant took his time leaving and seemed to be taking special note of the lavish appointments of the room as he made his way to the door, especially the hand woven carpet taken from a rich Jewish merchant's house. No doubt, this would be the Oberleutnant's office within the hour.

Mattias sighed deeply and looked at the Klimt on the wall behind him one last time. The painting was a beautiful view from beneath some autumn beech trees, circa 1903, and the sky behind them looked peaceful and full of light. There were worse places to do this. He sighed, pushed the despicable pill off the desk and shook his head. He would not die like a poisoned rat. He drew his Luger, pointed it at his temple, and smiled bitterly, apologizing to the Klimt and hoping the Oberleutnant would never get his bloodstains out of the priceless Turkish carpet.

CHAPTER 41

S PRITE, BERTIE, GERTIE, and Phoebe, only a few days out from
their ordeal, were escorted by four stern faced, spat wearing, fully
armed and helmeted MP's through the gray corridors of the new
five sided military headquarters in Washington DC known as The Penta-
gon. The silent guards took them through one level of security to the next
until they stood in front of General Hap Arnold. With Jackie Cochran by
the General's side, the debriefing began, and the girls each answered the
questions put to them until General Arnold believed he had the entire
story of their air battle with the Luftwaffe and the killing of Major Doyle
on the Giant's Steps.

"Well," said General Arnold, disapproval evident in his voice, "That's
one tall tale, ladies." Sprite, the twins, and Phoebe stood at ease, cleaned
up, a few days rested, and now silent after telling their story. "The Brits
collected most of the chromium after the storm played out, though some
of it now resides on the seafloor at the base of those undiveable cliffs," he
added, the scowl on his face softening a bit, when, behind the girls, the
door opened, and Captain Hal James was wheeled in by Lt. Pritchard.
General Arnold broke into a smile. "Ladies, Captain James wanted to be
present for your debriefing, but his doctors have only just released him, so
he is joining us a bit late. Welcome, Captain James."

Sprite could not help but grin, though when she felt the General's
eyes on her, she promptly straightened her face. Beside the General, Jackie
Cochrane winced and cocked her head at Sprite in warning.

Hal smiled, saying, "Thank you, General. How about these women?"

The General nodded but didn't smile back. "Yes, how about them? So it's all true, what they are telling me?"

Hal nodded. "Yes, sir, it is. I was there for a lot of it."

The General sighed. "You women realize that your actions in engaging combat with the enemy were never sanctioned and that you got your squadron leader, Mrs. Lowe, killed? She is a great loss to us all. And then there is the matter of Major Doyle. Since Captain James upholds your story, Sprite Shannon, you are absolved of any current or future charges of wrongful death in the shooting, but, and be advised that I mean every word of this: none of you will ever utter a word about what happened in the air or on the ground to a single living soul. This matter is now classified, and in as far as anyone else shall know, Major Doyle died from an accidental fall from those cliffs and was washed out to sea, his body never recovered. Do you understand, ladies?"

In unison, the girls answered, "Yes, sir."

"In the morning, I will be announcing that I am disbanding the WASP, ladies. I'm very sorry, but there it is. Despite your proven value to us *here at home when you do the jobs we give you*, we cannot have our women doing our men's jobs in combat. And now that the European theater is winding down and many of our pilots will be returning to the States, we'll no longer need you. I'm sure you understand. What happened with you four can never, ever, happen again, and the only way to prevent that is to cancel the program and send you all home."

Jackie made a sour face and looked down at her hands. Sprite could see the color begin to creep upward from her collar and tinge her face with red fury.

The General, if even aware of Jackie's anger, continued without pause. "Captain James, you have been promoted to Major for your part in exposing and disabling a Nazi plot that could have lost us the war. Congratulations. Medals to follow. That is all," he concluded, and stood up, thereby dismissing them.

X

At Sweetwater, the last graduating class was briefly addressed by the Colonel and a full parade review held to mark the occasion.

And just like that, the WASP was no more. The graduates packed, said goodbye, and boarded trains or were retrieved by family and friends, and the airfield and planes were taken over by official army operations.

At his far window, the Base Commander looked toward the west, the last place he had seen Chihuahua roaming the brush, taunting him. He would get that bull if it were his last act as Commander on this base, or die trying.

A buzz on his intercom sounded and he pressed the button. "Sir, there is someone from a previous class of trainees here to see you. She says her name is Liesel Ronguer. Shall I send her in?" the secretary said.

The Commander twitched his office door's blinds slightly open. He peered through the slits and saw the back of a young woman, her shape unmistakable, and the face of a few months' old child asleep on her shoulder. Also unmistakable.

Unmistakably *his!*

"I don't think so," he stammered, "No…keep her there for a few more minutes."

Quickly choosing between the evil lurking somewhere out beyond the window and the one at his office door, he took down his rifle, quietly eased out his back door, got in a jeep, and headed out into the vast, trackless scrubland.

ᚷ

Back as Santa Sabina, two weeks later, Sprite carefully opened a sealed letter.

> *Greetings to all,*
>
> *I am home again easy and have news. I get two days with Katya and brother Yevgeny, but we are sad. We go to bury cousins killed in recent bombing. Also I have told squadron of our*

adventure, and they are liking you with greatness now. I am hoping we fly same skies again some day.

Das Vadanya, my comrades.
Olga

Sprite folded the blue aeropostal letter back into its envelope shape and said, "I'm going to have to tell Olga about the WASP being disbanded. And that there's nothing we can do about it," said Sprite, dispiritedly. They all had given so much, risked their lives, and succeeded as well or better than any man in service, but the world would never know it. Now they were expected to go home and resume their lives as if none of it had ever happened. As if Nin and Meredith had not died in service of their country.

"It isn't right," agreed Hal from his wheelchair under an orange tree in the infirmary yard. "But it's the army, and the army will have its way. What will you do now?"

It was the same question she had been asking herself. "Hal, I don't know yet," Sprite replied, "We have a couple of weeks to clear out, and we can wear our uniforms until then, but after that, we are on our own again. I... haven't decided, is all I can say."

Sprite turned her head away so that Hal could not see her face. The thought of having to leave was almost more than she could stand. Flying—and Hal—were all that mattered in her life. She had no place to stay in California, no friends there other than the girls, and they were all going back to their homes. Sprite had no home to go back to, though she had thought about going back to Georgia and asking Lettie if she could stay with her until she could find work and a new place. Eventually, she could save the money to go to college. That would have made her father really happy. But returning to Lowland Mill seemed entirely too sad when she thought about how her house and hangar and plane were gone, and how the army had built its big chromium mining operation on her beautiful land. Sprite had had enough of chromium. She'd have to go someplace else. And as for Hal... he could be sent anywhere. The war was very much still raging in the Pacific and she truly might never see him again. Wartime romances hardly ever worked out. Usually, because somebody died.

She sat down heavily on the bench beside him and gave Hal a long, studied look. "So what's next for you, Hal? Where are they sending you?"

Hal took her hand and smiled. "Nowhere for a bit, at least. When I saw the doctor today, he said things were mending well, but couldn't be rushed. I have a long recovery ahead before I'm battle ready again. I have some R&R coming, so my folks have decided to come out and throw me a birthday party this weekend. I want you to meet my parents, so I hope you will come as my date. Please invite your other friends if you think they'd come," he said, looking into her deep green eyes.

Sprite smiled and touched his face. "Of course. I will be happy to be your date, Hal. I wouldn't miss it."

CHAPTER 42

"C'MON PHOEBE, YOU have to go," said Sprite, as Bertie and Gertie stood waiting behind her. Phoebe, still wearing her bathrobe, sat looking out the window of her quarters, and shook her head for the third time. "And is anyone else having a moment of déjà vu here? Phoebe, why do you make us beg you to go to dances?"

"No, I don't have to go," she said firmly. "And you can stop begging. I… don't feel like I'm part of anything anymore. I really, really let everyone down on the bomber mission, and now Meredith is dead because of me. You heard the General!"

"Meredith is dead… because Meredith chose to sacrifice herself so that we could make it," said Sprite, "and we'll not let you believe otherwise. Yes, you had some trouble up there. But none of us truly expected to see combat. We really weren't trained for it and it's a miracle any of us lived. The miracle that Meredith gave us. So don't cheapen her gift by making it about your failure, Phoebe."

"Her last words to you were that she believed in you," said Bertie, gently, "not, 'I'm going to have to die now to make up for your mess.'"

With that, Phoebe began to cry, but the other girls, rather than smothering her in sympathy, just waited for her to stop, and when she did, Gertie said brightly, "OK, if you are finished feeling sorry for yourself, how about now you wash your face, put your make up on, get into your Santiago Blues like the rest of us, and be a WASP for the last time together?"

Phoebe sniffed and blew her nose, looked up at them and said, "You really do want me to come despite everything?" They all nodded, smiling back at her.

"Well…OK, give me a few minutes," she said softly, "And I'll go."

X

"Would you look at this place?" said Gertie, peering upward at the soaring, Art Deco lines of the Biltmore Hotel as she climbed out of the cab. Hal paid the cabbie and Sprite helped him out, put his cane in his hand and herself on his other arm, and they joined the other three on the sidewalk, necks craning upward.

"It's stunning," said Bertie. She looked at Gertie wistfully and Sprite knew they were remembering Ninette and her love of architecture. Sprite sighed and smiled up at Hal, who was gamely attempting his first steps without the wheelchair.

He had gone a little white around the mouth but he smiled back at her and said, "I'm all right. Just stay close!" They both laughed and made their way through the Biltmore's front doors and into the huge lobby, which was festooned with fresh flowers at every niche and on every table. The arrangement in the center stood a good seven feet high and was stuffed with red roses, white carnations, blue statice, and fern. Enormous, glittering gold ornaments peeked out of the tight spaces between the blooms.

"It's meant to be a Christmas tree!" exclaimed Bertie. "And look over there—all the palms are decorated, too. It's a California Christmas!"

Sprite just stood stunned beside Hal, her mouth agape with the grandeur in front of them. Phoebe wandered over to the centerpiece and smelled a rose, her eyes closing in bliss.

"Let's go to the ballroom," Hal said, pointing to the arched doorway. Sprite nodded, still speechless, and began to walk forward with him, thinking how out of place she suddenly felt amid the lavishness around her. Music began to drift from the ballroom and Bertie and Gertie shared a look of pure joy—there would be dancing!

A few feet into the crowded room, a tiny, middle aged woman, dripping in diamonds and gold, her Chanel suit perfectly fitted to her lithe frame, came bounding toward them, her eyes on no one but Hal. She stopped short of him when she saw his cane, and then came in much more gently for a lingering, motherly hug. Sprite saw her eyes close as she pushed her face into her son's broad chest, a grateful tear shining on her cheek. A small, manicured hand wiped at the tear and Sprite caught sight of the most stunning diamond ring she had ever seen stacked atop two other diamond circlets. The brilliant stone was huge and encircled in an antique design of... rose and green gold! Sprite glanced down at her Claddagh ring, wondering what the chances were of ever seeing the same marriage of metals on another piece of jewelry. But there it was—a perfect companion piece to her own ring.

The woman winked sweetly at her, then drew back and, as if seeing the rest of them for the first time, said "I'm Halcyon's mother, Patricienne, and I am so glad you came! Hal said such wonderful things about everyone. And you must be Sprite!" she said, taking Sprite's other hand and pulling her in for a hug. Bertie and Gertie, standing behind Hal, simultaneously moved up on either side to catch him before he fell, then stepped back when Patricienne released Sprite. Sprite's head began to spin a bit at the sudden wash of Chanel No. 5 and the amazingly strong grip and exuberance of the little woman.

"Hello, Mother," said Hal, grinning ear to ear, "The party looks fantastic! You and Dad have outdone yourselves; this is beyond even that time at the Waldorf!"

Patricienne dropped her eyes in humility and said, "Oh, it's nothing, dear. Your Dad and I are so proud of you—he's out for a quick drink on the terrace with the governor, but he'll be back in a minute! And we were so happy to come to you this time that we just brought everyone else as well. They just made it their first stop before the golf at Palm Springs this winter. But it must hurt you to stand for very long, so let's get you to the table and then the guests can visit with you—Henry is here, and General Donovan, and oh, from what Hal tells me, Sprite dear, you will be especially pleased to meet one of our other guests! Come along!"

Sprite looked up at Hal, questions in her eyes, but Hal just shrugged.

"I don't know—they didn't tell me anything except the address!" he said. "I guess that was as close to a surprise party as they could make it."

Bertie and Gertie, already swaying a little to the big band's rendition of a Glen Miller song, sat down at the linen covered table and watched the musicians. The band was a full force big brass orchestra, led by an older man who wore a red silk triangle in the pocket of his dinner jacket. Phoebe slid in at Sprite's other side as Hal took the red leather chair Sprite and his mother held out for him. He leaned the cane on one side and settled back, looking around the room as Sprite dropped lightly into her chair beside him. Patricienne signaled a waiter, ordered them drinks and food, and then waved at Hal, saying, "I'll be around in a while, Darling! Enjoy yourselves, everyone!"

Hal looked up when the music changed and laughed aloud in surprise. The conductor was the same piano player at the jazz bar who had given him the tuning fork the night Hal had figured out the jet engine problem. As if the conductor could feel Hal's eyes on his back, he turned around. When he saw Hal's face in the crowd, he raised an eyebrow and winked at him. Hal shook his head and smiled back.

About the time the drinks arrived, a man in a three-piece suit disengaged himself from a circle of couples and made his way toward Hal. "Good God, boy, look at you!" he roared, shaking Hal's hand. "No, no, don't get up. Not necessary! Can I bring you anything? I want to hear your stories later, alright?" He glanced around and nodded at the girls around the table.

Hal cleared his throat and said "Secretary Stimson, these women are—sorry, were, part of the WASP. Meet Bertie, Gertie, Phoebe, and this is my girl, Sprite," he said in his most charming voice, looking at her adoringly.

Sprite almost fell into her plate—not from Hal's public declaration, although that would have been enough on its own to make her dizzy, but because the man before her was Secretary of War, Henry Stimson. Or just "Henry," if you were Hal's mother, apparently. The girls said their quick how-do-you-do's, and then "Henry" was gone, absorbed back into a passing, cigar scented crowd of uniforms.

"Hal!" Sprite whispered sharply, "Why didn't you tell me you knew the Secretary of War?! I might have…might have been a little more pre-pared and able to speak if I had known…and a governor is here? What kind of tony crowd do you run with?"

"Tony crowd?" said Hal, absently. "They're just my family's friends and business associates…I never thought of them as anything special." His honestly perplexed expression made Sprite a little ashamed that she had been cross at him and her cheeks colored from the private embarrass-ment. An awkward silence settled over the table.

"Uh, Phoebe, Bertie and I have our eyes on those three young sail-ors over there who look like they can dance—come on!" Gertie jumped up, her twin a second behind, but Phoebe just sat staring at them, puz-zled. There were no "three young sailors" anywhere she looked… "Hurry!" warned Gertie, grabbing Phoebe by the arm, "They just moved behind that couple!" When Phoebe still didn't move, Bertie stepped behind her and lifted her from the armpits while Gertie caught one elbow and steered her away from the table, purposefully leaving Sprite and Hal alone.

Watching them hijack Phoebe, Hal chuckled, "They really are pretty smooth, aren't they?"

Sprite had to laugh. "Yes, they are. And very kind," she added.

Hal took her hand in his and looked into her eyes. "I meant that, you know. You really are my girl. Forever." He ran a finger across the Claddagh ring on her right hand, happily noticing the heart was turned toward her, signifying she was "in a relationship."

"I am your girl," said Sprite, also touching the ring, "But Hal—the war… what if—"

"Let's just take this as it comes, Sweetheart," he said, squeezing her hand lightly. "This moment is all we ever have anyway. Enjoy the party."

Sprite nodded and sat back, deep in thought. A tumble of questions bounced around in her mind. What did any of this mean? All these peo-ple, these high born, educated, exorbitantly rich, and even *famous* people all around her—what would they think when Hal told them she was his girl? Would they laugh and think he was joking? Would they look down on her with disapproval, and worse, pity? And worst of all, would they think less of him? She never felt more like a farm girl than right now, she thought, amazed. But then the image of Liesel the Weasel calling her that name came back to her. She made a face and took a sip of her champagne to wash the bitter taste of the memory away. The bubbles got up her nose and she laughed, snorting, and Hal laughed, and then Sprite looked up when someone appeared at Hal's shoulder.

Someone who looked just like… Gene Tierney. Sprite blinked. Surely she was mistaken. And could that cold, wet feeling above her lip be snot trailing out of her nostrils? *Please, God, no.* She dabbed quickly at her nose with a hanky.

Hal felt the touch on his arm and looked up and behind, saw the woman, and received her embrace. "May I sit down?" she asked Sprite, who took a few seconds to realize the woman was speaking to *her.*

"Oh, of course," she coughed, "I'm so sorry; I just got champagne up my nose, and—" Then Sprite folded into embarrassment again, wondering why she was telling this elegant woman she had just snorted fizz, thereby proving she knew nothing about how to conduct herself in such rare company.

But the woman smiled, turning her beautiful face into an even more beautiful face, and said, "Darling, it happens to me *all* the time! By the way, my name is Gene. Gene Tierney." Gene held out her hand to shake Sprite's.

Sprite responded, eyes agog, mouth dry, and then Hal laughed and broke the spell, saying, "Hey, ladies, wounded man right here, needing attention!"

Gene flashed Sprite a big smile and a wink, and stage-whispered to her, "Men! They get shot a few times and then expect you to treat them like they're the only ones in the room! Hal, dearest," she added, turning to him, "I can see this girl is different and I hope you pay attention to that!"

Hal smiled. "You have no idea, Gene, and I certainly do!"

"Darlings, I have to see my next director over there while he is still sober, so please excuse me—so very good to see you again, Hal, and to meet you, Sprite," Gene said graciously, kissing Hal lightly on the cheek and bowing out of the conversation.

"So that's who mother was talking about!" said Hal, watching her leave, "How about that? Your favorite movie star in the flesh!"

Sprite nodded, still a bit awestruck at the encounter. Their food came and she discovered how hungry she was, so she tucked into the roast goose with single-minded vigor.

Across the room, Phoebe watched Bertie and Gertie tearing up the floor with a Congressman's son and an up-and-coming actor. She looked into her glass, swilled the champagne and watched the bubbles escape. When a shadow fell over their sparkle, she looked up and saw who was blocking the light. A tall man bent to her and said, "Hello, there. I'm told you are Phoebe Summerfield—would that be right? My name is—"

"General!" Phoebe exclaimed, eyes wide with surprise.

"Why, yes, that's the first part of it," he said, "The rest is 'Donovan.' Pleased to meet you." He held out his hand and Phoebe shook it. General Donovan pointed to a settee with a big flower arrangement on a table in front of it. Public, but also private. "Would you care to sit, Miss Summerfield? We can talk over here, if you would like. This isn't the kind of thing I want overheard...."

Phoebe nodded, intrigued.

When they had settled into the soft leather, General Donovan said quietly, "Phoebe, I am privy to certain classified documents and I know you had a hand in the recent radar transport operation."

"Yes, sir, I did," she said softly, and dropped her eyes, about to reveal her breakdown in the middle of the dogfight. "I think you should know—" she began, "that I had some trouble up there. I froze. I don't think I'll fly again, sir."

"Yes, well, I know everything," said the General. He let that sink in. "And I want to talk with all of your remaining squadron eventually tonight. I'm starting with you. I understand you are something of a languages expert, would that be right?"

"Well, I majored in them in college, but I don't know about expert," Phoebe demurred.

General Donvan smiled. "I am running a new kind of operations agency, for lack of a better word. I need operators for it. Operators with certain skills. Would you be at all interested in, say, becoming part of my team?"

"Your team, sir?"

"Yes," he replied. "The Office of Strategic Services. The OSS."

X

A man who looked like an older, slightly weathered, version of Hal came over to their table and pumped Hal's hand vigorously, saying, "Son! So great to see you! Happy birthday!" Hal's dad leaned over to Sprite and shook her hand as well, his bright blue eyes the same shade as Hal's.

If Hal were twenty-five years older, this is exactly what he would look like, she thought. Trim and tall, his sandy hair was streaked white at the temples, but his jawline was still clean and sharp. He had a permanent golfer's tan and his smile was genuine and unpretentious.

"Winslow James," he said, introducing himself. "Welcome to the party, Sprite."

Sprite smiled and thanked him, then endured the most awkward twelve seconds of silence she had ever experienced when Hal and his father exchanged a long, unfathomable look. Hal nodded wordlessly at his father as something understood passed between them. The elder James then broke into a smile and said, "Time for the birthday toast! I'll help you up to the platform!"

And with that, Hal was dragged up, hobbling on his cane, with his father clearing the path before them to the steps of the bandstand. Sprite shrank into her chair, feeling ever more like a duckling among swans. The party swirled around her, but without Hal there, she began to think she was invisible. She waited for Hal to make it up the steps and watched while his father toasted his son's 25th birthday, and then all the room broke into applause.

"Speech!" The demand rang out from the back of the room.

Hal blushed a bit, but then after a moment, said, "Thank you all for being here with me—with us." He stopped and looked around for Sprite, but couldn't find her. A sea of standing people obscured their table. He went on, "It means so much to me for you to celebrate a year of life with me. So, I propose a toast." He lifted a glass someone handed up to him. "To present company," he smiled, and then added somberly, "and to absent friends." Everyone clinked glasses and drank quietly in honor of the quick and the fallen. Bertie and Gertie caught Sprite's eye, and when Phoebe looked up at them all from her place by General Donovan, the remaining WASP shared a painful, sweet look as they thought of Ninette and Meredith.

Will anyone ever remember what we did in the war? Sprite wondered.

Someone then began to sing "Happy Birthday," to Hal, the orchestra joined in, and the guests lined up to shake Hal's hand. Someone placed a chair for him after the fourth person kept his conversation going for several minutes, and Sprite sat by herself and waited, becoming more and more uncomfortable.

She looked around to find the girls, thinking she'd talk to them for a while. Bertie and Gertie were having a great time on the floor, but where there was dancing, they always did—and Phoebe… was still sitting with that older man in uniform at the far end of the room, their heads together in earnest conversation.

Sprite sighed and found the ladies' room, where a Chinese woman sat in some kind of sofa-lined anteroom to the actual facilities, folding towels and offering a tray of perfumes and tissues and other items. Sprite passed her by, looking for the mirrors, and when she found one stretching all along a marble wall over *six* sinks, she stopped and stared at her reflection for a moment.

What she saw dismayed her. Looking back at her was a young woman with nowhere to go and nothing to do, wearing an out of service uniform. *A uniform that was kind of pretty, but now meaningless…kind of like me. All I can do is fly airplanes. What am I thinking, being with someone like Halcyon James! What will his life be like after the war? He'll probably go and be a banker like his dad. And what was that look between them about, anyway?*

What would I do if we got as far as a wedding? Stay at home in a big old house and pick out wallpaper and dinner menus? He runs with all these people I read about in papers or see in the movies… and who am I next to them that he won't just get tired of me when someone else catches his eye… he could have movie stars, for goodness' sakes! I don't even have a present for him today!" She thought bitterly, tears beginning to fall down her cheeks.

Well, I love him, but I can't give him the chance to hurt me like that. So, if I can muster the gumption to go right now, I can do it. I can't look at him and tell him, but if I slip away right now…that would be the best birthday gift I could possibly give Hal. To just disappear from his glamorous life and let him be free to choose one of his own kind.

She gathered herself to full height and strode out of the restroom, smiled at the Chinese woman, who for some reason did not smile back, and found the coat check attendant watching the party from her perch on a high stool. Sprite asked her to call a cab. She could apologize and say goodbye to the girls on the phone and ask one of them to send her things, most of which were already packed, to her wherever she landed. With a long look back, she opened her purse, saw enough money in it to buy a ticket to...almost anywhere else, and stepped out into the street to wait for the taxi.

CHAPTER 43

WHEN THE LAST hand had been shaken, Hal left the stage, limped back to the table and saw that Sprite had gone. Her napkin lay neatly folded by her plate and her cutlery bridged its rim, knife facing inward, fork tines down—the signal that the diner was finished. But the desert course—the birthday cake—had not been served and the party was nowhere near over. *Maybe she's in the ladies'* he thought, but knowing she wasn't. "Finished…" he said aloud as he looked at the plate. Hal's heart began to race and he reached for his cane. Bertie and Gertie saw and came to help him. "Where is she? Where is Sprite?" he asked urgently.

The twins looked at each other and shook their heads. "We haven't seen her since she went over to the coat check booth maybe twenty minutes ago…."

"She didn't *bring* a coat," muttered Hal, moving as quickly to the booth as he could.

The girl at the coat check shrugged. "She just asked me to call a cab that could take her to the trains. I sent her to Union Station. It's just a few streets over." Hal slammed his fist down on the table and made her jump, then apologized and stood thinking for a moment.

What happened? Why did she leave? Hal thought, the sudden sharp pain in his heart worse than his bullet wounds had ever felt.

Bertie and Gertie, following him, had overheard. "What can we do to help, Hal?" Bertie said.

"Go and find my father, and tell him I need his car keys, right now!" Hal answered, thinking to do the only thing he could.

Go and bring her back.

Ten minutes and a small accident later, Hal jumped from his father's Bentley convertible and slammed the door, then winced at the sound that told him the car would never be quite the same after that sideswipe against traffic he'd caught as he tried to take a short cut. He moved as quickly as his cane allowed all the way to the station gate, and then threw a few dollars at the attendant for a ticket to Idaho or somewhere else he never intended to go. It didn't matter. The ticket would get him on the far platform where he had seen a flash of blonde hair above a Santiago Blue WASP uniform.

From the bottom of the platform steps, he could see Sprite was boarding and that meant he had mere minutes to reach her, and the train tracks and two sets of stairs lay between them. He pushed against a crowd of sailors, shouting, "Make a hole, boys!" They almost started something with him for it, but then they saw he was a wounded officer, and let him through.

Huffing with the effort to climb the steep flight of stairs that bridged platforms, Hal said, "My girl…getting on that train!"

Two of the sailors exchanged a look and then came up behind Hal, who turned a stricken face to them. "We can help you out here, sir, if you'll let us!" said one of the Navy men.

Hal nodded frantically, and the sailors smiled at him and hoisted him aloft between them, racing up the stairs and over the archway, then down more steps to Sprite's train. In seconds, Hal was standing outside the doors he had seen her enter, the two sailors holding him up by the armpits.

Sprite looked out at the commotion beyond her window and saw the uniforms, but gave them no more thought than she would to any other bunch of servicemen playing a prank.

"Sprite! Sprite Shannon!" Hal called desperately.

She heard her name and jerked her head up to see Hal, waving furiously at her, supported by…a couple of Navy enlisted men? She lurched out of her seat and came to stand at the open door of the train.

"Hal," she began, "What are you doing here?"

Hal dropped his head with relief. "Thanks, fellas, I can take it from here," he said. The Navy guys patted him on the back, shook his hand, and left him swaying on his cane. "Sprite, please, why are you leaving? Where are you going? I thought we... I thought you... Sprite?"

"Yes, Hal," she sighed.

"Sprite, may I come aboard and sit down? Just until the train leaves?"

"Well...I guess, but Hal, it won't change anything," she answered.

Hal pulled himself up the steps and slumped beside her into the first seat by the door. The train car was almost full, but he didn't care if anyone overheard. "Sprite, what happened, Sweetheart?"

"I...guess I got scared, Hal," was all that would come out of her mouth.

"Scared? *You?*" he said, astonished. "You faced down a Nazi Stuka, raced after and disabled a V-1 rocket, shot a traitor to save my life...and you got scared at a birthday party?"

She smiled a bit at that. "I wasn't scared during those other things," she said, "They happened really fast and there was no time to think about anything but the next move. This is different—hey, I just needed to get out of there, Hal. I don't want to leave you, but I think it's best for both of us. Let's not make this harder, please. You know how I feel about you."

Hal took her hand and said, "Sprite, there is something I should tell you."

She stopped breathing, and waited for it.

"I love you," said Hal.

"What?!" she blurted. That was not what she had expected him to say.

"I love you."

Sprite was shaking her head and crying now. "Hal, this is impossible! What about your family? They see this sharp uniform and feel patriotic and proud now when they look at me, but they don't really know anything about me, do they? What happens to their smiles when the uniform is gone and they—and their fancy friends—learn where I'm from and what schools I didn't go to? That's what scares me! We are so different—maybe too different. Will they mock me? Talk about me? Laugh at me? They can't possibly approve of your little Georgia farm girl. I...I'm not in their league—your league," she added.

"That's right, Sprite, you aren't."

That, also, was not what she expected to hear. She turned to him full on and stared.

Hal smiled tenderly at her and said, "You are not in our league because you are way above and beyond our league. You are in a league of your own. I've never known anyone so brave and skilled and beautiful, all at once. They see it, too—and you're not being fair—they really aren't like what you're making them out to be. I know you can't believe they would like you. You can't trust us because anyone you let get close to you has abandoned you or hurt you on purpose. Your parents died, your relatives stole from you, and even Ninette and Meredith, your adopted big sisters, have left you. I have thought about this for a long time and I understand how it's hard for you to trust love. I know it will take some time for you to believe there is more to my love than a wartime, we-could-be-dead-tomorrow kind of desperation. I have dated socialites and beauty queens and one actress, and they were all nice girls. But there is no one like you, Sprite. I love you. I have loved you since I saw you sleeping under your plane at the Peach Festival. Even if you tell me to get lost, I'll still love you the same. I don't think I can help it. So...."

"So?" Sprite repeated, turning it into a question.

"So, will you get off this train and come back with me? Please give me a chance. It's all I ask. Just give me a chance and, if, after a while, you think you can't trust me to love you as you should and deserve to be loved, then I will bring you back here and buy you a ticket to wherever you want to go. It will tear my heart out, but I will not stand in your way, and I'll still love you the same."

She was still staring into his eyes, trying to fathom his words, when the train whistle blew and the first car lurched, its wheels beginning to turn. It was now or never. Either she took a chance and got off and went back with him, or she put him off and never looked back all the way to...she looked at her ticket...to Idaho. *Idaho!?* She had bought a ticket for the first train leaving, and hadn't even looked to see where it was going!

"Hal, the train is leaving," she said. "You should get off now."

"I won't get off unless you come with me," Hal said, pointing to his leg. "I need help with those steps."

Sprite sighed and said, "Get up. Of course I'll help you."

They stepped down just as the car started to roll forward, but there were another dozen cars moving slowly behind, and Sprite could reboard any one of them. "Darling," Hal said, pain in his voice, "I've done my best here. I guess it just wasn't good enough. But I will always love you. There is only one more way I can say it." He took her hand and twisted gently at the Claddagh ring. "May I?" he asked.

Sprite was puzzled. *What are you doing?!* she thought, and she nodded just to find out.

Hal worked the ring free of her right hand and looked long into her tear-rimmed eyes. Then without another word, he slipped the Claddagh onto her left hand ring finger, its heart pointing toward her fingertips. The ring now signaled, "My heart is taken. I am engaged." He was asking her to marry him!

Years later, Sprite would look on the moment and think about all the things Hal could have said or done, and not any other one of them would have changed her mind.

But this one did.

He had spoken his love in her language. And she finally believed him, not just with her head, but with her heart.

"Sprite, you know what I'm asking you. Will you marry me?" said Hal.

She kissed him, the tears spilling again, and he held her close, feeling their heartbeats slowly synchronize into one.

"Yes, Hal, I will. But just not tomorrow," she grinned, wiping the tears.

The last train car rolled past, leaving them behind.

Together.

✕

"You found her! Oh, thank God!" said Bertie, as Sprite and Hal entered the party room again.

"Yes," said Hal, looking around for his father and mother.

Gertie read his face and said, "They're over there. We'll get them!"

When Winslow and Patricienne came over, Hal was holding Sprite's hand and the Bentley's keys lay on the table. "Dad, Mom—I…we have some good news. Well, some good news and some bad news," Hal amended.

"Bad news?" said Winslow, perplexed.

"Yes. Your car, Dad—and I know how much it means to you—I had a little accident on the way to the station. But I promise to make it right."

Winslow began to chuckle. "I think that bad news is more for you than me, Son. I was going to give you that car for your birthday present!"

Hal's face went a little green, but he quickly rallied. "Wow, thanks, Dad. I think. But… now for the good news." His color returned to normal and he looked down at Sprite and hugged her close. "Sprite and I are engaged!"

Patricienne's mouth became a rosy "O," and she looked over to her husband, who was beginning to grin. She clapped her hands in joy and bent to hug Sprite while Winslow pumped Hal's hand. "He told us he was going to ask you tonight, Dear! We couldn't be happier, Hal!" said his mom. "Welcome to the family, Sprite! And call me Pats, everyone else does! Oh, and here, Hal—silly me! I should have given you this when I first saw you!" Patricienne removed the largest diamond—the one with the antique rose and green gold setting—from her overburdened finger and dropped it into Hal's hand. "This was his grandmother's ring. He asked me to bring it for you," she said to Sprite.

Sprite's eyes went wide. Hal turned to Sprite and picked up her right hand, a question in his eyes. She nodded. They both knew that, like her mother before her, she'd never take the Claddagh ring off her left hand again as long as she lived. Hal slid the diamond onto her right hand ring finger. He kissed her and the moment was sealed. Patricienne leaned in, her Chanel No.5 cloud enveloping them both, and hugged her. But this time, Sprite breathed it in its sweetness and hugged back.

Sprite looked over to see Phoebe, Bertie, and Gertie in a huddle with the old jazz pianist, and when they broke away, the band began to play a familiar song.

I Love You for Sentimental Reasons drifted over the party and Hal locked eyes with Sprite. With the help of the Phoebe and the twins, the floor around them cleared and they began to rock back and forth to the music, Hal dancing the best he could with Sprite as support. "Careful; you'll drop me," he whispered in her ear. She chuckled and looked up at him.

"Never," she whispered back, "Never."

EPILOGUE

Malta conference, January 1945—

FEELING DRAINED AND rushed, Roosevelt pressed on his forehead, trying to stop the throbbing that signaled his blood pressure had spiked again. He had barely arrived at Montgomery House in the little Maltese town of Floriana before the requests for audiences had begun. He had arrived on the last day of the conference and now, the British Chiefs of Staff Committee and the American Joint Chiefs of Staff wanted every minute of his time. Over the past week, they had been fervently discussing details of the ground war in Europe. It seemed that every general was breathlessly awaiting some form of approval or response from the President of the United States before anything resembling a cohesive strategy could be firmed up.

As it should be, Roosevelt thought. Still, he wished he'd had a few more moments to gather himself. The pounding in his head seemed to become much louder until he realized that this time, the noise was coming from the door. *Ah. Hello, Winston.*

Roosevelt nodded to his valet, signaling him to open the door for the British Prime Minister. Churchill strode in at once, accompanied by the now-familiar British MI-6 agent known as Gabriel. The two men took the seats in front of Roosevelt's wheelchair.

"Franklin, my apologies for the intrusion, but we have some news that should be heard before any meaningful strategy is formulated regarding Atlantic naval operations," Churchill said. "It's a new and credible threat. Of the worst kind."

Roosevelt knew that Gabriel's presence portended something both meaningful and ominous, so he mentally prepared himself for whatever new intelligence Gabriel had to report. "All right, Winston. I assume your man Gabriel here has something important to contribute," he said. Churchill turned to Gabriel, signaling him to begin briefing the President.

"Mr. President, as you know, British defenses of London have been flummoxed by our inability to effectively combat the V-2 rocket strikes. As the Allies advance toward German launch sites, we do believe that, in time, we can counter those strikes by eliminating them at their origin.

"However, I am in receipt of new intelligence which has been confirmed, to a degree, by a recent speech made by German Arms Minister Albert Speer. What it suggests is, quite frankly, horrifying beyond words," Gabriel said.

Roosevelt sighed deeply. Of course it was, otherwise Gabriel wouldn't be briefing him in person. "Please continue, Gabriel," Roosevelt said.

"The Germans have termed their plan '*Prüfstand XII,*' and what it entails, in brief, is the deployment of V-2 missiles through use of specially designed U-boats," Gabriel said.

Roosevelt sat straighter and gave Gabriel his fullest attention. "The Germans would launch V-2 missiles from submarines? From the *sea*? That means they could strike from practically anywhere!" Roosevelt said.

"Putting almost any target within range," Churchill interjected, "including Washington DC."

Roosevelt sank a bit in his wheelchair. Thus far, the United States had been singular among the world powers in that its soil had not seen combat, save for Pearl Harbor. Now, just as the ground war in Europe was speeding toward an apparent victory for the Allies, came this ominous bit of news. Perhaps America would not escape the war unscathed after all.

"There is more," Gabriel said softly. "Until your General Groves's ALSOS units seize more documents from captured German laboratories, we cannot be sure, one way or the other, of the progress of Hans Geiger's atomic bomb project."

As Roosevelt absorbed the words, he felt the specter of death's cold fingers touch his heart and his head throbbed harder. How much more of this war could he stand? He knew it was slowly killing him. "I understand," Roosevelt said, suddenly becoming very sober, even though he'd had only coffee to drink all day. "You are telling me that the Germans may soon have the ability to launch a V-2 missile at Washington DC, and that missile might be carrying the world's first viable atomic bomb...."

Gabriel and Churchill both slowly nodded.

Roosevelt all but crumpled in his wheelchair. He was so very tired; had been President so very long. An Allied victory had seemed imminent, but perhaps the war was not even close to being over. "What do you want to do about it?" he said quietly, his hands over his eyes.

Churchill gave the President a moment and then said, "Franklin, what my Chiefs of Staff Committee are proposing is something called 'Operation Concierge,' and it must be implemented in all haste, but first, there is a preliminary operation that must be carried out," said Churchill, "Gabriel will explain."

"Mr. President," began Gabriel, "Do you remember when we first spoke, that I mentioned one of our Archangels named Uriel had been killed and the one called Michael was missing?" Roosevelt nodded. "Well, according to my latest intelligence, Michael had been trying to get back to us, traveling in secret and posing as a German refugee, but was very recently captured. Sir, I believe we can stop this nuclear threat, but to do so, we will first have to find a way to rescue Archangel Michael, who has the specifics about the V-2 plans. Getting her out of Germany will be next to impossible and extremely dangerous. Time and secrecy are of the utmost importance—if the Nazis find out who she really is, Operation Concierge will be compromised. Sir, we'll need your help in this matter."

Roosevelt nodded slowly. "I see," he sighed. Then his eyes popped wide. Had Gabriel just said, "*her*" and "*she*?"

Gabriel smiled and nodded, seeing the reaction. "Yes, Sir. Michael is also known as Michelle, and in her photographic memory alone is recorded the complete list of names and places that we need. She's literally the 'keeper of the keys.'"

Roosevelt closed his eyes and thought, then said, smiling for the first time since they had begun, "Winston, I think I have the very man to help you. General Bill Donovan. His group, called the Office of Strategic Services, is perfect for this kind of operation."

We hope you enjoyed W.A.S.P. Sisters of the Sky by Teri McLaren & Bobby Garcia. Your reviews are important! Reviews provide valuable feedback for the authors, the publisher, the booksellers, and the larger reading community, and we welcome them at Amazon.com and Goodreads.com. Thank you, and happy reading!

Now, read on for an exciting preview of the next adventure for Sprite, Phoebe, Bertie, Gertie and others in:

SISTERS OF THE
O.S.S.

FROM THE "SISTERS OF ADVENTURE" BOOK SERIES

Coming in 2017

For status updates and exciting free bonus materials, visit:

www.mclarengarcia-saphirionpress.com

CHAPTER 1

Forty miles north of Berlin, Germany

MICHELLE AND TOVA moved like shadows through the ancient, quiet forest, pushing between the naked birches and snow-burdened pines toward the little river. Silently, their eyes and ears tuned to a painful awareness, they watched and listened for any sign or sound that didn't belong. A foot of fresh powder, with more coming down, hindered their speed, but still, they slogged forward in wide zigzags, never stopping to rest. They desperately needed to get to the other side of the icy water before dark.

As the wind picked up, bringing the smell of the moving river, Michelle felt the air change from cold to sharply colder, and shivered violently, biting the inside of her cheek hard. Blood poured into her mouth, the coppery taste filling her with revulsion, but she dared not spit the red gobbet into the pristine snow. Swallowing sickly, shoving snow into her mouth to dull the taste and staunch the bleeding, she prayed that it wouldn't be much longer until they came to the fording place. If they could cross, if they could just get to the other side, they would be picked up by their contact and taken to a safe house to recover for a day. Then they'd be smuggled back to Paris, where Gabriel would be waiting for them. But the patrols were out—they were always out now—and the contact had to be as careful as they did. She wouldn't wait for them after dark.

Their contact's code name was Violet, and like Tova, she was one of the Wildflowers, a group of women who helped the French Resistance from inside Germany. Violet had settled into her middle years and looked as ordinary as any red cheeked, plump, German *hausfrau*. But her only child, a son, had been killed early in a war she had secretly protested from its beginning, and she had become bitter in her heart toward the National Socialist party and its single-minded leader, Adolf Hitler. She had said no word against them, for that alone would have put her entire extended family in the camps.

Instead, Violet had been smart. She had wasted no time finding her place in the complex network of the Resistance, and now she moved under the cover of her real life, as a simple woodsman's wife, helping him run trap lines for small game for their table. One of Violet's trap lines lay along this river, a point of contact and travel for Jews, Gypsies, artists and professors, and even sometimes, Allied spies, running from the Nazis.

Michelle knew Violet's man was old and nearly deaf, and he liked his supper early. After dark, she'd have to go in with him, or there would be questions—he did not know her secret name or of her dangerous work, and was a staunch supporter of the Fuhrer. If he found out about her, he would turn her in himself.

Michelle stopped for a moment, waiting for Tova to catch up. They were so very dirty, cold, and tired. The hunger pangs had stopped yesterday, their third day on the run from the last Wildflower safe house, but the weakness that had replaced the gnawing hollowness threatened both of them with collapse.

The water smell grew stronger. Maybe a hundred yards now, and they could hear the smack of ice as the river, really just a deep, rushing stream, played at freezing over for the winter. Maybe seventy-five yards....

Michelle, in the lead, stopped short at the sudden, startled flight of a hawk a few trees away, and held up a hand for Tova to do the same. They both ducked down under a fallen limb and tried to still their breathing. Tova put her hand in Michelle's and looked over at her friend with wide, dark, eyes, and smiled sadly. Michelle nodded her understanding. If their week-long journey to safety ended now, with capture, they might never see each other again.

The bird circled her tree but did not return to it. Michelle's heart sank. That probably meant that the patrol had stopped near or under the bird's roost, and were likely spreading out to look for the fugitives from that point. She squeezed Tova's hand hard, their prearranged signal that she would run one way and Tova should run the other if they were found. No reason to make the Nazis' job any easier. Tova squeezed back her acknowledgment, and they both tried to sit still despite the pounding of their hearts.

Michelle stared through the softly falling snow from beneath the log and hoped their tracks, already disappearing beneath the touch of the rising wind, would not be spotted. Not the best choice for a hiding place, thought Michelle, but the fallen limb was huge and its snow bank had been the only ground cover within ten yards. The rest of the forest floor was almost a kind of desert—the old trees' dense canopy overshadowed any seed that ever sprouted, leaving a vast open space beneath the behemoths, and now, even their shed leaves and needles were covered in vacant whiteness. Suddenly, the wind gusted and the pine boughs overhead cracked and groaned. A huge clump of powder dropped with a muffled whump! right in front of them.

"*Ja!* I hear something!" The harsh voice of a German soldier carried on the wind.

Michelle and Tova heard something, too—the abrupt barking of a pair of Alsatians. The patrol always worked with dogs. They could find you anywhere. Even in a blizzard.

"They have us!" mouthed Tova, noticing a change in the tone of the barking.

Michelle faced Tova one last time, and whispered into her ear, "Thank you for staying with me after they killed Uriel and the others. We almost made it!" she smiled sadly. "Tova, you are a Jew and a known operative in the Resistance. They know nothing of me yet. Find help and get word to Gabriel. He will know what to do. You must run for all you are worth—now!" Tova had no time to protest before Michelle pushed her backward, sprang up from the snowbank, and stumbled forward through the heavy drifts. Tova scrambled on all fours in the exact opposite direction, obscured by the fallen log and the whirling snow.

"Help me! Help me!" Michelle screamed, waving her hands and slogging straight toward the Germans. She didn't dare look back. She had to convince them she had been alone so that they would not set the dogs after Tova. She fell at the soldier's snow encrusted boots and cried softly in her best Berliner German, "Help me, *Hundenfuhrer*, please help me. They are coming! They will kill me!" The two dogs, pure white and at least half wolf, strained at their leashes and barked, huge white teeth snapping within inches of Michelle's face. The soldier had been about to loose them when, startled, he'd pulled them in when he heard Michelle speak his own language. Nonetheless, he kept his pistol trained on her.

"*Fraulein*, who are you? What are you doing out here? Don't you know how dangerous it is? We are looking for Jews!" he said. "And who is coming to kill you?" He waited for her to answer and looked into her crystal blue eyes, searching for lies.

"The Allies, with their bombs! Can't you hear them?" she whispered, locking his stare. She gestured above her head and looked at him like he must be the mad one not to hear the imaginary planes. "I am so glad to find you. When I heard German, I came out of my hiding place. I am lost, *Hundenfuhrer*, and I thought I would die out here. I was separated from my family in Berlin during a bombing raid. I couldn't get into a shelter, so I started running, but the planes flew after me. The days, I hid in barns and walked all night and just never stopped because the planes are still following me!" She stopped for a moment and looked around. "Where am I? It is so cold here. I am hungry and tired. Oh, no, look!" she pointed above to a darkly clouded sky, empty but for the swirling snowflakes. "Do you see them? There! Flying right above me! Make them stop! Make them stop!" She clutched at her ears and fell into the snow as if she were hearing the screaming bombs falling all around her.

Her eyes went wild with fright and she looked pleadingly into the soldier's gray-green eyes. He couldn't have been more than twenty. The death's heads of the *Totenkopfverbande* adorned his uniform, and his lips, chapped white from the cold, stretched thin and bloodless in a long, straight line across a rawboned face.

He studied her for a moment, taking in her straggly blonde hair, slight build, and bare legs, chilled white by the cold. Michelle could almost hear him thinking that clothes were too thin and her shoes, though now ruined, had been too good for the countryside. She had nothing with her but a scarf, and her hands were gloveless, covered in wound rags torn from her skirt's hem. He might know what Tova looked like, but he might not. Quiet now, she let him come to his conclusion without any further help. Too much information was as deadly as too little. It had gotten Uriel killed only months before.

"Heinrich!" he called, not taking his eyes from her face. Heinrich, a portly, middle aged man, rifle trained on Michelle, stepped out of the shadows and the young *Hundenfuhrer* said, "She is possibly quite mad and does not match the description, so I want to question her back at the camp. She might know something. But it's too cold out here and getting dark. We will send Fritz out later to keep looking if we need to. Put her in the mule and wait for me."

"*Jawohl, Hundenfuhrer Klaus!*" said Heinrich, helping Michelle to her feet. His grip was firm, but not painful. She smiled up at him gratefully and a little madly, and let him lead her, hoping that Tova was now far enough away to be safe.

Heinrich lifted Michelle into the back of a mule, a kind of halftrack lorry suited for deep snow or mud, where the dogs normally rode. Most mules were open to the sky, but this one was enclosed, probably to keep the dogs clear of weather, she thought. He slammed the door and a lock snicked shut. Michelle could hear the crunching of his jackboots as he walked to the cab, got in and sat down heavily, his weight causing the vehicle to settle somewhat lower on its right side.

Michelle crept carefully around in the darkness, feeling around to see what her space contained. There was a blanket for the Alsatians, so she shook it out and pulled it around herself, not even minding its clinging, musty smell of wet dog. In a few minutes, out of the snow and wind, she felt slightly warmer, and began to rub her numb legs and feet back into feeling. They prickled painfully as the blood returned to them, but that was a good sign—no frostbite. All the running must have helped. In the dark, wrapped in the gritty blanket, she drowsed as fatigue swept over her, but she fought it off, rocking back and forth to stay awake. Until the mule was moving, she could not afford to sleep. *Tova, be safe! I hope you find help and please, God, let her get word to Gabriel that I did get the codes and the launch sites—*

The lock clicked, the doors swung open on well-oiled hinges, and Michelle scrambled to the far corner as the two Alsatians leapt gracefully into the back of the mule. The door closed instantly behind them. She quickly covered her head with the blanket, but they were on her in seconds, pawing at her and pushing their muzzled heads at her, sniffing. Sharp, strong claws dug into her arms as they stepped on her, but then, the mule's engine started and the vehicle lurched as it began to move forward in the snow.

The dogs settled on the wooden floor, panting. Michelle could feel their warmth begin to fill the space, and when there was no further attack, she drew the blanket from her head. Her eyes accustomed now to the darkness, she could make out the dogs' shapes. They were lying down in front of her, blocking the door, bodies tense and ready to spring. But they were quiet, and Michelle realized they had not tried to bite her through their muzzles. They'd jumped on her, been rough, but they were big dogs, and maybe that was some version of greeting to them. The blanket…it smelled of them, and she had wrapped herself in it.

"Hello, darlings," she whispered in German. "I will not hurt you, and I hope you will not hurt me." The foremost dog lifted his ears at her voice, but did not growl. She continued, "I want you to get to know me, so here is my hand to smell." She wrapped the blanket over her arm and carefully, slowly, put out one hand, palm down, and brought it close to the dog's muzzled nose. He sniffed it, sniffed the blanket, then let his ears drop and put his head down. The other dog threw her head over his neck and sniffed the blanket covered arm and the bare hand. Michelle could feel the warm breath of the animal, and when the dog had withdrawn, she moved her hand back as slowly as before. Then Michelle inched closer, put her head down on the wooden floor and breathed into each of their faces. They licked at her breath, relaxed and curled up, snuggled into one another, and slept as the mule bumped onto the highway and picked up speed.

Behind a giant spruce tree, Tova crouched in the snow, waiting for the patrol to leave. She had seen them take Michelle to the mule. The Hundenfuhrer had muzzled his dogs, loaded them up, and started the engine. Through the snowy branches, she could see him in the vehicle, looking around, checking one last time... If they didn't go now, it would be dark and Violet might have given up on them and gone home.

Tova sighed, grateful to be alive, but pained that Michelle had given her no choice in the matter. Michelle had known there would have been no quick bullet for Tova—the men would have taken their turns with her and then beaten her before they dumped her into the freezing river or set the dogs on her. Still it was a trade off Tova would not have made. Locked in Michelle's perfect memory was the detailed information the Allies so desperately needed, and even thought she was a trained MI-6 operative, it wouldn't take the Nazis long to get it out of her. What was one Jewish life next to the thousands Michelle's information would save?

The snow had let up and the last rays of a weak sun winked into dusk. The mule began to move. Tova shook the snow from her back and made her way down to the icy stream. She saw the fording place—a big log across the frigid river—and lost no time in scrambling over it, bending low and pushing the fresh snow away with her hands as she went.

"I thought you might have been picked up," said Violet, slipping from the shadows and helping Tova to her feet on the other side. "I am Violet." She briefly flashed a handkerchief with the little purple flower embroidered on the corner. "I was just about to leave. Why are you alone? I was told there were two." She looked around.

"No. The other woman gave herself up to keep them from finding me. There were dogs. The one with the death's heads has her. The other man called him Klaus, I think."

Violet's eyes widened with horror. "*Totenkopfverbande* Klaus? He was young? Very tall? A hard face? Two wolfdogs and a big man with him?"

"Yes, yes, exactly so," whispered Tova, "You know him?"

"Everyone knows him. He is the *Hundenfuhrer* of Ravensbruck."

ABOUT TERI McLAREN

Best-selling fantasy author Teri McLaren (HarperPrism's *Magic: The Gathering, The Cursed Land* and *Song of Time*; TSR's *DragonLance - Before the Mask*, and *The Dark Queen*) returns with writing partner Bobby Garcia, producer and screenwriter (*The Truest Valor, The Dead Princess*).

After thirteen years of teaching literature and fine arts at the University of Louisville, Louisville, KY, Teri currently teaches Humanities survey courses and Peace Studies at Jefferson Community and Technical College in Shelbyville, KY.

ABOUT BOBBY GARCIA

Los Angeles-based producer and screenwriter Bobby Garcia has worked in the entertainment industry for over 20 years, serving in various capacities such as producer, chief financial officer, business affairs executive, attorney, and production accountant in both feature films and television. Bobby holds an MBA from Cornell University's Johnson Graduate School of Management, a Juris Doctor from University of Louisville's Louis D. Brandeis School of Law, and a BA in Finance from the University of South Florida.

Stay in touch with the authors and receive updates on upcoming books at
www.mclarengarcia-saphirionpress.com

www.ingramcontent.com/pod-product-compliance
Lightning Source LLC
Chambersburg PA
CBHW031056260626
47172CB00001B/93